HOW NOT TO
Marry A
DUKE

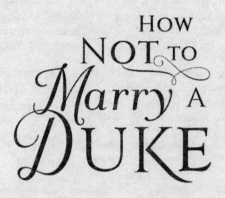

HOW
NOT TO
Marry A
DUKE

TINA GABRIELLE

Entangled Publishing, LLC
644 Shrewsbury Commons Ave., STE 181
Shrewsbury, PA 17361
Visit our website at www.entangledpublishing.com.

Amara is an imprint of Entangled Publishing, LLC.

Edited by Heather Howland
Cover design by Bree Archer
Stock art by David_Martin_Jackson/Gettyimages
Interior design by Toni Kerr

Print ISBN 978-1-64937-378-6
ebook ISBN 978-1-64937-379-3

Manufactured in the United States of America

First Edition May 2023

ALSO BY TINA GABRIELLE

For Laura,
I'm so proud of the young lady you have
become. May you always follow your dreams,
have the courage to believe in them, and may
your star always shine bright.

CHAPTER ONE

Daniel Millstone, the Duke of Warwick, tossed his quill on the desk in his study and pushed back his chair. He'd been trying to concentrate on his work, the mechanical drawings of a steam engine, but he'd been unable to focus.

What on earth is that terrible noise?

He went to the window and pushed aside the curtains. The shards of pain reverberating from the wound on his forearm that hadn't entirely healed only added to his agitation as he glared down the country road. He couldn't see his neighbor, but he could hear the cacophony coming from the cottage.

Barking, then howling.

A hound, or more aptly, *hounds*, were creating a racket. It had been three full days of it. The constant penetrating noise was enough to make him cover his ears and grind his teeth.

A muscle by Warwick's eye twitched. He'd chosen the small country house because it met all his requirements. Quaint, quiet village. A stream that powered a small waterwheel. A place where he could work without unwanted interruption.

Or so he'd thought.

Christ. He had a bevy of ducal estates from which to choose—massive piles of stone in Gloucestershire, Shropshire, and Hertfordshire. Not to mention a London mansion in Mayfair.

Instead, he'd settled on a country house in the small village of Chilham in Kent. Other than his trusted staff, no one in Chilham knew he was a duke of the realm, and he could tinker with his inventions in peace. He was also far from his matchmaking godmother in London who kept reminding him of his duty to produce an heir and spare for the dukedom and far from the bevy of scheming mammas of the *ton* who sought the prized title of duchess for their debutant daughters.

He'd turned the country house's study into his workshop. A high-pressure engine stood in the middle of the hardwood floor. Mechanical parts and tools were scattered across a worktable. The only other pieces of furniture were a sideboard with liquor and his desk—its surface currently covered with mechanical drawings.

Really, the country location and the house *should* have been perfect.

The incessant barking increased in pitch and fervor.

Making a quick decision, Warwick strode from his study, down the hall, then headed straight out the front door. His butler was busy elsewhere, another advantage of bringing along a sparse staff. His valet would have a fit if he saw him in trousers and no coat or cravat. Even his Hessians needed a good polish. No matter. He preferred to work informally.

He passed a fountain and well-maintained lawns, then progressed down a dirt lane. His steps quickened as he left his property, and a small cottage came into view.

His first impression of his closest neighbor was not a favorable one. A shutter on the house hung askew, and the hedgerows were overgrown. The door needed a good coat of paint and was missing its knocker. A cart loaded with baggage rested on the small patch of grass. A makeshift pen beside the cottage contained numerous animals—goats, sheep, and a cow. An old bay was hitched to a post and eating a bucket of grain. Two hunting hounds—the source of the disruption—were in a fenced kennel. Both resumed barking as soon as they saw him.

He glowered at the dogs. "What will it take to get you to stop that infernal barking?"

What is going on here? Where in God's name is the owner?

He quickened his pace until he was at the front door. Without a door knocker, he was forced to pound on the wood with his fist.

No answer. If the hounds hadn't alerted

the occupant that someone was on his property, what would?

"Hello!" he called out. When still no one answered, he pounded harder on the door. "Whoever is home, you must get your hounds to cease this racket!"

A laugh sounded from the side of the cottage.

His lips thinned with irritation. *Is someone laughing? At me?* Fists clenched at his sides, he marched full steam toward the noise and collided with a body.

A very soft one.

"Oh!" a feminine voice cried out.

Instinctively he reached out to grasp the woman's arm before she tumbled to the ground. "My apologies, I—"

"My goodness! You gave me a fright, sir."

She lifted her face to look into his eyes. His heart pounded as he took in her features one at a time. A curly mass of long dark hair and an oval face with an aquiline nose and full, pink lips. Her complexion was a dusky shade, not as fair as the ladies of the *beau monde*. But it was her blue eyes that captivated him. The irises were lined with a darker blue and framed by thick, dark lashes.

"I was in the garden." She held a basket of newly pulled carrots balanced precariously on one hip.

She met his gaze, and for the first time in a

long time, he found himself speechless. The contrast of those blue eyes and midnight hair against olive skin was stunning.

He cleared his throat. "Pardon, miss," he said as he dropped his hand and stepped away. "I am looking for the owner of this cottage."

"You found the owner, sir."

Truly? How was it possible one small woman, no matter how beautiful, could own the dogs that had distracted him from his work for three long days?

"I'm Miss Adeline. How can I help you, sir?"

He'd had his speech prepared, or rather his list of complaints for the fellow who owned such unruly dogs, but he'd been taken aback by the fact his neighbor was a young woman—a very pretty one. Was she married? It would be easier to confront a husband.

She looked up expectantly at him, waiting.

"The truth is, I'm here because of your—"

A blur from around the corner of the cottage drew his eye. *What the devil!*

A giant pig barreled full speed toward them with no sign of slowing. Unthinking, Warwick hauled the woman behind him. "Watch out!"

"Wait—"

With the cottage to one side and Miss Adeline behind him, Warwick's options were limited. Heart hammering, he had just enough time to angle her away from the attack and brace himself as about two hundred pounds of solid farm animal barreled head-first into him.

The threesome tumbled to the ground, man, woman, and swine. He took the brunt of it, cushioning the lady's fall with his body. They landed in dirt and a patch of mud.

A sharp pain raced down his arm. Through the roaring din, he swore.

His prior injury hadn't fully healed, but at least the pain had eased to a constant dull ache. But now, the stabbing pain was like a rasp on his skin, and he knew the wound had reopened.

He sat upright and eyed the corpulent beast. White with black spots and a spotted black-and-white snout with a tail that curled upward, the animal had charged him like a bull. As far as pigs went, he was ordinary, except for the glimmer of intelligence in his beady black eyes. Rather than wander off, the pig snuffled in Warwick's face.

The woman shoved herself from beneath Warwick to sit. "Henry, no!" She wagged a finger at the pig. Her tone was one of pure admonishment.

Amazingly, the pig responded, and, with a snort, he turned away from Warwick to waddle to her side. Her lips curved in a fond smile as she gave him a pat on the head. The pig snorted once more, then wandered off to his pen and started guzzling food from a bucket of feed. Warwick noticed the door to the pen was ajar.

He rose and reached down to grasp the woman around the waist and help her to her feet. Her waist was trim and fit the curve of his hand, her curves soft as she briefly pressed against him.

She stood straight and looked up at him. "I apologize. He's never done that before and is quite docile. I believe you frightened him when you shouted."

Warwick's eyes widened. He couldn't fathom her defense of the animal. His arm began to throb, and his already strained temper flared. "*I* frightened *him*? Your pig is a nuisance and attacked me." Just saying it out loud was ludicrous. His clothes were ruined, and he didn't bother to wipe away the dirt, dust, and mud from his trousers and once-white shirt. Mud clung to the skirts of her dress.

Her eyebrows drew together. "Only to greet you. Henry is friendly and wouldn't harm anyone."

Warwick cradled his arm. "Henry is over-sized and dangerous."

She glared. "He is *not* fat! He was the runt of the litter. He's also my beloved pet."

His heartbeat hammered. "Your pet? A pig cannot be a pet. It's a farm animal."

"That's untrue. They are quite affectionate."

"I doubt a pig can express affection." His tone was surly.

"You, sir, don't have much experience with pigs."

"Only the bacon or pork they provide on my table."

She gasped and her eyes narrowed.

As angry as he was, he couldn't help but notice she was beautiful. Bits of straw clung to her hair and his fingers itched to pluck them out. Still, she was either mad or simply illogical, and arguing with her over a pig was not why he was here. He'd been managing his injury, and now it hurt anew. He needed to return home, remove the bandages, and inspect the damage.

"The pen is not secure," he pointed out.

"Henry has a knack for releasing the latch."

"You don't say."

Her chin lifted at his flat tone. "You have yet to state your purpose here, sir. I told you my name. What is yours?"

He'd chosen this village for a reason. Far from London, no one knew him here, and he had no intention of revealing his true identity. "Mr. Daniel Millstone. I reside down the lane."

Her eyes lit and her expression softened. "A neighbor! Well, Mr. Millstone, I had hoped to meet you under different circumstances. As you can see," she said, waving to the cart on the patch of grass he'd noticed earlier, "my belongings have just recently arrived."

He eyed the overloaded wagon. Whoever had packed the rickety contraption had done a sloppy job. Warwick's mathematical mind excelled at geometry, and he inwardly cringed at the way the baggage and valises had been haphazardly tossed into the wagon. If they had been properly loaded, much more could have fit. A portrait was strapped to the back of the wagon with a rope. A ten-year-old child could have secured it better. How it hadn't fallen out during its jaunt down the bumpy country road was beyond him.

Wait.

Warwick's brow furrowed as he gazed at the portrait. The man's image was vaguely familiar, like a specter in the back of his mind. Where had he seen him before?

"I apologize for a most unusual welcome. I had planned on stopping by to introduce myself with a basket of baked goods, but along with unpacking, there is much to be done around the cottage." She let out a sigh. "Perhaps we can start anew, and if you'd be kind enough to return another time, I'll be sure to have tea ready so I can properly say hello."

"You misunderstand. My visit is not for social purposes."

Her brow creased. "It's not?"

"No. Your dogs are a nuisance; they bark at all hours of the day and night."

"My dogs? Oh, I understand." She walked to the makeshift fence and placed two fingers between her lips and let out a loud whistle. Both hounds loped to her side. Tongues lolling, they sat back on their haunches. She stroked the top of the dogs' heads and ears. "Remus and Romulus are not my hunting hounds; I'm treating them for digestive problems. The barking isn't their fault. You'd bark as well if you suffered from the same condition."

Only his manners prevented him from laughing at the ridiculousness of that statement. Surely, she was mad. First a pet pig, now the ill dogs. "You are not the only person in this village, madame. Your animals are disruptive."

Her lips thinned. "*Disruptive*?"

"Is it your habit to repeat everything?" he asked.

"To repeat…" Her spine stiffened and she faced him, blue eyes blazing. "I assure you, the barking will be temporary. Just until the dogs fully recover. As for you, Mr. Millstone," she said, placing a hand on her hip, "I can honestly say that I have never encountered such an arrogant man in my life, other than my own aristocratic brother. You and Edwin would get along nicely."

My aristocratic brother. Edwin.

His gaze returned to the portrait. With pulse-pounding awareness, he realized why it disturbed him. The man looked like an older version of someone from his past, someone he didn't recall with fondness, and there was only one titled man he knew with that name.

Lord Edwin Cameron, the current Earl of Foster. The portrait must be of Edwin's father, the old Earl of Foster.

His gaze raked over Adeline. She looked nothing like her fair-haired and pale-skinned father and brother. He'd believed she was a country mouse, not an earl's sister. She'd even introduced herself as a miss and not a lady. The Earl of Foster may not be a friend, but he was still a part of the aristocracy, and Warwick had no intention of continuing to argue with an earl's sister, a lady.

"I see," he said.

"Do you?"

It was best if he left. From his physical discomfort, he suspected his arm had started bleeding and needed to be attended to. Even though he was never one to back down from an argument, no good could come from confronting the unusual woman facing him.

His voice was gruff. "I'll leave you to your business, and bid you good day, miss."

. . .

How could such a handsome man be such an arrogant arse!

Adeline let out a held-in breath as she watched Mr. Daniel Millstone walk away. Her arrival at her cottage in the quaint Chilham village was not as she'd expected, and her neighbor was no exception. He hadn't even spared a backward glance as he strode down the dirt lane toward his home. He may possess a sour disposition, but she'd have to be blind not to notice his tall, muscular build—a build she had closely encountered in the garden during the Henry incident. With his tawny hair, chiseled jaw, aristocratic nose, and vivid green eyes, he had the face and form that could make a lady glance back on the street or a barmaid linger as she offered him a tankard of ale.

Fortunately, Adeline knew not to be fooled by a handsome face. Her half brother, Lord Foster, was attractive…and spiteful. Mr. Millstone seemed to be cut from the same cloth.

As for Edwin, he'd never accepted Adeline or her mother, who'd been an untitled daughter of an Arabic rug merchant. Not a day went by that he didn't express disgust over her "mixed blood." As she'd grown, Edwin's prejudice had never changed, and he'd taken every chance to bully her and make her feel inferior.

Despite the lack of affection from her half brother, Adeline's father, the old earl, had loved her mother and had doted on Adeline. Her mother's death had devastated her father, and he'd passed less than five years after. Edwin had inherited the title and all the wealth that accompanied the estate. The former Earl of Foster hadn't set up an allowance for Adeline. Rather, he'd left her the unentailed country cottage. Before Edwin got the satisfaction of tossing her out of their childhood home, she'd packed up the cart and left.

Her father had used the country dwelling as a hunting cottage when he'd wanted to escape the hectic pace of London. She'd accompanied him to Chilham several times as a child. Her memories were of a warm and colorful home with rustic furniture, a cheery fireplace, comfortable bed, and maintained grounds.

As such, she'd expected a well-kept and quaint cottage. Instead, she'd arrived in Chilham to find a dwelling that—even described in the most favorable terms by a seller—was in much need of repair. A future owner would see it for what it was: dilapidated. The roof leaked in spots and should be replaced, and almost all the rooms needed carpentry work on the creaky floorboards and the crown molding, as well as a fresh coat of paint. Rugs needed to be replaced where the roof had leaked, and even the furniture was in poor condition. Her father hadn't visited in years, and the condition of the cottage had deteriorated. No wonder Edwin hadn't complained when the solicitor had read her father's will and bequeathed her the cottage without any funds for the repairs.

Still, she was determined to follow through with her plans of helping the country folk with their ailments. Adeline was a healer and she'd learned her mother's Middle Eastern knowledge of herbs and medicinal techniques to help the sick and injured. Her experience extended to the hunting dogs, Remus and Romulus. Their owner, a country farmer, had planned to shoot the dogs. Adeline had convinced the farmer to let her treat the young hounds first. She could never refuse a person or animal in need of aid.

Her handsome neighbor be damned.

Adeline opened the cottage door and set the basket of carrots on the small table. She'd been pleased to find them in the garden. The previous hired gardener had planted vegetables and only the carrots had survived. The table wobbled from the small weight of the basket. She glanced underneath and sighed.

One of the legs was definitely shorter than the others. She added it to the ever-growing list of repairs, just as the door burst open.

"Adeline!"

Adeline turned to smile at an older woman. "What took you so long, Hasmik?"

"I found the yarrow you were searching for."

Adeline took the herbs from her. "Wonderful! I intend to use it to treat the shopkeeper's wound."

Half Egyptian and half Armenian, Hasmik had arrived with Adeline's mother from Egypt and had served as Adeline's nursemaid. She was now her companion and dear friend. Hasmik was knowledgeable in herbs and invaluable to Adeline. Thin with reddish hair that she dyed with henna—a natural dye her mother's people often used—Hasmik had intelligent brown eyes and a wide smile. Hasmik was loyal and had often shielded Adeline from Edwin's cruelty when her mother was not able to do so. But with her dark skin—much darker than Adeline's olive complexion—Hasmik had known prejudice, and Edwin had treated her as one of the lowest servants.

"The shopkeeper won't die, but he is making a fuss about a cut on his hand. He is like an overgrown child," Hasmik said.

Adeline hoped to treat the shopkeeper in

exchange for a new chair in her parlor. With limited funds—which included her remaining pin money—she planned to find other ways to repair the cottage.

"He's not the only one to complain." Adeline's neighbor came to mind. Insufferable man.

Hasmik eyed her, then arched a brow. "Oh? What troubles you?"

Adeline blew out a breath. "What doesn't? My plans to aid the villagers are in jeopardy. The cottage is in disrepair. The roof leaks. Every piece of furniture is broken. The yard is overgrown. And my neighbor is disgruntled."

"Pardon?"

"The cottage is in—"

Hasmik held up a hand. "Not the cottage. What's this about your neighbor?"

Adeline attempted to prop a hip on the table, then remembered the uneven leg. "Mr. Millstone may be handsome, but he's just as difficult and arrogant as my half brother. Even more so."

"How handsome?"

Adeline threw her hands in the air. "Hasmik! Did you not hear me? Mr. Millstone is *rude*. He arrived on my property and rudely accused me of disturbing his peace because of the dogs."

She chuckled. "Perhaps there is some truth to his accusation. Those hunting dogs bark too much."

"As I told him, it's not the dogs' fault. The farmer gave them chicken bones that upset their stomach. Romulus is doing better on his own. Thank goodness I was able to treat Remus's vomiting and he has been drinking more and more water. Soon, we can begin feeding him boiled meat. His barking and howling has already lessened."

"Good news indeed. But is the barking the only reason your neighbor is upset?"

Adeline bit her bottom lip. "At first. But then Henry charged him."

Hasmik's jaw dropped. "Your pig attacked a man?"

"I wouldn't say *attacked,* per se, though Mr. Millstone believes differently. You know Henry is friendly. The pig reacted to Mr. Millstone's harsh tone. Mr. Millstone pushed me behind him and attempted to stop Henry. And then we…fell." More like she fell on top of him. Heat throbbed in her cheeks as she recalled their encounter. The press of her neighbor's body against hers was hard to forget. Not a touch of fat softened his hard chest.

And then there were his large hands on her waist as he'd helped her up…

"That was chivalrous of the man, but there must be more to the story."

Adeline let out a huff. "He said pigs cannot be pets."

"Most would agree. What else?"

Adeline shook off her inappropriate thoughts and tried to focus on the conversation at hand. "Henry, in his overly affectionate manner, may have hurt the man."

"Hurt him? Where?"

"When we got to our feet, Mr. Millstone flinched and cradled his forearm. I don't think it was entirely due to the force of stopping the pig, or the fall, based on the way we... landed." Heat rushed to her cheeks again, and she cleared her throat. "I suspect the man has a prior injury." Another person may not have noticed, but Adeline had seen the signs. Mr. Millstone's reaction, his flinching at the contact, then the way he'd held his arm, had alerted her.

Hasmik shook her head in disapproval. "Hmmm. Perhaps you should pay this neighbor a visit."

Her neighbor's face flashed in her mind. He'd left abruptly, but not before he'd expressed his ire. Was it possible his anger was exacerbated by pain?

Adeline shook her head. "I do not think he would appreciate seeing me. Best if I focus on the cottage's repairs so I can attend those who seek my help."

"But you are already thinking of him, aren't you? You have a soft heart, *habibti*."

Hasmik used the Arabic endearment

sweetheart—that Adeline's mother had used. And Hasmik knew her better than anyone. Adeline had difficulty turning away people in need. Her empathy superseded her stubbornness. She'd even once brewed Edwin a medicinal tea when he'd had a bad cold.

Not that Mr. Millstone was in need or would accept help.

But if her instincts were correct, then he'd had an injury and the incident with her pig had exacerbated it. Her stomach roiled. *Damn*.

Was he suffering as they spoke? Was she responsible for his pain? Had protecting her made his injury worse?

Still, she knew when she was unwanted. "My efforts are best served elsewhere. I need to gather enough funds for the cottage repairs."

"You can ask Lord Foster for aid."

Adeline laughed out loud, a harsh sound to her own ears. "Edwin wouldn't spare me a shilling."

Hasmik clucked her tongue. "Your father would disapprove of how your brother is treating you."

"Our father is dead." Her heart squeezed in her chest. A day didn't pass that she didn't think of him. At least her father had thought to leave her the cottage.

A cottage in disrepair.

He wouldn't have done so if he'd known of the poor condition of the dwelling. The more she thought about it, the more she concluded that her father must have forgotten to pay a groundskeeper to keep up the cottage.

"We will make do, *habibti*. I'll enlist the aid of the locals in the village to help with repairs. I noticed two young boys while shopping this afternoon."

"How will I pay them?"

"The boys may be willing to work for a bit less than the town carpenter."

Adeline looked about her. The leaky roof and creaky floorboards. The fencing in need of repair. The overgrown garden. Even the shutter hanging askew. "I hope so."

Hasmik's eyes twinkled with mischief. "If all else fails, maybe the man next door will come to your aid. Again."

Adeline rolled her eyes at the ludicrous notion. He may be handsome, but he was maddeningly arrogant. "That will never happen."

· · ·

The following morning, Adeline woke to loud pounding on the front door. Heart jolting, she bolted upright in bed. Blinking, she glanced at the mantel clock.

Six o'clock in the morning.

Who in God's name could it be?

For a single flustered moment, she wondered if it was her neighbor, the handsome Mr. Millstone. His visit yesterday was still fresh in her mind, thanks to an unsettling dream where he touched her waist for no protective reason at all. His nearness made her senses spin, and she was entirely caught up in her own emotions until she abruptly woke.

He wouldn't visit again soon, though, would he? If so, he had no reason to complain. Romulus's condition had improved after the third dose of the tonic she'd administered to ease his nausea. And with his relief his barking had ceased.

So who could it be? Other than the pounding, the cottage was eerily quiet. As was her habit, Hasmik had already risen and left for the village for fresh cream and eggs.

Adeline threw off the covers and slipped out of bed. She didn't bother with a night rail. She slept in loose-fitting white linen Arabic pants and a tunic that fell to her hips. She dressed as a proper English lady in the day, but behind closed doors, she preferred her mother's traditional, comfortable garb.

She padded barefoot through the cottage and opened the door.

She wished she hadn't.

Edwin stood on her front step. His gaze raked over her from head to toe, and a look of disapproval, one that she was accustomed to, flashed in his eyes. She swallowed hard as old fears and uncertainties arose, and her fingers tensed on the door handle. She was conscious of her unpinned dark hair in disarray on her shoulders.

"Hello, Adeline." Her name rasped across her half brother's lips like a curse.

"Edwin." She chose not to address him using his newly minted title. Her beloved father had held that title, and to address Edwin with it seemed like an abomination.

She wasn't ready. She'd never be ready.

"I realize we are in the country, but must you dress like a heathen?"

Her practiced smile disguised her anger. "I was sleeping. And need I remind you that *you* are the one knocking on my door at this very early hour. Why are you here?"

Edwin pushed the door fully open and stepped inside the cottage. "I wasn't aware the country had respectable calling hours. To answer your question, I am here on a matter of family urgency."

Adeline's pulse leaped as she shut the door. "Is Mary unwell?"

Mary was Adeline's beloved half sister, almost a year older than her, but Adeline had always thought of Mary as a twin.

Mary was the one person both Edwin and Adeline cared for. Mary had a sweet disposition and was terribly shy, night from day compared to Edwin. She had been all nerves in anticipation of the upcoming Season, whereas Adeline had chosen to travel to the country to work as a healer.

Mary had her own secret talent. She was a prolific writer and had published short stories under a pseudonym. For almost a year, Mary had been working on a full-length novel. Edwin had no idea. Adeline had always marveled at Edwin's ignorance of Mary's publishing endeavors, considering Mary would disappear for hours in her room to write.

"Mary is fine," Edwin said. "This does not concern her."

A knot in Adeline's stomach eased. "Then what matter of family urgency?"

His lips curled in a crocodile smile. "It's simple, dear sister. I've arranged for you to marry."

CHAPTER TWO

Adeline gaped. "Pardon?"

"You are to marry a man by the name of Mr. Slade," Edwin said, his tone light, as if he had announced she was to attend a frivolous garden party hosted by one of the ladies of the *ton*.

Of all the asinine things she'd expected her half brother to say, that he had arranged her marriage to a stranger was not one of them.

"You arrive here unannounced to tell me I'm to marry? Have you lost your mind?" In contrast to his offhand delivery, her voice was high-pitched and laced with irritation.

"I have little choice. Believe me when I say that I would be anywhere else if I were able." Edwin walked past her and into the small parlor, his eyes darting to the sparse furnishings, consisting of a couch with sagging cushions, an end table in need of sanding and refinishing, and peeling wall coverings. Hasmik had picked a bouquet of bright yellow buttercups and placed them in a porcelain vase on the end table to add a splash of color to the drab room.

Edwin took no notice. His lips twitched in distaste as he picked up a pillow, tossed it aside, and sat on a chair with fading upholstery. She wanted to scream that he wasn't welcome and that he shouldn't make himself comfortable.

She also wanted an explanation.

"Do not expect me to go along with whatever mad plan you have concocted." She remained standing and didn't offer refreshment. At least she felt some small advantage standing while he sat.

Edwin stretched his legs and crossed his booted feet at the ankles. "It's not a mad plan, but one of necessity. My hands are tied."

"Perhaps it's best if you explain."

His eyes darted over her dress. "I can wait until you dress properly."

"I am dressed properly." He may not like her Middle Eastern garb, but she wouldn't change on his behalf.

"I should expect no less from you. Your mother was a camel-riding foreigner."

Her temper rose by the second. She should be used to his insults of her and her mother by now, but the truth was, the barbs still stung.

She raised her chin a notch. She'd overheard him and his aristocratic friends speak in the study of her family home when they'd believed the ladies had been occupied elsewhere. They'd smoked their cigars, consumed whisky, and talked about women. The mixed bloods were worthy of mistresses, never wives, and their bigoted beliefs had tormented her with confusing emotions of shame and simmering anger.

She'd never believed a title made a gentleman. In fact, her experience with Edwin and his friends had pointed to the exact opposite. "Do not try to change the subject."

"Fine," he snapped. "The truth is that Father left the estate in debt."

That admission seemed preposterous. Her fingers twisted in her pants. "Father wasn't a gambler. You inherited all of the earldom's estates and its wealth."

She wasn't aware of any financial hardships. Had Edwin gambled it away so soon? But that didn't make sense either. For all his faults, her brother was not a gambler. At least not to her knowledge.

Edwin snorted. "I inherited a steep mortgage for the remodeling of the London home as well as merchant debt."

When her mother was alive every luxury had been afforded them. Her father, the old earl, had spared no expense, and Adeline recalled his purchasing her mother jewels and fashionable gowns. She also recalled them hosting lavish parties and hiring master carpenters and decorators to remodel their London home in Berkeley Square. Growing up, Adeline had always thought the earldom's coffers were plentiful.

Her father's death a month prior had

changed her life. Had the former earl sheltered her from any hardship? Other than Edwin, only Mary resided in the London home. "What about Mary?"

"I did my duty for my sister and funded her Season—gown, shoes, jewels—and I haven't touched her dowry. Mary is unaware of the situation."

She was grateful he'd looked after Mary. She shook her head. "Why not tell Mary everything?"

"Do not be obtuse. Gentlemen do not speak to ladies of their financial concerns."

"You are speaking to me," she blurted before realizing the truth. He didn't consider her a lady, even if their father had married their mother and she was as legitimate as Mary. In his eyes, she was of mixed blood and a stain on the family name. It didn't help that the old earl never loved Edwin's mother, but had adored Adeline's mother, the daughter of a Middle Eastern merchant. A commoner.

Even more damning, the old earl had married Adeline's mother two weeks after his first wife's death. It was a sin Edwin could never forget or forgive.

She was aware of Edwin watching her, waiting for her response. "I'm pleased you did right by Mary, but what's this nonsense about me marrying?"

Edwin stood and went to the parlor

window. Hasmik had removed the curtains to wash them, and they currently hung on a line drying in the spring breeze. As a result, Edwin had a clear view of the overgrown hedgerows and the makeshift pen that housed Henry, who was currently rolling in a patch of mud.

"Well?" Adeline prodded.

Edwin turned away from the window. "I seized an opportunity to improve things by investing in a shipping enterprise that promised to return with goods from China."

Chinoiserie decor was all the rage with the *ton*, and Adeline knew such a venture had the potential to be quite lucrative. She recalled attending a ball where two ten-foot-tall statues of Chinese warriors flanked the ballroom entrance like silent sentinels. Even the ballroom walls had been decorated with wall coverings depicting images of pandas and bamboo. She'd thought the statutes ostentatious for a London ballroom, but the guests had marveled at the decor.

Edwin folded his hands behind his back. "I borrowed money from a moneylender for the investment. Mr. Slade's interest on the loan was exorbitant, but the benefits outweighed the risks."

"And did they?"

"The ship sank at sea."

A soft gasp escaped her. "I assume Lloyd's of London insured the cargo."

He winced. "I didn't see the need. Purchasing insurance was an extra expense."

"I see." Only she didn't. No halfway responsible businessman would make that mistake. Why had he traveled all this way? Edwin must know she didn't have funds to aid him, and what did all of this have to do with her marrying—

"The moneylender, Mr. Stan Slade, seeks respectability and entrance into Society this season. Despite your mother's lineage, you are the daughter of an earl. Your marriage to the moneylender assures he gets what he needs. Fortunately, he had seen you walking in the park and finds no objection to you. In exchange for your hand, he has graciously agreed to forgive the entire debt."

She blinked. A sinking sensation settled in her stomach. For all the bad blood between them, she'd never believed he would treat her with so little regard. "You're jesting. Tell me you are jesting."

Edwin turned to fully face her. He was tall, a good foot taller than she, and he used it to his advantage as he towered over her. "I am the head of the family now, Adeline. Father is no longer here to coddle you. You will do as you are told."

Her anger rose, and her fingers clenched at her sides. She refused to be cowed. This was her future and her happiness they were discussing. "No, I will not. Since your bad business decision caused the problem, it's up to you to find a solution."

His lips curved into a smug smile. "From the looks of your new home, you aren't in a position to argue. The roof may fall down upon your head this winter."

"Then I'd rather live in a barn. My answer is still no."

His eyes narrowed to slits. "You were always ungrateful. You will marry the man. It will be done before the end of the Season. Nothing else will satisfy Mr. Slade."

Her temper flared, hot and vivid. He was supposed to protect her, to have some amount of responsibility for her happiness, not to bargain her off to a moneylender. "Get out."

When he didn't move, she picked up the vase of buttercups and tossed it at his head. Edwin ducked and it crashed against the wall, shattering into shards of porcelain and splotches of yellow flowers across the wood floor. Panting with rage, she pointed to the door and bellowed, "Out!"

• • •

Warwick settled behind his desk in his study and reached for the stack of correspondence that Nelson had delivered. He had come to the country to work on his inventions. Never one to neglect his ducal responsibilities, his ledgers were already balanced, he met regularly with his stewards, and he ensured the multitude of staff that oversaw his numerous estates were cared for.

His duty to produce an heir and spare was another matter entirely.

Warwick sorted through the letters, then froze. On the fifth one, he recognized the flowing script as belonging to his godmother, Lady Heywood.

With hesitation, he broke the seal and read.

Warwick,
Your desire to remain in the country during the Season is ill-timed. If you do not hurry and return to Town, all the good ones will be taken.
Lady H

Good riddance, he wanted to write back to his well-meaning godmother. *Let them be taken.* He felt the beginnings of a headache at his temples, an irritable throbbing. If he didn't love his godmother, he'd rip the letter in half and toss it into the wastepaper basket.

But Lady Heywood had never abandoned him, even when those closest—those with a stronger responsibility—had cruelly neglected him. She'd been there when his mother had sent him away to Eton soon after his eighth birthday. His keen intelligence was apparent at an early age and, rather than encourage his inquisitiveness, the duke and duchess had never understood him, viewed him as odd, and had treated him coldly.

Lady Heywood had been his mother's best friend when they'd attended the same finishing school for ladies. They had stayed friends and his mother had chosen Lady Heywood to be his godmother upon his birth. Things had changed between them, however, when Lady Heywood had disagreed about his upbringing.

It was his godmother who'd come to visit him during holidays and invited him to her residence over the summers. His godmother who'd never once forgotten his birthday, and his godmother who'd been proud when he'd received the highest marks at Eton and then at Oxford. And his godmother who'd stood by his side at the burial when he'd lost his parents years later in a carriage accident.

How could he deny her now?

Warwick scowled at the letter. He knew he'd eventually have to concede. He was a duke, after all, and the continuation of the title required an heir. To get an heir, he needed a wife.

But he sought one more Season of freedom. One more Season to focus on his work.

Was that too much to ask?

An image of a dark-haired virago flashed

in his thoughts. Frustrated, he rubbed the back of his neck. He kept thinking of his neighbor when all he wanted to do was shove the memory deep in the recesses of his mind.

The headache shifted to the base of his skull. He covered the letter with a stack of other papers. If he didn't see it, he wouldn't have to address it.

Childish? Yes. Did he care? Not today.

A strange noise sounded outside. He lifted his head and squinted at the study's open doorway. Other than Nelson and a limited staff, there was no one to disturb him here. So what was that sound?

It almost sounded like…like a *snort*.

Good God, was his headache causing hallucinations?

The snorting grew louder and then—to his complete shock—a pig entered his private domain.

No. Not just any pig.

Henry.

He'd be able to pick that spotted nose out of a pen full of pigs. Bloody hell!

Warwick pushed back his chair and stood. Henry approached and, as if in a daze, Warwick reached out to touch the top of the pig's head. Sharp, intelligent eyes met his. If he didn't know any better, he'd swear the pig greeted him.

"Nelson!" he bellowed.

The butler appeared in the doorway in seconds. "Your Grace?"

"Explain." Warwick pointed to the pig. Henry had waddled to the sofa and begun nibbling one of the ruffles of a pillow. Soon, stuffing puffed out of the ripped seam.

Nelson's eyes bulged in his pale face. If Warwick's temples weren't throbbing, he would almost consider his butler's expression comical.

"How did a pig get inside my home?" Warwick's voice sounded harsh to his own ears. He supposed being pressured to marry and a giant pig wandering into his study in the span of a few minutes would do that to a man.

"I must have left the front door ajar, Your Grace."

"You must have indeed."

Nelson hurried forward then stopped a foot away from the pig. It was clear the proper butler had no idea what to do. Henry dropped the ruined pillow and nudged the butler's hand.

Nelson jumped back as if he'd been bit. "I have no idea where the pig came from, Your Grace. I shall look for its owner at once."

"Do not trouble yourself, Nelson. I know the owner. I'll deal with her. Meanwhile, help me get that pig out of my study."

• • •

Warwick massaged his temple. Beads of perspiration dotted his brow. Even with Nelson's help, attempting to shove a two-hundred-pound pig out of his study and his house had been unsuccessful. It had finally taken a good amount of bribery with lettuce, carrots, and apples to lure the blasted pig outside.

Taking matters immediately into his own hands, Warwick used the leftover apples to cajole Henry down the country lane.

"That's it," he spoke to the pig. "If you want more, keep coming along." Good God, if his friend, the Earl of Drake, saw him now, he'd never let him live it down.

At last, his neighbor's home came into view. Warwick halted long enough to rub the back of his neck again where his headache had settled. He needed to calm his temper before he saw the woman.

He'd been well on his way to a foul mood before the pig had paid him a visit. Despite Lady Heywood's demands, marriage was far from his mind and not one of his imminent goals. He had much more pressing matters. When he did marry, it would be a business-minded choice. Not much would change in his life. He'd still work on his inventions, visit booksellers, and attend science meetings where he'd enjoy stimulating intellectual conversations. During this time, his wife could occupy herself with whatever nonsensical society events the *ton* devised. His godmother didn't understand his reasoning, of course, and nothing would make her happier than if he were betrothed.

As Warwick got closer to the house, Henry spotted a bucket of slop in his pen and meandered to the food.

"All it takes is kitchen scraps to distract you and make you happy?" he asked the pig.

Henry looked up from his meal and snorted. Warwick shook his head as he approached to secure the pen when shouting sounded from the cottage. He turned to the sound, his pulse quickening. What the devil was going on?

"I said get out!" Warwick's muscles tensed as he heard a woman's voice, full of rage.

The front door was ajar, and a man's angry response was clear as day. "No. You will do as you're told. You shall marry Mr. Stan Slade before the end of this Season!"

"Perhaps *you* should marry the money-lender. It's your debt that needs to be satisfied, not mine."

"You ungrateful bitch!"

Warwick sprinted to the porch and pushed the door all the way open. Lady Adeline stood in the center of the parlor arguing with a man. But not just any man.

Edwin, the Earl of Foster.

Warwick avoided London society, but he

could pick his childhood nemesis out of a thick crowd. Tall with pale hair and brown eyes, Edwin had an arrogant air, a smugness of expression that bordered on narcissism. Warwick's blood pounded. He'd been right about the painting in the back of the wagon. Edwin's resemblance to his father was uncanny.

Engaged in a heated argument, neither noticed him standing in the doorway. He used the opportunity to take in the scene. A broken vase and flowers lay scattered on the floorboards in a puddle of water.

He'd overheard enough of the argument to understand the situation between brother and sister. The Earl of Foster sought to arrange his sister's marriage to a moneylender named Mr. Slade. Adeline refused.

His gaze was immediately drawn to Adeline. Her blue eyes flashed with anger and her mahogany curls cascaded across her shoulders and down her back. She was dressed in a strange garment. Her breasts heaved beneath the low neckline and a silk sash was cinched at her slender waist. Her legs were encased in loose-fitting trousers. Whatever she was wearing, it was definitely not English, and he suspected that she had been unprepared for her brother's early morning visit. She folded her arms across her chest in a protective motion. She looked alive, lovely…and vulnerable.

Her beauty was exquisite. Thick, dark lashes framed blue eyes. Her lips were full and rounded over even teeth. Her garment emphasized her figure, and her curves were singed in his memory as he'd hauled her against him in the yard. But it was her spirit that called out to him, unafraid and fiercely challenging as she faced the earl. Warwick couldn't look away.

A man who easily mastered complex mechanical devices, he often struggled to interpret emotions. But any difficulties he'd had in the past didn't apply now. Adeline's brows were drawn downward, and she lowered her hands, her fingers clenching the sides of the loose-fitting garment. She was furious and frightened.

Clearly, Edwin was the cause of her distress. Warwick didn't like it, not one bit. His own fists clenched, and he wanted to pounce forward and tear Edwin away from Adeline and toss him out the door.

He inhaled, then slowly exhaled. Violence wouldn't do. Not here. He disliked Lord Foster, but this wasn't Eton, and they were no longer boys. His breath may burn in his throat at the sight of the earl, but whatever occurred in this cottage had nothing to do with him. He should walk away.

Instead, he took another step into the

parlor and cleared his throat. "Pardon the intrusion."

Two pairs of eyes met his. One brown, one bright blue.

Adeline blinked and her lips parted. "Mr. Millstone. What are you doing here?"

"Your pig decided to visit me in my workroom."

"Henry?"

"Do you own another pig?"

"No."

Lord Foster's brows slashed downward. "What on God's earth are you two talking about? And why are you here, *Your Grace*?"

Adeline's gasp echoed through the parlor, and she pressed one hand to her heart. "Your Grace?" She shook her head. "You must be mistaken. This is my neighbor, Mr. Millstone."

"Your neighbor? You're the one who is mistaken, Adeline." Edwin's lips twisted with dislike. "May I have the pleasure of introducing you to His Grace, the Duke of Warwick."

Bloody hell. Of all the people to expose his identity, he'd never dreamed it would be Edwin. The man seemed to relish revealing his title. Christ! Lord Foster had been an ass as a youth. Nothing had changed.

Warwick's gaze clashed with Edwin's. "May I inquire what's going on here?"

Edwin waved him away like an annoying fly. "This is a family matter that has nothing to do with you, Your Grace."

Warwick's already surly mood veered sharply to anger. "Ah, but you have a grating voice, Foster, and I could hear it all the way down the lane. It sounded much like your failed argument in the House last year when you wanted to limit soldiers' pensions. You were outvoted and outranked as I recall." He enjoyed putting the earl in his place. "As for today, I feared the lady was at the mercy of brigands or thieves and in need of aid." Warwick eyed the shattered porcelain vase on the wood floor. "I wasn't far off."

Edwin's eyes narrowed. "As you can see, there are no brigands or thieves. My discussion with my sister is not your affair."

Warwick had already overheard Adeline's objection to Foster's plans of marrying her off to a moneylender. Would her will, or the earl's, prevail?

Despite his dislike of the Earl of Foster, he knew the man was right. Warwick had no standing to interfere. The pig was in its pen, and her hounds had ceased howling. He had no reason or right to stay. No reason to concern himself with the drama unfolding before him.

Then why am I hesitant to leave? Was it because of his animosity toward his childhood bully? Or something else?

It's not my concern.

He needed to extricate himself from the family drama taking place. It was not his fight, no matter how intriguing he found his neighbor. Warwick started to turn away just as the earl reached for Adeline's arm. She winced.

Warwick's gaze met hers, pain and anger and fear flashing in the blue depths of her eyes. Something tightened in his chest, something uncomfortable and unexpected, and, before he could stop himself, he turned back, his booted feet solid and square on the hardwood floor. He shot the earl a penetrating look as the words escaped his lips.

"You're wrong, Foster. This matter has everything to do with me. You see, I'm courting your sister."

CHAPTER THREE

I'm courting your sister.

Comprehension came slowly for Adeline. She'd barely begun processing the shock of her ornery and handsome neighbor being the Duke of Warwick, and now he announced they were courting?

Confused thoughts and feelings tumbled through her. What on earth was the duke thinking? They'd met only once, and it hadn't been pleasant. Oh, she recalled their physical collision before Henry had charged. The shock of the heat and hardness of him when he'd hauled her against him had been quick, but unforgettable. The shock on his aristocratic face as the pig had nuzzled him after the fall had been just as remarkable. She also remembered the first time she'd seen him—the golden brown hair, the chiseled profile, and the piercing green eyes—were not ones a woman could easily forget.

Until he'd opened his mouth. She'd thought him arrogant and high-handed.

So why would Warwick claim that he was courting her?

Adeline stole a quick glance at her brother, and he looked just as taken aback.

"What did you say?" Edwin released her arm.

The duke arched an imperious brow. "I said I'm courting your sister. If you'd given her a chance to explain, I have no doubt that she would have told you herself."

"I see." Edwin turned to Adeline. "Is it true?"

The words were thick as molasses in her throat. "I...I—"

"She is obviously speechless from happiness," Warwick interrupted. "It has been easy to keep our secret in the country far away from the gossipmongers of the *ton*. We realize it will have to come to light soon enough when we return to Town."

Edwin eyed him with a critical squint. "This is...unexpected."

The duke held his gaze. "Unexpected, indeed."

"From what I've heard, Warwick, you're interested only in intellectual matters and associate with scientists. Not women."

"That's because I never met a woman like your sister." The duke flashed a wolflike smile at Adeline that suddenly caused her heart to thump in her chest and her frayed nerves to tighten.

"Who knew the country air could inspire such sweet romance?" He motioned to the scattered flowers across the floorboards. "I see my flowers have fallen victim to your...discussion. I gave them to the lady only yesterday."

Edwin's eyebrows shot up, even as his mouth curled in a sneer. "Your flowers? Do not tell me you have written poetry as well?"

The duke shrugged. "Her beauty inspires me."

"From what I've heard, steam engines inspire you."

Understanding dawned as Adeline watched the exchange between her brother and the duke. Clearly, they had a past—and it was not pleasant. And somehow, she'd become a pawn in whatever standoff they were now engaged. She wanted to demand an explanation from the duke but couldn't until her brother departed.

Warwick sighed. "I find you tiresome. What will it take for you to believe us?"

Foster tore his attention from Warwick to glower at her. "Is there a witness to this courting? You are a maiden alone in the country and your virtue is at stake."

Adeline shook her head, heart pounding. The notion that he was suddenly concerned with her virtue was ridiculous. He couldn't wait until she'd left their Berkley Square home. He'd never inquired about her whereabouts or what she'd been doing in the small country village.

"I'm not alone. Hasmik is with me," she said.

Edwin glowered. "That dark-skinned heathen is hardly a proper chaperone."

Adeline's temper spiked and she glowered. "Do not speak of her that way! She has been with the family for years and is my devoted companion. Father always treated Hasmik with respect and kindness."

"Only because your mother had bewitched him with her Middle Eastern concoctions."

"Enough!" Warwick roared. "Don't disparage your sister's family that way."

Adeline gaped, completely taken aback at Warwick's unexpected defense. He may be an arrogant aristocrat himself, but it was clear he could not abide her brother's prejudice.

Her gaze returned to Edwin, a cold knot forming in her stomach as she faced him. "As for my mother's 'concoctions,' they saved lives." Edwin had never understood her mother's healing abilities, and the fact that Adeline followed in her mother's footsteps had irked him even more.

Edwin pointed a finger at her. "This isn't resolved, Adeline."

She raised her chin a notch and met his icy gaze. "It is for today. I think you should leave, my lord." Of the two men in her home, she wanted Edwin gone more. Both had surprised her this morning, Edwin with his demand that she marry a stranger—a moneylender, no less—and the duke with his mad outburst that he was courting her.

Her brother's jaw tightened, his frustration evident in his blotched complexion. He looked like he wanted to throttle her. Until today, he'd never placed a hand on her. His cruel comments had been sufficient barbs.

Still, she was aware of Warwick standing to the side, tall and solid, and for several passing heartbeats, she was relieved for his presence.

Edwin turned on his heel and stormed out of the cottage. She held her tongue until his carriage door closed, and the conveyance departed down the winding country road before whirling to face her neighbor.

"Pray tell me what were you thinking, *Your Grace*?"

• • •

As far as questions went, the lady's was succinct and to the point. It was the same question Warwick had been asking himself in the few moments since Lord Foster had departed.

What the hell had I been thinking to claim I was courting her?

A logical man thought things through. Spontaneity was not in his nature. Impulsiveness led to dangerous experiments and failed laboratory results. The burn on his arm was evidence of this fact. He'd been pressed to show his results with his experiment of a fast-burning gunpowder, and he'd experienced the consequences of his haste. Perhaps the heightened pain of the burn had affected his behavior.

It was suddenly quiet in the cottage, and he was aware of Adeline's gaze. The shade of blue was unlike any other he'd seen. Not quite sapphire. Not cornflower blue. A deep azure with chips of black.

Good God. Why am I thinking of her eye color?

There had to be a good reason for his behavior. Except, there wasn't.

Which left him one option—bluff.

"It makes perfect sense." His voice held an entirely fabricated note of confidence.

"How so, *Your Grace*?"

The sarcasm in her tone when she used his title was apparent. He couldn't fault her. He'd had no intention of revealing his identity; he'd planned on residing in the small village with no one the wiser. But he'd also never anticipated that his neighbor would be the Earl of Foster's sister. Of all the rotten luck.

She tapped a toe. "Well?"

How to explain his behavior? "*Well*, I overheard your predicament with your brother, Lord Foster."

"My *half* brother." Her brow furrowed. "You eavesdropped?"

"Not quite. A person eavesdrops only if they have intent to do so. I had no such interest. Your argument was loud enough to wake the dead."

Indignation lit her eyes. "I beg your pardon. You're the one who trespassed on my property, not once, but twice."

"I had no choice. Your pig trespassed on mine."

Her eyebrows arched. "I find that hard to believe. Henry has never wandered away before."

"Not only did he wander, but he also entered my home." The memory of the pig helping himself to the pillow on the sofa in his study was not one he would easily forget. "I had to bribe him with food to return here."

"He must like you. Otherwise, Henry wouldn't have visited." She bit her bottom lip, and his gaze lowered to her mouth. She had kissable lips, plump and pink.

Do not think of her lips. Or her eyes, no matter how fascinating the color.

"As I told you before, I doubt a pig can express affection." He heard the surliness in his voice.

"As I told *you* before, you don't have much experience with pigs. Henry is my pet. I allow him in my own home at times. He must have thought he was welcome to enter yours."

"That's the most ridiculous thing I've ever

heard. You may be a lady, but you need a lesson in manners."

"Me! What about you? I do not care if you are a duke. You are truly ill-mannered."

Her eyes were dazzling with fury. Rather than respond with anger, he found himself entranced. His heart thundered as his eyes raked boldly over her. There was no rationale behind these feelings. None at all. He cleared his throat. "If the former duke and duchess were alive, I believe they would agree with you."

His parents had hired numerous tutors in Greek, Latin, mathematics, geography, and other subjects the young men of the aristocracy were expected to learn. His tutors had lasted only a few weeks, some even less, before departing—often fleeing—the ducal mansion. Warwick had swiftly mastered the subjects and grown bored and restless. His inability to focus had often been interpreted as a challenge to their authority and a lack of discipline. Those hired to teach him gentlemanly manners often became even more frustrated by his lack of interest.

Her expression softened momentarily, but then she let out a huff. "Do not change the subject. Why did you tell Edwin that you are courting me?"

He hadn't a clue. But he needed to find an answer not just for the lady but for himself.

True, his godmother's letter had been rattling
around his brain, but that wasn't enough to
blurt out their courtship to Edwin. It had
been something more that had made him act,
and—after more thought—he precisely knew
the cause. The moment Edwin had grasped
Adeline's arm and her blue eyes had met his,
a tightness had spread within his chest. He
couldn't leave her at Edwin's mercy, couldn't
allow him to force her against her will. All
rational thought had fled and had spurred
him to act.

"You do not wish to marry the moneylender, Mr. Slade. My godmother, Lady
Heywood, is pressuring me to marry."

"So? Your godmother is right. You are a
duke and must produce an heir and spare.
And what does that have to do with me? I do
not want to be your wife."

"I understand my duty all too well.
However, I wish to put off marriage for the
Season to finish my work."

Her delicate brows drew together, and she
threw her hands up in exasperation. "*What*
work? Dukes don't work."

He took offense. "Untrue. Other than the
management of my estates, overseeing my
staff and tenants, my seat in the House of
Lords, and other ducal matters, I am an inventor. My current innovations are the sole
reason I'm in the country. I seek temporary

peace and quiet away from the hubbub of London."

She eyed him warily. "What types of inventions?"

He shook his head. "They are of no importance to you."

She folded her arms across her chest. "You don't think a woman is intelligent enough to comprehend your work?"

"More that I don't have time to explain my work."

A flash of anger lit her gaze. The tension stretched even tighter between them. "Then let me see if my simple female mind can summarize your dilemma. You wish to avoid your matchmaking godmother and the bevy of debutantes who are no doubt after your title and wealth? A duke *is* the ultimate prize, after all."

He didn't miss the continued censure in her voice. He chose to ignore it. "Precisely. Which leads me to my offer. If we agree to a fake courtship, Society will believe I have every intention of proposing marriage and you have every intention of accepting. As you said, what woman wouldn't want to catch a duke? It's the perfect plan."

"Oh, really? The perfect plan, you say?"

"Yes."

"You are forgetting one glaring question."

"Which is?"

"What happens at the end of the Season?"

That part felt easy enough to understand. "Mr. Slade is seeking to marry by the end of this Season, correct?"

"Apparently."

"Then after the Season ends, we go our separate ways. You return to the country and your home here." He tried not to flinch as he waved a hand around the disheveled parlor. "I shall finish my work, then return to my London residence. It's a logical plan. What do you say?"

Adeline unfolded her arms and shot him an incredulous look. "Logical? I don't think there is one smidge"—she held up a forefinger and thumb pressed tightly together—"of logic in your outrageous plan."

He bristled at her choice of words. No one had ever had the nerve to challenge his decisions. "I'd hardly call it outrageous."

She held up a hand and started to pace. Warwick imagined all the scenarios flitting through her pretty head. As she moved, his gaze roved over her face, and lower to the swell of her breasts above the foreign-looking garment. From the side, the curve of her breast was visible beneath the fine linen.

Her eyes. Her lips. Now her breasts. He tore his gaze away, but the image was hard to scrub from his mind. What was wrong with him?

Biology. What red-blooded man wouldn't notice?

She halted and measured him with a cool, appraising look. "If I agree to this, we'd have to return to Town."

The simple statement had the same effect as if she'd tossed a bucket of cold water over his head. His gaze snapped back to hers. "What? Why?"

This was unexpected and unwanted. He hadn't intended to return to London during the current Season, but to remain in Kent until all his work was completed to his specifications.

She planted her hands on her hips. "Don't be daft! How else are we to convince both Lord Foster and your godmother of the charade? We must be seen together in London. Do you have a better idea?"

He felt as if a suffocating hand was closing around his throat. She was right, dammit. Still, he loathed to consent. He had no wish to return and face the *beau monde*...or his godmother. He hated Society events. "A week at most."

She tossed a lock of dark hair across her shoulder and shook her head. "Two, at least. We have to attend balls, garden parties, and be seen together by High Society."

He narrowed his eyes. "How many balls and parties?"

"As many as needed. And you'd have to woo me with flowers, chocolate, and poetry."

He scrunched his nose at the last item on her list. "You cannot be serious."

Her lips twisted upward in a half smile. "You told Edwin as much regarding poetry."

Among other things, he regretted ever mentioning poetry to Lord Foster. He supposed he could hire someone to write a blasted poem or two. Starving artists were plentiful in town. He needed all his spare time to improve the efficiency of the high-pressure steam pistons.

She bit her full lower lip. "We must rehearse. Get to know basic facts about each other."

"Such as?" He had made the offer, but she was quickly taking over with stipulations. Had he made a mistake? At each item she listed, his nerves tightened incrementally like one of his workshop screws. Clearly, he hadn't thought everything through. Another first for him.

She waved a hand. "Oh, all the ordinary things couples know about each other. Our favorite pastimes, favorite colors, funny stories about our childhoods. Lord Foster will not easily be misled."

And his godmother was far shrewder than Edwin. He supposed it was a good idea to know these things about each other before he introduced Adeline to Lady Heywood. He anticipated that she would have dozens of questions for him and Adeline. His godmother was not an ordinary lady and could be quite eccentric. If anyone could ferret out their charade, it would be his godmother.

"You agree?" Adeline folded her hands before her and waited.

The initial idea had been his own. As for her terms, he had quickly realized that he had little choice. "I suppose."

"You suppose? Do you consent or not?"

Christ! She was bossy and argumentative. "Yes. Yes, I agree."

She nodded. "Good. It's settled then."

The tightening in his chest eased, but at the same time, the burn on his forearm began to throb anew. It was as if now that they had an understanding, he grew more aware of his own discomfort.

The wound was tightly wrapped beneath his shirtsleeve, and he couldn't wait to remove the constraining bandages. He needed to get back home. His trusted butler, Nelson, had been following the doctor's orders, and Warwick needed another treatment. And a glass of whisky. Or two.

"How did you injure your arm, Your Grace?" Adeline's voice was soft and inquisitive. Her tone was different, and it caught him off guard.

She was no longer looking at him, but her gaze had lowered to his arm. He realized he'd been clutching his forearm just above the wound. He dropped his hand.

The burn was hidden beneath his shirt-sleeves. "It's nothing. An old injury."

"I don't believe that. You flinched when Henry first greeted you."

"He didn't greet me, he charged me."

Her eyes flashed blue fire. Whatever softness had touched her voice was gone. "You are in the country. Mishaps with farm animals are a risk."

"A risk! You said he was a pet, remember?" He shot her a stern look. Once more, she seemed to ignore it.

"I remember. Now may I see?"

"No."

Her brow furrowed. "If it's nothing, then you shouldn't mind if I take a look."

"Do not trouble yourself."

"Are you this stubborn about everything, Your Grace? If so, then I don't think our plan will work."

Warwick's jaw tightened. He knew when he was outmaneuvered. He was also aware of his faults…and sheer stubbornness was one of them. He was a duke. His word was all but law, and his staff and acquaintances never questioned his requests.

Clearly, this woman was not easily cowed.

She spoke her mind and challenged him. He almost admired her courage. Almost.

She came close and reached for his sleeve. "Let me see."

CHAPTER FOUR

Adeline rolled up Warwick's shirtsleeve and unwound the bandage. She was aware of the tenseness in his large body and his muscled forearm. He didn't want her to touch him, to see beneath the bandages.

When the last of the cotton strips fell away, she stifled a gasp at the unsightly burn. She'd seen worse. It wasn't just the injury that caused dismay, but the ineffective treatment. The skin had never properly healed and was raw, angry, and seeping.

Good God, how had he managed the pain?

"I'm treating it." The duke's voice was gruff as if he anticipated her surprise and disapproval at the sight of his wound.

"How?"

"Flour. My butler applies the treatment."

She pursed her lips. She'd heard of the use of flour to treat burns by English doctors. Her mother had called many of their Western techniques ineffective, sometimes barbaric. Looking at the duke's injury, she wholeheartedly agreed.

Her voice was brisk. "Flour smothers the burn but does not heal it."

"How would you know?"

"I am a healer."

"A healer? You are an earl's daughter."

She had lost count of the number of times a man had dismissed her abilities. From his condescending tone, the Duke of Warwick was no exception.

"So? You are a duke and an inventor," she pointed out.

"That's different."

She made a sound of disgust. "Why?"

"I attended Oxford and studied physics and mathematics."

"I studied Eastern medicines from my mother."

"Your mother was not from England?"

She was surprised he didn't know. Many members of the *beau monde* knew of her heritage. Warwick had isolated himself from Society more than she'd thought. Or he'd never bothered to read Debrett's like some religiously read the Bible or the scandal sheets. Maybe he just didn't care. He had spoken up for her when Edwin had disparaged her mother and Hasmik, but the duke didn't know all the facts.

She wasn't ashamed of her heritage, and it was best if he learned the truth now. If he wanted to rescind his offer of "courtship," then he must tell her. She'd have to make an excuse to Edwin, of course, but he wouldn't shed a tear over the loss of the Duke of Warwick as her suitor. The two men seemed to barely tolerate each other. Besides, Edwin would be more than eager to pressure Adeline to marry the moneylender.

Heavens. She suddenly found herself hoping Warwick *didn't* care about her mixed blood.

"My mother was the daughter of a traveling Arabic rug merchant. She was a skilled midwife and learned healing techniques from her own mother and her mother's mother in Lebanon. Oftentimes, her father—my grandfather—would trade rugs for healing herbs and bring them back to England for her use."

"You have an interesting background. I'd like to travel to the Mediterranean and Middle East in the future. If one is able, they should experience different cultures."

No hint of concern, or worse, prejudice, tainted his handsome features, and a tenseness eased from Adeline's shoulders.

"It makes sense that Foster is only your half brother. You two look nothing alike," Warwick said.

"The old earl married my mother weeks after his first wife died."

His eyes sharpened. "Foster didn't like that, did he?"

"I'd rather not speak of him." She forced an even tone, despite her pounding pulse. Her family discord was not something she wanted to share. Having overheard her argument with Edwin, the duke had already witnessed more than any outsider. "Now, sit and rest your arm on the table so I may properly examine your wound."

She was conscious of the duke's gaze. He wanted to object. She shouldn't care and shouldn't be upset if he chose to leave. He could continue listening to the English physician and apply the flour. It was not her concern.

But the healer in her could never ignore someone in pain or in need.

And the duke was hurting. She'd sensed it after Henry had charged him and he'd protected her—a stranger—by pushing her behind him and then breaking her fall to the ground. She also grudgingly admitted that she owed him gratitude for sending Edwin away.

Still, he was a stranger, and she was uneasy with their agreement.

Warwick must have decided to take her up on her offer. He pulled out a chair, sat, and rested his forearm on the kitchen table. He frowned when the table wobbled a bit. One leg was an inch shorter than the others.

He shook his head. "Your entire cottage needs repair, including the furnishings."

It was rude to point out the obvious. "You're very critical."

"Only when I'm right."

"You're a duke. Raised with privilege. It is

easy for you to point out these things."

His square jaw tensed. "I meant no insult."

"Yes, you did." At his silence, she felt compelled to explain. Pulling out a chair, she sat across from him. "I hadn't expected the cottage to be in such disrepair."

He snorted. "You purchased it sight unseen?"

Did he believe her to be a complete idiot? "No. It was bequeathed to me upon my father's death."

"Lord Foster, the old earl, gave you this place?"

"I don't believe he knew of its condition. He hadn't traveled here in many years. All the times I'd visited in the past with my father, it had been well-kept and cozy."

"Most likely his steward stole whatever money he'd been allotted to maintain the cottage and should be fired."

She shrugged a shoulder. She didn't know much about her father's stewards. "Perhaps."

"Why move here? Why not stay in London?"

"My half brother is the new earl."

"From what I've overheard, I take it you two do not have a pleasant relationship."

"You are observant." She refused to elaborate.

"You are missing a London Season and the marriage mart," he said. "I thought all young women from the aristocracy wanted a match."

Her decision to depart Town was her business. Still, she found herself explaining her reasons once more. "I never said I didn't wish to marry. I seek a love match like my own parents."

"Lord Foster says otherwise."

She lowered her lashes. Despite years of knowing how Edwin felt about her, it was humiliating to admit the truth to a stranger — a duke no less. She felt her cheeks warm. "My brother has never viewed me as worthy of the family name."

"For all his intelligence, your brother is an idiot."

She raised her gaze. Warwick's eyes were fierce, like chips of green glass. For the first time, she found herself in complete agreement with the duke.

He motioned toward his arm. "How will you treat the burn?"

"Not with flour, Your Grace. First, I need to cleanse the area. The wound is seeping pus and the bandages need to be changed." Confidence infused her voice. Healing was a topic she was comfortable discussing, even with the argumentative and maddening duke.

She stood and made her way to one of the cabinets, opened the door, and removed clean cloths and bandages. Hasmik always ensured that fresh bandages were on hand. Adeline filled a porcelain pot from a pitcher of fresh water and carried her items to the table and sat across from him.

She began to gently cleanse the wound and remove the thick layer of flour. She was especially careful to avoid the angry, seeping blisters. "How did you injure yourself?"

"It was an accident during one of my experiments with gunpowder."

She focused on her work. "Why would you experiment with gunpowder?"

"To find the cleanest burning powder, of course."

She glanced up. "That sounds dangerous. And reckless."

His dark eyebrows slanted in a frown. "My work is not reckless. It's wise, well thought out, and necessary."

She rolled her eyes. "Who was this *wise* experiment for then?"

"For the soldiers in the King's army. It could be the difference between life and death."

She'd treated her fair share of impoverished soldiers who'd returned from war, men who'd lost limbs, had festering wounds, had lost not only their health, but their pride after sacrificing everything serving their country. Men who were treated no better than stray dogs in return. Men who never protested when a female healer offered them relief from their suffering and pain.

"Tell me, Your Grace, was your work with the gunpowder worth the wound?"

"It was. I gave my findings to the Crown."

"I see," she said, although she did not. Why would a duke of the realm trouble himself with such matters?

She rose once more and went to her medicine chest. Made of mahogany, the two front doors opened to reveal dozens of vials of herbs and poultices. The chest was embossed with vines and Arabic writings.

Warwick shifted in the chair to see. "That's an interesting piece."

Adeline rested a hand across the top. Her fingers passed over the smooth wood. "It's a medicine chest that belonged to my mother."

"I'm still curious. As Lord Foster's half sister, why move to this remote village?"

She stared at him, her heart tripping in her chest. Dare she share her plan? Would he think it a woman's fancy, like Edwin did? Warwick was a duke, and from her experience, titled men had preconceived notions for highborn women. In her opinion, it was all suffocatingly restraining. "My plan is to help the village folk with their ailments. The traveling doctor who used to come here was much older and has died. The people are in need of a skilled healer."

And more willing to accept a woman.

Not waiting to see his response, Adeline selected a vial from the medicine chest, then went to the windowsill for a potted plant. When she returned holding the plant, he shifted in his chair. "What kind of strange plant is that?"

"Are you always this curious?"

"Always."

She could understand, and she had an inquisitive mind when it came to anything that dealt with medicine. She set the plant on the table. "The aloe vera plant grows in the wilds of the Arabian Peninsula, near the Al-Hajar mountains of Oman. My mother brought the plant to London with her after one of her travels. It will not thrive outdoors in English soil, but it grows well in clay pots indoors. The plant's sap can be made into a poultice to treat your burn."

She assumed satisfying his curiosity would make her work easier. His brow furrowed as he studied the plant, turning the clay pot as he eyed it. "The leaves are thick and fleshy and deep green color. There are white spots on the leaves, and the edges are sharp to the touch. It is quite unusual."

His observations sounded like something from a scientific journal. Adeline broke off two of the thick leaves and a clear juice appeared.

"Interesting," he said.

She placed a pestle and crucible on the table. "Other herbs are helpful for burns as well, such as chamomile and lavender." She added drops of chamomile from a vial and the juice from the plant to the crucible, then reached for the pestle. All the while, she was aware of his penetrating gaze watching her.

The aloe vera didn't have much of a scent, but the chamomile and lavender both perfumed the air with a delicate floral fragrance. Once the poultice was ready, she reached for his injured arm. He held up his other hand. "Will it sting? The flour doesn't."

"No. The poultice is soothing. But for it to work, it must be applied twice a day. The bandages must be changed as well."

"Does that mean you will be the one to change the dressing?"

"Who else? If infection sets in, I don't want you to blame my pet pig on your suffering. Besides, your butler isn't a healer."

His lips quirked and he nodded. She carefully applied the poultice to the burn, then began to wrap his arm in clean bandages. His free hand touched hers, light as a butterfly. His fingers were long and tapered, strong. "You were right," he said. "It didn't hurt."

She froze and stole a glance at his face beneath lowered lashes. Warwick looked at her intently, something alarming in his green gaze. An unwelcome awareness tingled through her, and she forced an even tone despite her thumping heart. "Do not remove the bandages until I visit. You will find some relief, but it will take time for the burn to fully heal." As she secured the last of the bandages, she was aware of the breadth of his chest, the warmth of his skin.

"Thank you."

She swallowed, suddenly unable to find her voice. *Goodness.* Why did he have to be so attractive? He was the type of man who could make a woman forget herself and do foolish things.

A frightening thought crossed her mind. If he wasn't maddening, she just might find herself one of those women.

. . .

Just as the Duke of Warwick was to leave, the front door creaked on its ungreased hinges.

"Adeline! I found the peppermint and hyssop." Hasmik's face, which was flushed from her journey, turned a shade of pink as she spotted the duke alone with Adeline. Wisps of red hair had escaped from her turban and created a frizz around her round face. "I didn't realize you had a visitor!" she said breathlessly.

"Come sit, Hasmik. I'll fetch you water," Adeline said.

Hasmik shook her head, her gaze never leaving Warwick's face. "I'm fine. Good day to you, sir. Are you ill?"

"No," Warwick said.

Adeline pursed her lips. "Hasmik, may I introduce you to our neighbor, His Grace, the Duke of Warwick." Adeline motioned to the older woman. "Your Grace, this is my companion, Miss Hasmik."

Warwick bowed. "It is a pleasure to meet you, Miss Hasmik."

Hasmik gaped and the basket of herbs slipped from her fingers to scatter across the floor.

Hasmik looked awestruck. Standing in the middle of her parlor, the duke was striking in a dark, captivating way. If only he wasn't so frustrating. If only she wasn't embroiled in a fake courtship with him. How were two such different people supposed to pull it off?

Adeline's gaze lowered to the floorboards, and she sighed. She hadn't had a moment to clean the shattered vase and buttercups on the parlor floor. With the addition of the herbs, she didn't look forward to cleaning the mess.

Warwick picked up the basket and handed it to the older woman.

"Forgive me for my clumsiness, Your Grace. It's not every day that a duke visits." Hasmik's gaze settled on the duke's bandaged arm. "Ah, I see. You are not ill but injured. Has Lady Adeline treated you today?"

"I won't take any more of your time." Warwick turned to Adeline. "Shall I expect you later today to change the dressing? Miss Hasmik is welcome as well, of course."

The country was a refreshing change from the stifling stiffness of London. Other than Hasmik, no one here knew that Adeline had been alone with a bachelor for a good part of the afternoon. Still, manners prevailed, and Adeline would never visit the duke's home unaccompanied. Hasmik would act as her chaperone.

Adeline nodded. "You can expect us before dark."

Hasmik waited until the door closed behind Warwick before whirling to face her. "A duke! Our neighbor is a duke?"

"It appears to be true." Adeline suppressed the urge to press her palms to her overheated cheeks. Too much had transpired, and she needed time alone to process her thoughts. From the rapt look of fascination on Hasmik's face, she knew that was unlikely.

"Is he the man who rudely demanded you keep quiet just yesterday?" Hasmik said.

"Yes."

"Why treat him at all, *habibti*? A duke is like a pasha, entitled and powerful. You are too kind."

"I understand it's a shock. But there is something else you should know." Adeline took a deep breath. "Edwin paid a visit."

Hasmik's gaze traveled over Adeline's Arabic garment, and her lips twitched in humor. "Dressed as you are, I can only imagine Lord Foster's reaction."

"He called me a heathen."

"Esheg." Donkey. Curses in their mother tongue often translated into colorful sayings. Adeline didn't disagree. "I blame him for making you feel unwelcome in your childhood home."

Leaving her father's home—the only home she'd known—had been painful but necessary. Adeline had many fond memories of time spent with her mother, her father, and her half sister, Mary, in their Berkley Square townhome. They'd had tea parties with their dolls, played hoops in the garden. When they were older, they'd attended musicales, and laughed around the dinner table. But now that both parents had passed away, Edwin had made it no secret that he wanted her gone...had wanted her gone for years.

"Leaving Mary was the most difficult," Adeline said. Her sister remained under Edwin's care. At least she knew he loved Mary in his own way. They were full-blooded siblings, and he paid her the respect she deserved.

"Did Lord Foster bring Mary to visit?" The hope in Hasmik's voice rang out.

Adeline scoffed. "Edwin would never."

"Then why was Lord Foster here? I assume it was not to check on your well-being after your father's death."

A shiver ran down Adeline's spine. The shock of Edwin's visit and demands had not yet worn off. "He wants me to marry a moneylender, Mr. Slade, a man who seeks entrance into Society through marriage to an earl's daughter." Edwin's words echoed in her head and made her brain hurt.

"Tell me it isn't true."

"Edwin is in financial trouble. He's in debt to the man."

"You didn't consent to his demands, did you?"

"Of course not!"

"Then what does your neighbor have to do with the matter?"

Adeline shifted her feet. How best to explain? Their implausible arrangement was fresh in her mind. "The Duke of Warwick unexpectedly showed up when I was arguing with Edwin. He overheard much of the conversation. Rather than leave, he intervened and told Edwin that he was courting me."

Hasmik gaped. "He *what*?"

"I was just as surprised as Edwin. It took a while for me to speak. Warwick sent Edwin on his way. It was gratifying to watch my half brother storm out of the cottage." She'd relished that moment.

"I do not doubt it. But what of this courtship with the duke?"

"It is a fake courtship, of course. He wishes to avoid his godmother's matchmaking for a Season. I wish to thwart my brother."

Hasmik's eyes lit, and she rubbed her chin with her thumb and forefinger. "Well…well. What a surprise."

"Imagine my *own* surprise when Warwick made the announcement to Edwin."

"The duke is a handsome man."

Yes, he is. Too handsome for her own good. Too bad he was arrogant, highhanded, and argumentative, to name a few. "Hasmik! Do you understand? It is a fake courtship. Nothing more."

Hasmik pursed her lips. "I am old, not blind."

"Then you must know that we agreed to go our separate ways after the Season. I can return here and to my plans of becoming the village healer."

"Yes, yes. I understand," Hasmik muttered.

"Do you? Because I need you to be on my side. Our plan will not work without your understanding and support."

"You know I will always stand by your side. Your mother asked it of me, and I love you."

"Thank you."

"But I also must inquire. What if a false courtship turns into more?"

Adeline's stomach tightened. "No. Warwick is stubborn, selfish, and insensitive. He called Henry *bacon.*"

Hasmik shrugged. "He isn't wrong. The animal is a pig."

She had to understand. There was no future, no *more*. "He insinuated that women lack intelligence."

"He sounds like most Englishmen. You must educate him."

Adeline's frustration grew by the second. How could she convince Hasmik that there could never, never be anything between her and the duke other than a business arrangement? She didn't want a titled man, let alone a duke. She wanted to marry for love. Her future husband would most likely be a commoner who accepted her mixed race, her profession, her ideals. "I do not like him."

"Then why treat his wound?"

Hasmik had a good point, but she also knew Adeline better than anyone. "You know I cannot let anyone suffer."

Hasmik smiled broadly. "Ah, but the duke is not just anyone, is he? He is the duke who is courting you."

. . .

"Pardon, Your Grace?"

Warwick leaned back in his chair in his workshop cum study and contemplated how to explain the turn of events to his longtime butler. He preferred things to be logical and well thought out, like solving a mathematical problem. But he'd recently acted uncharacteristically *illogically*. How best to tell his staff?

"I am courting a lady, the half sister of the Earl of Foster," Warwick said.

To Nelson's credit, the only reaction was one arched eyebrow. The butler's posture was ramrod stiff. "I wasn't aware you had met a lady, Your Grace. As the head of the household, I can also speak on behalf of the staff to say that no one was aware."

Warwick's staff at Chilham consisted of his butler, housekeeper, a maid, two gardeners, and a cook. He required little else. This handful understood that he despised interruption and sought quiet to concentrate. Warwick had even left behind his valet. He was perfectly capable of shaving and dressing himself, although Nelson could aid with his clothing in a pinch.

"No need to be concerned," Warwick said. "It was a decision made quickly."

"I have never known you to act quickly. In anything. And certainly not in matters of the heart."

Warwick frowned. He knew what Nelson

meant. Warwick had previously avoided social events and the ambitious mothers of the *ton*. He'd also never expressed the slightest hint of interest in a lady. He wasn't a monk, and like any man he had biological urges which had led to liaisons—satisfactory interludes with widows and older women.

Never young ladies like Adeline.

"When can we expect the lady?" Nelson asked. "Mrs. Posner will need to be notified straightway."

"Before we notify Mrs. Posner, you should know something else. Lady Adeline has treated my wound. She will continue to do so."

"Your wound?" This time Nelson looked utterly confused.

"She is a healer."

All pretense of formality seemed to drop as Nelson squinted at him. "You are courting a lady, the daughter of an earl, who is a healer?"

"Yes."

"What about the treatments from your London physician, Your Grace? I've been applying the flour."

Warwick nodded once. "You have done an exemplary job, Nelson."

"But this lady has other ideas?"

Warwick rolled up his shirtsleeve to reveal his freshly bandaged forearm. "Yes."

As Adeline had promised, the ointment was soothing and hadn't stung, burned, or caused additional pain. Warwick was willing to continue her treatments for a week or so.

"I see." His butler's disapproval was stamped across his face.

"One more thing. I'm expecting Lady Adeline today." He'd best get the worst over with.

Nelson gaped. "Today? You cannot."

"Whyever not?"

"The place is not fit, Your Grace."

"What's wrong with it?"

"It's not presentable for a lady who is the daughter of an earl, and who is a healer, and who you are courting, Your Grace." Nelson's cadence didn't miss a beat as he managed to cram each of Adeline's attributes into one sentence.

Warwick settled back in his chair and stared at the man. "I do not see why."

Nelson's eyes darted to the worktables spread around the room. A flash of distress crossed his features as he spotted the high-pressure steam engine. "There are mechanical devices and grease and tools and—"

Warwick held up a hand. "I assure you; the lady will not mind." Adeline's cottage was, to his mind, in much worse condition. She also seemed like a woman who was more concerned with the state of her medicinal chest than her housekeeping abilities.

Nelson didn't agree. "With all due respect, Your Grace, *every* lady would mind."

Warwick frowned. "Even if you are correct, there is no time for Mrs. Posner and the rest of the staff to move everything."

As if he had conjured her, Mrs. Posner appeared in the doorway. His housekeeper was a plump elderly woman who had been a loyal member of the Warwick household for as long as he could remember. It took a bit of convincing for her to leave the ducal mansion in town, but she knew Warwick needed her here.

She clearly had heard enough of their conversation, for she clasped her hands to her ample chest in excitement. "You are courting a lady? A daughter of an earl? Your godmother will be happy, Your Grace!"

"Lady Adeline is to arrive today," Nelson said, his voice dry.

"Today! Oh, my goodness, there is no time to waste." She tsked as she scanned his workshop. "It cannot be done. It simply cannot be done. She must visit only the parlor. We must get everything in order. Your other work must be removed to this room, Your Grace."

Warwick was at the end of his patience. He'd forgotten about the mechanical drawings he'd left in the parlor. "Nothing will change!" he roared. "May I remind you that my work is the reason we are here."

"Yes, but now you are courting an earl's daughter." Mrs. Posner spoke as if he were a child who'd snuck into the kitchens to steal a slice of one of Cook's prized pies and sorely needed a lesson on how dukes were to behave.

Warwick ran a hand through his hair in exasperation. "Lady Adeline knows I'm in Kent to work. She will understand this," he said as he swept a hand toward the tables holding his tools and machinery.

"I doubt any woman would understand." Mrs. Posner's comment echoed Nelson's.

It was on the tip of his tongue to tell them both that Adeline wouldn't complain—she didn't have the luxury. Their courtship was false and entirely for show. He couldn't admit it, since to make their farce work, they needed to convince everyone, not just Adeline's half brother and his godmother.

They needed to convince the world.

CHAPTER FIVE

"I need your help, my lady."

Adeline had opened the door later that afternoon to find a middle-aged woman from the village wringing her hands, a look of distress creasing her brow. Hasmik stood by her side.

"How can I aid you?" Adeline asked.

"My name is Emma Taylor. My husband is the village blacksmith, and he is ill. Your companion"—her eyes traveled to Hasmik—"was in the village early yesterday morning. I overheard her say that you are a healer."

Adeline opened the door wide. "Please come in and tell me more about Mr. Taylor's sickness."

The cottage's appearance was much improved. Gone was the shattered vase of buttercups and the scattered basket of herbs. Adeline and Hasmik had tidied up, scrubbed the floorboards, aired the sofa and the pillows, and hung the now clean and fresh-smelling curtains in the parlor. They'd removed their belongings from the baggage cart, and a plush Wilton carpet covered the floorboards. A rocking chair rested by the fireplace, and the parlor now exuded a cozy atmosphere. Much work remained, but it was a good start.

Hasmik brought out a silver tray with a pitcher of lemonade and handed Mrs. Taylor a glass. The tray and glasses had belonged to Adeline's mother and had arrived on the cart from town. "For me to help, you must describe your husband's symptoms."

Mrs. Taylor sipped the lemonade. "My husband suffers from a lingering cough. A traveling physician came to the village after our Doctor Latham passed away, but he did not help, and my husband is still ill."

"I cannot promise a cure, but I'd like to examine your husband to see if I can help," Adeline said.

A look of unease crossed the woman's face, and she lowered her eyes to the glass in her hands before continuing. "You should know Mr. Taylor is a stubborn man. I haven't told him I've come here."

"You mean because he does not trust a woman healer." Adeline spoke aloud what Mrs. Taylor was uncomfortable confessing.

Mrs. Taylor's brown eyes appeared large in her face. "Like I said, he can be stubborn. But I'm worried. He's been coughing a fit and hasn't been able to work for days."

After learning more from Mrs. Taylor about her husband's sickness, Adeline packed her medicinal bag. "Your husband may protest at first, but let's see if we can convince him."

Gratitude flashed across the woman's face. "I'd be grateful."

Less than fifteen minutes later, they were in the village. The heart of the village was quaint and lovely, much of the architecture of its square dating back to medieval times. St. Mary's Church boasted a tower that allowed great views of the surrounding countryside and, on a clear summer day, one could even see Canterbury Cathedral six miles away. Pubs, two tearooms, and several shops, which sold everything from clothing and shoes to flowers and fruits made up the commercial streets. Passersby regarded Adeline and Hasmik, and Adeline was careful to meet their gazes and smile.

Leaving the village square, they took a path and soon a dozen cottages came into view. They were much smaller than Adeline's with timber frames and thatched roofs. Mrs. Taylor stopped outside one of the cottages, and Adeline could hear coughing from inside.

Adeline gave Mrs. Taylor a sideways glance. "It's good you came for me."

Mrs. Taylor took a deep breath, opened the door, and the trio stepped inside. The Taylors' cottage was less than half the size of Adeline's. A man lay on a bed in the corner. The room was warm with a coal brazier burning low, but he was still covered from neck to toe with a colorful quilt. As soon as he saw

Adeline, he rose on his elbows. "I told you not to fetch her, woman!" he bellowed at his wife, before a fit of coughing forced him to lie back down.

Mrs. Taylor planted her hands on her hips. "You need help, and the traveling doctor made you worse with those leeches."

"Leeches?" Adeline asked.

Hasmik *tsk*ed. "All those so-called fancy doctors can do is suck a man's blood."

Hasmik was right. Leeching was used all too frequently for fevers, boils, ailments of the joints, digestive disorders, and much more. Adeline knew leeching had it benefits, but she disagreed with how often English doctors made use of them.

Adeline approached Mr. Taylor's bedside. She would have to be blind not to notice the wariness in his gaze. But any strenuous protest was cut off by another bout of coughing.

"You have a buildup of phlegm in your chest. I could hear it from outside the door."

"What would you know?" he asked between coughs.

"I am a healer and I believe I can help you."

"Ha! I heard talk when you moved into the village. You are the daughter of an earl, not a doctor."

If she had a shilling for every time someone had made that observation, she'd be able to purchase more medicine. "Yes, I am the old earl's daughter. That fact has nothing to do with my abilities."

He scowled as he glanced at Hasmik. "And she's a…a dark-skinned Arab. A foreigner."

Adeline's voice was sharp. "Miss Hasmik has been with me since I was born and is as much a lady as I am."

"I don't want her touching me."

Hasmik raised her chin. "You would rather suffer?"

Mr. Taylor kicked off the quilt and attempted to sit up and holler. He coughed instead.

"Enough!" Mrs. Taylor stepped forward, then lowered her voice. "Please allow the lady to try. For me." She smoothed her husband's hair back from his forehead. The simple act of affection seemed to have an effect. After several heartbeats, he finally nodded his assent and lay back down.

"Go on," he said. "I won't have a moment's peace until you are allowed to try."

Adeline bent forward and lowered her head to his chest. "Take a deep breath."

He inhaled once before he began coughing.

"Like I thought. You have much mucus in your chest. The cough will not subside until we treat it." She glanced at Mrs. Taylor. "Please put on the kettle for some medicinal tea." The woman hurried to do her bidding.

Hasmik removed a glass jar containing a thick syrup from Adeline's medicine bag. Adeline often prepared the syrup, made from lemon, honey, and horehound leaves and flowers. Horehound was a bitter herb that acted as an irritant to cause coughing and loosen the mucus and phlegm in the chest. The mixture was boiled until it thickened, then cooled. She had also brought along the ingredients to prepare a fresh mustard plaster.

She poured a good amount of the syrup into a cup and handed it to Mr. Taylor. "Drink. It will allow you to cough up the phlegm in your chest."

He took a tentative sip, then wrinkled his nose. "It's bitter."

"The honey helps with the bitterness of the horehound. You must drink all of it," Adeline instructed.

Under the watchful eyes of Mrs. Taylor, he drank. Meanwhile, Adeline worked on the mustard plaster, a thick paste of mustard powder, flour, and water. She spread a good amount on a cotton cloth and folded it in half. Just as the plaster was ready, the syrup worked, and Mr. Taylor coughed up a large amount of phlegm.

Adeline placed an ear to his chest once more. "Good. You sound a bit better already."

Hasmik handed him a cup of medicinal thyme tea. "This will soothe your throat." He grumbled his thanks.

He offered no protest when Adeline pressed the cloth with the mustard powder to his chest. "Mrs. Taylor, I will leave the mustard powder with you. Never apply it directly to the skin but spread it on a cloth and press it against his chest. Along with the syrup and the thyme tea, it will bring him relief."

"See? No leeches," Mrs. Taylor said.

"His recovery will take time." Adeline didn't want either to believe the cure would work overnight. "Coughs are stubborn and tend to linger."

Mrs. Taylor took her husband's hand. "We do not expect a miracle."

Adeline touched her patient's shoulder. "I will return daily to check on you."

Hasmik helped Adeline gather her medicine bag and they stepped outside. It was late afternoon. They had much more work to do at her own cottage before the sun went down.

"He still mistrusts us," Adeline said.

"Fool. He'll think differently when he coughs less," Hasmik said. "You have a special touch with those in need."

Another patient came to mind. A swath of tawny hair and green eyes. She needed to visit the duke to change his bandage. Her stomach tumbled wildly at the idea of continuing to touch him, to treat him. Goodness, what had she been thinking to accept his proposition?

It was simple. Edwin had left her little choice.

"My lady!"

Adeline halted to see Mrs. Taylor hurrying down the path to catch up with them.

"I want to thank you." Mrs. Taylor's cheeks were flushed. "The truth is that the people in the village are wary about an earl's sister who claims to be a healer. I shall tell them you are not to be mistrusted, my lady, but to be embraced."

• • •

"You have a visitor, Your Grace."

Warwick set down the wrench and looked up from where he knelt on the floor. The high-pressure steam engine he'd been tweaking for hours had been close to the desired modification. His butler knew he hated distractions.

"It is still too early for Lady Adeline to visit to change my bandages. Tell me it isn't the local vicar." He was in no condition or mood to entertain visitors, especially a religious man who would most likely invite him to attend his weekly sermons or participate in local events.

"No, Your Grace," Nelson said.

Another thought came to mind, and Warwick felt a wave of unease. Could his godmother be paying him an unannounced visit? He stood and wiped the grease from his hands on a nearby clean rag. Once again, he was dressed in breeches and a loose linen shirt without cravat, waistcoat, or jacket. The high-pressure engine rested in the middle of his study's hardwood floor. Tools and mechanical parts cluttered his worktable. He'd been inspecting mechanical drawings and making markings before taking apart one of the engine's pistons.

"Lord Drake waits in the parlor." A pained look flashed across Nelson's face. Along with his housekeeper, Mrs. Posner, they were both disgruntled he hadn't removed the engine from the study before Adeline's visit. He had no intention of doing so.

Warwick stood and let out a held-in breath. He may love his godmother, but he was more than a bit relieved that his friend, the Earl of Drake, waited instead. "See Lord Drake here."

Lord Drake entered just as Warwick returned the wrench to the rest of the tools on the worktable.

Drake approached and eyed the engine Warwick had been toiling over. "Are you still working on that contraption?"

"If by that contraption you mean the

high-pressure engine for the first steam-powered locomotive, then yes. Richard Trevithick obtained the patent for it. I'm improving the efficiency of the engine's pistons." Warwick folded his arms across his chest and leaned against his worktable. "What are you doing in this backwater?"

Drake's lips twitched with humor. "What do you think? I miss my sparring partner. No one else at Gentleman Jackson's has your nimble footwork."

The two had met as boys at Eton, then attended Oxford together, and were long-time friends. The two were alike but had their differences. Warwick didn't seek out new friends; he preferred books and tinkering in his workshop. Drake, on the other hand, could be charming and outgoing, but he preferred duty over gambling, drinking, and carousing. They'd shared a kinship. As for their favorite pastime, Warwick considered sparring as a way to exercise the body to help with the mind. Drake looked at it as a way to relieve stress. They were a good match in and out of the ring.

Warwick went to a sideboard in the corner of the study. It was the only piece of furniture not covered by mechanical tools or parts. He poured two whiskies and handed Drake one. "I'd be pleased if I didn't know better. Let's try again. Why leave your lovely wife for the country visit?" Drake had married Lady Ana Woodbridge last year and she was expecting their first babe.

Drake accepted the glass. "I'm on my way to one of my estates in Kent to meet with my steward. Since I'm one of the few who have the privilege of knowing of Your Grace's presence here, I thought to stop by."

Warwick's lips twitched at the hint of mockery in his friend's voice. "I'm flattered."

Drake took a step closer to peer down at the engine. "I thought you were working on developing a faster burning gunpowder."

"I was."

Warwick excelled at mechanical engineering and mathematics, and nothing excited him more than taking an ordinary device and modifying it or designing a completely new device.

"You suffered a burn from that gunpowder invention, didn't you?"

"Less than a month ago." Warwick turned over his forearm.

"Those bandages are fresh. Did you burn yourself again?"

"No. I was accosted by a farm animal."

Drake blinked. "Pardon?"

"You heard correctly. It was a large pig."

Drake set the whisky on the worktable. "Of all the crazy things you've said over the years—about your inventions and such—that might top the list."

"It wasn't my fault. My neighbor is a nuisance."

"Is your neighbor the pig?"

Warwick snorted.

"Ha! Now you sound just like one."

Warwick's frown deepened. "I first went over to politely ask her to get her hunting hounds to stop barking and howling. I couldn't focus on my work."

"Barking, you say? I thought she owned a pig."

"She does. Along with two hunting hounds who barked all hours of the day and night. She was treating the dogs for digestive problems."

Drake's lips twitched. "That sounds messy. But what does that have to do with a pig exacerbating your injury?"

"She keeps the pig as a pet. She claims 'Henry' is overly affectionate and sought only to greet me. I didn't know this, of course. All I could see was a charging two-hundred-pound farm animal. I acted automatically. I pushed the lady behind me, then defended myself. Do you have any idea how heavy a barreling pig can be?"

"Not precisely."

"Rather than apologize, she told me it was my fault for bellowing and startling Henry."

Drake laughed. "I should like to meet her.

Is she old? Bent over? Wrinkled? I'm struggling to picture a woman who keeps a pig as a pet, lives in the country, and is treating two hunting dogs who howl all hours of the day and night from digestive disorders."

"Her name is Lady Adeline. She's young. And beautiful." The words slipped from his lips before his mind could stop them. A vivid image of mahogany hair, a straight nose, and striking blue eyes appeared before him.

Drake's dark eyes gleamed with renewed interest. "Well, then I'm quite intrigued."

"You'll be even more intrigued. I'm courting her."

Drake arched one dark eyebrow. "Bollocks. I don't believe you."

"It's true. You know my godmother has been insistent on my engagement. Her half brother wants her to marry some moneylender. Why not agree to a temporary courtship?"

Drake's mouth dipped in a frown. "I've never known you to be an idiot."

"It's well thought out. We part after the Season. We both get what we want. I would think you'd see the strategy in the plan."

"Christ. It's a plan full of complications. As your long-time friend, can I talk you out of it?"

"No."

"You were always inflexible. But this idea

is as dangerous as a landmine. What if you get stuck with the woman?"

"I won't." Warwick was certain of this fact. Neither of them wanted a temporary court-ship to turn into more. Not to mention that Adeline was the most stubborn, argumenta-tive woman he'd ever met. When he did choose a wife to beget an heir, she would have to be pleasant, pliable, and agreeable. Someone who would leave him to his work, and, in exchange, she could engage with the Society ladies and attend as many *ton* func-tions as she desired. Without him, of course.

Drake watched him with a critical squint. "*Hmm.* When can I meet this mysterious pig-owning woman you're courting?"

"It's likely you have met her. She's Lord Foster's half sister."

Drake stiffened and his upper lip curled in distaste. "Now you *must* be jesting."

Warwick didn't blame his friend. The two had an unsavory past with Edwin. Warwick had excelled at academics at Eton, and before either Warwick or Drake had grown into men, when they were just skinny boys, they'd been teased by a group of school bullies.

Bullies led by none other than Edwin, the current Earl of Foster.

Edwin had been one of the smartest in the class until Warwick had arrived and outshone everyone. A jealous Edwin had hated

Warwick from the beginning and plotted against him.

One instance, when he was ten years old, was hard to forget. Edwin, accompanied by his two lackeys, had cornered Warwick returning from the evening meal. Outnumbered, Warwick would have suffered a beating. But Drake had shown up and, together, they fought tooth and nail and managed to send the three bullies scurrying. Both Warwick and Drake had suffered black eyes and had been close friends ever since.

"You never lacked arrogance," Drake said. "But this tops the list."

"Funny you should say so. The lady accused me of possessing her brother's arrogance," Warwick said.

"Edwin is not only arrogant, but an arse." Drake rubbed his chin with his thumb and forefinger. "On second thought, I'm curious to see the outcome of this courtship."

"Why the change of heart?"

Drake flashed a crocodile smile. "It's simple. It will be a pissing contest to rival all others. Can you imagine Edwin's ire as you escort his half sister all over Town?"

• • •

Adeline clutched her medicine bag as she walked up the winding path to the duke's home. It wasn't a cottage like her own or one of the villagers' smaller dwellings, but a fine manor house of red brick with black shutters. The hedgerows were meticulously trimmed, and the flower boxes overflowed with colorful spring blooms. She heard the rush of a stream and the churning of a waterwheel by the gardens.

It was not as fine as the Grosvenor's Square townhomes in London occupied by the aristocracy, but no doubt the Duke of Warwick owned a grand mansion himself. As the daughter of the Earl of Foster, Adeline had been raised in a fine townhome.

Which now belonged to her half brother. *No sense mourning the past.*

Her country home may be a work in progress, but Adeline loved the freedom it offered. London was stifling, and an earl's daughter could accomplish only so much. If it were up to Edwin, she would marry a stranger, a greedy moneylender to satisfy a family debt.

"Are you having second thoughts about the duke?" Hasmik asked as they reached the porch.

Adeline's step faltered. She didn't bother to deny it. Hasmik always knew what Adeline was thinking. "I don't have the luxury of second thoughts."

"You mean because of your brother?"

"Edwin was quite adamant about my future. The duke's offer, no matter how shocking, came just at the right time."

"A lady can always reconsider."

"How? My brother would love for me to return to him with my tail tucked between my legs."

"Harumph! Your brother isn't worthy of the title."

"Perhaps. But there is nothing to be done for it. My father is dead."

"Do not think sad thoughts, *habibti*. The greatest future is for those who are courageous enough to seize it." Arabic proverbs were inspiring and could be daunting at the same time, and Hasmik had a habit of spouting them.

"I pray you are right." Adeline lifted the shiny brass knocker and rapped the door twice.

The door swung open to reveal a middle-aged butler with a receding hairline and brown eyes. "May I be of assistance?"

"My name is Lady Adeline Cameron, and this is my companion, Miss Hasmik. His Grace is expecting us."

She didn't miss the slight flare of his eyes as he took in her features first, then Hasmik's. "Please come in, my lady, and I will see you both to the drawing room."

The vestibule was welcoming with a black-and-white marble floor and fresh vase of flowers on an end table. No priceless paintings from masters graced the walls, nor were there gilt mirrors or massive chandeliers holding hundreds of candles. Yet the walls were freshly painted a cream color. The drawing room was lovely with yellow and blue striped settee and matching chairs, a pianoforte, and a curiosity cabinet in the corner. Large windows overlooked the gardens, the stream, and the waterwheel.

"I will inform His Grace that you are here, my lady, and will send for refreshments." The butler bowed and departed.

"It may not be a fancy London house, but his servant is just as proper," Hasmik said, a note of approval in her voice.

"I never would have believed he was an aristocrat, let alone a duke, the first time we met." She'd noticed his face, of course. Who wouldn't? His handsome features belonged on a painting, only she wasn't an artist. Then there was their physical encounter, and her cheeks felt warm at the memory of his body pressed against hers as they had collided outside her home.

Adeline and Hasmik sat side by side on a plush sofa. The door opened and Adeline's pulse leaped, then settled when an older woman entered the drawing room. She wore a black dress with a starched white apron and cuffs. A ring of keys hung at her waist.

"Good afternoon, ladies. My name is Mrs.

Posner and I'm the housekeeper here. We have prepared refreshments for you both." She motioned behind her, and a young maid wheeled in a cart with tea and scones.

"Thank you," Adeline said.

Mrs. Posner's expression was friendly, and Adeline had the sense the woman's gaze lingered on her a bit longer than necessary, as if she were a curiosity.

"We are glad for your visit. His Grace has not had much company during his country stay."

How much did the housekeeper know? Adeline knew servants gossiped. She also knew the value of a loyal housekeeper. When her mother had married the earl, the housekeeper had been loyal to the former countess and despised her mother. She had been a thorn in her mother's side for a full year before her mother had let her go and retained a different housekeeper. Edwin had used it as another excuse to resent his stepmother.

Even if Adeline's arrangement with Warwick was temporary, she needed an ally. She smiled at the housekeeper. "The scones look delicious."

Mrs. Posner returned her smile. "I'll be sure to tell Cook." She bobbed a curtsy and departed.

"She knows something," Hasmik said.

"You think Warwick told the staff and they

are waiting for Warwick to make a proper announcement?"

"I don't know exactly, but one knows when one's nose itches."

"Your nose is itching? It is most likely an unpleasant reaction to the flowers in the vestibule."

Hasmik glowered. "That isn't what I meant, and you know it. Either it's uncommon for the Duke of Warwick to have female visitors, or it's too common."

Adeline didn't want to think about the duke's dearth of women, or their abundance. The less she thought about his personal relationships the better. Meanwhile, she was here today to treat his injury, nothing more.

Booted heels sounded on the marble vestibule. Adeline set down her teacup on the saucer just as Warwick appeared in the doorway. Awareness rushed through her, and her pulse leaped in her chest at the sight of him. Dressed in a navy coat of superfine, a waistcoat, snowy cravat, and buckskin breeches with shiny Hessians, he cut a striking figure. He looked very much like…like a duke.

A strikingly handsome one.

Despite her efforts not to think about his private life, she wondered how he hadn't married. Surely women threw themselves at him.

Then she remembered his peccadilloes. He preferred to put off his duties to the dukedom not because he wanted to indulge in gaming, drinking, or ladybirds at bordellos, but because he wanted to finish his work. She still wasn't certain exactly what work that was.

He bowed. "Lady Adeline and Miss Hasmik. Thank you for coming."

It wasn't just his dress that impressed. His manners were much improved from their first encounter. He wasn't yelling or throwing accusations, and her pig was nowhere in sight.

Adeline stood and curtsied. Proper manners were also second nature. "How is your arm, Your Grace?"

"Your treatment is better than the flour."

She pursed her lips. "Anything is better than the flour."

"My butler, Nelson, didn't approve at first."

"Why?"

"He has been applying the flour from the London physician. Only after I received some relief from your initial treatment has he reconsidered."

"It's good to know I've somehow proved myself to Nelson." She reached for her medicine bag. "Your wound needs to be tended to and dressed."

"Here?"

"It would be inappropriate for me to visit your bedchamber, Your Grace." Her cheeks flushed. What made her even mention his bedchamber? And why would she care?

She'd treated men before without this tingling in the bottom of her stomach.

Because none had looked like him.

Meanwhile, he appeared entirely unaffected.

He slipped off his coat and tossed it across one of the chairs. His shoulders were broad and, clearly, his tailor didn't need to pad his coat to enhance his frame. He rolled up his shirtsleeves to reveal the wrapped bandage. Even his forearm was muscular with fine golden hairs.

"I will search for Mrs. Posner to see about more clean cloths," Hasmik said.

Adeline's eyebrows drew together. They always brought along their own dressings that they'd boiled and dried, but Hasmik sailed out of the drawing room and shut the door before Adeline could argue.

"Where shall I sit?" Warwick asked.

Adeline turned to face him. "The chair is fine." He pulled the chair close to the settee so that she could sit and tend him at the same time. At this proximity, his cologne filled her senses, a tantalizing sandalwood and cloves. As she unwrapped bandages, she made the mistake of glancing into his eyes. They were a mesmerizing green like a roiling ocean on a windswept day. Her already warm cheeks grew hotter. What was wrong with her? She needed to calm her rapid heartbeat and focus on the task at hand. She cleared her throat. "The blisters are looking a bit better, but the skin will take time to heal."

"You brought more of your salve?"

"I made it in advance." She was aware of him leaning down as she gently applied the fragrant salve to the angry burn. She hadn't lied; it would take numerous treatments before the wound healed. She couldn't hold her tongue at the incompetency of the prior treatment.

"Who was the London physician?"

"Why?"

"I should like to know his name to warn any future patients away from the man."

"He came highly regarded."

She pursed her lips. "I wouldn't listen to whomever recommended him on any subject."

One dark eyebrow rose. "You are quite opinionated, aren't you?"

"Only when I'm right."

His hoarse laugh filled the room. "Fine. I grudgingly agree regarding the physician's treatment."

Beneath his gaze, awareness rushed through her, and she lowered her gaze. It was safer to focus on her work rather than the man. Once she finished, she bandaged his arm with clean cloths. If he noticed that she already had her own and Hasmik's departure was unnecessary, he didn't mention it.

She sat back on the sofa. "I've been thinking about what you said."

"You mean my offer to court you for the Season." The degree of warmth in his voice caused her heartbeat to leap.

She bit her lower lip and raised her gaze to his. "I'm uncertain how we are going to convince the world, let alone my half brother."

"It does pose a minor dilemma."

"Minor! I'd hardly call it that." She glared and pressed her lips together. If Warwick believed it would be simple, her concern tripled. Edwin was no fool and—if he was in as much debt as she thought—then he had strong motivation to want her to marry the moneylender.

"What can I do to ease your mind?"

"Like I said before, we know little about each other." It was only a start. She feared they'd need to know *a lot* about each other before they ventured to London.

Warwick hesitated for a moment before nodding once. "Then we must address that." He stood and offered his good arm. "Come with me."

• • •

Adeline placed her fingers on Warwick's sleeve. Without his coat and her gloves, she could feel the heat of his skin beneath her fingertips. She had an overwhelming urge to run her hand up and down his arm, to feel each muscle and the warmth of his skin. She hadn't bothered to ask where he was taking her. She supposed it didn't matter, as long as it wasn't his bedchamber. She swallowed her earlier annoyance. If he truly believed it would be only a minor problem when they returned to London, he was not as intelligent as she'd thought.

He passed several closed doors, a music room, a dining room, a library, and stopped outside the last door in the hall. It had to be either another library or a study.

He opened the door and she gasped.

It was unlike any other study she'd seen.

It wasn't a study at all, but a large workshop. A carpet had been rolled and pushed aside. A long wooden worktable lined the entire length of the back wall, its oak surface scarred and stained. Tools, nails, oil pots, and iron parts were haphazardly strewn across the table. Smaller worktables held various machines and objects that she assumed were inventions or ideas he was working on.

"Welcome to my workshop."

Her jaw slackened. "You moved all this from London?"

"I have a much larger workshop in my London home. To my butler's chagrin and my housekeeper's disapproval, I brought only the necessities with me to the country."

The necessities? She couldn't imagine what he'd left behind and the size of his London workshop. "You are like a mad professor." The statement left her lips before she could catch herself.

Rather than take offense, he chuckled. "Others have called me worse." He leaned on a workbench and spread his arms wide. "Medicine may be your passion. This is mine."

She still wasn't sure what *this* was. Her breath caught in her lungs, and she stilled. The shock of walking into the room hadn't fully worn off. He'd told her he was an inventor. She hadn't anticipated the extent of his ambitions.

"I see you are confused."

She walked to one of the tables and scanned the contents. "Perhaps if you tell me what these things are, I may understand."

"Come and I'll explain." He stopped by what looked like a large iron contraption and waited for her to follow. "This is a high-pressure steam engine. It was invented by a man named Trevnick years ago, and I've been perfecting the efficiency of the pistons."

"What is it intended for?"

"The engine powers a train. His invention was too heavy, and it broke the rails. But I believe trains are our future and that someday they will change our everyday lives."

His passion for his work was clear. "How?"

"We'll be able to move everything by railroad—goods, fuel like coal and wood, as well as people. The cost of goods will be cheaper for the everyday man and woman."

She squinted at the black, greasy contraption and tried to picture all he'd described. His enthusiasm was evident in his voice and his intense gaze. A slow swirl built in her chest. What would it be like to have his undivided attention?

She shoved the thought aside. She needed to understand more. Much more. "Tell me about the other items."

He pointed to another object. "This is an electric battery invented by Sir Volta of Italy. It can provide electricity."

"What is that?"

"Electricity is a form of power that forward thinking scientists believe can make things work and move. Sir Volta discovered it could be generated chemically. He has inspired the study of electromagnetism, and even Napoleon honored him with a medal."

She recalled hearing about scientific accomplishments, but the device and field of study appeared complex. She reached for a round object on one of the tables that looked like a ball she'd seen the country children use. "And this? What is it?"

"A ball."

Her brow furrowed. "A simple children's toy?"

"Yes. We played football with it all through Oxford."

"Why is it here? Do you plan on playing with the countryfolk?"

He looked at her like *she* was irrational. "The ball is made of an inflated pig's bladder and covered with leather. When it gets wet, the leather is heavy...so heavy it could cause harm to the players. When I was at school, I once saw it break an opponent's arm."

She supposed it was possible if it hit a man with enough force.

He ran his hand over the ball's surface. "I've been experimenting with different materials to cover the ball. It must be sturdy enough for a game, supple like leather to cover the ball, but not as heavy when wet."

It seemed like a worthwhile endeavor. She continued perusing the objects in the room. Some were on tables, others on the floor. Her initial shock had ebbed, and she found herself more and more curious. "What's this?" A mannequin like one a Bond Street dressmaker would use to display a garment in the bow window of her shop lay on its side.

"I've been working on a self-tying corset."

A lady's maid assisted a woman in this task. She didn't think they would use such a contraption but held her tongue.

Another device caught her eye. An iron box with what looked like a smaller box on top with a long handle. She had no idea as to what it could be.

"And this?" she asked, pointing to the box. "What is it?"

He rubbed his chin with a thumb and forefinger. "That invention is in the early phases of development. If successful, I hope it can be used to maintain a well-kept lawn."

"How?"

"Only the wealthy can justify the expense of dozens of scythe-wielding gardeners to maintain their vast lawns. My own gardens in town and at Warwick House in Hertfordshire comprise ten thousand acres. Not all acres are maintained by my gardeners, but it takes a small army and a lot of coin."

She had memories of her father's gardeners out at the break of dawn. "You are right that dozens of gardeners are required, but they also rely on the work to provide for their families. Wouldn't this contraption eliminate many of the staff?"

"That's the idea. You see, once this is perfected, it will save time and money."

"But what about the staff, those who desperately need their wages? Their families? The owners of these grand manor homes can spare the expense. You can spare it. The workers cannot."

"It is progress. You cannot fight it." His voice was full of conviction and confidence, as if no one could see otherwise.

"I dislike it."

"Then we must agree to disagree."

Yes, they did. Still, he was showing her a part of himself, and she needed to know as much as she could.

"I can show you more machines when we return to Town," he said. "This is just the beginning."

She may not agree with his idea of machines replacing workers, but she was struck by his intelligence and ingenuity. He was no ordinary aristocrat. No ordinary man, for that matter. She gave him a sidelong look. "You studied mathematics?"

"Mathematics, physics, and engineering at Oxford. However, not all these inventions are my own. I enjoy taking a prior invention, then improving it. Innovation, I believe, is the best way to help others."

"I never thought of it that way."

He tapped his temple. "I can't think of it any other way. Every time I look at a piece of machinery, a simple household item in the kitchens, or a tool used in my stables, my mind churns with ways to improve that device."

Ordinary people never gave such items a second glance. She couldn't imagine the thoughts swirling in the duke's head. What must it be like?

"I also like to collect things," he said.

What else captures his interest? She scanned the crowded room. "What type of things?"

"Archeology rarities. Historical books. Anything that interests me."

"I like to collect herbs and plants." She wasn't sure why she added that fact. Perhaps she wanted him to know that she also desired to help others and had vast interests, as well.

"I'm not surprised. When I return home, I plan to research the aloe vera plant."

Her mother had brought other plants and herbs from the Middle East. Would he be interested in them or judgmental like Edwin? And why did his opinion matter? The less she cared, the better. Their arrangement was a matter of expedience, nothing more.

"You told me you burned your arm doing an experiment with gunpowder. Is that invention here?" She turned the topic of conversation to something more clinical.

He shook his head. "No. That mishap occurred in my London workshop. As I said earlier, my workshop is much larger in Town, and most of my work is housed there."

She couldn't envision it. How many more items had he collected? She'd never paid much attention to London gossip, but she vaguely recalled hearing the whispers of a reclusive duke. A mad duke. As far as she could tell, Warwick wasn't mad, but highly intelligent and eccentric.

Her stomach churned, and a different type of apprehension coursed through Adeline. He'd shown her his workshop because she'd insisted that they get to know more about each other. Never in her wildest dreams had she expected a study turned into a mechanical workshop.

What exactly have I gotten myself into?

"Do you see why I'm drawn to my work?" he asked.

"Not entirely, but I suppose I'm catching on. What is your favorite project?"

"A favorite? I've never thought to identify one."

"Really? What about the train?"

"Trains highly interest me, of course. But truth be told, I have trouble focusing on one thing at a time. Every project calls to me, and oftentimes I find it difficult to focus on one and complete it."

She tilted her head to the side and regarded him with renewed interest. She'd initially believed him to be high-handed, self-entitled, and rude. While he might possess all of those qualities—he was a duke, after all—he was also supremely knowledgeable about an array of topics and exhibited a strong work ethic.

Others likely had shared her first impression of him. Those people also viewed her as odd for having her own ambitions. Her half brother, Edwin, would be first in line.

Still, the Duke of Warwick was unlike any man she'd known. Mad duke and professor? Eccentric intellectual? Arrogant, privileged aristocrat? Perhaps all of the above. He was too different, too dangerous, and he'd dragged her into this mess when he'd announced to Edwin he was courting her. His outburst had left her with little choice but to consent to his crazy plan, and her future remained more uncertain than ever. Her wariness of the man remained, and she needed to be careful.

She wondered how this would all work out in the end. Her only conclusion was that it would work out badly. For her.

CHAPTER SIX

As Warwick escorted Adeline outside, he was conscious of her slim, graceful form. The first time he'd met her, he'd nearly bowled her over when he'd run into her outside of her home. He'd also never imagined she was a lady. But here and now her proper breeding was unmistakable. She clutched slim hands before her as she walked gracefully, looking straight ahead.

He cleared his throat. "Now that you've learned a bit about my work and seen my country workshop, does that alleviate your concerns?"

She shot him a disbelieving sidelong look. "Not entirely, Your Grace."

He wondered what more she wanted to know for her to be comfortable with their arrangement. He'd shown her a glimpse into his life. She should be grateful he'd rescued her from Lord Foster's plans.

They walked down the gravel path, and sunlight glinted off her hair. Pulled back in a bun, it was a glorious rich chestnut. Stray wisps curled around her cheeks and nape, and he knew—from the time he'd interrupted her argument with her brother—the curly tresses reached her waist.

Her skin was a shade darker than the porcelain complexion of the London ladies of his acquaintance. Because of her coloring, one might assume that she had deep brown eyes. Instead, her eyes were a remarkable vivid blue. He could spend a good amount of time deciding on the precise shade.

He swallowed and refocused on the task at hand. He was never one to be distracted by a woman's beauty. God only knew, he'd been surrounded by plenty of lovely debutants and widows ever since he'd come of age. A duke, especially a duke as rich as Croesus, was a catch. He recalled, at his first ball, feeling as if he were a fox pursued by an avid pack of hounds. His anxiety hadn't improved at his second ball. He never gave a third a chance.

Science had called to him and, despite his godmother's displeasure, he'd isolated himself as much as possible and avoided the bevy of balls, routs, garden parties, and whatever trifling entertainment members of the *ton* flocked to each Season.

Yet here he was trying to persuade the daughter of an earl, the sister of his former school nemesis, to agree to a false courtship. A thought occurred to him. "I shall visit you tomorrow."

She blinked. "Why?"

"You have seen my work. I have yet to see yours." His reasons were simple and rational.

"I do not have a workshop."

"You have herbs and medicines." He touched his freshly bandaged arm. In two days' time, his arm felt better and her treatment had proven more effective than a month's worth of an expensive London doctor.

Adeline pursed her lips as they passed by well-trimmed hedgerows. "Let me see if I understand. You would like to learn about my herbs, tonics, poultices, and medicines?"

"Yes."

"And you believe that will help with our ruse?"

"I wouldn't define it as a 'ruse,' but yes. You pointed out that we know little about each other."

"Your workshop and my herbs are not exactly what I had in mind."

"What else is there but our work?" Science was an important part of his life. He thought she understood.

She halted and glowered up at him. "Are you serious? Our work is not everything. We must be able to pass muster when we return to Town. You are no stranger to London."

"Since I rarely attend functions, it's normally not a problem."

"But you must attend family dinners. Go out with friends. Escape to your clubs. Make an appearance at *some* social events. You are a duke, after all!"

"My title has nothing to do with our arrangement." At times he resented inheriting
the dukedom. If he were a commoner, he
would have more personal freedom and
could choose whether or not he married.
There would be no pressure to produce an
heir and a spare.

She shook her head. "For a man who says
he values rational thought, you are speaking
nonsense."

"How so?"

"Even in the country your title is important. It's not something you can shed or
ignore. Villagers will respect you and address
you differently. Once we return to Town, everyone will be abuzz that the Duke of
Warwick is engaged."

A muscle twitched by his eye. She could be
infuriating. He didn't need reminding of the
gossipmongers. "What I mean to say is that I
pick and choose which Society events to attend. I've never found dinner parties, garden
teas, and most manner of London events entertaining. Especially balls." He hated the
small talk, the crush of the crowd, the odor of
perspiring bodies and heavy perfume, the
awkwardness of asking wallflowers to dance.
Frustration was evident in his voice.

"Entertaining or not, we will have to attend them together," she said.

"Fine. Meanwhile, expect me mid-afternoon tomorrow."

Her two delicate eyebrows drew together. "That's feeding time for Henry."

"Who's Hen—" He stiffened. "Oh," he said, unable to come up with a coherent justification for disturbing the feeding time of her pet pig.

"Would you like to watch me feed my pig?" Her tone was light.

"To be truthful, no."

"Good." She ignored his response. "Then you can help."

His gut tightened at her sweet smile. He may be inexperienced when it came to feminine wiles, but he could identify the glint of mockery in her gaze.

To his dismay, it had the desired effect.

• • •

News of Adeline's treatment of the blacksmith spread in the village. The next morning, she'd been summoned to help a young mother whose baby suffered from croup, a woman with painful menses, and a man with dysentery. Adeline returned home in the afternoon and was changing into a clean gown when a knock sounded.

Hasmik opened the door and, a moment later, Adeline heard the Duke of Warwick's familiar masculine voice. The deep, vibrating sound rumbled through her body. He'd arrived earlier than expected. She pressed a hand to her hot cheeks. This wouldn't do at all. She needed to remember how irritating the man could be. Taking two deep breaths, she smoothed her hair and skirts, then hurried to the top of the stairs as Hasmik led him inside.

"Welcome, Your Grace," Hasmik said. "Lady Adeline will be just a moment and—"

"Tell His Grace I'm ready." Adeline clutched the banister as she descended when a frantic knocking echoed in the parlor.

"Now who could that be?" Hasmik hurried to crack open the cottage door to find a middle-aged man with wiry salt and pepper hair and a long face, leaning on a younger version of himself. A tourniquet had been applied to the man's upper thigh, and blood had seeped through the bandages and ran down his leg. A cart had been haphazardly parked in the middle of the yard where the injured man had been transported.

"I was told there is a healer here," the wounded man said.

Hasmik nodded. "You've come to the right place, sir."

"My name is Max Simmons. I'm the village carpenter and this is my son and apprentice, Jonathan. I cut myself while working." He was clearly in pain and his face was pale as bone. His brow was furrowed, and his lips were pinched together revealing fine lines around his eyes and mouth.

"Let them inside," Adeline instructed.

Mr. Simmons leaned heavily on his son as they shuffled awkwardly into Adeline's kitchen. A chair was pulled out for the injured man, and Jonathan stood by his father's side.

"It's my fault, miss." Jonathan's voice cracked with strain, and he appeared on the verge of tears. "I distracted my dad, and he hurt himself, he did."

"Quiet, Jon," Mr. Turner said, then winced as Adeline crouched down to untie the bandages to reveal an ugly gash across the top of his thigh. His trousers had been shredded where it appeared a saw had made a nasty cut through muscle but hadn't reached the bone or nicked an artery. She was able to cut the rest of the material away to get a better look at the damage.

"Good God, that's a bloody mess," Warwick blurted out.

The duke had followed them and stood in the corner of the kitchen.

Adeline's patient turned an even more alarming shade of white, and his son started sobbing.

Adeline stood and stared at Warwick. He could be an unwanted distraction. "Perhaps you should come back another time, Your Grace."

The duke had the good sense to look apologetic. "Please forgive me. How can I help?"

"That's not necessary and like I said—"

"He may be able to help," Hasmik interrupted.

Adeline hesitated. She knew what Hasmik meant. If her patient needed to be held down, she couldn't do it and the son didn't appear able.

Adeline nodded briskly. "If I need your assistance, I'll ask."

The duke nodded his understanding and wordlessly removed himself to the corner of the room.

Adeline turned her attention back to her patient. "Mr. Turner, how did the accident occur?"

"With a saw."

Her assumption had been correct. The cut didn't concern her as much as the chance of infection this type of wound could cause.

"It's my fault, it is!" Jonathan cried out. "Father told me to hold the piece of wood straight, but I was distracted, and it slipped from my hands. That's why the saw slipped and sliced him open."

"If you weren't looking at the potter's daughter, you wouldn't have been distracted,"

Mr. Turner said.

"No sense arguing over what's done," Adeline said. "You'll need to get onto the table." She tugged the tablecloth off and tossed it aside.

The man rose from the chair and shuffled to the table. He'd have to pull himself up—

"I'll help." Warwick was by the man's side and hoisted him up from under his arms until he sat on the table with his leg extended. Then the duke returned to his place against the wall.

Adeline proceeded to cut away the rest of the shredded trouser. "Hasmik, please fetch my suture kit."

Hasmik had it before Adeline could finish the sentence. The woman also carried a bottle of whisky and poured two glasses, one for the patient and the other for Adeline's needles. She then offered the bottle to Adeline.

Adeline held the bottle above the wound and eyed her patient. "Take a deep breath. This whisky is going to sting."

He grit his teeth then cried out at the first dribble of whisky on the wound.

Out of the corner of her eye, she saw the duke shift his feet. If the wound hadn't been worrisome, Adeline might have been amused by Warwick's squeamishness. Most men didn't have the stomach for this type of work. She surmised Warwick was one of them. The last thing she desired was for the man to keel over. "Do you need to step outside, Your Grace?"

Warwick shook his head. "You may need me."

Adeline returned her attention to her patient. The first stitches were always the trickiest. The jagged skin had to be gathered and oftentimes slightly overlapped. It was also the most jarring to the patient. She had nothing to numb the pain except a strong bottle of whisky that Hasmik had already offered to the man. The wound would take dozens of stitches.

Focused on her task, Adeline carefully pulled the thread through the skin.

• • •

Warwick stood in the corner of the small kitchen and watched as Adeline spent the next two hours stitching the carpenter's nasty wound. She bent over her patient, her fingers sure and deft, a look of sheer concentration on her face. Surely her back would be sore afterward.

Her patient moaned. "Bloody hell! It feels like a hundred pinpricks."

"Please try to be still." Adeline didn't look up from her task. "Hasmik, give him more whisky."

Warwick reached the bottle before Hasmik. He splashed a good amount into a glass. To Warwick's surprise, his hand shook slightly. In contrast, Lady Adeline Cameron was solid as a rock as she staunched the flow of blood with a clean cloth, then returned to her work. A basin of bloody rags rested on the table.

He had been wrong about her. She wasn't just a healer, but a surgeon. A talented one, too.

Good God, she was fabulous.

At first, he'd wondered if he'd made a mistake to "court" her. He'd found her stubborn and argumentative. She still was. He knew she had talent as a healer, as she'd helped him with his own wound, but this was different. He leaned as far forward as he could without blocking the light. He was fascinated by her ability.

He'd known women to faint at the sight of a paper cut. He'd witnessed others flutter their fans at balls and claim exhaustion from a crowded room. In contrast, the temperature of the small cottage had climbed higher, and it was uncomfortably warm. Beads of perspiration formed on Adeline's brow. She had to be exhausted, mentally and physically, but she continued, making sure the carpenter had the best chance to heal.

A man she didn't know. A man who most likely couldn't even afford to pay her for her services.

Warwick continued to watch her as she worked. Her curly dark hair was pulled back in a braid that brushed her low back. Her lips were full and rose-hued. The dark arches of her eyebrows accentuated her long lashes. It was no longer just the brilliant blue color of her eyes that captivated him, but that they shone with determination and intelligence.

She was dressed in a plain blue dress without a hint of adornment and a blood-stained apron. As she bent over her patient, her gaze narrowed with intent focus. He was fascinated and couldn't tear his gaze away from her. She was unlike any lady he'd ever known.

If all went according to plan, and there was no reason to think otherwise, then they'd soon travel to London, and he'd introduce her to his godmother. He'd escort Adeline to a ball under the watchful eye of her half brother, Lord Foster. Adeline would dress in fine gowns with pearls at her throat and in her hair and, once others learned he was courting her, they would look upon him with envy.

But none of that would matter because here—now—she was remarkable.

Get a hold of yourself. He could not afford to look at her as he was. Hers was not a quiet grace, but fearless and fierce. Her half brother could have ruined her, financially and emotionally. Adeline hadn't allowed it. She'd moved all the way to a remote village to pursue her purpose—her driving need to help others. He saw it clearly now.

If his interference had helped her in any way with Edwin, then he was even happier for it. For the first time, he thought about how it would feel to have Adeline on his arm as his true fiancé. How would she taste when he kissed any argument from her lips when they inevitably found themselves at odds? Christ. Kissing a woman with this much latent passion would steal his breath and all rational thought. He was fast realizing Adeline was no ordinary lady, no ordinary earl's daughter.

He tamped down his desire. His challenge was to resist this unwanted stirring in his chest and to stay the course for the duration of the Season. Then they could part ways with mutually beneficial outcomes.

It was that simple. He owed her that much. She wanted to marry for love, not convenience. And that was not his goal. He wanted to focus on his work.

When she was finally finished, five dozen neat stitches closed the wound.

"It stopped bleeding, but there is risk of infection." Adeline straightened, the first time in more than two long hours. She rubbed her lower back and Warwick had to clench his fists to prevent himself from stepping forward to massage the muscles for her.

"You must visit daily so that I can check

on the sutures. If you feel fevered, send your son to fetch me no matter the hour, even in the middle of the night."

Mr. Simmons nodded. His son spoke up. "Thank you, lady! We don't have much to pay you but a chicken and—"

Mr. Simmons slowly slid off the table, then sagged against it, leaning heavily on his uninjured leg. "This table wobbles. I can make you a fine new table and fix your shutters. I noticed a crooked shutter outside."

Warwick was impressed he'd even noticed the shutters when he'd arrived here with that nasty wound.

"A table would be wonderful, Mr. Simmons. But not until you are completely healed."

Adeline's smile caught Warwick off guard, and he froze, his heart pounding in his chest.

Bloody hell. Their simple ruse was becoming more complicated by the minute.

. . .

"You arrived earlier than expected today, Your Grace," Adeline said.

After Hasmik had accompanied Mr. Simmons and his son back to their home to see the father comfortably settled, Warwick stayed behind. Adeline disposed of the dirty rags, then slipped the bloodstained apron over her head. She was bone weary, her whole body limp with fatigue, and she wanted nothing more than to collapse on her sofa and rest her feet on the ottoman. Her back ached from bending over her patient and her eyes were tired from focusing on the needle in her hand.

Warwick pushed away from the wall and came closer, his steps measured, his gaze steady. Adeline's heart thumped an irregular beat. "I finished my work on the engine for the day, and I longed to see you."

Adeline stared at him as he stood before her. An unwanted warmth flooded her body, her skin tingling beneath her blue dress. Sunlight from the parlor window cast his chiseled features half in light, half in shadow. What in heaven did he mean when he said he *longed* to see her?

"You have seen my workshop. I was interested in your herbs—local and mid-eastern ones—as well as your medicinal concoctions," he said. "But I learned much more than I thought I would. I was also taken by surprise."

"Oh? What do you mean?"

"Your abilities, for one. You are much more skilled than a simple healer with a batch of medicinal herbs at your disposal."

The way he looked at her—intense, heated, and full of something akin to suspicion—made her nervous. She began putting away her suture kit, her movements quick and measured. "I don't know whether to be insulted or pleased by your assumptions."

"Pleased. My comments were meant to be complimentary."

She arched an eyebrow and met his gaze. "And here I thought you took me seriously after treating your burn."

His jaw tightened. "I did. I do. But then I watched you stitch up that man's jagged and bloody wound with calm and precision. You have done that before."

She had. Five times to be exact.

"You are a surgeon." The statement was more accusation than fact.

"No. You are mistaken. I am no surgeon. I am an herbalist and healer who helps people who cannot afford or do not have access to a fancy London doctor. I still have much to learn."

The tightness in his expression eased. "So do most of the men who call themselves London doctors."

She grinned. She couldn't help herself.

"The carpenter's recovery will be due entirely to your ability." He crossed his arms over his chest. It was a very broad chest, and she found it hard to tear her gaze away.

She inwardly shook herself. "I've learned to wait and see. I meant what I said about the risk of fever."

"It's expected." He bowed, then moved to the door. "You must be tired, Lady Adeline. I will leave you to recover."

To her surprise, she wasn't ready for him to leave. Questions remained and she wanted answers from the elusive duke. "Wait. I still want to understand your motives. Why the interest in my herbs in the first place?"

He turned back. "I told you. I haven't forgotten your concerns over our 'courting.'"

He'd already appraised her of his plans. As if by talking about the contents of her medicine chest any worries she harbored over their "courting" could be dispelled.

Good grief. Learning the layout of his country workshop and the contraptions he toiled over was one thing. Feigning an amorous courtship and fooling Edwin, his godmother, and the rest of Society was something else entirely.

"I appreciated the tour of your workshop, but Your Grace's visit to learn about my daily activities did little to alleviate my concerns."

"Perhaps if you'd be more specific, I will be able to address your hesitancy."

He sounded like a professor making an inquiry of his student. The man was maddening. He completely misunderstood her "hesitancy." How to phrase it?

Physical contact.

Touching.

Holding hands.

Kissing.

No! She shouldn't be thinking about kissing him, should she?

His lips were perfectly formed, like the rest of the man. The more she stared at the enticing divot in his chin, the more she wanted to reach out and touch it, press her lips to it…

No. No. *No!*

"Well?" he asked.

She cleared her throat. "First, my half brother is perceptive. He also has a strong motive for me to marry Mr. Slade."

"Ah, the moneylender. Edwin plans to use you as payment for a debt."

She tried not to cringe. Warwick was right, of course. No matter her discomfort. The duke's straightforward manner was unlike any of the aristocrats she'd known. That's because *he* was unlike any other. "You make it sound like I'm a commodity for sale."

"When you look at the entire marriage mart of the *ton* from an economic lens, is it any different? Most marriages are an equitable exchange for dowry, title, status, or all three."

There it was again. His method of rational thinking. Only this time he'd mentioned economics instead of science. It all was bookish without any sensitivity or heart. "Not all marriages lack emotion. Some even wed for love." Her parents had. Granted, her father's first wife had a dowry, title, and status. His second marriage to her mother, a commoner, was for love.

"You speak of a minority of the *beau monde*," he argued.

"Whatever Lord Foster's reasons, I don't think we can fool him," she said. That much was true. Her half brother had been angry that she'd refused him, and his ire had increased when Warwick had disrupted Edwin's plans.

"I disagree. I know the man better than you think."

"You cannot know him in just one brief meeting." She'd noticed the hostility between the two men; it couldn't have been missed.

Warwick waved a dismissive hand. "Not from the morning confrontation."

"Then from where?"

"We attended Eton together, then Oxford."

This was interesting but not uncommon. Many aristocrats sent their heirs and spares to the prestigious Eton. What she really wanted to know was what bad blood existed between the two men.

"Edwin, Lord Foster, is arrogant and dislikes a challenge—whether physical or intellectual," Warwick said.

"I take it you challenged him at some

point. Or vice versa?" Warwick was highly intelligent. Oh, her brother was smart, and he'd never been a fool, but she didn't believe he could rival Warwick when it came to book learning.

But there were other traits she was more concerned with now. Shrewdness. Worldliness. Instinct. Edwin had all three.

"My godmother, Lady Heywood, is far more observant than Foster."

She sighed. "If that's true, then you should understand. If we are to return to Town as planned, our families will suspect something is wrong."

"There is one sensible solution."

She took a deep breath. "Pray tell me."

"We must practice."

"Practice?"

He couldn't mean…wouldn't dare.

"Yes, practice acting affectionate toward each other."

He did mean it. At least to some extent. She'd already noticed his mouth, the fuller bottom lip and the divot in his chin. Was he proposing kissing? A restless tension coiled inside her, and she felt her face flush with color. "How on earth are we to accomplish that?"

"I can't imagine it would be that difficult. You are a skilled surgeon who has the knowledge to treat my arm."

Her heart thumped an irregular beat. "I'm not a surgeon," she protested once again.

"Regardless, we have already had physical contact." He extended his hand. "What is the harm in a bit more?"

CHAPTER SEVEN

Adeline stared at Warwick's outstretched hand and wondered if she had the nerve to accept.

Don't be a ninny. She reached out and slipped her hand in his. His grip was sure and firm, and her palm tingled with warmth.

"We have already taken the first step," Warwick said.

"We have?" Adeline's voice sounded strained to her own ears.

"Touching. You have touched me."

She had. She'd also noticed the clear-cut lines of his perfect profile, his shoulders, his chest. She'd treated men before, of course, but never had she been as aware of a patient as she was of Warwick.

To her horror, she was thinking those same thoughts now. It must be due to her exhaustion. He was still holding her hand and she couldn't find the strength to pull away from the comfort. Soft prickles of pleasure coursed up her arm. "We will have certain expectations when we return to Town," she managed to say.

He nodded. "You refer to the Society functions you require."

She didn't miss the "you require" at the

end of his statement. If it was up to him, they would never be seen together, and that wouldn't work. "Those functions are necessary, if we are to succeed. We will have to touch in different ways when we are out and about."

"Like dancing?"

"Yes."

His mouth turned downward. "I don't dance. I especially avoid waltzing."

He released her hand. To her dismay, she felt a sense of loss.

Foolish, Adeline! Either he was a master at seduction or completely ignorant of the effect he had on her.

She folded her arms across her chest. "That isn't acceptable. All gentlemen dance. You are a duke."

"I know *how,* of course. My mother made certain it was part of my education. I choose not to."

She knew it wasn't just girls that mothers hired dance instructors to teach. Still, he had to have taken a spin on the dance floor at one time. She eyed him anew. He probably drew every eye in a ballroom when he was announced by a majordomo. Tall, dominating, and ridiculously handsome, he acted as if he couldn't care less what other men thought of him or what ladies whispered about him behind fluttering fans. Mad, eccentric, or simply elusive, whatever they called him didn't matter. He was a duke, one step below royalty, and he carried himself with the command associated with his title.

"Then we shall practice looking at each other with amorous attention, as if we are at a ball or strolling in the park or sitting across from each other in a crowded dining room," he said.

A prickling grew in the pit of her stomach. Touch him. Look longingly at him. Meet his gaze and smile. It would be torturous. Exciting. Thrilling.

Dangerous.

"We will still have to dance," she insisted. "I received an invitation to Lady Furlong's country dance. It's the same day as the village fair. It's an opportunity for us to dance before a larger London ball."

"Fine. I'll attend. Meanwhile, we can practice dancing now if you'd like," he said.

Suddenly he pulled her close and she found herself pressed flush against him. Her hands landed on his arms for balance, her fingers curling around his biceps. The muscles flexed beneath her hands, and her breath caught. She looked up into his eyes, and his grip on her waist tightened. She was highly conscious of the placement of each finger on her ribcage. Warmth billowed up inside her, heating more than where he touched her. She felt it in the strangest places. Fluttering in her belly. A tingling between her legs. She sucked in a breath. "That won't be necessary right this moment." Her voice rose an octave.

He released her at once. "As you wish. I apologize. You must be exhausted."

She had been. Until she'd slipped her hand in his and he'd pulled her against him. Her exhaustion had blown away like dry leaves in a strong gust of wind. Eyes wide, she stepped back, a tumble of fear and excitement knotting in her chest. With slightly trembling fingers, she smoothed her skirts to gather her wits.

"You needn't worry. I will be sure to visit you with roses and poetry in hand at Lord Foster's home each day," Warwick said.

Her stomach jolted in an unpleasant manner that had nothing to do with the man standing before her.

"You cannot," she blurted out.

"Why? Will your brother deny me entry? I hadn't thought of that." He rubbed his chin with a thumb and forefinger.

"It's not that. Edwin will deny *me* entry."

"Pardon?"

"My brother all but forcibly removed me from the London home."

"You're jesting?"

She shook her head.

"Son of a—" Warwick caught himself

before he emitted what she assumed was an obscene curse in front of a lady. It would have been amusing had it not been about her very real circumstances.

Warwick's lips thinned in a grim line. "I hadn't believed it possible. My dislike of your brother has increased."

"Half brother," she corrected.

"Why would he toss you out?"

Her face heated once more, but this time it had nothing to do with the man standing before her. "I already told you of my mother's Arabic background and how she married the old earl soon after the death of his first English wife, Edwin's mother."

"Edwin didn't approve."

She nodded once. "It was a crime Edwin could never forgive. He despised my mother. He never accepted her Arab roots and believed her beneath our father. It was not just prejudice on his part, but a deep-seated resentment that his parents had a cold, unloving marriage, whereas our father adored my mother."

"So he holds it against you?"

A brief shiver rippled through her. "Yes, I'm of impure Arab blood as well."

"This changes things."

A cold knot formed in her stomach. Had the duke changed his mind about helping after learning how Lord Foster treated her?

Would her half brother's prejudice taint the Duke of Warwick's perspective?

"I had planned to write my godmother and tell her of our mutual admiration," Warwick said.

"You will no longer write her?"

"I will. But I shall have to add a request. Knowing Lady Heywood, she will be happy to have you and Hasmik reside with her. Her Piccadilly home has many rooms."

"I couldn't possibly impose upon your godmother."

"Once you meet the lady, you will understand. She will be more than thrilled that I've finally lost my heart to a lady."

• • •

True to his word, Warwick showed up to escort Adeline to the village fair, followed by Lady Furlong's country dance. By the time they arrived in the heart of Chilham, the village was abuzz with activity. A quaint village green was surrounded by an old stone church, a tavern, and rows of small cottages with thatched straw roofs. Torches blazed and illuminated vendors who had set up temporary stalls selling a wide array of goods including children's toys, clothing, candles, jewelry, farming tools, and furniture. Others offered mouthwatering grilled meat on skewers, mincemeat pies, and pastries. Fairgoers could purchase spiced wine and ale for a coin. A group of children giggled in delight at a juggler who managed to toss eight small apples in the air and catch each of them. Others on the green laughed and danced to festive music, while those interested in purchasing goods wandered from vendor to vendor, eyeing wares and sampling food. A torch popped and the aroma of grilled meat and burning candles scented the air.

Hasmik had accompanied Warwick and Adeline. "I'll leave you two to attend Lady Furlong's dance. There is much for me to see and buy." She waved as she departed, leaving them alone.

Adeline glanced up at Warwick. It was their first public outing and a test of sorts. Together, they entered the village green and soon, they were surrounded by people.

"Come. I see something I want to buy," Warwick said.

She shook her head. "We should go to Lady Furlong's dance. We don't want to be late."

He looked back at her. "I thought fashionably late was desirable."

How could she explain? Fashionably late in London, yes. The country was different. She didn't know what to expect here. The villagers were enjoying all the fair had to offer. The upper class of Chilman was most likely different.

He took her hand. "We have time."

She had no choice but to follow. His hand was warm and engulfed hers. After passing three stalls, Warwick stopped at the fourth one. An old husband and wife manned the stall, which offered scarves, lady's fans, frilly garters, gloves, and other articles of clothing. Warwick pointed to a blue apron embroidered with vines on the border. When the man took it off a hook and handed it to Warwick, he turned to Adeline. "I believe you will make good use of this."

"An apron? It's pretty, but I'm a horrid cook."

"I didn't mean it for the kitchen. At least, not in that respect. When you stitched up that man's thigh, you had blood on your apron. You need another. I chose this one because of the vines. It reminds me of your herbs."

A flush heated her cheeks, and she looked up at him in surprise. He wanted to buy her an apron for healing patients? It was the first time anyone had purchased her a gift for her work. He threw her off balance, thoughtful one moment, agonizingly argumentative the next. "Thank you." Her voice sounded soft to her own ears.

He flashed a grin. "Now let's head to Lady Furlong's event, shall we?"

She rested her hand on his uninjured arm,

aware of the strength beneath his sleeve and
the coiled power of the tall man beside her.
"You should know that I had my butler reveal my true identity in the village," he said.

"Why?"

"To start our story, I had to come out of
hiding."

She gave him a sideways look. He was
right. She was surprised and appreciative that
he had the foresight to "come out of hiding"
as he'd phrased it. It would make their presence at the dance easier as well as much more
interesting. "I think it was a good idea."

Lady Furlong's home was a short walk
from the village green. It was a stately country home with white stone pillars and a small
circular drive that could hold one carriage at
a time. Many of the genteel country neighbors had walked from the fair. Torches
illuminated a large wooden front door. Music
sounded from the ballroom, not the same
country music that played in the village
green, but from an orchestra.

The formalities were relaxed here, and
thankfully, a majordomo was not required to
announce the guests as they arrived. Adeline
and the Duke of Warwick were careful not to
walk in together, but separately. They were
not yet engaged. Rather, this was the perfect
opportunity for them to practice a courtship—to pretend to be enamored of each

other and have their first public dance. If rumors of their affection reached London before they'd had a chance to arrive, then all the better.

A footman led them to their hostess, Lady Furlong. A wealthy middle-aged widow two-times-over in her forties, she'd grown richer after each marriage and could carry out her eccentricities. She was dressed in an extravagant gown of yellow with billowing skirts and an overlay of gold tissue. A low bodice embroidered with Brussel's lace did nothing to hide her large breasts. Her cheeks and lips were rouged, and a towering wig of blond hair contained a small gilded birdcage and peacock feathers.

Lady Furlong fluttered her fan. "Lady Adeline Cameron. What a wonderful surprise to meet your acquaintance. Is your brother accompanying you?"

Adeline lowered her gaze from the headdress to the lady's necklace. A chain of diamonds with an emerald the size of a walnut rested between her ample cleavage. "No, my lady. He is in London."

"'Tis a shame. My youngest niece is visiting. Perhaps she will meet him in Town."

Adeline smiled smoothly. "I'm sure." The best thing for the niece would be to avoid Edwin. He wouldn't treat any wife with the respect she deserved.

Their hostess's eyes lit with excitement as she traveled to the next guest in line. She pressed a beringed hand to her chest. "The Duke of Warwick! I daresay, I was surprised to learn of Your Grace's presence in Chilham, and I am most honored to have a duke attend my country gathering."

"The honor is mine." Warwick bowed over her hand.

Adeline let out her breath in relief. For a man who hated Society functions, he was charming and polite.

Warwick folded his hands before him. "Do you have an interest in ornithology, my lady?"

Lady Furlong looked at him questioningly. "Pardon? I'm not sure what that is, Your Grace."

"Ornithology is the study of birds. Scientists study their flight patterns, visual appeal, even their birdsongs."

Lady Furlong repeatedly blinked. "Why would you ask, Your Grace?"

"Your headpiece is of a birdcage."

The lady's mouth gaped as her hand fluttered to her extravagant wig.

Oh my God. Adeline's cheeks flushed hot, and her heart galloped with embarrassment. Any relief over his manners dissipated like a puff of smoke. What was he thinking? Could he be that socially inept? An awkward silence stretched between the parties, and Adeline wanted to melt into the crowd.

Thankfully, the next guest in line approached.

Thank our lucky stars!

Warwick bowed and stepped aside. As he walked away from the receiving line and into the ballroom, Adeline hurried to follow and touched his sleeve. He turned and she motioned for him to meet her behind a pillar.

Eyes wide, she looked up at him. "Why on earth would you ask that of Lady Furlong?"

"Just as I said. Because of the towering birdcage upon her head."

She scowled. "It's fashion!"

"Why would a birdcage in one's wig be fashionable?"

She threw up her hands. "I don't know. I know only that gentlemen don't go around asking ladies offending questions." If she was truthful, she'd had a hard time tearing her gaze away from the ridiculous headdress herself. The difference was that she'd kept her thoughts to herself, and her mouth shut.

"I didn't mean offense."

The ballroom was warm, and Adeline opened her fan and began rigorously fanning herself. "I understand…but—"

"I feel compelled to point out that you were the one who suggested we attend Lady Furlong's country gathering to practice, remember? I'd rather be in a library with a good book," he said.

"Clearly."

He arched one dark eyebrow. "You also insist we attend a London ball," he said.

"Balls. More than one." She began to wonder if that was a mistake. Insulting a lady in the country was one thing. A glittering London ball hosted by a renowned Society hostess, or a powerful patroness of Almack's was another thing entirely.

She felt queasy at the thought.

He rested a hand on the pillar by her head. "While we are here, we should dance."

The change of topic and his nearness made her head spin. Her anxiety veered into a heightened awareness of him. Dressed in a well-tailored navy coat, snowy cravat, and checked jacket, he looked every inch a duke. A very handsome one. Her insides tugged and twisted. She snapped her fan shut. "Can you?"

"Don't be ridiculous. I already told you I could. Come."

Once more, he took her hand and rested it on his forearm. She resisted the urge to squeeze and feel his muscles. On the way to the dance floor, she spotted Hasmik in the corner. She must have arrived from the village fair. She nodded and offered Adeline an encouraging smile as the duke led her to the hardwood floor.

The musicians began a country dance. The dancers paired off and other dancers joined them in a line. Her feet moved to the music. She risked a glimpse at his face, and she tripped but caught herself. Across the way, Warwick moved with ease and never missed a step of the dance. For some reason, that irked her.

He can dance. She should be grateful. It was his social ineptness that needed refinement. He'd spoken like a scientist to their hostess. He was right: he'd do better in a library full of books rather than a ballroom.

Out of the corner of her eye, she spotted women watching them as she met and separated from Warwick during the dance. This was practice for London. This was what they needed. The women gossiped like magpies behind fluttering fans.

If they were lucky, the gossip would travel like wildfire and reach London before they did.

Warwick may be awkward with social mores, but he was handsome enough to draw every eye. His prized title was icing on the cake. They must pull off their ruse long enough to survive the Season.

• • •

"What ails you now, Your Grace?"

Warwick dropped the wrench he'd been

using to adjust the pistons. Nelson was showing more and more familiarity toward him.
The country air must have loosened the rigid-
ity of his proper English butler.

"Pardon?"

"You forgot your notes." Nelson held up a
leather-bound book. Warwick always meticulously inscribed his progress with his various
machines. He was religious about carrying the
book with him when he worked.

"I must have misplaced them."

"Are you unwell? In pain? I can continue
with the flour." Deep furrows marred
Nelson's brow.

Nelson's concern was obvious. Warwick
often became engrossed in his work and
could take his long-time staff for granted.
Only his work wasn't the reason for his distraction today. It was entirely due to his
attractive and argumentative neighbor.

Warwick had been trying not to think
about the prior evening but his efforts were
in vain. He *couldn't* stop thinking about
Adeline—how her slender hand had felt on
his arm as he'd escorted her around the country fair. Or how she'd looked up at him, blue
eyes wide with wonder, when he'd given her
the apron. No one had ever looked at him
that way, and it had stirred a long-buried
pang in his chest.

It hadn't lasted long, though, before they'd

crossed the village green and entered Lady Furlong's ballroom. Oh, he knew he'd said something wrong to their hostess. But who could help it after seeing that ridiculous contraption of a birdcage teetering on the lady's head?

Then there was later during the evening. He'd told Adeline that he knew how to dance, but the flash of surprise on her face was unmistakable. The country dance hadn't offered enough opportunity to touch her, only the briefest moment to feel her lithe body brush against his. His gaze had been drawn to her full lips, the graceful lines of her neck, and the glimpse of smooth skin above her bodice. It was enough to distract him then...and now. For a man who had never had trouble focusing on mechanical drawings and machinery, his baffling emotions were frustrating.

Warwick grew aware of Nelson waiting for his response. He leaned forward in his chair. "No. I'm not ill or in pain. The burn is healing nicely." He hadn't been in pain for more than a week, thanks to Adeline's treatment.

"You have been unusually quiet, Your Grace."

"Have I?"

He was to return to London with Adeline soon, and they'd both have to deal with their families. He knew how to handle his godmother but Lord Foster was an entirely different challenge.

When he'd first discovered she was Edwin's sister, he'd believed she would be like her brother. Arrogant, self-righteous, judgmental of everyone. He realized he'd been just as judgmental during his first encounter with Adeline. Oh, she was quick to put him in his place when she'd deemed it necessary, but her reactions hadn't stemmed from a belief she was superior to everyone, like Edwin, but from a deep intelligence and sharp wit.

She was nothing like her brother.

Half brother, she'd been quick to point out.

The same half brother who had tossed her out of her home.

Adeline was brave and courageous and driven to help others—villagers who couldn't afford to pay her for her services other than to fix a broken shutter and make a new table. She hadn't asked for coin in return.

Mrs. Posner appeared in the doorway of the study. "The morning post arrived, Your Grace. A letter from Lady Heywood." She handed it to him.

Nelson scowled, his displeasure obvious that the housekeeper had answered the door and intercepted the morning post.

"Let me see."

Warwick broke the seal. As he'd expected, his godmother was surprised but thrilled to learn of his interest in Lady Adeline Cameron, and she was even more excited for Adeline and her companion, Miss Hasmik, to reside with her.

I was against your decision to abandon the Season for the country. Never did I anticipate that you would meet a lady in Kent. I eagerly look forward to hearing your love story.

His love story? Damn! He'd have to concoct a believable tale of how he'd met Adeline. She'd have to approve. "Well?" Mrs. Posner wrung her hands. "What does the countess say about your romantic interest?"

Warwick grew aware of Nelson and Mrs. Posner awaiting his answer. "It seems we are to return to London with Lady Adeline. My godmother eagerly awaits our visit."

•••

"We just finished unpacking our belongings and now we find ourselves packing once again," Hasmik said.

Dresses and shoes were scattered about the bed and the floor of Adeline's bedchamber. Two trunks were half full. "Not everything. Just our clothing and necessities. If all goes according to plan, we will return soon enough. Meanwhile, Lady Heywood was kind enough to invite us to stay in her home."

"How do you feel about living with the

duke's godmother?"

Adeline picked up her silver hairbrush. It was a small item, but she'd have to find a space for it where the bristles wouldn't get crushed. "Warwick says she is a widow and eager for companionship. She believes her godson is courting me. I'm not certain what he told the countess about us."

"The lady will undoubtedly welcome you. You are the daughter of an earl."

"As well as the daughter of an Arab commoner," Adeline pointed out.

"I'm not concerned how *you* will be received. As for myself—"

"Do not even think it." Adeline's eyes flashed as she tossed the hairbrush down on her bed. "You're my dearest friend and my companion. If you are unwelcome, then I will not stay."

"You are young and full of righteous fire, Adeline. You must learn the world does not see everything through your eyes."

"Nonsense. Let's not worry until we meet Lady Heywood."

Without another word, Hasmik returned to packing Adeline's gowns.

Adeline did worry, but she didn't want Hasmik to see her trepidation. Surely God wasn't so cruel that He would take her mother, then her father, and then force her to separate from Hasmik?

Adeline's jaw clenched. They'd experienced the bitter bite of prejudice far too often from Edwin. She wouldn't allow it from anyone else.

An hour later, the duke's crested carriage came to a stop before the cottage. The black lacquered conveyance gleamed beneath the sun and the magnificent matching bays stood in unison. A second baggage coach halted behind the carriage. Warwick stepped out of the carriage. He was an impressive sight in a moss coat with blue and green striped waistcoat and buff trousers.

A coachman loaded their baggage. "Why the second coach?" she asked the duke.

"My inventions, including the high-pressure steam engine."

"You are moving an engine?" Adeline had packed just her medicine chest and a few other items.

"My work on the pistons can be completed at my London home. On my way here, I thought of your pig and the hounds. Who will care for them?"

She was surprised by his inquiry. Was he truly concerned for the animals or was he worried *she* would be worried and not wish to spend sufficient time in Town to accomplish his purpose?

"I made arrangements for a local farmer to care for Henry and both dogs. Mrs. Taylor will keep up the cottage." Adeline couldn't leave her animals without the villagers' help and was happy that her animals would be looked after. The people of the village had grown to mean much to her, and they had stepped up to aid in her time of need.

"Is Mrs. Taylor the blacksmith's wife, the man you helped heal from a persistent cough?"

She tilted her head to the side. "How did you know?"

"I heard."

Had he inquired about her in the village? Any chance to ask was cut short when his coachman approached to lower the step. But Warwick waved the man away. "Allow me," he said, extending his hand.

For the second time, she rested her hand in his. And for the second time, a tingling warmth, an unwelcome awareness, sent her stomach into a wild swirl.

Hasmik took a seat in the corner of the carriage. Warwick sat across from Adeline on the padded leather bench. With a jingle of harness, they were off. As they drew farther and farther away from the country, her misgivings increased. How could she convince others of their courtship when she was having trouble convincing herself?

CHAPTER EIGHT

A benefit to their agreement was the duke's carriage. The green velvet curtains covering the windows matched the padded back of her seat, and the conveyance was well-sprung on the bumpy country roads. One wouldn't think a luxurious carriage would make a difference, but then it wasn't every day that one traveled the distance from Kent to London. The two-day trip could play havoc on one's disposition and temperament.

The only drawback of the conveyance was the fact that the duke came with it. Her unease had nothing to do with the journey and everything to do with the tall, broad-shouldered man seated across from her, and his presence seemed to occupy every square inch of space. Warwick's long legs brushed her skirts whenever they took a turn. His features were only half-illuminated, and she couldn't gauge his reactions.

With Hasmik acting as her chaperone, all was proper. But her companion's presence did little to alleviate Adeline's discomfort. After the first half hour, Hasmik had fallen asleep, and her head lolled against the padded side of the coach. There was no one to speak with but Warwick.

"We shall stop at an inn for a meal," Warwick announced. "You look like you need a respite."

Adeline shifted on the bench and glanced at him beneath lowered lashes to find him watching her as if she were a curiosity, as if he were trying to solve a perplexing problem in one of his complex machines.

On some level, she felt the same about him.

"What do you mean? Do I look weary?"

His look was quick and keen. "No. You appear nervous."

She bit her lower lip. "Aren't you?"

"No."

"You aren't the slightest hesitant at our return?"

"When you put it that way, then yes," he said briskly, "but I suspect for different reasons. I didn't want to move my steam engine back to Town until my work was finished."

Heat throbbed in her cheeks. "That's the only reason for your agitation?"

"What else is there?"

Was he serious? "We will soon be back in the fold of Society."

"And?"

She wanted to slap her own forehead in exasperation. She took a breath instead. "We could be discovered."

"We won't." His voice was infused with confidence.

"How can you be sure? What of your god-mother, Lady Heywood?"

"What about her?"

She cleared her throat and tried for patience. "I know little about her."

"She was my mother's distant cousin. They were good friends until later."

"Later? What occurred between them?"

"Me."

She met his green gaze. "Why?"

He shrugged broad shoulders. "Their discord had to do with my upbringing. The duke and duchess had certain expectations for their heir."

"And Lady Heywood disapproved?" Warwick was being particularly vague. He obviously didn't like to talk about himself.

Warwick sighed, as if recounting the memory was bothersome or…difficult. "I was young, but I recall an incident. I ran to my mother after discovering a book on the topic of physics in my father's library. Even though I was not permitted in my father's domain, I was excited to find the book and even more excited to learn something new. You see, there was a whole world of thinkers, as I had called them back then. Thinkers who wondered about the universe just like me."

"How old were you?"

"Seven."

Goodness. She pictured a little boy with a

shock of fair hair and big green eyes full of curiosity and wonder. In essence, he'd discovered a new world.

"What did the duchess say?"

"My timing was unfortunate. She was entertaining friends, ladies of influence in the *beau monde*, in her private drawing room. She found my exuberance embarrassing. She snatched the book from my hands and admonished me for sneaking into my father's library."

"That was unfair." He'd been terribly young and of tender feelings.

"Then she grasped my hand, dragged me into another room. She snatched the book from me, smacked me across the cheek, and sent me to my room without dinner. I never saw the book again."

Adeline gasped. "That was horrid." She swallowed a lump in her throat at the image.

"Not as horrid as what was planned for me thereafter. My father took me on a hunt the next day. And the day after that. And for the next month. He made me shoot game. 'It's the best way to become a man,' he'd said. Looking back, I believe I was too tender-hearted to kill anything."

"That was unfair as well."

"Perhaps. I occasionally shoot, like many gentlemen, at Manton's, but I dislike hunting."

"The duke and duchess were wrong."

"It was not all bad. Lady Heywood was one of the ladies in the drawing room that day and witnessed everything. She confronted the duchess, and they had a terrible row. Thereafter, my godmother became my champion. She protested that just because I didn't express interests in the same activities as other boys my age—rolling in the dirt, spending hours tormenting their siblings, and stealing sweets from the kitchens—it was nothing to be ashamed of but encouraged. She snuck me books and I kept them hidden beneath a loose floorboard in my bedchamber."

Adeline pictured a young boy on his hands and knees retrieving books from a hidden cavity and reading by candlelight in secret.

"The duke and duchess may not have understood me," Warwick said, "but I didn't fault them. I was not what they expected as their heir. Eventually, I found others with similar scientific interests at Oxford, men of great learning."

"I see why Lady Heywood means much to you."

"Yes. She is intelligent in her own right and a bit eccentric in her thinking. She is also determined to see me settled, not so much for the continuation of the title, although that is of great importance to her, but because she wants me 'to be happy.'"

Adeline had a better understanding of his godmother. But learning more about Warwick's past didn't put her worries to rest. Her nerves were wound tighter than clock springs. If the lady was that protective of Warwick, then she'd be especially watchful of Adeline.

• • •

Adeline's fingers clenched on the handle of the carriage the first time she saw Lady Heywood's home. She knew her anxiety was unwarranted, but her nervousness increased the nearer they got.

It was a lovely Piccadilly home with cream-colored stone. She caught a glimpse of the well-maintained gardens through the gate. Flowering shrubs of azaleas and wild roses climbing trellises perfumed the air. A liveried footman opened the carriage door and Adeline climbed stone steps into the home. The vestibule was welcoming with cream marble and expensive artwork on the walls. She spotted a sporting painting of a stallion by George Stubbs, and a landscape from Thomas Gainsborough of ladies promenading through a park, their shimmering dresses capturing the light of a pink sunset. The drawing room was a pretty shade of pale yellow with striped yellow and gold drapes and a matching yellow velvet settee and sofa.

It was a luxurious and welcoming home, yet Adeline's heart thumped madly, and she felt a terrible tenseness in her body as she awaited the arrival of Warwick's godmother.

"What's wrong?" Warwick turned away from a tall window overlooking a garden maze to address her. Dressed in a coat of navy superfine with a ruby pin in his cravat, he looked every inch a duke.

Adeline chose to sit on the yellow-striped sofa.

"You have nothing to fear from my god-mother."

She hoped her smile was noncommittal. "What makes you think I fear your god-mother?"

"I've come to know you. For someone who can stitch a man's gaping wound with nerves of steel, I find your current nervous state un-necessary."

She'd thought she'd done a better job of hiding her distress upon their arrival, but ap-parently, he could tell. They hadn't spent weeks together. She'd tended to his burn and toured his country workshop. They'd attend-ed one country dance. He'd watched her work. How had he come to know her that well? It bothered her. She'd only begun to understand his complex mind.

As for his comment about her nerves of

steel when she'd stitched the country carpenter's thigh, those circumstances were completely different from this and—

Adeline stood and lifted her chin and met Warwick's enigmatic green gaze. Her lips parted just as the drawing room door opened and a middle-aged woman walked inside, a smile upon her face.

"Welcome," Lady Heywood said as she came forward to greet first Adeline and then Hasmik, before giving Warwick a hug and a kiss on his cheek.

Lady Heywood's golden hair, fading gently to gray, was artfully coiffed, and her brown eyes were alert. Tall, slim, and dressed in a stylish blue gown, she carried herself with grace and command. Adeline knew the lady was a countess and a widow, and she must have been exceptionally beautiful in her youth.

"Thank you for allowing us to stay with you," Adeline said.

"Her family home is busy with tradesmen coming and going. Building and repair is necessary, but quite noisy and disruptive," Warwick added.

It was the excuse he'd given for Adeline not staying at her family's home during her time in Town. She wondered if the countess would ask questions, but instead she simply nodded.

"I can only imagine," Lady Haywood said.

"But it is my pleasure to have you and Miss Hasmik. This house has many rooms and I'm happy for the company. Besides, it will give us time to get to know each other, my dear."

There was kindness in the lady's gaze, but clear curiosity as well. Another emotion mingled with Adeline's discomfort, and she acknowledged it for what it was: a pang of guilt. She had no such feelings when it came to lying to Edwin, but the countess had done nothing to deserve her deception.

Adeline forced a smile. "I look forward to it, my lady."

The countess looked between Warwick and Adeline, her eyes sharp and assessing. Adeline clutched her hands before her and forced a gracious smile.

"I was thrilled to hear of my godson's interest in a lady," the countess said.

"Ah, it was quite unexpected," Adeline said.

"You must tell me all about it, my dear. But I cannot be selfish. You must be tired and wish to change. Your rooms are ready, and my housekeeper will escort you." Lady Heywood turned her attention to the duke. "Meanwhile, I can catch up with my godson."

Adeline nearly sagged in relief. It was a reprieve, albeit brief. Now that she was under the countess's roof, she would have to pull off a performance worthy of Drury Lane.

· · ·

"Tell me the truth, Daniel."

Warwick placed his hands behind his back and faced his godmother. She'd known him since he was in leading strings and was the only one who addressed him informally. "Whatever do you mean?"

"How have you managed to keep Lady Adeline a secret?"

He walked to the sideboard and poured himself a glass of madeira. "May I get you a drink?"

"I suppose the occasion calls for a celebratory drink."

He grinned. It was one of the things he liked about her. She was a true lady, but she also knew when to loosen the rules. He'd broken many rules as a young boy. He handed her a goblet.

Her smile faded and she gave him a matronly look. "Now answer my question."

"I didn't keep Lady Adeline a secret. I wrote you about her, remember?"

She sat on a sofa, her back straight and her gaze direct as she sipped her wine. "Nonsense. You must have met the lady in Town before seeing her again in the country."

He settled in an armchair across her and sipped his own drink. "What makes you believe that?"

"Her father was an earl, and her family isn't known to be recluses. You were out and about somewhat before your country sojourn. You had to have met Lady Adeline somewhere. A bookshop? A scientific presentation? A museum?"

She'd named his three favorite pastimes. As for her observation that he'd attended events while he'd been in Town, she was right, to some extent. Other than the places she'd mentioned, he had memberships to all the gentlemen clubs—White's, Brook's and Boodle's. He frequented Gentleman Jackson's boxing salon where he sparred with Drake and, as he'd mentioned to Adeline, he even attended Manton's to shoot. He was an excellent marksman, as long as the targets were not live animals.

"You are mistaken about how I met Lady Adeline. The first time I set eyes upon the lady was in the country. You of all people know I do not attend balls, Almack's, or parties where young ladies gather." From what Warwick knew of Adeline, she didn't favor those events either.

Lady Heywood eyed him. "Lady Adeline is beautiful, but not what I expected."

"What do you mean?" For a moment, he wondered if his godmother recalled the bad blood between him and Adeline's half brother, Edwin. Their feud had begun years ago when they were at Eton.

"I always thought you would end up with a tall, willowy, fair-haired blonde."

He lowered his glass. "Why would you think that?"

"When you were young, you thought Lady Whistle was pretty and would trail behind her."

He rolled his eyes. "Good grief. I was twelve. Everyone thought Lady Whistle was pretty."

"Hmm. Well, Lady Adeline is quite lovely with her raven hair and blue eyes."

"She is lovely," Warwick found himself saying.

The countess's expression changed. He should have seen it coming. Whether she'd unwittingly elicited a reaction, or he had loosened his guard, the effect was the same.

"Why do I get the feeling that you are keeping things from me? What exactly have you been up to in that country cottage, Daniel?"

"I didn't know you wanted a detailed accounting of my daily activities. I have made progress on my work, specifically the pistons of the high-pressure steam engine—"

She raised a hand and leaned forward in her seat. "I may be old, but I am no fool. The lady is Lord Foster's sister."

She *did* recall. "Ah, you remember."

"Of course I remember! You were disciplined by the Eton headmaster. It was only your third year at school. The duke was most pleased."

He scoffed. "Most fathers would have been angry."

"Yours was satisfied that you gave Lord Foster's son a black eye."

Edwin had stepped on his astronomy project. It had taken Warwick days to make the planets and stars from small sticks, acorns, and a golden painted apple as the sun. Warwick had experienced a thrill of satisfaction after putting the bully in his place, but he'd dreaded his father's reaction. He should have known better.

"My father was proud I fought and made a boy cry. I didn't know whether to be horrified or relieved that I had finally gained my father's approval. All I'd done was escalate a deep-seated rivalry between Edwin and myself."

"And yet you are courting Lord Foster's sister?"

"Half sister. And no, I do not hold it against her. I didn't think you would either."

"Of course I don't. I shall plan a party to celebrate your upcoming engagement."

"We are not engaged."

Her gaze glimmered with mischievous intent. "Not yet, Daniel. But if the way you looked at the lovely Lady Adeline is an indication, then it will happen soon."

. . .

Adeline's mind was awhirl as she descended the grand staircase. A maid waited for her at the bottom of the stairs. "Lady Heywood awaits your presence in the blue drawing room, my lady."

The first drawing room had been yellow, and she wondered as to the significance of meeting the countess in a different room. She followed the maid, a young girl by the name of Beatrice, down the corridor and stopped outside a closed door. Beatrice bobbed a quick curtsy, then opened the door. This drawing room was just as lovely as the first one. The drapes were a pale blue and matched the shade of a well-padded sofa and two armchairs. The white marble mantel had two blue porcelain birds on either side of a gilded mantel clock.

The countess rose from her seat. "Good morning. I trust you had a restful evening?"

"Yes, my lady. My room is lovely. Thank you again for your hospitality." A tea tray had been delivered with a tray of fresh scones with jam and clotted cream. Warwick was notably absent this morning.

Adeline joined the countess on the sofa and the woman poured her a cup of steaming tea. She could do this. She could smile and lie and maintain her poise, staying as close as possible to the story she'd concocted with Warwick.

Her gaze darted around the room, taking in the rich paneling and rosewood furnishings. The painting above the mantel caught her eye. An older man with gray hair and wrinkles by his eyes. His expression was softened with a slight smile.

The countess noticed her interest. "The Viscount Heywood, my late husband."

"You loved him?" The question slipped from her lips before she could stop it. Her nerves had returned.

But the countess didn't seem to take offense. "I loved him very much. He was twenty years my senior and we were married for only two years before his passing."

An ache centered in Adeline's chest. "I'm sorry for your loss." Didn't she long for a love match for herself? Her parents had loved each other. Her father had adored her mother, and he hadn't cared that she was the daughter of a commoner.

Lady Heywood's gaze remained on the portrait. "I hated him at first."

Adeline blinked. "Truly?"

The countess turned back to her. "Oh yes. I thought him too arrogant, too selfish, too much a wastrel."

Adeline felt the same about Warwick, except the man was no wastrel, just an academic. "What changed?"

"We gave each other a chance. It happened while we were leaving a ball. A driver had lost control and his carriage was about to strike an elderly woman. Charles sprinted in the path of the runaway carriage and saved the woman just in time. He hadn't a care for himself. I never saw anything like it."

"It must have been shocking."

"It was! I knew I had been wrong about him. I approached him at the next ball and asked him to dance."

"You didn't!" Adeline covered her mouth with her hand.

"It's not something I readily confess, but it's true. Charles quickly bowed and took my hand, and no one at that ball knew of my boldness save the two of us. He asked my father for my hand in marriage a week later."

Adeline smiled. She took a bite of scone and chewed. Her nervousness eased. Lady Heywood had an easy manner, and she understood why Warwick cared for her. She was different, and just what a highly intelligent young boy had needed to survive beneath his parents' roof. The duke and duchess hadn't understood their son.

But his godmother had.

Adeline was different as well. She'd rather

help a villager than gain a coveted Almack's voucher for a Wednesday evening assembly.

"You care for my godson?"

Adeline swallowed a lump of scone. The woman was direct. "Yes."

It was true. She did care for the duke, though not in the manner that this woman wished to believe. She admired him for his intelligence, and she owed him a debt for dealing with Edwin. God only knew how Edwin would have retaliated had she continued to refuse his demands. Would she already be betrothed to the moneylender? The truth was she could be grateful to the duke and still find him maddening.

"Warwick never gave me a straight answer. How did you meet? At the theater? A dinner party? A country ball? I asked him, but he never answered."

Adeline set down her teacup. "We didn't meet at a country ball."

"I'm not surprised. Warwick dislikes them and avoided them in Town. I never believed he'd begun attending balls while he was away." The countess set down her own teacup. "Do not leave me in suspense, child. Was it through friends?"

"I'm a healer and we met when he came to me for a healing salve." They'd decided to stay close to the truth without revealing the *entire* truth. It was more believable, and

Adeline would be a horrid liar if they concocted a wild story of love and romance.

The countess pursed her lips. "Truly?"

"The burn on his forearm is healing well."

The lady threw her head back and laughed.
"Oh, that's rich and not what I'd thought at
all!"

"You are shocked?"

"It takes much to shock me, my dear, but I
admit I'm surprised. Where did the daughter
of an earl learn how to heal wounds?"

"My mother was a healer and midwife before she married the earl. Oftentimes, I
accompanied her."

"Fascinating. You said you helped treat
Warwick. Pray tell me, was his injury due to
one of his inventions?"

"Yes."

She *tsk*ed. "Stubborn man! I understand
his need to pursue his intellectual passions,
but he forgets his position. He is a duke, after
all!" The countess looked her over. "You are
quite unexpected, my dear."

"Is that good or bad?"

"You're what my godson needs. He was
not what his parents *expected*." She reached
out to touch Adeline's hand. "I shall enjoy
hosting you for the remainder of the Season."

"I'm grateful."

"Nonsense. I've been alone for far too
long. It will be a pleasure to have you and

your companion. I've already received invitations for garden parties, dinners, as well as the Kirkland ball, which is the social event of the Season." She leaned forward, her green eyes alight with excitement. "And from the way my godson spoke of you, I believe it will be an interesting few weeks. I hope the gossips wag their tongues."

CHAPTER NINE

"I like her. I fear it will be a problem," Adeline said.

"Why?" Hasmik asked.

It was a pleasant spring afternoon as they walked in Hyde Park. The promenade hour had just begun, and ladies with colorful gowns and carrying parasols strolled arm in arm together, some accompanied by gentlemen, while others rode in carriages and on horseback. Tall trees shaded the walking path, and a slight breeze blew from the Serpentine River and ruffled the tendrils of hair that escaped Adeline's pins. The scent of shrubs and evergreen filled the air.

"Because we are living beneath Lady Heywood's roof, and I must continue with this charade with her godson." The countess was unexpected in a pleasant way, and Adeline enjoyed her company.

Hasmik touched her arm. "She likes you and that's all that matters. You should just try to enjoy London."

"I suppose you are right. It's been a month since I've seen my sister. I'm eager to catch up with Mary." If she timed it right, perhaps Edwin would be out of the house at one of his clubs. It would be heaven to spend time with Mary without the dark shadow of Edwin hovering over them.

"Do you plan to tell Mary the truth? We never discussed it," Hasmik said.

Adeline hesitated before shaking her head. She was close with her sister, and they had grown up almost as twins. It never mattered to either of them that their birth mothers were different. But her situation with the Duke of Warwick was unique, and Adeline didn't want to involve her sister in the subterfuge. Mary was kind and tenderhearted, and she would be shocked at Adeline's arrangement and might let the secret slip to Edwin.

"No. The fewer people who know, the better. Appearances are everything if our plan is to succeed."

Hasmik scanned the crowded park. "Well, you were right about this interlude at the park. Many eyes will be upon us."

Most of the well-dressed people in attendance were here to be seen rather than to enjoy the refreshing outdoors. As the daughter of an earl, Adeline was familiar with the fickle nature of the *beau monde*. Warwick may not care about Society's rituals, but he was a duke, and as such, he would attract the most attention.

As if she conjured him, she spotted Warwick's tall frame heading down the gravel path toward them. Sunlight glinted off his golden brown hair and illuminated his striking features. Even from this distance, he made her breath catch.

"He is prompt," Hasmik noted. "It is a good quality in a man."

Adeline forced herself to smile and raised her hand to give a jaunty wave at the same time her voice lowered. "He had best be on time. It is our first planned London outing together, and we need to get a few tongues wagging before our first ball."

Hasmik chuckled. "Just the sight of that man will get tongues wagging."

Adeline had no time to answer before Warwick approached and bowed. "Good day, ladies."

Adeline curtsied. "Good day, Your Grace."

"It would be my honor to escort you about the park, Lady Adeline."

A couple a few yards away took notice of the duke and began to whisper to each other.

Good. Let them all see.

"It is a lovely day for a stroll, Your Grace."

Warwick offered his arm and Adeline rested her fingers on his sleeve. Hasmik trailed behind at a proper distance. A chaperone wasn't needed in a crowded park, and the woman knew how to make herself scarce.

Adeline tilted her head to the side and gifted Warwick with a smile. His green gaze met hers and he grinned. They began to stroll together, his long legs setting a slower pace so that she could walk beside him.

A group of riders noticed them and slowed their mounts. Another couple in a gentleman's high-perched phaeton watched them.

"Your idea was a splendid one," Warwick said. "I do believe that lady almost fell off her sidesaddle ogling us."

Adeline laughed then, a rich and genuine sound to her own ears. "I do believe you have a sense of humor."

Warwick's eyes gleamed. "Only for those I'm most comfortable with."

The toe of her shoe caught on a stone, and she stumbled. Warwick's hand was quick to cover her own hand on his arm and steady her. She was highly aware of the heat of his touch. Sensations rippled through her and, despite the warm weather, she shivered. "Careful. The path isn't even here."

It wasn't the path, but his words that had made her trip. Goodness, had he just confessed he was becoming comfortable around her? They had spent time together. She'd treated his wound; he'd watched her work.

But *comfortable* implied a level of intimacy as if they were a true couple, which they were not.

Definitely *not*.

She swallowed the lump in her throat and turned the topic of conversation. "We are fortunate today. Lady Hobson is a notorious gossip and she is here with Lady Whittaker, her close friend." She glanced at the women. Lady Whittaker was wearing a dark blue gown with a matching blue parasol; Lady Hobson, a green gown with a high collar and no parasol. She wondered how Lady Hobson wasn't perspiring in the warm spring day.

Warwick arched an eyebrow. "Is that so?"

"Oh yes. They are standing by the park bench and watching us intently. News of our stroll will surely make its way around the proper circles before the Kirkland ball."

"Then we must make every second count."

Before she could ask what he meant, he faced her, then lifted her hand, tugged her glove aside just enough to reveal a few inches of skin and placed a soft kiss on the inside of her wrist. She gasped. The feel of his lips on her naked skin sent her stomach in a wild swirl. Just as quickly, he raised his head, his green eyes capturing hers for one second, then two…then three…before his lips curled in a tantalizing smile.

"Save me a dance at the ball, Lady Adeline."

• • •

"My! My!" Lady Heywood waved a paper in hand after bursting into Warwick's study. "When was the last time you enjoyed a stroll in the park, Daniel?"

Nelson stood in the doorway. "The Viscountess, Lady Heywood, Your Grace."

Warwick scowled at the butler. The man was to announce a guest *before* anyone walked into his house. Apparently, his godmother was the exception. Nelson pulled the door closed on his way out.

Warwick pushed back his chair and rose from his desk. He'd been working on his engineering drawings for one of the inventions he'd mentioned to Adeline—a mechanism to cut the acres and acres of lawn at his estates. The one invention he'd claimed as progress and she'd pointed out would deny workers their wages.

"What's this about my walk in the park?" Warwick asked.

"The *Scandal Sheet* arrived this morning," Lady Heywood said.

"Why would I care?"

"Because, Your Grace, you are the main topic." His godmother held up the paper and read out loud:

The elusive Duke of Warwick has returned to town from Chilham just in time for the Season. Eligible ladies, be warned. His Grace, the man who has shown more interest in intellectual pursuits than the pursuit of a wife, has suddenly shown a keen fondness for Lady Adeline Cameron, daughter of the late Earl of Foster. The lady has also recently returned to town from Chilham. Coincidence or country interlude?

Warwick scowled. "Must you read that nonsense?"

"It isn't nonsense," Lady Heywood retorted. "All the Society ladies read it."

"Precisely my point," he said. "Pure gibberish and a waste of ink."

But Warwick was pleased. Adeline was right. The park had been the perfect place to set the tone of their relationship and start important tongues wagging. Warwick didn't care what the scandal sheets said, but he was smart enough to understand the benefit of gossipmongers. He hoped Edwin had the salacious paper delivered to his home.

Warwick would pay good coin to see the reaction on Edwin's face when he read the gossip sheet. The insufferable bully would have to find another way to pay back his loan, other than to sell his sister to a moneylender.

His godmother roamed his study, her skirts swishing as she turned. "Hmm. You kissed Lady Adeline in the park."

It was hard not to relive what had happened between them. The way the sun had glinted off the richness of Adeline's hair. The tinkle of her laugher as they'd strolled beneath the canopy of trees. The glint of mischief in her blue eyes as they noticed others watching them. Then the darkening of her irises as he'd slipped the glove away from her hand to kiss her skin. He'd wanted to do much more than that—he'd longed to kiss her lips. Would they be as soft as they looked? "I most assuredly did not kiss her. I placed a kiss on her wrist."

"*After* you removed her glove." She wagged a finger at him. "*Tsk!* How scandalous."

"She is hardly ruined."

The viscountess froze. "Was that your intention?"

Warwick stiffened beneath her stare. "Of course not. I haven't even kissed her."

She tapped a toe. "Oh? Why not?"

"Now *you* are being improper."

"Oh posh! I'm not an old lady. I loved the viscount dearly and we had a robust—"

He raised a hand. "Stop! I do not wish to hear more."

She planted her hands on her hips and studied him. "Is this an elaborate ruse, Daniel?"

He stiffened. "Whatever do you mean?"

"It is no secret that I have wanted you to marry. God only knows, I've listed all the eligible debutantes in my recent letters to you. Not once have you expressed an interest in any of them. Then you travel to the country and come home with a lady three weeks later.

Why wouldn't I be suspicious?"

Damnation, she was too perceptive. "I would hope you would trust me." His voice was hollow.

"Hmm. If you were any other man, I wouldn't bat an eyelash. But I know you, Daniel. Better than most." She came forward to wag a finger at him. "I know how smart you are. Others may underestimate your intelligence. God only knows, your own mother and father didn't understand your keen mind, but I do."

"I have never outright lied to you, godmother."

"True. You were never one to be manipulative, but then again, you were never pressed with your responsibilities to ensure the progression of the ducal line."

He'd never shirked his ducal responsibilities, but he had yet to take a wife and produce an heir. That responsibility was like a festering thorn in his side. It wasn't as if he'd had a stellar example growing up. His mother and father had a cold, loveless marriage. They'd never shared the same bedchamber, let alone the same wing in the massive mansion. He'd often wondered if they'd slept together only once to conceive him. His mother had also been cold toward *him*, and as a child he'd believed she never truly loved him. How could a mother not love her son? Her lack of affection had left him with a bitter taste for marriage.

Warwick knew he couldn't put off choosing a duchess forever. He sought only to delay the inevitable until he could complete more of his work.

Beneath the steely stare of his godmother, Warwick's resolve grew. If his plan with Adeline was to work, his godmother had to be convinced.

"I assure you that Lady Adeline and I share true feelings for each other." At least, that was not a lie. He did admire Adeline's healing ability and compassion to help others. His own recovery was proof of her skill.

Lady Heywood's expression shifted from suspicion to satisfaction. "I'm pleased."

"I hope you will sponsor Adeline for the remainder of the Season."

His godmother clutched her hands to her chest. "Now that I know you care for the lady, I am looking forward to it. I never had my own children, and I will treat Lady Adeline as my own. As for the upcoming Kirkland ball, leave the rest to me. I know just what to do to inspire romance."

Inwardly, Warwick caught his breath. *Good grief.* What romantic-inspiring plans did she have spinning in her sharp mind? Her words did more to concern than comfort him.

• • •

Warwick raised his fists and circled his opponent in the boxing ring, staked off at its four corners.

"I wasn't sure you'd come today." Lord Drake's right fist jabbed out and Warwick ducked, then shifted.

"What made you think I wouldn't show?"

Sweat beaded on Warwick's brow and chest. Both fighters were bare-chested and wore gloves. Their footwork was nimble, as they shifted back and forth, their shoes scraping the hardwood floor.

"You've been in Town only two days."

"A body must exercise to keep the mind sharp." Warwick believed in this truth. Otherwise, he wouldn't have spared the time away from his workshop.

"You're already the sharpest mind I know," Drake said.

"Are you flattering me to distract me?"

"Flattery isn't needed to best you in the ring. Besides, you are already distracted."

"How so?"

"The lovely Lady Adeline Cameron."

"Don't tell me you read the gossip rags?"

"My wife does."

Thankfully, the conversation ended as they focused on their sparring. Gentleman Jackson himself was present today. The tall, broadshouldered champion rotated among the rings in his boxing salon and shouted encouragement and advice to his gentlemen pugilists.

After several rounds, Warwick and Drake stepped from the ring. A boy rushed forward to untie their gloves and offer them water. They wiped their brows with cotton towels and slipped their shirts over their heads.

"Ana and I are holding a garden party. Invitations have been sent out to Lady Heywood and her new prodigy."

Warwick knew he meant Adeline. "Am I to expect an invitation as well?"

"You have always avoided Society events in the past, but I told Ana that you are a changed man."

Warwick tossed the towel aside. "You do realize my tendre for Lady Adeline is entirely for show."

Once again, the time they'd spent together in the park came to mind. He'd wanted to kiss more than her wrist. Much, much more. She tempted him more than any other woman he'd known.

A glimmer of humor lit Drake's dark gaze. "So you say."

"And she feels nothing for me either. Only the burgeoning of a friendship."

"I cannot begin to fathom the lady's thoughts," Drake said. "I'm not certain you can either."

Warwick rolled his eyes. "As my best

friend, you are sworn to secrecy."

Drake nodded. "I haven't told a soul."

Warwick eyed him. "Even your wife?"

Drake dropped his towel on a bench. "Now there—"

"Everyone must believe my budding romance with Lady Adeline to be real for our plan to work."

Drake swung his gloves over his shoulder and faced him. "Are you doing this just to spite Edwin?"

Warwick scoffed. "No. Although I admit to a certain satisfaction in thwarting that arrogant arse's plans for his half sister."

Drake eyed him with a critical squint. "Careful, Warwick. You may end up thwarting yourself."

• • •

Knocking on one's own front door felt strange, although Adeline supposed the Piccadilly townhome was no longer *hers*.

The door swung open, and her family's longtime butler answered the door. "Lady Adeline! How nice to see you." He held the door open. It was a good sign—she'd feared he'd shut the door in her face at the direction of the new Earl of Foster. Either Edwin hadn't anticipated she'd visit, or he hadn't thought to instruct the staff to turn her away if she should darken the doorstep. If her timing was right, Edwin would be out of the house and at one of his usual haunts.

"Is all well, Bertram?" Adeline asked.

"We all miss you, my lady. Especially Lady Mary."

"I miss her as well, and I'm here to pay her a visit."

"She'd love it, but—" He lowered his voice and glanced behind his shoulder. "If you'd come another—"

"Who is it, Bertram?" A booming voice sounded behind the butler's shoulder.

Adeline froze. *Damnation.* Her timing had been poor after all. She stiffened her spine and clutched her reticule before her like a shield.

No. She gathered her resolve. This may no longer be her home, but she had every right to visit her sister. She swept past Bertram and into the vestibule. Everything was familiar, from the crystal chandelier and the gilded sconces to the classical paintings on the flocked papered walls. Edwin strode into the vestibule carrying a walking stick. He was dressed in a coat and hat and clearly on his way out. If she had arrived just five or so minutes later.

She met his dark gaze. "Hello, my lord."

He gaped, then his dark eyes narrowed, and his mouth screwed into a sour expression. "So it's true, and you have returned to Town.

Did that dark-complected heathen accompany you?"

She held onto her anger at the insult. "You mean Miss Hasmik? Yes, my companion accompanied me in the duke's carriage from Kent."

His eyes narrowed in obvious disapproval. "Why are you here?"

"To visit Mary, of course. I wouldn't waste my time to see you."

His fingers tightened on his walking stick. "You have nerve."

"Whatever do you mean?" she asked innocently.

"The Scandal Sheets have been abuzz about you, Adeline."

"I thought you never read the gossip rags."

"And to think," he said as he walked close, "I thought you were as dried up as one of those herbs you used to hang in the cellar. Maybe that is why that mad duke likes you."

The barb hurt, but she refused to give him the satisfaction. Her chin jutted out as she faced him. "His Grace and I informed you of our affections toward each other when you rudely burst into my country cottage to attempt to marry me off."

She was aware that although Bertram had disappeared, he was never far. Her mother had once told her the walls had ears when it came to the servants. She could only imagine what they were thinking now.

"As for the duke's affections toward you, sister, I'm not entirely convinced of your so-called courtship. It was too quick and unexpected. The duke is engrossed in his silly inventions, and you are just as obsessed with your herbal potions."

"So? We are like-minded." She felt light-headed from his scrutiny. She forced her gaze to meet his cold one.

"Hmm. I've given it much thought after I left you that day. Your courtship is too convenient for both of you."

"Your mind is playing tricks on you, my lord."

"But, if by chance, your courtship is true, I'm still not concerned. Even Warwick will come to his senses eventually and toss you aside."

She fought the urge to strike him with the reticule she clutched. "Why would you care? Are you so deeply in debt that I am your last hope when it comes to the moneylender? I pity you, Edwin. You'll have to find another way."

"How dare you speak to me that way under my—"

"Adeline! Is that you I hear?" A soft voice sounded from the landing of the staircase.

"Yes, it's me, Mary." Adeline attempted to rush to the bottom of the winding staircase when Edwin's hand snaked out to grasp her arm.

"I'll be watching you and Warwick," Edwin hissed, then just as abruptly, he released her and stormed out of the house.

Adeline took a breath, resisting the urge to rub her arm. She forced a smile as she met Mary at the bottom of the staircase and embraced her sister.

"I've missed you terribly, Adeline!"

"And I've missed you too, Mary."

The sisters were night from day. Mary's blond hair, brown eyes, and fair complexion were in striking contrast to Adeline's raven hair, blue eyes, and olive skin. Mary was less than a year older than Adeline, but Adeline had always felt like the protective older sister.

"How long will you stay?" Mary asked.

"For a while, darling."

Mary looped her arm through Adeline's, and they passed through the French doors leading to their favorite place, the outside gardens. They sat in chairs on the terra-cotta terrace where a maid served them lemonade. Fragrant daffodils and forget-me-nots bloomed in the garden and birds chirped. It was a pleasant day, and the sun warmed their cheeks. For the first time since arriving at her brother's home, Adeline took a deep breath and relaxed. Thankfully, Edwin had left and she could visit her sister in peace. She had fond memories of playing with hoops with Mary as children in the gardens, and then when they were older, sitting on the terrace and gossiping about how the brothers next door had changed from awkward youths to handsome men.

Mary sipped her glass of lemonade. "I've missed you terribly. I've been writing, but I wish you were here for me to share my story ideas."

Mary had published short gothic stories under a male pen name that had been successful. "Tell me about your writing—what are you working on now?"

Mary's lips curved in a smile. "I've finished my first novel."

"Wonderful! What name will you use?"

"My short stories have been published under the pseudonym M.J. Price, which was my mother's maiden name. I've always dealt with Mr. Elder, the publisher, through correspondence, and he believes I am a man. But this time, I want to meet him in person and deliver my novel."

"Are you ready to reveal your true identity?"

Mary raised her chin. "I am. Will you accompany me?"

"Of course. I'd be honored."

Mary clutched her hands. "Oh Adeline. I've missed you so. The house has been lonesome without you, and I've been melancholy."

"Has Edwin spent time with you since Father's death?"

Mary's gaze lowered to her glass. "He hasn't been around much."

"Then it was doubly unfortunate that he was here this afternoon."

Mary rolled her eyes. "Will you two ever get along?"

"It's unlikely. Especially after he showed up in the country to demand I marry a complete stranger."

"Edwin would never!"

"He would and did."

"Who is this strange gentleman?"

"It no longer matters."

Adeline was careful to keep the details from Mary. Not because Mary was incapable of understanding Edwin's financial strains, but because she didn't want to ruin her sister's relationship with her brother. Mary and Edwin were full siblings, and Edwin treated Mary well. He'd never evict *her* from their home or force *her* to marry an unscrupulous moneylender.

"You have been keeping secrets yourself." Mary gave her a sly look.

Adeline trailed a finger down the frosted glass. "You read the gossip rags!"

Mary leaned forward in her seat. "A duke!

You should have written to me."

"The post is slow and there was no time. Warwick and I had decided to return for the remainder of the Season."

"You traveled together?"

"Nothing scandalous occurred. Hasmik was in the coach."

"I never thought otherwise." Mary set an elbow on the table and rested her chin in her hand. Her eyes widened in rapt interest. "Now tell me. Is your duke handsome? Charming? Courting you with flowers and chocolates? Penning you love letters?"

Adeline laughed. She couldn't help herself. "Too many questions!"

"I'm sorry. It's just that little is known about the Duke of Warwick. Is he a recluse?"

"He is an intellectual. He prefers books to balls."

"It sounds like a good match. You prefer preparing herbs and poultices to parties."

Adeline didn't want to think about the ways the two of them aligned. She didn't want to look for any more in common with Warwick. She didn't want to like him or admire him any more than she already did. It only added to her frustration when they bickered…and they often did. Besides, their dealings were temporary. Nothing more.

"What about my other questions? Do not think to avoid answering them," Mary said.

"He is handsome." *Strikingly so.* "You will meet him soon enough. I'm staying with his godmother, Lady Heywood. Despite our dislike of balls, we both must attend a fair number of the *ton*'s upcoming entertainments."

"Oh Adeline. Is it true romance? Like Father and your mother?"

"I could only hope for a sliver of what they shared." Adeline's gut tightened with guilt. She hated lying to Mary, but she also understood her sister. Mary would struggle to keep the secret and she'd most likely slip in front of Edwin. Her integrity and innocence would make it difficult not to confess the truth, and Adeline couldn't risk the chance.

"Lady Kirkland's ball is the event of the Season. You will attend, won't you?" Adeline asked.

"I wouldn't miss it for all the world. Do you think you will waltz together? Many say it's scandalous to dance so close to each other, but it was performed at the last two balls, save Almack's, of course. Will you waltz with Warwick?"

Adeline tapped her chin with a forefinger. "I hadn't thought of it." But now that she had, it was another opportunity to fool Edwin and for Warwick to convince his godmother of their amorous relationship.

"Your duke's affection is fortuitous for

me," Mary said.

"How so?"

"If Edwin is focused on you, then he won't watch me."

Once again, regret pierced her chest. She was convinced that keeping the secret from Mary was the best course of action. If Edwin learned the truth, he'd be relentless and find a way to force Adeline to accept the money-lender's proposal. Edwin could contest their father's will in court and claim the cottage as his own. She wasn't naive and she knew what happened to young, unmarried ladies without a steady source of income. She wouldn't be able to afford a solicitor or barrister to take her case. Her hopes of healing villagers would never be realized.

No, keeping Mary in the dark was the only way. As for her own future, she'd rather trust Warwick than Edwin.

CHAPTER TEN

On the day of Lord and Lady Drake's garden party, Adeline was filled with a strange sense of anticipation. Not dread, but excitement, and she was unnerved by the change.

Was she looking forward to another public encounter with the Duke of Warwick?

"This is your first function since your return, Adeline," Lady Heywood commented as a liveried servant opened the garden gate to allow them entrance into the Drakes' gardens.

"I confess I find myself a bit anxious." Adeline scanned the well-dressed guests. The gentlemen wore tailored coats, colorful embroidered waistcoats, and starched cravats. The ladies, never to be outdone, were dressed in delicate muslin or silk in all the colors of the rainbow from bold blues and violets to pale pastels. It was a warm afternoon and stately oak trees provided shade.

"You have no need to fret, my dear. You look exquisite in that pale blue. It brings out your magnificent eyes."

Adeline smoothed the silk fabric and managed a small smile at the lady's kind words. "It's not the dress, but the people. They are all staring."

"Let them ogle and talk."

"I'm not sure their looks are friendly. Most ladies do not want to appear in the *Scandal Sheet*."

"Posh! Most ladies are not courted by a duke." She looped her arm with Adeline's. "Come now. I wish for you to enjoy your afternoon, my dear. The hosts, Lord and Lady Drake, are exceptionally proud of their gardens. They even have an orangery that produces fresh oranges throughout the year."

The gardens were impressive with flowering shrubs, a complex maze, and a pond with a small waterfall. As they walked closer, she noticed colorful fish in the clear water. A table had been set outside, and a stream of servants carried out trays of food.

Lady Heywood smiled at passersby. Adeline was conscious of their appraisal, and she was careful to nod and smile.

"You will find our hosts most welcoming," Lady Heywood said.

Adeline knew Lady Drake from the section of the city where Mediterranean and Middle Eastern Londoners resided—Arabs, Greeks, and Armenians. Then she'd been known as Anahit, the daughter of a Middle Eastern woman and an English baron. Now she'd married the earl and had become a countess. Adeline and Anahit had been close to an elderly lady named Queenie who'd since passed away.

When it was their turn to greet the hosts in line, Lord Drake bowed. "Lady Adeline, you are as lovely as my friend, the Duke of Warwick, has described."

Adeline flushed. She was aware of the interest of others waiting in line. "His Grace spoke of me?"

"Of course, we are good friends. He tells me many things."

A flash of unease traveled down her spine, and she studied the earl beneath lowered lashes. Had Warwick told Lord Drake about their "planned courtship"?

If so, how humiliating.

Lord Drake was handsome with dark hair and sinfully dark eyes. She supposed some would find his dark countenance intimidating. Adeline knew better. Any man who befriended Warwick had to understand the duke's eccentricities and inventive work and, therefore, must be of high intelligence himself.

Tall and beautiful, Lady Drake had dark hair and eyes that were not quite green nor brown, but an intriguing hazel. She was expecting their first child and her hand rested on the curve of her abdomen. She hugged Adeline. "Hello, Adeline. Do not let my husband tease you. Drake and Warwick spend hours together in a boxing ring at Gentleman Jackson's. They are hardly gossiping magpies."

"Boxing?" Warwick hadn't mentioned his

interest in the sport. The duke was fit, and she'd noticed his muscular chest when she'd first treated his wound. It wasn't as if she'd been looking—the muscles of his forearm and biceps were hard to ignore.

Lady Drake leaned close and smiled. "You must visit for afternoon tea. Ladies need to plan."

She wasn't sure what planning she referred to, but Adeline wanted to learn more about both Warwick and Drake. What exactly had he told his friend?

Lady Drake leaned forward to observe the line of guests waiting to greet her and her husband. "Warwick is expected, of course."

Adeline anticipated the duke's arrival at any moment. Their walk in the park had gone as planned and the gossip paper had aided their cause. Adeline knew that Edwin, too, could appear. If he did, it was important that Warwick be present to allay any suspicions her half brother still had.

Adeline stayed by Lady Heywood's side as they mingled with the guests. She recognized many members of the *beau monde.* Lady Heywood knew many more. Adeline nodded as they passed Lady Strathmore and Lord Sheldon, and she stared at the towering turban of Lady Hubert, then the swaying ostrich feathers of Lady Stewart's hat.

Her hopes of the duke appearing dwindled

as first a half hour passed, then an hour, then even longer. Fashionably late was becoming a distinct improbability.

Warwick was not coming.

Beneath the warm afternoon sun, Adeline felt the beginnings of a headache. Her smile became as brittle as glass.

She wasn't the only one who noticed Warwick's absence. Each time the garden gate opened, Lady Heywood turned to see if the new arrival was her godson.

Adeline rubbed her right temple. She mumbled an excuse and headed for the refreshment table for a glass of lemonade.

"May I get you a drink?"

Adeline glanced up at a young gentleman, a man close to her own age. Thin and of average height, he had brown hair and brown eyes. "Yes please."

He handed her a glass of lemonade, and she sipped the drink. It was refreshing, not too sour or too sweet, but it still didn't help her headache.

"Lord Bowen at your service."

"Lady Adeline." She recalled hearing the name from Edwin. He'd recently inherited a viscounty.

"Are you enjoying yourself?"

"To be truthful, not as much as I'd hoped."

He gave her a curious look. "To be truthful, me either. It is rather warm out." He watched as she sipped her lemonade. "I've heard that you are recently returned to London from Kent?"

"Yes. I'm staying with Lady Heywood."

"Did something lure you to the country?"

"My father bequeathed me a country cottage. I found the small village of Chilham refreshing." She finished the lemonade and placed the empty glass on the table.

"I'd prefer the country to London this time of year as well. Once the weather warms, it's hard to ignore the stench of the river. Although Hyde Park is pleasant this time of year with its abundance of shady trees. Perhaps we can stroll the park together?"

For a pulse-pounding moment, she wondered if the young viscount had read the *Scandal Sheet*. Did he read about her intimate episode with Warwick in the park?

And where was the duke?

Lord Bowen smiled. "I consider myself fortunate to have met you, Lady Adeline. The other ladies are far from intriguing."

"You must say that to all the ladies." She found him oddly charming but not attractive. He reminded her of one of her friend's big brothers growing up.

"Honestly, no."

The hosts of the garden party, Lord and Lady Drake, were Warwick's friends. If the duke failed to make an appearance here, then what hope did she have for any other party or ball? Or for the future?

Warwick risked his matchmaking god-mother.

Adeline risked much worse—her brother's machinations and an unwanted betrothal to an unscrupulous moneylender. She lowered her lashes to hide her thoughts.

"Am I being too forward?" Lord Bowen's brow furrowed.

"No. You have been nothing but kind."

"Would you do me the honor of joining me at one of the tables to eat?"

She raised her gaze to his. She saw interest in his brown eyes. She wasn't unfamiliar with male attention. And she was hungry. She'd only nibbled on dry toast and drunk a cup of tea that morning. Her foolish thoughts had been filled with the upcoming garden party... and the duke. If the man wasn't coming this soon after their return to Town, then she saw no harm in having the viscount escort her.

They helped themselves to the lavish buffet and then joined a middle-aged couple on one of the blankets that had been spread out on the vast lawns. It was proper and no one paid them attention. Lady Heywood smiled and waved. Adeline nibbled on teacakes and strawberries and her headache subsided. She barely noticed when the couple rose and left the blanket. It was a pleasant day and—

A hush came over the crowd, and Adeline turned to see what had occurred just as she spotted Warwick enter the gardens. Her pulse quickened. Lady Heywood waved, and he made his way to his godmother's side.

He commanded attention. His reputation as a recluse was well known in Society—the *mad duke*, he was called. None of it mattered. With his light brown hair, green eyes, and muscular build, he cut a handsome figure—the type of man women swooned for. Watching the crowd, it was a toss-up as to whether it was the mammas of the *ton* or their young daughters who eyed him more rapturously. For the first time, Adeline truly understood why he'd fled to the country to live in a modest home.

"May I visit you at Lady Heywood's home?" Lord Bowen interrupted her thoughts.

Her gaze flew to the man beside her. "I...I..."

She opened her mouth, then closed it. How should she answer? A deep part of her felt slighted, offended at the duke's late appearance. Hadn't they come to an agreement? He was to attend balls, parties, dinners...numerous functions to flirt and dance with her. If this was to work at all, he had to participate and not wait until the end of a party to show.

Just then Warwick looked past his godmother to see her sitting with the young viscount. The corners of his mouth turned downward, and his eyes met hers.

If the duke was unhappy, then he had no one to blame but himself. He'd left her to fend for herself for the duration of the party. If only he hadn't led her and his godmother to believe he'd come, it wouldn't have been so disappointing. Anger, frustration, and wounded pride made her brow furrow. It was ridiculous, really. She was not the type of woman to experience such useless emotions.

Lord Bowen shifted and touched Adeline's arm. "Do you prefer chocolates? Or flowers?"

• • •

Warwick pulled his godmother aside. "Who is Adeline sitting with?"

"That is Lord Bowen. He has been entertaining her for the past hour."

"I don't like it."

"You do not own the lady, Your Grace. She is free to speak with any gentleman she desires. Especially when the man courting her fails to make a timely appearance." Her disapproval was evident in the inflection of her voice and the steel of her eyes.

Warwick chose to ignore both. His gaze returned to Adeline. She was sitting close to Lord Bowen on the blanket, too close. "She cannot desire the dandy."

"I never thought I'd see the day, Daniel. I had my doubts, but I see I was worried for no reason."

"What on earth are you talking about?"

"You are jealous."

Warwick's eyes snapped to hers. "That's preposterous. Jealousy is a waste of mental energy."

"Is it?"

"I'd rather spend my time and energy reading scientific journals." He sounded like a petulant child—completely unlike himself. *Dammit. What is Lord Bowen saying to Adeline?* He was restless and irritable and had a ridiculous urge to march over to the blanket and yank her away.

"Hmm. You could always leave and allow Lord Bowen to continue to entertain Lady Adeline."

"No."

She gave him the I-told-you-so look that had bothered him as an adolescent. It infuriated him even more now. "I'm sure Lord Bowen wouldn't mind if you simply departed."

"Come to think of it, I did meet Lord Bowen at White's once. He didn't make a good impression; he is empty-headed and lacks so much as two brain cells."

"Then what will you do about it, Your Grace?"

He knew she was manipulating him. None of it mattered when Adeline laughed at something Lord Bowen said. He should be the one to make her laugh. "Pardon me, my lady."

Warwick was aware of the stares and whispers behind fluttering fans as he moved through the crowd. He was aware and he didn't care. He avoided these events, even those hosted by his friends, Lord and Lady Drake. But he'd made a promise.

His gaze focused on the woman seated on the blanket ten feet away. Sunlight glinted off her glorious mass of dark hair. The smooth curve of her cheek was turned toward another, and she gifted Lord Bowen with a smile that should have been meant for him.

He halted at the edge of their blanket. Two heads turned up to look at him. Adeline's blue eyes were clear; Lord Bowen's, questioning.

"Hello, Bowen. I had an agreement to meet with the lady. If you do not mind?" He stared at Lord Bowen, a man five or so years younger than himself. It wasn't respect for Warwick's age that made the viscount blanch. Bowen must have read the menacing intent in Warwick's gaze.

Lord Bowen stood and bowed. "If you will please pardon me, Lady Adeline. I must say hello to a cousin."

Adeline rose. "Of course."

Warwick watched with satisfaction as the viscount scurried way.

Her lips thinned with displeasure. "That was terribly rude."

"Was it? I didn't realize."

The spark of anger in Adeline's eyes brought out the chips of black around the blue irises. "I don't believe you. Regardless of your chosen social isolation you were raised as heir to a dukedom. Proper manners would have been part of your tutelage."

"I don't care about my tutelage. You forget our agreement."

"Our agreement! How dare you!" At her raised voice, several people looked their way. As if she realized the attention they were drawing, she lowered her voice and grit her teeth. "It is you who is forgetful."

"Perhaps we should continue this conversation elsewhere. The gardens are vast." He offered his arm.

She stared at it for several moments before placing her fingers on his forearm. He escorted her away from the gawking men and women and toward the maze. Once they were isolated by shrubbery and out of earshot, she spun on him.

"As I said, our understanding will not work if you do not participate."

"I was not the one sitting beside another lord, flirting with him."

"Oh!" She stomped her foot. "You are too arrogant, for sure. You forget your end of the agreement."

"Which is?"

"To attend events together, to make tongues wag. To convince your godmother and my half brother that we are madly in love."

"And how am I to do that when you spend time with another lord?"

"You make an appearance. That's how."

"I'm standing here, am I not?"

"If you haven't noticed, Your Grace, some of the guests have already departed. I've been here for three hours."

Had he lost track of that much time? It was a problem he'd had since he was a child. "I had something of importance to attend to."

"More important than me?"

His heart pounded in his chest as he met her clear gaze. *No, not now,* he wanted to say. He'd never been good with words. How could he explain?

"The pistons of the high-pressure steam engine didn't overheat." His discovery didn't seem as important now.

"Congratulations." She began to turn away, but he grasped her arm.

"Wait! Forgive me."

"Pardon?"

"I often lose sense of time when I'm working."

She stood still. He could hear the chirping of the birds and feel the slight breeze through the trees. At that moment, her response meant more to him than all his work for the day, for the week, even longer.

"This once."

"Yes, I promise to do better. But you should know something else. I didn't like seeing you with another man." His heart thundered at the confession. Her lips parted, then closed, and he wanted to know what she was thinking.

She sighed. "I didn't enjoy spending time with Lord Bowen."

Male satisfaction coursed through him. He offered his arm once more and she took it, and they turned to go back. "Will you visit me at my home soon?" he asked. "There is something you should see."

"Why? I've already toured your country workshop."

She worried her bottom lip with her teeth, and he found it near impossible to tear his gaze away from the full, pink lips. If he hadn't arrived when he had, would Lord Bowen have taken the opportunity to escort her into this very maze and attempt to steal a kiss?

Bloody hell. When she'd slanted her blue eyes up at Lord Bowen, smiled and laughed at something the bloke had said, his heart had hammered and his fists had clenched and he'd feared he'd do something barbaric—something he'd regret.

Only fools would behave that way. Rogues with nothing else but lust and debauchery on their minds. He was not like those men. He had a purpose, a brain, and self-control.

Then why was he still staring at her mouth with hunger? He must not think of kissing her. Any kind of intimacy could change things between them, and she didn't want that. Nor did he. He was simply trying to get her to understand him in case he was late in the future.

"Ah, but this is different. If you see, perhaps you will understand my challenge with the clock. Miss Hasmik can accompany you."

She tilted her head. "Fine. I'm visiting the dressmakers with your godmother tomorrow. But I shall come the day after, at noon."

"I look forward to it." Together, they left the maze and he escorted her back to where his godmother awaited. Dozens of eyes seemed to focus on them, followed by hushed whispers.

Her fingers tightened on his sleeve. "It seems we have caused an unintentional stir, Your Grace."

Warwick's gaze never left her upturned face, and he grinned. "Aren't they the best kind?"

• • •

"Well, well, if you were trying draw more attention, you and Warwick certainly accomplished your goal." Lady Heywood sat cross from Adeline as their carriage progressed through the busy London streets. It was the following day, and they were on their way to the dressmakers. Afterward, Adeline planned to see Mary.

"It was unintentional, I assure you," Adeline said.

"I don't blame you for spending time with Lord Bowen, my dear. My godson is often tardy, although not *that* tardy. He must have been delayed by one of his inventions."

"He assured me as much."

"Well, the *Scandal Sheet* is brimming with gossip about both of you. Shall I read it to you?" Lady Heywood opened the paper that sat upon her lap.

Adeline didn't believe she was being asked. More like being prepared. "Will it cause me discomfort?"

"That depends, my dear, on how sensitive you are."

"Go on then. It's best if I know what it says."

The countess raised the paper and read out loud.

A lover's quarrel? It appears as if Lady Adeline Cameron is causing quite a stir when it comes to the gentlemen this Season. A viscount or a duke? The Duke of Warwick may

have been notoriously late to a garden party,
but the lady may have been the one to steal the
show.

Adeline felt herself flush. "That is hardly accurate!"

The countess's lips twitched. "I never said it was."

"I didn't speak with Lord Bowen to make the duke jealous," she insisted. "If Warwick had arrived on time, none of this would have occurred."

"As I said, you need not defend yourself to me, my dear." She glanced outside the carriage window. "Look. We have arrived."

The coach rolled to a stop on Bond Street, and Adeline spotted Mademoiselle Helene's Dress Shop. A wooden sign with a large *H* and a silhouette of a lady in a gown swung in a slight breeze. A large bay window displayed two mannequins, one with a day gown of lavender lace and the other with a navy riding habit. Any chance she had to explain what had happened was gone. Moments later, the door opened, and the driver lowered the step. Lady Heywood descended, followed by Adeline. The little bell above the shop chimed as they opened the door.

Adeline had accompanied her mother and Mary here when her sister had prepared for her debut. The Bond Street dressmaker was a favorite with the ladies of the *beau monde*.

Today, she was shopping for herself. Adeline needed a gown for the upcoming Kirkland ball, and the countess had insisted on accompanying her.

The shop was a feast of color and texture and Adeline stepped forward to run her fingers over various fabrics—brocade, damask, velvet, muslin, chintz, sarcenet, and bombazine. Lady Heywood joined her. "Which is your favorite?" Adeline asked her.

"Anything but the heavy brocade. After Lord Heywood died, I wore black brocade mourning gowns for a full year. I wish never to wear anything like it again."

Adeline admired Lady Heywood for her honesty and courage. It must have been very difficult after his loss. The countess was still a beautiful woman, and Adeline wondered why she'd never remarried. Had she not wanted to give up her freedom? As a widow, she didn't need a companion to accompany her everywhere she went and she could live independently.

A middle-aged lady with dyed auburn hair, dressed fashionably in a pale green dress with a heart-shaped bodice and ruffled hem, greeted them.

"Bonjour, Lady Heywood. I received your note."

"Hello, Mademoiselle Helene. This is Lady

Adeline, my houseguest."

The dressmaker's gaze swept over Adeline from head to toe in a professional appraisal. "Is this the young lady who needs a gown for the ball?"

"It is."

"Oui, oui! You make my task easy. With that dark hair, bronze skin, and blue eyes, sapphire will look exquisite. I have sketches to choose from, but I must first take your measurements. Come along."

Adeline was led into a private room and stripped of her dress and left in her chemise. She stepped upon a pedestal as the dressmaker took her measurements. "Raise your arms. Stand still. Turn." The dressmaker had the efficiency of a headmistress of a finishing school.

Once she was done, Mademoiselle Helene led her to the back of the shop where three separate areas had been created with curtained partitions. "You may dress here." She gestured toward one. "My assistant will arrive to help with your stays and buttons. Then we can pick out the fabric."

The curtain was closed, and Adeline was left in the dimly lit space. She reached for her dress on a hook on the wall just as she heard female voices enter the room. Two ladies stepped into the partitioned area to her right.

"Did you witness the spectacle at Lady

Drake's garden party yesterday?" a woman with a high-pitched voice asked.

"Sadly, I was not there," a second woman said.

"Lady Adeline Cameron has returned from only God knows where in the country, and she has two men vying for her attention—one of them is a duke."

"I read the *Scandal Sheet.* He's not just any duke, but the Duke of Warwick! He hasn't attended a function in almost a year."

"Mamma says he's half mad."

"Who cares? He's bloody rich. And *gorgeous.*"

"Maybe he has a string of women who visit his mansion under cover of darkness."

"I wouldn't mind being one of them."

"Don't bother! He has eyes for the Earl of Foster's sister, remember?"

"*Half sister.* She's not a pure Englishwoman. Her mother was from the Middle East, an Arab foreigner. God only knows what heathen religion or traditions she practiced behind closed doors."

"Maybe the duke prefers the exotic. Her skin is darker, her hair is black as pitch."

"You'd never compare."

"I would never want to, although Warwick could have his pick. What does he see in her?"

"I don't know. She probably learned tricks

from her mother like a harem girl who entices men."

Adeline's heart pounded in her chest, and bile rose in her throat. She swallowed. Her temper flared hot and heavy. How dare they speak of her mother in such a derogatory fashion! Her mother was more educated in ways they couldn't equal. She'd healed a lady ill with fever from childbirth. Helped a man who'd suffered a stroke. A child who had weak lungs. All three patients had been left to die or waste away by English doctors. There had been many others as well.

So why did the prejudice of these two women bother her? Her mother had also taught her not to care.

Do not let harsh words upset you, Adeline. Some will never accept us. Most will. Be proud! You come from a long line of healers. Find a man who loves you for who you are.

Despite her mother's words, Edwin's taunting was never far from her mind. The cruelties suffered as a child were hard to forget.

Warwick had never mentioned her family history. He didn't seem to care. But then again, he had no intention of proposing. Would a man of his station seriously consider marrying her? And why was she even thinking about it? She had no intention of becoming his duchess. She would settle for nothing less than love.

Adeline raised her chin and swept the curtain aside to face the two women, one blond and the other brunette. She didn't recognize either of them. "These curtains are not very private, are they?"

The blonde looked as pale as a glass of sour milk. She opened her mouth, then closed it like a fish caught on a line.

Adeline's gaze dropped to the yellow gown clutched in the woman's hand. "I would avoid that bold color. It would look good only on a woman with darker skin and hair."

The blonde gasped and pressed a hand to her chest.

Adeline turned to the brunette. "You are right about the Duke of Warwick. What woman wouldn't sneak into his house at night?"

Head held high, she swept by them.

• • •

"Mr. Elder will want your novel, just as he has published your short stories," Adeline said.

Mary squeezed her hand. "You are the best sister I could ask for. Thank you for coming with me today."

"You can thank me after you are a success."

Adeline and her sister sat in a small room

waiting to meet Mary's publisher. Mary held her bound manuscript on her lap. A young assistant sat behind a desk, his gaze darting to the sisters every so often. Adeline suspected he was surprised when Mary had appeared for her three o'clock appointment. Clearly, the assistant had expected a man. Adeline wondered how Mr. Elder would react.

Mary clutched the manuscript to her chest as a young assistant escorted them to the publisher's office. He eyed them with a critical squint, then closed the door behind them.

Mr. Elder sat behind a large oak desk littered with stacks of paper. A tall cabinet to the left of the desk, and a settee across from a small fireplace were covered with more papers. The coal brazier had burned out long ago and there was a slight chill in the room. He lowered a page he'd been reading when they entered and removed a pair of wire-rimmed spectacles.

"Well, I expected M.J. Price to look a little different." A middle-aged man with fleshy jowls and a bulbous nose, Mr. Elder had dark eyes and thinning dark hair. A walrus-style mustache hid his upper lip.

Not waiting for him to stand, Mary hurried forward and took a chair across from his desk. Adeline occupied a chair to her right.

"Good day, Mr. Elder. As I wrote in my letter, my manuscript is complete," Mary said.

"Is that it?"

His gaze lowered to the manuscript she held. "Yes." She set her novel on his desk. The top sheet was written in neat handwriting.

The springs of Mr. Elder's chair squeaked as he leaned back and rested his hands on his ample stomach. "Things have changed."

"How?"

"Your short stories have not sold as well of late."

Mary's eyes widened. "But...but you advised otherwise in your last letter. Your precise words were, 'We cannot print them fast enough.'"

Mr. Elder waved a dismissive hand. "Publishing is a fickle business and changes day by day, miss. I will still accept your manuscript, of course, but my terms will have to be different."

"Precisely how different?" Adeline spoke for the first time.

His eyes flicked to Adeline, then returned to Mary. "I can no longer offer a royalty. I will pay ten pounds for the novel."

Mary gasped. "Ten pounds! But it has taken me a year to complete. It is my best work to date."

His mustache twitched. "Time is money in my business as well."

A trickle of dread ran down Adeline's spine at the man's obvious prejudice, followed by a simmering anger. The situation reminded her of the two women at the dressmakers—oh, their bias was different—but they were similar in one important respect—both were demeaning to one's self-worth.

Adeline couldn't, wouldn't, allow the publisher to take advantage of Mary or to cause her suffering. She leaned forward in her chair, pressed a palm flat on his desk, and eyed him. "You seek to steal her work."

"Pardon?"

"You heard what I said. Offering her ten pounds is akin to robbery!"

Mr. Elder's face turned a mottled shade of purple. "How dare you!"

"My sister is right," Mary said, her voice firm. "I refuse your terms." She reached for the manuscript on the desk.

Mr. Elder's hand snaked out to land on the manuscript. "You will regret this. No publisher will take a woman's book. My offer is the best you'll receive."

Mary tugged the manuscript from beneath his hand. "Come along, Adeline. It's time for us to leave."

The man pushed back his chair. "Don't be a fool. You will regret this!"

Mary glanced back, her face pale. "I don't believe so."

Once the two sisters were in the carriage, Mary began shivering. A tear slipped down her cheek. "That didn't go at all as I'd expected."

Adeline's heart ached for her sister. "He is a cad."

"I know. But I can't help but think that if I had submitted my book through correspondence, like I had my short stories, this would have ended differently. Mr. Elder would know me only as a man, and I would have seen my work published."

"Do not doubt yourself. Mr. Elder is a jackanapes."

"He isn't the only biased publisher."

"You don't know that for certain. Do not allow that man to ruin your dreams."

Mary didn't seem to hear her. She shook her head, her brow tight with strain. "What was I thinking? All men are alike. If Edwin even knew I wrote, he would prohibit me from pursuing publishing."

"You know how I feel about Edwin. He's a step below the measly Mr. Elder. If you want to continue to publish as M.J. Price or as Lady Mary, sister of the Earl of Foster, or any other pseudonym you fancy, then I will support you. We will find another who will value you work."

Mary wiped a tear with the back of her hand and managed a weak smile. "Oh,

Adeline. I wish I had half of your determination."

Adeline squeezed her hand. "It's not determination. It's plain stubbornness!"

CHAPTER ELEVEN

Adeline hadn't forgotten Warwick's invitation to his home. After attending the dressmaker's with the countess, then the publisher with her sister, she was finally free to see him. The Duke of Warwick lived in a pile of stone in Berkley Square. Lady Heywood's home was grand, but the duke's residence dwarfed every home she'd so far visited. Made of gray granite, a mermaid fountain greeted guests in the round driveway, and well-maintained lawns with Roman statues lined the drive. At the sight of the perfect lawn, she immediately thought of Warwick's lawn trimming invention. How many gardeners did he employ?

"I've never been in such a grand home," Hasmik said.

"After the country, I can't picture Warwick living here," Adeline said.

The poultice she'd prepared was in the basket she carried. Adeline lifted the brass knocker and rapped. Warwick's butler opened the door before she could knock twice, and they stepped inside a magnificent vestibule with a crystal chandelier holding a hundred candles, a priceless Chinese vase, and artwork from Gainsborough, Rowlandson, and Hogarth on the walls.

"Hello, Lady Adeline. Miss Hasmik."

Adeline smiled. "Good to see you again, Nelson." He'd appeared a proper English butler in the country and his bearing hadn't changed here, except for a slight flush to his cheeks at her greeting.

He took their cloaks, then hesitated. "I owe you an apology, my lady."

Adeline looked at him anew. "Whatever for?"

"I believed your treatment of His Grace's wound unorthodox."

Caught off guard, she blinked. He wouldn't be the first man who'd believed a woman incapable of doctoring. "I understand."

The butler cleared his throat. "You misunderstand. I had been the one applying the London doctor's treatment."

"Ah yes, the flour."

He nodded.

"There is nothing to apologize for. You looked after His Grace."

"But I didn't help him." Nelson's voice was strained. "The flour made it worse and caused His Grace pain."

"You followed the doctor's instructions, and you care for the duke. I find that most admirable," she said.

"You are too kind, miss. I misjudged you, and for that I apologize as well."

She was speechless in surprise, and she

stared wordlessly across at him, her heart pounding. Praise from a proud servant who served the duke was not expected and meant much to her. It also made her feel better after overhearing the cruel words of the two women at the dressmaker's shop, and after Mr. Elder's treatment of Mary.

"Kindly follow me, ladies. His Grace awaits."

Hasmik cleared her throat. "I would like a word with your housekeeper. Mrs. Posner, is it? I would love the recipe for Cook's scones, and she offered for me to see her during my next visit."

Adeline's attention snapped to Hasmik and she eyed her warily. She'd never mentioned the scones before, and she knew her friend was scheming for her to spend time with the duke alone.

"Stay here, miss," Nelson said, "and I'll summon Mrs. Posner. Now if you will please follow me, Lady Adeline." If Nelson suspected Hasmik's motives, he didn't show it.

The butler led Adeline beyond the vestibule, along several corridors and past numerous rooms—two drawing rooms—one green and one pale blue, a music conservatory complete with pianoforte, violin, and a flute, and a dining room with a table that could seat more than fifty, before halting outside two large double doors.

The butler turned to her and cleared his throat once more. "Most find His Grace different, my lady."

Adeline tilted her head and looked up at him. "I know of his intellectual pursuits."

"Some of them."

"I've seen his country workshop," she countered.

"I imagine you were surprised."

"I was. But I now know what to expect."

"Perhaps."

She arched an eyebrow. "What makes you say that?"

"You will see."

What was the man trying to tell her? She didn't fully understand the complexities of Warwick's mind or his work, then again, she didn't expect him to fully comprehend or tolerate her own work. The memory of Warwick turning sickly pale when she'd stitched the carpenter's wound was hard to forget.

"Come, miss. His Grace specifically instructed that you join him in the ballroom."

The ballroom? More questions arose, but she held her tongue. Warwick had asked her to visit, and she'd brought along her healing poultice in case his wound needed a final treatment.

Nelson opened the double doors and Adeline stepped inside. And froze.

It was a ballroom unlike any other she'd

ever seen, and her eyes widened at the sight. Shelves had been built against the walls, and machines, tools, and bits of machinery crammed every surface. The high-pressure steam engine had been moved from the country, but other pieces of machinery were also displayed in the sizeable room. Workbenches lined one wall and the surfaces were crammed with tools. On the opposite wall, rows of shelves held glass jars containing various chemicals. Some were colorless, others were blends of the color spectrum from yellow to green to blood red. Sunlight streamed through French doors, and the light reflected off the jars, creating a kaleidoscope of color on the hardwood floor. She recognized some of the other inventions—the electric magnet, the rifling of a gun barrel, his lawn-cutting machine. There were others, of which she had no idea as to their name or function.

Warwick turned away from a wall of shelves. Dressed in linen shirtsleeves, his coat and waistcoat discarded on a chair, his broad shoulders strained against the linen. "Thank you for coming, Adeline." His green eyes intense, he grinned as he came forward to greet her.

Her stomach fluttered and her pulse leaped. Why did he have to be one of the most arrestingly handsome men she'd known? As he approached, she was conscious of his tall, athletic physique and the power that coiled within him. He exuded a confidence in his domain. She swallowed.

"You seem surprised. I told you I would visit." She scanned the shelves. "You took over the entire ballroom."

"It's the largest room in my home and serves my needs. It otherwise would have been a wasted space."

Her brows knotted. "It's a ballroom. Its purpose is to accommodate dancing."

"Which I do not do."

"Has there never been a ball here?"

"Yes, this mansion belonged to my parents, and they had lavish parties, balls, and gatherings in this room with hundreds of guests. None of them were true friends. The mansion was not a warm place to grow up as a child. I've managed to make it my own."

Her heart ached at his words. She pictured him as a neglected young boy while his aristocratic parents entertained Society. Had he hovered at the landing of the grand staircase, listening to the revelers, longing for the duke and duchess to visit and read him a bedtime story or tuck him in bed?

No! She shoved her concern aside. His past was not her concern. She shouldn't care about his upbringing, whether it was full of love or devoid of it. She shouldn't care.

But she did.

She envisioned a clever boy who'd loved learning and adored books. Rather than be praised for his intellect, he'd been chastised by his own father and mother for his interest in book learning over riding, hunting, and shooting. She couldn't help but wonder: if he'd been loved and accepted, would he have turned out differently?

"Lady Heywood cared for you. She still does," Adeline said.

"The lady is special."

Her stomach twisted, a different feeling than the heightened attraction she'd experienced walking into the room. "Yes, she is. I feel guilty lying to her."

He ran a hand through his hair, ruffling it, his fingers holding back the golden brown strands before releasing them. A lock fell rakishly across his brow, and she had a strong urge to smooth it in place. To touch him.

"I'm sorry for that part of our agreement. I assure you that you will not be misleading my godmother for long. I understand perfectly well that I will have to pick a future duchess sooner rather than later."

For some reason, his comment pricked her conscience more. She must greet Lady Heywood each morning with a smile, knowing she was lying to the woman. And Warwick's admission that he would take a wife caused a different discomfort in her chest. An ache she wanted to rub away. *What in God's name is wrong with me?*

Perhaps she was still upset over the ill-behaved ladies at the dressmaker's, or even more likely, over the distressing exchange with her sister in the publisher's office.

Warwick tilted his head and regarded her. His piercing green eyes seemed to penetrate her soul. "What's amiss? I understand misleading my godmother is concerning, but I sense something else is wrong."

Could he tell? Not for the first time she found his perception startling. She'd spent much of her life protecting herself from society, from those who didn't understand her cultural roots and treated her differently—oftentimes rudely. And here was a man who could look past her barriers and pluck her thoughts from her head.

She paused to catch her breath, her misgivings increasing. Could sharing her concerns with him be beneficial? What would he say about the publisher?

"My sister Mary wrote a novel," she blurted out.

Warwick arched a dark eyebrow. "That's an achievement."

Once she began, the words flowed easier. "She's published short stories under a male pseudonym. For the first time, she went to see her publisher with a full-length novel she'd written. I accompanied her. The visit was not a good one."

"Why?"

Adeline rubbed her temple as she envisioned the encounter. "Mary had corresponded with the publisher, Mr. Elder, for her short stories only as M.J. Price."

"M.J. Price? I've read his…or her short stories. They are well-written and entertaining."

"Mr. Elder rescinded his initial offer for the novel once he discovered Mary's true identity."

"You mean because she is a woman."

"Yes."

He let out a slow breath. "Mr. Elder was wrong. I'm sorry for Mary."

Her fingers twisted in her skirts, and rancor sharpened her voice for the unfairness of the situation. "It was difficult to witness. Mary tried to hide it with bravery, but the flash of despondency and despair that crossed her face was painful. I love my sister, and it was heartbreaking. I fear she will toss aside her quill and never write again."

"Then we will purchase her another quill. She must not give up on her dreams because of a tyrant."

She watched him closely. "You think so?"

"I know so."

Gratitude welled in her chest. And relief for being able to share her burden. She stole a glimpse at him beneath lowered lashes. His confidence as a duke spoke volumes and infused her with renewed hope. She may not be able to aid Mary with Mr. Elder, but she could keep encouraging her sister. "Thank you for listening."

"Of course. It's reasonable to share a distressing experience. You care for Mary. Does Edwin know?"

"That Mary writes? Or that Mr. Elder turned her away based on her sex?"

"Both."

The notion was laughable if not so upsetting. "No. Edwin would never approve of Mary's writing endeavors. The sister of an earl shouldn't dabble in trade, and he would consider an author a tradeswoman."

"One more reason I consider him a bore."

She couldn't agree more.

Warwick motioned to one of the tables. "May I show you my latest findings? It may distract you from your problems. At least for a short while."

She followed him to one of the tables and spotted a rifle. "Is this it?"

Warwick shook his head. "No. That is an older invention and not the one that I wish to—"

She ran a finger along the barrel of the rifle. "Is this how you injured yourself?"

He shrugged, rolling his muscular shoulders before her. "If you must know, I was experimenting with both the gunpowder as well as the rifling of the barrel to increase the accuracy and distance of a single shot. The gunpowder burned too hotly, and I was injured. I still consider the invention a success."

She looked up at him. He stood close, and the fluttery feeling in her chest returned. She clenched her fingers and imposed iron control on herself not to rest a hand on his arm. "I wouldn't consider the extent of your burn a success. How is your injury, by the way? I brought along more of my poultice."

He rolled up his shirtsleeve. "Much better thanks to you."

She raised his forearm for inspection. She was aware of the warmth of his skin and that he was standing inches from her, not feet. "Hmm. No sign of infection, but you will be left with a nasty scar."

His quick grin made her heart beat faster. "I had the best of care."

Her heart pounded, and she wondered if he could hear it. Suddenly flushed, she turned away. She followed him to a different table where he picked up what looked like a hollow tube and handed it to her.

"This is what I wanted to show you," he said.

She studied the tube, then looked up at him, her eyebrows drawn together. "Is this a flute or some other musical instrument?"

He chuckled and reached out to touch her hand before she raised the tube to her lips to blow through the smaller end. His warm fingers lingered, and her eyes locked with his as he spoke. "It's called a stethoscope and was invented by the Frenchman, R. Laennec. It's used to listen to the heartbeat or inside the chest of a patient."

Her interest was suddenly piqued tenfold. She lowered her gaze to the tube in her hand. "Truly? How does it work?"

"You place the flat end to the chest and the other end to your ear. The hollow wooden tube conducts sound."

"I'd like to try."

He stepped back and waved a hand to himself. "As you please."

Without a waistcoat, the linen shirt offered little barrier. He was giving her permission to touch him, to use the instrument to come close, very close. The scent of his cologne, sandalwood and cloves, tickled her senses. She inhaled and stepped near. She was suddenly hot, and a tingling awareness zinged in her veins. She was caught between sexual attraction and intellectual curiosity. Most women wouldn't find both dangerous. She did. She placed the flat end of the tube on his chest, the other to her ear, and concentrated. At first, she didn't hear anything, then the strong beat of his heart came through the hollow tube.

"Oh my goodness! I hear your heartbeat!" A lurch of excitement made her cry out.

He gazed down at her quizzically. "You have a look of rapt fascination on your face. I'm pleased you like it."

Her heart rate galloped, and she felt a little breathless. "I do." She returned her attention to the wooden tube in her hands. "For such a simple device, it has much potential. I could have used it to help Mr. Taylor."

"Mr. Taylor?"

"A man with a bad cough I treated. I had to place my ear to his chest, but he was overweight, and the sound was muffled. But this device," she said as she held up the stethoscope, "would have helped me." Her brow furrowed as she studied the device. "Although I wonder if Mr. Taylor would have allowed me to use it on him."

"Why wouldn't he? You said you helped him."

"He was reluctant to allow a woman to examine him. You were the same at first."

"I was not."

She pursed her lips. "Don't be stubborn. I'm a woman and you thought less of me because of my sex." It was like the way Mr.

Elder had treated Mary. But she couldn't compare the two. Warwick was different. He *had* allowed her to treat him, and he'd acknowledged her ability. Still, she wanted to hear him admit his initial bias.

He had the grace to concede. "You are right. I was hesitant. I didn't know you then."

"I do not blame you. I want you only to acknowledge it. You will never understand the prejudice women face daily, let alone a woman who is a healer." *Or an author like Mary.*

His silence seemed to echo in the room. They remained, silent and motionless—inches apart. Finally, he nodded. "I will never fully comprehend your battles. But I do know what it feels like to inherit a dukedom but wish to work on something to which only a tradesman or a man of lesser title should aspire."

She blinked. "What do you mean?"

"A duke who is expected to spend his days gambling, drinking, and whoring rather than tinkering on inventions in a ballroom converted to a workshop. Are we very different?"

The frustration in his voice touched a deep part of her soul. She didn't want to think of them as similar. She couldn't. He was a duke, and her mother was a commoner. Even if her father was titled, she was still far from his station. Edwin was her half brother and he'd treated her like the dirt beneath his boot, and she'd learned not to trust titled men.

He reached for her hand. "I want you to have the stethoscope."

Her lips parted in surprise. Her awareness of him hummed beneath the surface. She studied his features one by one. "Why?"

"Because you will make much more use of it than if it sits on my workbench. Because you have a talent that must not be wasted, and if this device can help you to help others, then it is a simple gift."

His words struck a vibrant chord in her chest as her fingers wrapped around the device. She felt a curious swooping pull at her innards. Perhaps it was too late. Perhaps her resolve to keep herself at a distance had already begun to crumble and her heart was at risk. Her voice was a soft whisper. "Thank you."

He was close, so close and the urge to touch him—to touch his perfect lips—could no longer be denied. She set the stethoscope on the workbench, then reached for him. Her fingers found the divot in his chin, then her forefinger traced his full bottom lip.

"Adeline." His voice was full of rich promise and temptation. The sound of it seemed to vibrate along her spine.

"Yes."

"We shouldn't. Remember our agreement." His voice was strained, hoarse.

"I remember. But no one needs to know.

Just us."

His green eyes darkened, and she recognized his need. It echoed her own. "Just us."

Then, blessedly, he lowered his head and kissed her.

• • •

Warwick was keenly aware of the softness of Adeline's lips as she met him halfway. Need raced through his veins as he shaped his lips to hers, learning the texture. Her lips parted on a sigh, and he took advantage to deepen the kiss. His tongue slid between her open lips, and she shivered in his arms.

Sweet. So sweet.

She was everything he'd imagined and more. Much more. He'd had lovers. Widows and even a divorcee. Women who knew what they'd wanted and understood what he'd wanted as well—a way to ease the urgings of the body without complications.

Adeline was entirely different. He didn't kiss virgins. Daughters of earls. A half sister of his former rival.

None of it mattered. He wanted her with a fierceness that was irrational. Her tongue met his, tentative at first, then bolder. She tasted like a brilliant summer day in the country— warm, enticing, seductive. She moaned and came alive in his arms, angling her head to eagerly increase the contact of the kiss. His restraint snapped, and he was suddenly a starving man wanting to taste and take as much as she offered. Her fingers clutched his arms, moved higher to his shoulders, then buried in his hair. Her nails scraped his scalp, and it was like a lit match to hay.

The kiss increased in intensity, and his hands ran down her back and pressed her flush against him. At the first contact, silk sizzled against broadcloth. He longed to pick her up, place her on his workbench, and lift her skirts to reveal her pretty, long legs. To skim his hands up her stockings to discover the warm flesh of her inner thighs. His cock hardened in his trousers at the image.

Christ! What was he thinking? She deserved better. More.

He had to stop this madness before the remnants of his control shredded entirely. He tore his mouth from hers. Her eyes were closed, her lips glossy and plump from his kiss. He was breathing as hard as if he'd dug a deep ditch around his country home. "Adeline." His voice was hoarse.

She lifted her long lashes. Her eyes were enormous and bright blue. She sucked in a breath and her breasts strained against her bodice. "Oh my. I hadn't expected it to be quite so…enjoyable."

"Neither did I." The truth. Just his luck. She was just as passionate about kissing as her healing. Who would have thought?

Her cheeks colored. "Your Grace, we should—"

"Ah, right." She was still pressed flush against him. Her breath brushed his throat and a renewed hunger to kiss her again raged inside him. He was a blackguard to take advantage. He was the more experienced and should have control. Instead, he'd lost every sense of reason at the mere taste of her tempting lips. Releasing her was no easy task. His chest felt like someone squeezed a fist inside it.

He picked up the stethoscope and placed it in her hands. "I promise, Adeline, it won't happen again."

• • •

"Well, well," Lady Heywood drawled. "Warwick showed you his ballroom workshop and you haven't taken the first coach back to the country. I consider that wonderful news!"

"I admit it was a bit shocking. Then he showed me some of the inventions, even gave me one called a stethoscope, and I find it fascinating."

Fascinating was a more proper way to describe their kiss. Her thoughts skittered as she recalled their heated encounter. She'd been shocked at the first sight of his workshop but drawn to the man as soon as she'd entered. He'd captivated her with his virility and his inventions. And that kiss…heavens…that kiss. Hungers she hadn't known existed had thundered in her veins. Heat had rippled under her skin as their tongues had touched and tasted. She'd wanted it to continue, to last forever. Yet he was the one to end the kiss, then promise it wouldn't happen again. She should be relieved at that promise. Only she wasn't.

What is wrong with me? The countess clapped her hands. "Even better news."

"Pardon?" She'd already lost track of their conversation.

"That you find some of his work of interest, my dear."

A different pang settled in her chest that was due to lying to her host. "What about the gossip rags? Is it causing you unwanted attention to have me reside with you?"

"Goodness no! I do not care what others say. It has taken this long, but my godson has developed an unexpected flair for attention. I never would have guessed it of a man who prefers the comforts of his workshop and the familiarity of his tools over the excitement of a party. I owe it all to you, my dear."

"You must know that paper embellishes the truth," Adeline said.

"Yes, but in your case, I hope the truth is

much more exciting." A twinkle lit the lady's eyes. "Warwick cares for you. I see it clearly. If my godson needs a nudge, all you need to do is ask me for help, my dear."

Before Adeline could answer, there was a knock on the parlor door. The lady's butler announced His Grace a moment before he walked inside.

"Hello, Warwick," Lady Heywood said with a smile. "To what do we owe this pleasure?"

"Good morning, ladies." Warwick bowed. "I'm here to ask Lady Adeline to accompany me to a scientific gathering."

It was hard not to stare. Warwick looked incredibly handsome dressed in a blue coat, snowy cravat, and buff trousers. His green eyes blazed. Memories of their passionate kiss returned in a rush, and it took great effort not to reach up and touch her lips.

"Must it involve science, Warwick?" Lady Heywood asked in a motherly voice. "Ladies enjoy Gunther's for ices. Or riding in the park. Or even chaperoned visits here."

"I wouldn't ask if I didn't believe Adeline would enjoy it," Warwick said.

Adeline cleared her throat. The pair spoke as if she were not in the room. She stood and crossed the room to stand before them. "What sort of scientific gathering?"

Warwick turned to her. "A group of

experts in varying fields gather to discuss their intellectual pursuits. Oftentimes, a presentation is given by one of the members. It isn't a ball, garden party, or social event, but I believe you will find it invigorating."

She was intrigued. What did that say about her? "Should Hasmik attend?"

"Your virtue will be well guarded. To my knowledge, no debauchery has every occurred at these gatherings. The most wild and unpredictable behavior was when Mr. Hannings, a renowned taxidermist, was to give a presentation, but his preserved dogs were sent to the wrong house. The Duchess of Powell's screams could be heard throughout the park."

Adeline burst out laughing. "Since I have no plans this afternoon, I would like to attend one of your meetings."

"Splendid."

Warwick helped her into his crested carriage and took the seat across from her.

"Did you have a chance to read the *Scandal Sheet* after the garden party?" she asked.

"I've never subscribed to the gossip rag, but I sent Nelson out to fetch it. It was quite enlightening. I seem to have made an impression."

She pursed her lips. "I thought I was the one to steal the show."

For a heart-stopping moment their eyes met, then they burst out laughing. Whatever anger his behavior at the garden party had engendered had long since dissipated.

"Have you used the stethoscope?" he asked.

"Not yet. But I'm excited to try it on a patient."

It wasn't the only thing she'd thought of last evening. He didn't mention their shared kiss, but it was there, hovering between them. She'd touched her lips in remembrance, and it had been a long time before she'd fallen asleep.

Warwick cleared his throat. It was an awkward sound that drew her attention. "Listen, Adeline. About yesterday."

"I thought we weren't to speak of it."

His square jaw hardened. "I did say that. Now I'm saying otherwise."

"Why?" Had he thought of it all last night as well? Even in the close confines of the carriage, he was difficult to read. Enigmatic. Had heated kisses flitted through his head rather than mechanical drawings?

"It shouldn't have happened. I...we can't let it happen again."

Her stomach sank. She forced her expression to remain serene, as stoic as his. "It was a moment of weakness. Nothing more." Still, his rejection stung. Stupid, Adeline. He didn't have feelings for her, other than perhaps friendship, and she couldn't allow herself to have feelings for him. Anything more would be perilous for her.

He nodded once. "Good."

She shoved her hurt feelings aside. Thankfully, the carriage came to a stop before a Piccadilly townhome, and Warwick helped her alight and escorted her inside. A group of ten men and two women sat in chairs in a large library. Leather-bound books lined the walls and the room smelled of their particular scent, and that of expensive port. At the front of the room a table stood, a drape thrown across its surface covering whatever was beneath.

Warwick held out a chair for Adeline and seated himself beside her.

"What is your field?" an older gentleman with salt-and-pepper hair and wire-rimmed spectacles asked her.

"Medicine."

"Ah. A good and helpful specialty. Needed both in Town and in the country."

His gaze was direct and without judgment. If he thought it unusual for a woman to study medicine, he made no point of it.

"And you?" she asked. "What is your field of study?"

"Civil engineering. Bridges and roads and tollbooths." He pointed to a red-haired man across the way. "Sir Dragan is a biologist. The lady beside him, Miss Wagner, is a mathematician. Mr. Updike studies astronomy. Mr. Lagrou is a barrister who has a mechanical mind and helps inventors obtain patents. We have an architect who works with Mrs. Walter, a skilled draftswoman. And Mr. Levins is an expert in heat transfer. Warwick is especially interested in his work."

A jolt of excitement surged in her stomach. Adeline had never been in a room with such a vast array of experts. Warwick was right. This was more scintillating than a garden party.

"Where did you meet all these intellectuals?" she asked Warwick.

"They had been gathering for years before I attended the first meeting. We are all judged on our work, not our titles. Everyone here knows that I'm a duke, but it's unimportant. What is important are our discoveries and advancements to the fields of science."

She looked around, her gaze scanning the others. "There are women in the group."

"Yes. Miss Wagner is a brilliant mathematician," Warwick replied with clear admiration. "She aided with a chemical formula I was working on a year ago."

Miss Wagner was young and beautiful with honey hair and blue eyes and porcelain skin. She appeared as day to night with Adeline's dark coloring. Pressure built in Adeline's chest, and she was honest enough with herself to recognize the uncomfortable feeling as jealousy.

Had the lady and Warwick shared more than mathematical formulas?

Blast! It's none of your concern! His rejection was fresh in her mind.

Then why did the thought bother her?

"We have a presenter today," Warwick said, oblivious to her discomfort. "Someone I believe will capture your interest."

"Who is it? Do not keep me in suspense."

"An anatomist."

She shifted in her chair and craned her neck to look at the doorway. "Truly? Here? How is that possible?" Eagerness thrummed in her veins. An anatomist's presentation would allow her to forget the duke. When Adeline was thirteen, and her father, the earl, had been on a hunting trip in the country, her mother had taken her to observe a surgery. The surgeon was from Arabia and had been her mother's friend since childhood. He'd been training others in Eastern medicine. The patient had expired by the time they could arrive, and the surgeon had decided to dissect him to learn why his liver had failed.

Adeline had stood by her mother while three out of five of the surgeon's aspiring students had turned green. One had to leave, and she'd heard him vomit outside the room. Adeline's mother had held her hand during the dissection and had explained that a healer should know what was between skin and bones to best treat a patient.

Adeline had later learned that surgeons, anatomists, and artists needed to dissect corpses to study and create accurate models, and grave robbers were notorious for providing corpses for profit.

Warwick chuckled and raised a hand. "He will not dissect a flesh-and-blood body, but a model made of wax. When I heard that he would be presenting today, I thought of you and knew you must come."

Warwick's consideration made the pressure in her chest bloom like a hothouse flower. Most men would disparage her interest in medicine.

But not the duke.

He was confident enough in his own knowledge and masculinity not to be intimidated by her intelligence.

She knew firsthand it was a rarity in a male.

Edwin had never encouraged her healing endeavors. Looking back, her own father had never fully embraced Adeline's interests, either. As for Adeline's mother, she had been a healer and midwife before marrying the Earl of Foster. But she'd ceased working soon after her marriage.

Adeline had always believed her mother had stopped treating others because she wanted to spend all her time with her husband.

Had Adeline been wrong? Had her mother slowly stopped going to houses simply because her father had disapproved?

Her mother had agreed to her father's demands. *Mostly.* There were exceptions, and her mother had taught Adeline what she'd known about herbs and healing and had taken her along when she'd slipped out of the house to help a friend in need or a sick servant. She'd acted clandestinely. Adeline had thought it was because she didn't want payment, but maybe there was another reason. Maybe it had been because of her husband's demands.

Warwick would never demand his wife give up her dreams.

Good God, why was she thinking such thoughts?

Because of their kiss. It had changed things between them. At least, it had for *her*.

Despite their conversation in the carriage, she couldn't forget their heated encounter. She licked her suddenly dry lips, and her stomach fluttered as her mind helplessly relived the velvet warmth of his lips. She'd wanted to kiss him, and she hadn't been disappointed. For a man who isolated himself in his workshop, he certainly knew how to kiss. From what she could discern, he had enjoyed the kiss even though he had been the one to pull away.

Sweet Jesus, despite everything, she wanted to kiss him again.

"He's here."

She jumped in her seat just as a dark-haired man entered the library followed by two assistants who carried jars of unidentifiable specimens floating in clear fluid. The anatomist was short with a wiry mustache and beard.

"Welcome, ladies and gentlemen. Many of you already know me. If you are new to the group"—his eyes rested briefly on Adeline—"my name is Mr. Morton, and I will be dissecting a human male for you today." Once he had the group's attention, Morton drew back the sheet to reveal a male model, leaving a portion of the sheet over the model's nether parts in consideration to the ladies in the room.

The model was painted to appear extremely lifelike. Its brown eyes were open, and the artist had paid meticulous attention to each facial feature; its eyebrows, eyelashes, nostrils, lips, and earlobes all were rendered in vivid detail. The muscles of its chest and arms were clearly delineated, and a line, which looked like an incision, ran down the center of its breastbone.

Morton waved his arm at the model. "This specimen is my male model, Paul. As you can observe, his anatomy is scientifically accurate. Paul is made of a mixture of wax from bees and other insects; other inferior models are made of wood, ivory, and papier–mâché. Now, if you feel like my model is staring at you, it's because he has the preserved eyes of a pig."

Adeline wrinkled her nose. She'd left Henry safely behind in the country under the care of one of the farmers. She'd always believed her pig's eyes were expressive. She disliked the thought of an artist using a real animal's eyes, specifically a pig's.

Morton pointed to the jars his assistants had carried into the room. "I also brought along examples of animal anatomy that I will discuss at the end of my lecture. I will pass the jars out then as well."

From the "incision," Morton proceeded to remove two sides of the chest to reveal the organs beneath. The model was cleverly made—the heart, lungs, liver, and kidneys, all made of painted wax, were visible. When he removed the organs and held them up for the audience to have a better look, Adeline leaned forward in her chair, eager to see.

"Interesting, isn't it?" Warwick whispered in her ear.

Adeline nodded, not wanting to look away or miss a word of the presentation.

Morton held up a wax heart. "The heart is comprised of four distinct chambers and pumps blood to the entire body, including the brain." One of his assistants raised a glass container. "This is an ox's heart," Morton said.

The assistant walked around with the specimen so everyone could see. It was a well-preserved heart, and Adeline spotted the chambers. Some of the members turned away, including Mr. Updike and Miss Wagner.

"Many believe the brain is the most important organ, but Egyptians believed it was the heart," Morton continued. "They inserted a hook into the corpse's nose to break up the brain, then removed the pieces and discarded them. But they treated the heart with value and placed it in a special urn for the afterlife. Without it, the deceased would be in danger of not ascending to the afterlife."

The anatomist's presentation lasted for the rest of the hour. When he was finished, Adeline turned to Warwick. "Thank you for bringing me. I enjoyed the presentation."

"I doubt our afternoon together will end up in the *Scandal Sheet.* These scientific gatherings never do."

She brought a hand up to stifle a laugh. "But a dissected model is much more interesting than a garden party. Don't you agree, Your Grace?"

His grin made her stomach swirl. "You are an oddity, Lady Adeline. I have never met a woman who would think that, let alone speak it aloud."

She cocked her head to the side. "An oddity? That makes me sound unpleasant."

He reached out, gently clutching her fingers. He looked down at her, something akin to a striking possessiveness flaring in his green eyes. "To the contrary. It makes you priceless. A shining, polished diamond among a pile of carbon."

She gasped as a tremor unfurled through her. It was the highest regard coming from him.

Priceless.

Was that how he saw her? No one before had gifted her with such a compliment. Not even her father.

A tangle of alarm and emotion swelled in her chest. He'd already disarmed her with a kiss. Then with an anatomist's presentation. Now, Adeline wholeheartedly agreed with the Egyptians. The heart was the most valuable and dangerous organ of all.

CHAPTER TWELVE

After Warwick dropped Adeline off at his godmother's home, he headed to a coffeehouse in the Strand. It was part of his normal routine to have coffee, read the *Morning Post* and the *Times,* and talk politics with jobbers from the London Stock Exchange, merchants, and aristocrats who had an interest in the Exchange or politics or both. Sometimes Drake joined him after they'd spent an afternoon boxing.

The main salon of the coffeehouse was busy today. He'd barely made it to a table when a man called out his name.

"Warwick!"

He turned to see Matthew Jacobson, a member of the scientific group. Jacobson was an inventor who dabbled with mechanical devices, and he shared common interests with Warwick. He'd been absent from today's presentation.

Jacobson's right eye was black, and his left arm was in a sling. Either the man lost heavily at Gentleman Jackson's, or he'd been attacked by footpads.

"What the hell happened to you?" Warwick asked.

Jacobson's gaze darted around the room as

if he expected an enemy to leap out at any moment. "May we speak in private?"

Warwick motioned to a table in the corner of the coffeehouse. Jacobson sat across from him and clenched the fist of his good hand on the table. "I'm in trouble."

Warwick eyed him. "You were attacked?"

"No and yes."

"Which was it, man?"

Jacobson glanced around as if to see who was near, then lowered his voice. "I was attacked, but not in the street. I needed money to continue working on my innovation of the miner's headlamp. I'm close...so close to a workable prototype."

"What did you do?" Warwick had an idea what the man's answer would be.

"I went to someone I'd heard about, a moneylender."

"You should have come to me first."

"I wish I had, but it's too late."

"Go on," Warwick urged.

"I didn't go to the lender on Bond Street, the one the fancy lords use when they've heavily gambled. That moneylender wouldn't take a risk on a simple inventor without much success. I heard of another." Jacobson scrubbed a hand down his face, then flinched as he remembered the black eye. "A lender who is unscrupulous and charges high interest. But I was so sure about the success of my miner's lamp that I was willing to take the risk and took the loan. But it didn't work as I'd hoped." He sagged in his chair. "When I couldn't pay the interest, there was no sense reasoning with Mr. Slade, and he sent a burly man to collect. A man who used his fists and—"

Warwick's gut twisted, and he shot Jacobson a penetrating look. "Good God, man! What did you say?"

"When I couldn't make the exorbitant payment, he beat—"

"No. The name of the lender. What is it?" It took all his effort not to reach across the table and shake the answer out of him.

Jacobson's eyes widened. "Mr. Slade. Stan Slade."

Warwick's throat tightened, and panic snaked in his chest. Edwin had mentioned Slade's name when Warwick had first overheard him arguing with Adeline in the country. Edwin was more than eager to trade Adeline in exchange for release of his debt to the moneylender.

No wonder Edwin was desperate. Slade was a dangerous man; one the new Earl of Foster didn't wish to cross.

The bastard is in over his head.

Warwick should have known. Bartering Adeline's hand in marriage to Slade was stooping low, even for Edwin.

Warwick's fingers fisted on the table. Their kiss had left him hard and wanting, desperate to claim her. It had taken all his will to pull away. An image of Adeline absorbed in the anatomist's presentation sprang to his mind. Upswept raven hair had revealed her swan-like neck. Her lovely blue eyes had sparkled. Like him, she thrived from knowledge, and Warwick found her bewitching. Despite his resolve to not touch her, he'd wanted to pull her into his arms and kiss her right then and there for his scientific peers to see. To stake his claim.

Over his dead body. His heart thumped like a battering ram. He'd be damned if Adeline was sacrificed to an unscrupulous man like Slade. When he'd first struck a bargain with Adeline, he'd thought only of himself—to remain a bachelor for one more Season. But sitting across from Jacobson, observing the black eye and broken arm, the man's injuries were alarming and infuriating.

The stakes had risen, and the simple had become more complex.

He needed to persuade everyone of their fake courtship, for certain—and to protect Adeline, no matter the cost.

• • •

After a quick breakfast of toast, jam, and poached eggs, Adeline sent Warwick a note explaining she would be busy for the day. A hired hack dropped Adeline and Hasmik off at Threadneedle Street. From there, it was a short walk to a smaller part of the city where her mother's people and Londoners of Mediterranean and Middle Eastern descent worked and resided.

Adeline's pulse thrummed with excitement. It had been too long since she'd visited. This area of the city was a hubbub of activity. Merchants in outdoor stalls sold foreign items—goods that had recently been shipped into the port, such as rare carpets, vases and pottery, artwork and jewelry. Customers bartered with merchants using their hands to articulate as well as a blend of different languages—Arabic, Turkish, Armenian, and Greek. She sidestepped a man who unrolled a carpet, a magnificent handwoven piece with colorful peacocks, green vines, and lush flowers. A husband and wife immediately began bargaining with the merchant. Others sold spices like cumin, anise seed, and za'atar, a Middle Eastern mixture consisting of thyme and sesame seeds.

Adeline had a fondness for za'atar mixed with olive oil and she purchased the spice along with freshly baked pita bread and a small flask of olive oil from one of the merchants. Hasmik haggled with another for sumac, turmeric, and tahini. Adeline was not a cook, but Hasmik was talented in the kitchen and would use the tahini, a sesame seed paste, to make hummus and other savory dishes.

With their packages wrapped and under their arms, they made their way to a small house close to the end of the street. The door swung open and two young women, twins, smiled in unison. Both had long, dark hair and wore simple dresses with embroidered aprons. One was plump, the other slim.

"Look who's here!" the heavy-set twin cried out.

"Hello, Araz and Isa," Adeline greeted the sisters.

The slender twin grasped Adeline's arm and pulled her inside. "You are both here just in time. Armen and his friends arrived earlier."

They were led around the side of the house and into a yard. Armen and his friends were musicians, and Adeline could hear the music before she stepped through the garden gate. One played the dumbek, a small drum held under the arm, and another played the duduk, a deep-toned double reed instrument made from apricot wood. A third strung an oud, a pear-shaped, short-necked string instrument.

More than a dozen people had gathered; many had been friends of Adeline's mother.

Hasmik immediately joined a group of women and began speaking Arabic. In the corner, a man grilled skewers of lamb shish kebab over coals, and the delicious smell wafted to Adeline and made her mouth water. As the musicians played, a group of men and women held hands for line dancing. They circled in the yard, kicking their feet to a choreographed rhythm, their laughter echoing off the garden's stone wall.

Memories returned to Adeline in a rush. She'd visited here with her mother when her father was away. *These are your people, too, Adeline,* her mother would say.

Warm. Welcoming. Without airs. They didn't reside in lavish townhomes with servants or attend glittering balls dressed in fancy gowns. But they were just as thriving and happy. Many even more so.

As Adeline joined the dance, she wondered what Warwick would think. He was a duke, but he had no apparent qualms about spending an afternoon with scientists and intellectuals without titles. What would he think about these people?

His world was different, but so was he. Would he be accepting or awkward and uncomfortable? And why did it matter?

Born of an aristocratic father and a Middle Eastern mother, she straddled two worlds. She wondered where she fit in herself.

The dance ended and Adeline walked away.

"Smile, Adeline." Hasmik materialized by her side. "Are you not happy? Or are you thinking of the duke?"

"Why would you think he is on my mind?"

"Because I know you better than anyone, and you have a dreamy, faraway look on your face lately."

"Dreamy! I do not look dreamy," she protested.

"If you say so." Hasmik's dark eyes watched her.

Adeline raised her chin. "Let us speak of other things."

"Fine with me. You should know that people have asked if you can help them with their ailments. Many cannot pay for the English doctors."

As Adeline scanned the group, their discussion of the duke was immediately forgotten. "Of course. Spread the word that I will do all I can."

Hasmik nodded. "One woman in particular is asking to speak with you now. I had to look twice, but you wouldn't believe who it is."

"Who?" Adeline scanned the crowd.

"Lady Drake."

Adeline swung around to see the earl's wife sitting at a table chatting with a group of women. Adeline hadn't even noticed her among the other dark-haired women. It wasn't the first time she'd forgotten they had a common background. Ana's father had been a collector of Middle Eastern antiquities, and, like Adeline, her mother hadn't been English.

Lady Drake rubbed her swollen abdomen as Adeline sat beside her. "Hello, Adeline. Is everything they say about you and Warwick true?"

Adeline wasn't sure how to explain her relationship with Warwick to her, and she spoke the first thing that came to mind. "We are friends. Have you heard something different?"

The lady flashed a smile. "My maid is obsessed with the gossip rags."

Adeline rolled her eyes. "Do not believe all you read."

"Some say the duke is eccentric, but he is a good man. Warwick admires you. That alone is telling. The duke is particular."

If Warwick admired her, it was because of her healing knowledge, not as a woman.

"The babe is almost due. I do not trust English doctors. Will you come for the birth if I send word?"

"I'd be happy to."

Lady Drake's eyes widened. "The babe is kicking. Do you want to feel?" Not waiting for an answer, she grasped Adeline's hand and placed it on her abdomen. Sure enough, Adeline felt a ripple of movement.

Pure joy crossed the Lady Drake's face. "Lord Drake believes it's a girl. I want a boy."

Adeline experienced an unexpected stab of jealousy. She cared for others, but she longed to marry for love and have children of her own, just like Lady Drake had. Would it ever happen for her?

A dangerous vision sprang to mind of tawny-haired, devilish boys with green eyes. Little Warwicks running around the ducal mansion, tugging on Lady Heywood's skirts, chasing each other across the manicured gardens, and making her heart swell.

. . .

On their way back to Lady Heywood's home, Adeline stopped to see her sister. Mary was sitting at an escritoire in the corner of the parlor, a paper before her and quill in hand. She rose to hug Adeline.

"What's wrong?" Adeline asked as soon as she joined Mary on the couch. Her sister's fingers were twisted in her lap, and her face was pale as a wax candle.

"I cannot bring myself to write. No matter how hard I try, the words will not come. Worse, I almost tossed my completed manuscript into the fireplace last night."

"You will do no such thing. And you will not stop writing. I will not hear of it."

Mary's face crumpled, and she choked back a sob. "Oh Adeline. You have always been stronger than me."

Adeline's stomach dropped at her sister's distress. "That isn't true."

"Yes it is, and you know it. You have stood up to Edwin for years, and you have managed to pursue your own aspirations."

Those dreams were in jeopardy. She couldn't confess the truth to her sister—that Edwin wanted her to marry a moneylender. Or that Adeline had entered into a false courtship with a duke of the realm to avoid it.

Adeline sat next to Mary on the sofa. "Writing the novel is the hard part. A smart publisher should jump at the chance to publish your work."

Mary squeezed Adeline's hand. "You inspire me! One day I shall even gather the gumption to tell Edwin."

As if he heard his name, boots clicked on the tile floor and Edwin entered the parlor. As soon as he spotted Adeline, a cold, congested expression crossed his face. "What a surprise."

Mary jumped to her feet and stood between her brother and half sister. "Do not say anything insulting. I invited Adeline."

"And you are also aware that I now own

this house."

His arrogance had increased tenfold since their father's death. Adeline stood. She could not give a fig about Edwin, but she didn't want to cause Mary discomfort. She'd already experienced enough distress from the publisher.

"Don't fret, my lord. It's unbecoming to you. I shall leave at once." Adeline kissed Mary on the cheek and reached for her reticule, then hurried out the parlor door.

Edwin was hot on her heels and stopped her in the vestibule. "A word, Adeline."

She gave him a backward glance. "I'm a busy woman, my lord."

"So busy you have yet to be betrothed?"

Adeline turned, her blood simmering in her veins. "What is it you want to ask?"

Edwin took two steps forward, a smirk marring his handsome features. "The duke has not come to me."

She lifted her chin, knowing that cowering before him only fed his sense of superiority. "Why would he?"

"Why else? To ask for your hand in marriage."

She faced him squarely, an anxious shiver racing down her spine. What would it take to get Edwin to leave her be?

"Perhaps you should talk to His Grace."

A crude laugh crossed his lips. "Why would

I do that?" He came close and his hot breath scalded her cheek. "Don't fret, Adeline. When your duke fails to act, Mr. Slade will be waiting."

...

Over the course of the week, Adeline kept herself busy. During the mornings, she took Hasmik's advice and began treating people from the diverse section of the city. Society events didn't occur until late afternoon or evening, and Adeline used her earlier free hours to meet with patients. Her supply of herbs was depleted, and Hasmik had made trips to the apothecary and around Town scouring for calendula, chamomile, elecampane, peppermint, lavender, and whatever else she could find in the London markets.

Adeline helped deliver a babe, treated a case of gangrene, alleviated a man's indigestion disorder, set a broken arm and bound it, and prescribed a poultice for a rash. Her most challenging patient had come when she'd arrived at a house at Hasmik's urging.

"Thank goodness you've come." A young mother had spoken from where she'd been sitting by her seven-year-old son's bedside.

Adeline had learned the boy had been ill for two weeks before he'd developed an earache that caused him to cry out in pain. It was worse at night, and he'd been unable to sleep.

The local doctor had prescribed leeches, which hadn't helped, but only made the boy weak. Soon after, the boy's illness had progressed into a raging fever. The boy's parents were at their wits end with worry. The physician continued with the bloodletting until the mother had reached out to Hasmik.

Adeline recalled her mother talking of a patient with similar symptoms. At the protest of the doctor, Adeline put a stop to the bloodletting. Thereafter, cool cloths and constant sips of bone broth lowered the fever. She used drops of thick olive oil to temporarily lessen the ear pain, then applied a warm compress to the infected ear. As she'd anticipated, the pressure from pus within the middle ear discharged. Adeline had kept the ear clean and drained, and over the course of the next few days, the infection had subsided, along with all the pain.

The young boy would live and his mother was grateful.

On her last visit, the boy sat by a table, eating bread and cheese, and smiled at Adeline. "It doesn't hurt!" He touched his ear.

"Good news indeed." Adeline smiled and patted the boy's shoulder.

"Thank you." The mother grasped Adeline's hands. Tears streamed down her cheeks. "Vasken is better because of you."

The boy's father was just as grateful. "We

cannot pay you much, but please take this."
He thrust a small gold cross into Adeline's
hands.

Adeline looked up at the father. "Thank
you, but I cannot take this."

"Please, we will be upset if you do not. The
cross is from a traveling merchant from
Jerusalem and was blessed by the local priest.
It will look after you as you looked after our
son."

Adeline knew the gift was beyond precious. This was a proud, working family. To
refuse the gift would be an insult. To accept
seemed too much.

Hasmik understood. "She will wear it with
pride."

Soon after, they arrived back at Lady
Heywood's home.

"You did well, Adeline. That boy will live
because of you," Hasmik said.

"We were fortunate the mother summoned us when she had. The fever was the
most worrisome."

"The family will be indebted to you. The
others you have helped since your return to
London are grateful as well. You are needed,
whether you are in London or the country."

It was a sobering thought. The villagers
needed a physician, as did an entire commu-
nity here. As for all of London, she wouldn't
have to search far for patients. The lower

classes and poor seemed endless in the city streets.

"Your family should be proud."

"Mary is, yes. But not Edwin. If I were still living beneath his roof, he would prohibit my work. As things stand, Edwin may still be able to stop me from healing patients."

Hasmik waved a dismissive hand. "The Duke of Warwick will not allow that to happen."

Adeline's brows drew together. "You have much faith in our plan."

"I am old and wise. I have faith in the man."

Adeline scoffed. "Since when have you become the duke's champion?"

"Since when have I not? Let's get you home and to sleep. You look tired, and you must be refreshed when His Grace comes for you tomorrow."

• • •

Her next outing with Warwick was not another garden party, but a bookstore.

"The Kirkland ball is coming swiftly, and I thought we might go elsewhere in advance to stir up gossip," Warwick said.

Adeline glanced up at the sign above the Mayfair shop. "Hookham's Bookshop. Are you certain, Your Grace? I don't believe this is the best place to find magpies." The bookseller was located at 15 Old Bond Street and tended to cater to the wealthy and titled.

He offered his arm. "A chaperone isn't required here, and it suits our intended purpose."

"Truly?"

He winked. "Trust me."

Butterflies fluttered in her chest. His teasing nature had its intended effect. She followed beside him, her attention drawn to his profile from beneath lowered lashes.

The bookstore was not a hubbub of activity and didn't seem like a hotbed of gossip. Once more, she wondered if Warwick knew what he was talking about. Still, she did enjoy the surroundings. Hundreds of books were on display for the establishment's patrons. When her father was alive, he'd had a membership to Hookham's. A yearly fee of forty-two shillings entitled a member to take out twelve books from the circulating library. Visitors could browse the collection, and if they found a novel they wanted to own, a special arrangement could be made with the bookseller to purchase a book. It was a wonderful arrangement for both the patrons and the bookshop.

Warwick escorted her to a reading room where tables and comfortable armchairs and settees were arranged before a fireplace with a marble mantel. A large window allowed for plenty of sunlight. Patrons could peruse newspapers, magazines, and books in casual comfort here. It was also an area where a patron might wait while one of the books they'd selected was fetched by a clerk and delivered to the reading room.

The door opened and a servant wheeled in a tray and offered both coffee and tea to those reading or waiting for their reading material to be delivered.

Adeline could spend an entire afternoon here, drinking tea and reading books. Mary would love it as well, and Adeline made a mental note to bring her sister here soon. Mary could even bring her notepad and pencil and write her next novel while Adeline read beside her. It would make for a lovely afternoon.

Warwick brushed her sleeve, and she was reminded of their purpose here today. "Are you certain we will attract attention?" she asked.

His lips curved in a smile. "Leave it to me."

He motioned for her to sit in a settee then sat close beside her. Her nerves tingled with awareness. Several ladies eyed them above the edges of their magazines and novels.

"Do you see those two in the corner?" he asked.

She did. Either the pair of middle-aged women were not as engrossed in their books or the presence of the dashing duke was enough to draw their attention away from their penny romance novels.

He opened a newspaper and raised it for them to read together. For all pretenses, it looked like they were using the paper to cover a romantic interlude. Warwick waggled his eyebrows and Adeline giggled. She was enjoying herself. He inched even closer on the settee until his muscular thigh brushed her skirts. Her heart leaped wildly in her breast. A lock of hair fell rakishly across his forehead and gave him a boyish appeal. Only he was a man, one who was "courting" her. Sitting on the settee, heads together behind the newspaper, it would be easy to ignore the outside world and focus entirely on him.

Except that would be reckless.

She could hear the two women in the corner whispering, no doubt about them. Soon after, the ladies stood and left the reading room.

Warwick lowered the newspaper. "No doubt they will spread gossip."

She pressed a hand to her heart and giggled. "I anticipate tomorrow's edition of the *Scandal Sheet.*"

The door opened, and two different women entered the room.

Adeline's smile faded along with her joy. A sinking feeling settled low in her stomach.

"What is it?" Warwick asked.

Adeline lowered her voice to a whisper. "Those two. I overheard them gossiping at the dressmaker's the other day."

"About us, I assume."

She shook her head. "Not at first. They were too busy talking about my mother."

He looked at her quizzically. "Your mother?"

"They called her an Arab foreigner who practiced a heathen religion and traditions. I'm no better in their eyes, you see, because I'm a harem girl who enticed a duke to court her."

His eyes widened and he visibly stiffened. "Bloody hell."

At his anger, her cheeks grew warm, and her lashes lowered. "It's not the first time others have insulted my mother. Or me. My mother understood their prejudice. She said it was from fear and ignorance. She also told me to ignore those who chose to spew nonsense. Not everyone holds hatred in their hearts."

"You mother was a better person than I am, and I cannot begin to understand the prejudices your mother had to face. Or that you do."

"What should I do? Confront them? Lash out?" She shook her head. "No matter how badly the urge to retaliate, I do not want to give them the satisfaction."

"If they were men, I would challenge them to a duel." Warwick's voice was hard, cold.

"Duels are illegal."

"So? They are still conducted."

Her fingers fisted. A part of her wanted to confront them here as she'd done at the dressmakers. She stayed seated. They weren't worth the effort. She also knew that if she fought back, the *Scandal Sheet* would print negative nonsense about *her,* not them. Worse, any recourse Adeline took would hurt her sister, and Mary didn't deserve any part of it.

She reached for his arm. "Please. I just want to leave."

"Not yet."

"Why not?"

"If they are vicious gossipmongers, then we should use them to our advantage."

"How?"

"Like this." He leaned forward and brushed his lips against her cheek. The touch was brief, and his warm breath fanned her skin. Stunned, Adeline turned and met his eyes. He lowered his head and pressed his lips to hers. The kiss lasted an instant, but all her earlier emotions rushed back in a delicious avalanche. Heat swirled in her veins and her stomach tumbled wildly. Her palm rested on his chest. Under it, his heart thumped hard. He raised his head and captured her eyes. His smile nearly took her breath away.

The gasp from the two women could be heard across the room.

Warwick took Adeline's hand in his much larger one and stood. "Follow me."

Her legs were weak, but at that moment, she would have followed him anywhere. He stopped before the two wide-eyed women. "Ladies."

"Your Grace," they said in unison, staring up at his chiseled features.

"The answer to your question is yes," he said.

"Your Grace?" Again in unison.

"Dukes find women from different cultures fascinating and they offer much more scintillating conversation than simple English gossips."

Speechless, their lips parted.

With a hand on Adeline's back, he ushered her out of the reading room, then out the front door. Adeline was speechless as a strange sense of satisfaction swept through her.

As Warwick escorted Adeline across the street, his mouth was set in a grim line. "If I could have challenged them another way, I would have."

"I do not doubt it."

He grinned. "Instead, I decided to use them, rather than for them to insult you. Malicious gossip or not, tongues will wag."

CHAPTER THIRTEEN

The following afternoon, Adeline returned to the countess's home after treating a patient. She removed her cloak and handed it to the butler just as Lady Heywood rushed into the vestibule.

"Adeline! You are just in time. The sapphire ballgown was delivered by the modiste's assistant this afternoon. You must try it on."

"But I was already fitted at the dressmaker's shop," Adeline protested. She'd returned to the dressmaker's as soon as the gown had been sewn.

"Posh! I missed the fitting. I want to see it on you. Besides, the invitation to the Kirkland ball arrived today, and a lady can never be careful enough to ensure that everything is in order."

Adeline was tired and wished to rest in her room. She pushed her fatigue aside. Lady Heywood seemed overly excited, and Adeline wanted to please her.

"Shall I summon my maid?" Adeline asked.

"No need. I shall assist you. Hurry along now!"

Adeline followed the lady up the grand

staircase and into her bedchamber. A package wrapped in delicate tissue rested on her bed.

"I took the liberty of removing it from the box." Lady Heywood tore the tissue, removed the gown, and shook it. A shaft of sunlight illuminating the silk as it rippled made the dress appear like a shimmering lake.

She bit her bottom lip. Why was the countess so interested in seeing her dressed in the gown? Did the lady have late-blooming concerns about the color or style? Adeline thought the dress was beautiful, but she was not as knowledgeable of current fashion. She'd never been interested. Lady Kirkland was one of the most important hostesses of the Season, and it had been a long time since Adeline had attended a ball as lavish and important as the Kirkland ball. Everyone who was anyone would be there.

Including the Duke of Warwick. Her nerves tensed anew. "Maybe you are right. It is best if I try the gown on for your inspection."

"That's a good girl." The countess spun Adeline around and began to unbutton the muslin walking dress she currently wore.

"Tell me about Warwick," Lady Heywood said as she worked.

"The duke is well."

"Not about his health, my dear. I do see

him often."

Different nerves tensed. "You are inquiring about our courtship?"

"A godmother can never have enough information."

Adeline felt her face redden as the lady worked the buttons of her walking dress. How best to answer? The trip to the bookstore was fresh in her mind. She'd never believed a room full of books could result in scandal, but then she'd never known a man like Warwick.

"The *Scandal Sheet* is abuzz about us. I think it will continue." After the kiss in the bookstore, she was sure the two women would also spread the word.

The lady's fingers halted for a moment before continuing. "Ah, but I know better than to trust gossip if I want to know the truth. Why not ask the source directly?"

With her back to the lady, she couldn't see Adeline's flushed complexion. "Have you spoken to His Grace about us?"

Adeline stepped out of the walking dress. Lady Heywood helped remove her stays and stockings. Dressed only in her thin shift, her skin prickled from the cool temperature in the room. The countess reached for a black corset the dressmaker had provided and tied the laces. The new corset pushed her breasts up and cinched her waist. Black stockings followed and were secured by red ribbons at her thighs. A lock of dark hair escaped her pins and landed on her bare shoulder.

Lady Heywood picked up the sapphire gown. "Men do not like to be questioned about their romantic intentions."

Adeline could only imagine the elusive answers Warwick would give his godmother.

"We spent time together at a bookstore," she offered.

"Hmm. That does sound like Warwick. First a meeting with his intellectual friends and then a bookstore." She clucked her tongue. "Things are progressing much too slowly. I must tell him to take you for another spin in the park or to Gunther's for ices."

"But the bookstore was rather pleasant."

The way Warwick had stood up for her with the malicious women sprang to mind. His displeasure was obvious when she'd told him the cruel gossip she'd overheard in the dressmaker's shop. His temper had risen, and he'd reacted in a most unexpected way. His kiss still caused a tug deep in her belly and a pang in her heart.

"It wouldn't hurt for a lady to hurry things along," she said.

Something about Lady Heywood's tone set off alarm bells. Adeline eyed her with a critical squint. "What do you mean?"

"You must understand my godson.

Warwick is a passionate man, far more passionate than any rogue or scoundrel mothers generally mistrust when it comes to their young daughters. The duke has channeled all his passion into his creativity and his inventive work."

Adeline understood firsthand. The duke's ballroom workshop was hard to forget.

"Because of his interests, I often worried Warwick would never marry. Then he appeared in London with you by his side. At first, I didn't know what to think. But seeing the way he looks at you, my dear, tells me everything I need to know."

"Perhaps you know more than I do," Adeline said.

"Warwick desires you."

Adeline felt her face grow warm. "Pardon?"

"I may be much older, but I was young and married once. You have power, my dear. A lady's future is not entirely in a man's hands."

"You are talking in riddles."

"I'm talking of seduction."

Adeline's lips parted. *Seduction.* Just associating the word with Warwick caused butterfly wings to flutter in her chest.

"It's not a good idea," Adeline managed to squeak.

"Why not? I'm not talking *outright* seduction, mind you, simply encouragement. A few stolen kisses when no one is looking is sufficient to inspire a man to act. Nothing more."

Their shared kiss was far from simple, and had left her burning with need, yearning for more. The idea of seducing…encouraging… Warwick went against their arrangement and all good sense. So why did her heart skip a beat at the thought?

Warwick's words—*It shouldn't happen again*—were never far from her mind.

It was a quandary because she wanted it to happen again.

Longed for it.

The sound of the front door opening and closing followed by an all-too-familiar, deep male voice reached them.

"Oh dear. I forgot that His Grace is expected for luncheon," her ladyship said.

"Here? Now?" Adeline's eyes widened.

She shrugged. "He's on time for once."

Suspicions arose. Lady Heywood was sharp as a tack. She was not forgetful. What was her game?

"Do not think mothers, or in this case godmothers, cannot have a hand in hurrying things along, my dear."

Hurrying things along!

"Pardon me for a moment." The lady walked out, not bothering to shut the bedchamber door behind her.

Adeline stood in the black corset, chemise,

and silk stockings waiting for the countess to return to help her slip into the sapphire gown while absorbing everything she'd told her.

Booted footsteps sounded on the marble vestibule floor, then became muffled on the carpet runner on the stairs. Adeline hurried to shut the bedchamber door just as Warwick strode inside.

"What in the world is so important that—"

It was like colliding with a solid wall of masculine perfection. Adeline tilted her face upward to meet his shocked gaze. "Warwick."

"Adeline."

He held her by her upper arms, and she was grateful for his support. His sizzling green gaze lowered to her chest, where her breasts swelled above the corset. Her chest expanded, and she found it hard to breathe.

"Good God. What's going on?" His voice was rough.

"I'm getting dressed." Her voice sounded weak to her own ears.

"I can see that. Why call me here?"

"I didn't."

"Lady Heywood's servant said I was needed to…" He shook his head as if clearing his thoughts or his vision or both. "Never mind. I'll leave."

"Wait! We have a dilemma. I'm guessing her ladyship is responsible. She told me to seduce you."

His nostrils flared. "Seduce me? I should walk right out this door." He made no move to leave, and his thumbs traced circles on her upper arms. Her skin prickled pleasurably.

"I would agree, however, I fear she would doubt everything if you depart now."

His eyebrows drew together. "You're right, dammit. We need to convince her."

"She said we should find stolen moments to kiss."

"Did she?"

"And that other young ladies find ways to entice prospective gentlemen to act." Adeline licked her lips and his gaze immediately lowered to her mouth.

"By *act* I assume she means to propose marriage?"

"I'm certain of it."

"It wouldn't shock me." He released her. "Still, I'll go and—"

"No!" She held up a hand. Her initial panic from Lady Heywood's machinations veered into a heightened awareness of the virile man standing before her. Lady Heywood may have gone about it badly, but if she had even a sliver of doubt, then they needed to douse all her suspicions once and for all.

Shockingly, the thought didn't frighten her. Rather, a traitorous anticipation snaked through her body as she looked up at him. "Perhaps we should oblige her." Heart

pounding, she walked to the entry, shut the
door, then leaned against the wood and faced
him. Their gazes met, sizzling hot awareness
tingling down her spine.

"Perhaps we should." His green eyes were
captivating.

She stepped away from the closed door.
Then they met halfway, and she was in his
strong arms. He swooped down to capture
her lips. She was just as eager, just as greedy
to kiss him. Openmouthed, their tongues
tangled. The need that had been building between them for days combusted. He kissed
her like a man consumed, and her fingers dug
into his shoulders, then burrowed into his
hair. His strong arms lifted her up and
pressed her against him. Her soft curves
molded to every hard angle of his body. Her
breasts swelled and her corset grew even
tighter as she dragged in a breath.

He was not satisfied for long, and soon hot
kisses traveled down her throat to the swells
of her breasts above the corset. "You are a
sight for sore eyes. I never stood a chance
walking into this room, did I?" His breath
was a rasp against her skin.

"Do you want a chance?" She tilted her
head to the side to give him better access. Her
nipples hardened beneath silk from his hot
breath.

"Not right now, no. Thank God you shut

that door." He dipped a finger inside the corset and dragged a thumb across a taut nipple. Then he lifted the entire breast out and sucked it full into his hot mouth. Her limbs turned weak, and she sagged against him. The slick rasp of his tongue warmed a secret, aching place between her thighs. She dug her fingers into his hair and cradled him against her breasts.

He moaned. Or was that her? "Oh my, Warwick."

"Does it feel good?"

She clung to him, unable to think. If it felt this good to have his mouth on her breasts, what would it feel like to have him touch her elsewhere? "Goodness, I can't breathe. My corset is too tight."

"Take the blasted thing off." His fingers were at her back in a flash, and he nearly ripped the laces until she was free of the corset and it fell to the carpet. Her silk chemise was a wispy barrier between them. Her breasts swelled and her nipples strained against the sheer fabric.

"Is that better?"

"A bit." She was still breathless. She wanted more. More kissing. More touching. And definitely more of him. Her hands landed on his waistcoat. He dressed as a gentleman in town—waistcoat, cravat, and jacket—and she longed for the simplicity of the country where he'd often dress only in a shirt and trousers. She fidgeted with the waistcoat's buttons. His hands landed over hers, halting her.

"I want to see you," she protested.

"It's not wise. This wasn't supposed to happen again. I'm trying to remember our agreement." His breathing was harsh. Despite his words, he held her tight, and his green eyes blazed with desire as he watched her.

"I remember it, too, but we have to convince everyone."

"I thought we were doing that."

"Wise has nothing to do with how I'm aching right now."

His lips were a whisper away from hers. "Good God. You are everything a man could desire and more."

He picked her up, cupped her buttocks, and pressed her softness against his erection. A shiver of excitement pulsed in her veins. Taking two steps he lay her on the mattress and climbed on top of her. Her lids slid open. He was a towering hulk of dominant, virile male. She should be frightened. Instead, she wanted him with an intensity that was startling.

"I want to study you. Every inch of your flesh."

"Like one of your experiments?"

"No. Never like that. I want to savor you."

He buried his head in her breasts, teasing

and laving first one nipple, then the other. Each tug of his lips was like a lick of flame causing the aching bud between her legs to throb. He lifted the edge of her shift, and his palm skimmed the silk stocking and fingered the red bow where the stocking ended and the soft flesh of her thigh began. Inch by inch, he peeled off one stocking, then the other. If he didn't touch her where she ached, she would go mad.

Her eyelids fluttered open. "I feel like I'm going to combust."

"Where?"

"Everywhere."

"I can help with that."

His fingers found the aching bud between her thighs. The rough pad of his finger made her slick with need.

"Is that the spot?"

She whimpered. "Oh yes. Right *there*."

The fervent need on his face rivaled her own passion as he rose above her. He slipped his hands beneath her, cupped her buttocks, and lowered his head between her legs. She squealed in surprise and rose on her elbows.

He glanced up at her, his eyes darkening with lust. "Relax. Trust me."

He gently parted her tender folds, and his hot breath brushed her swollen, sensitive nerves. Then he kissed her *there*. His tongue licked, laved, and sucked, leaving her a

quivering mass of nerves. Her thoughts frag-
mented from the erotic pleasure, and molten
need exploded in her veins. She grew wild
beneath him, her fingers tangling in his hair,
holding him close. Blessedly, he knew just
where to touch and where to stroke. She'd
been cold and now she was fiery hot, and she
surrendered completely to his masterful seduction. He dipped a finger inside her, sucked
her aching bud, and the hot tide of passion
raged. She quivered at his low growl of approval against her skin. Then she dug her feet
into the mattress, arched into his mouth, and
her world upended as passion radiated from
the soft core of her body.

He cradled her in his strong arms and
whispered words of praise against her throat.

For something that was wrong, it felt so
right.

. . .

Warwick held Adeline in his arms as they lay
on the coverlet of her rose canopied bed. His
heart pounded in his chest, and he kissed the
top of her silky hair. The lavender scent
teased his senses. "This wasn't supposed to
happen."

Blue eyes looked up to meet his. "Do you
regret it?"

"No." He brushed her lips.

She sighed. "Good. Neither do I. I wouldn't

take back a single moment."

"Heathen."

Her smile was brilliant and breathtaking. A siren's smile that could easily lure a man to her side. It was just his luck. He'd entered a pact with the most enticing, intriguing woman in all of England. Smart, determined, independent. Giving and sensual. Looking at her swollen lips and flushed cheeks, she was burgeoning with sexuality, and he was far from immune. For a man who prided himself on his control and had never fallen victim to a woman, he'd lost all restraint.

"How long have we been alone?" she asked.

He glanced at the mantel clock. "Almost twenty minutes."

She sighed and stretched. His gaze was riveted on her sinuous limbs. "Only twenty minutes? I feel like I've reached the moon and the stars and fallen back to Earth."

He was hard as rock in his trousers. Sexual need raged with protectiveness. He was aware of where they were—in her bed in her bedchamber. Christ, he hadn't known what type of feminine trap he'd walked into. He truly hadn't stood a chance.

His godmother may have concocted the encounter, but he wouldn't put Adeline in danger of discovery by servants.

She wiggled her backside against him. He

grit his teeth against a rush of desire.

"What about you?" Adeline turned in his arms and traced a finger down his waistcoat. "I know enough about what occurs between a man and a woman to know that you haven't—"

"I'm fine." His voice was hoarse. As a healer and midwife, he knew she knew.

But she didn't really *know*.

She bit her lush lower lip. "Do you think your godmother heard?"

His gaze dropped to her mouth and his skin grew tight and hot. Did she realize how she affected him? "You were quite loud. Besides, she is smart enough to know her machinations worked, and she shouldn't feel the need to stage another."

A beautiful flush crept over her cheeks. "What will you tell her?"

"Nothing. I will leave all to her imagination. Meanwhile, you should know that I'm escorting you, my godmother, and Mary to a party tomorrow."

"I hadn't heard. I'm not sure Mary will attend."

"She already confirmed with my godmother."

"I'm surprised and grateful." She reached up to give him a quick kiss.

Her lips were whisper soft against his, and she looked at him like she wanted him to kiss her again. What he wouldn't give to stay in bed with her in his arms. To make slow, satisfying love to her. To possess her and mark her as his own.

His own.

God, what was he thinking? That wasn't part of their arrangement, none of this was. She was a virgin, and it wasn't fair to her. One day she would find the man of her dreams, a man who loved and adored her—a man she loved in return. That was what she wanted, had always wanted. He couldn't give her that. A strange sense of disappointment hammered at the thought. He shoved it aside and rose first.

"Let me help you with your dress." It took several attempts with the tiny buttons. For a man who could fine-tune an engine with ease, his fingers felt like sausages.

"Thank you." She turned and made an attempt to smooth her hair.

If she knew his thoughts, she shouldn't thank him, but run. His gaze traveled over her from head to toe, drinking her in. Disheveled hair. Swollen lips. Heavy-lidded eyes. She looked like a fallen woman, completely different from her normal appearance. *Warwick's woman.* Rather than be shocked, the selfish part of him rather liked it.

CHAPTER FOURTEEN

"Thank you for escorting me to Lady Trehorn's party, Your Grace," Mary said as she looked up at the duke. "My brother, Lord Foster, could not attend."

"It is my pleasure. Besides, I've wanted to get better acquainted. Lady Adeline speaks highly of you," Warwick said.

Adeline watched the pair as they waited in line to greet their hostess, Lady Trehorn.

Mary's gaze scanned the mingling guests. "This gathering is a refreshing change from the other events this Season."

The party was a guise for an art viewing where a hundred guests had been invited to see the new statue of the hostess's late husband, Lord Trehorn. A large cloth was draped over the statue in the center of the large garden. The white cloth billowed in a slight breeze and reminded Adeline of a ghost.

Mary must have thought the same. "It looks like the late lordship is present in spirit."

"It is disconcerting," Adeline agreed.

Their hostess was a ridiculously wealthy widow and Warwick's godmother's close friend. Lady Heywood waved from the refreshment table where she was speaking with a group of ladies.

The guests were an interesting mix of titled and gentry. One didn't need a title to secure an invitation to one of Lady Trehorn's parties.

"Lady Trehorn is known to be a bit different. It's no wonder my godmother is friends with her," Warwick said.

Mary smiled. "Then our hostess is someone I'd like as well."

Adeline let out a breath of relief at her sister's lightened mood. Mary had been despondent ever since the experience at the publisher's office. To see her sister smile, even a small smile, lit Adeline's heart.

"I see Miss Hart," Mary said. "We both had the same pianoforte instructor and we met at a recital years ago."

"Go ahead and say hello," Adeline urged.

Adeline waited until Mary was out of hearing before giving Warwick a sidelong glance. She'd relived memories of their heated encounter in her bedchamber in her dreams. She'd experienced passion in his arms. He hadn't been unaffected, either, and she'd never forget the fire that had heated his green gaze. Awareness thundered through her, hot and unwelcome. She couldn't think of that now. Not here.

She gave a slight tug on Warwick's sleeve to gain his attention. "Why are we really here?"

The corner of his lips tilted, and he lowered his head. "Whatever do you mean?"

A tremor unfurled through her at his closeness. She shoved it away. "This is hardly the event to cause gossip. Lady Trehorn usually manages that all on her own. It's rumored the statue of her late husband is scantily clad."

Warwick arched a dark eyebrow. "Fascinating."

"Not all rumors are true, of course." Adeline tilted her head and studied him. "Are you thinking to distract me from my question?"

A gleam of humor lit his eyes. "I'm not surprised you noticed. Wait and you shall see."

Adeline's breath caught. She couldn't help herself. His mischievous expression had captured her interest and made her heartbeat quicken. *What is he up to?*

Just then, Lady Trehorn clapped her hands twice and gained everyone's attention.

"I know you have all been impatient to see Lord Trehorn's statue. I wouldn't dream of making my guests wait until the end of my party." With the aplomb of an experienced auctioneer, the lady tugged the cloth away from the statue. The cloth billowed in a white cloud before settling at the foot of a bronze replica of her husband. The crowd drew in a collective breath. The rumors were partly correct. The late Lord Trehorn wore an open shirt, no cravat, and his shirtsleeves rolled up to his elbows. The muscles at his throat and chest were delineated. His thigh muscles were clearly visible beneath his breeches. His hunting dog sat at his bronzed feet.

The crowd grew silent. The artist was skilled, but the portrayal was far from the reality. Lord Trehorn had been middle-aged with a sagging middle. And he certainly never wore an open shirt. Lady Trehorn's memory was flawed.

"Let us celebrate with champagne!" Lady Trehorn waved a hand and a group of liveried servers carrying trays of flutes of bubbly champagne marched outside in a well-orchestrated line. The guests let out an audible sigh as they availed themselves of the alcoholic refreshments.

Warwick fetched two glasses of champagne from a passing servant and handed one to Adeline. "At least she waited until her husband had passed to commission such a statue. Had she not, I think the portrayal would have caused his heart to give out."

Adeline stifled a laugh with her free hand. The champagne bubbles teased her nose. "You are probably right."

Out of the corner of her eye, she noticed a man wave down a server to place his empty champagne flute on a tray and snatch up a full one.

Her stomach tensed. "That's Mr. Elder, the publisher! The one who wanted to pay only ten measly pounds for Mary's novel."

"Is it?" Warwick's voice was light.

Yet something in the duke's voice made her turn and eye him suspiciously. "Did you know Mr. Elder would be here?"

"Perhaps. Go and fetch Mary."

Her sister was smiling and talking with the friend she'd seen earlier. Adeline shook her head. "No. It will upset Mary to see that horrible man, and I don't want to ruin her happy mood."

"Trust me. This time will be different."

There was a visible harshness in the set of his chiseled jaw and the narrowing of his gaze, but a raw honesty as well. He wouldn't go out of his way to hurt her sister. She was sure of it. She did trust him.

His nod of encouragement was all it took. Adeline hurried to her sister and tapped her on the shoulder.

Mary turned away from Miss Hart. "Is something amiss, Adeline?"

"The duke is asking for you."

"Whatever for?"

"I've learned to just go along with some of his requests. They can be surprising. I believe this may be one of them."

They returned to Warwick's side. Adeline knew the moment Mary recognized Mr. Elder by her quick intake of breath.

Mr. Elder looked just as surprised as the trio approached. "Your Grace. Miss…"

"Lady Adeline," Warwick said. "I believe you are already acquainted with her sister, Lady Mary."

"Ah, yes." Mr. Elder cleared his throat. "The writer." Turning away from the women, he looked at Warwick, clearly uncomfortable.

"I was told you tried to steal Lady Mary's manuscript, offering to pay her a pittance for it." Warwick's tone was conversational. Adeline wasn't fooled. His green eyes were like ice.

Elder shifted his feet. "I beg your pardon, Your Grace," he sputtered. "As I told them before, they are mistaken. I do not steal."

"Ten pounds for the work of M.J. Price is theft to me."

"Publishing is a complex business."

"So it seems. I've heard that Mr. Winter, another publisher I assume you are familiar with, as he is your rival, has expressed interest in the lady's novel."

"Mr. Winter!" Mr. Elder straightened his spine, but even so reached only to Warwick's chest.

"Yes, the gentleman has asked for Mary to send him the manuscript for consideration.

As a smart businessman, I suspect he realizes Lady Mary's book will earn the publisher a good deal of money. I'll also be sure to tell my godmother, Lady Heywood, who is a fan of M.J. Price. I anticipate her friends will be thrilled to discover M.J. Price is a woman."

Elder rubbed his chin with his thumb and forefinger. "Perhaps I was a bit hasty."

Warwick clucked his tongue. "It's too late. What is the saying? One man's loss is another man's gain."

Mr. Elder blinked.

Mary's blue eyes twinkled, and Adeline knew it took heroic effort for her not to laugh in the man's face.

"Come along, ladies. Servants just wheeled out more refreshments. I've heard Lady Trehorn's hired a French pastry chef."

"Is it true?" Mary asked once they had left Mr. Elder behind. "Has Mr. Winter expressed an interest in my manuscript even knowing that a woman wrote it?"

"Yes," Warwick said. "Mr. Winter has yet to read your manuscript and you will be competing with other writers to gain publication, but he is genuinely interested in your work."

Mary's enthusiasm was clear as she leaped forward to hug Warwick and place a chaste kiss on his cheek. "Thank you for the introduction to Mr. Winter, Your Grace. I will submit my best work and dazzle the publisher."

"I have no doubt," Warwick said.

A tingling warmth rushed through Adeline. She waited until Mary left to return to Miss Hart before asking what was on her mind. "You did that for Mary?"

"Do you want an honest answer?"

"Of course."

"I did it for you. I do not like to see you unhappy, and I know you care for your sister."

"I—"

"I also happen to think Mary is a charming and talented young lady. Mr. Winter has attended my scientific group on occasion. He isn't an inventor but is a highly intelligent man who enjoys reading scientific journals in the evening. All I had to do was mention Mary's pseudonym. He has read her short stories and is a smart businessman who isn't afraid to acquire a talented female author. I was truthful. I'm confident Mary will be able to sell her manuscript to Mr. Winter on her own. Besides, it was a pleasure for me to aid her."

A familiar tug and twist centered in her chest when she looked up at him. Warwick had gone to the trouble of making her sister happy. She'd initially thought the duke selfish, engrossed in his own strange world, a man too preoccupied with himself to care for others. But there was so much more to him.

And the more she discovered, the more she liked, despite herself.

. . .

"When you visited Mary the other afternoon," Hasmik began, "Lady Heywood had a group of ladies over for tea."

"I assume you attended the gathering," Adeline said.

They were in Adeline's bedchamber and Hasmik was helping her change from a morning walking dress into a serviceable dress without lace or trim. She was to travel to the home of a Lebanese woman who suffered from repeated morning nausea from pregnancy.

"Yes. Lady Heywood treats me as a guest." Adeline stepped out of the walking dress, and Hasmik shook the garment, then hung it in the wardrobe.

"She's a kind woman." Adeline wasn't surprised. Lady Heywood could be a bit eccentric, especially when it came to her views of the sexes, but she was not prejudiced and would have included Hasmik with her friends.

"The lady isn't just kind. She makes one feel like a loaf of freshly baked bread."

The Arabic saying was not lost on Adeline. She could never be upset with Lady Heywood for artfully arranging her encounter with Warwick the prior afternoon. As Warwick's godmother, she meant the best for the duke, even if the lady's machinations had resulted in Warwick walking in on Adeline half dressed in her ballgown. As for what happened afterward...that passionate encounter was entirely their doing.

"It's not the tea I want to talk about, but what the other women discussed. The talk was not just about you and the duke, although you two did come up once or twice. They talked about the upcoming Kirkland ball." Hasmik helped Adeline into the plainer dress and began working on the row of buttons on the back of the garment.

"It is a big event. The last big ball of the Season."

"Many of the *beau monde* will stay in London for a short while, then leave for their lavish country estates. It made me think of your future."

Adeline knew Hasmik was referring to the end of her "courtship" with the duke. "The Season isn't over yet."

"Hmm. Why do I sense you are glad there is more time?"

"Not glad. Just pointing out the truth. There are a few less formal events remaining, and most do not immediately seek the relief of their country estates." Once fully dressed, Adeline reached for a pair of well-worn brown boots that allowed her to stand for long periods of time in comfort while she worked.

"How long will you wait after the ball?" Hasmik asked.

Adeline sat on the edge of the bed and began lacing the boots. "Wait for what?"

Hasmik shook her head. "To return to Chilham and the cottage. Or have you forgotten about your plans to heal the villagers?"

Hasmik watched her carefully. The woman was wise, and she knew Adeline better than even her own mother had. Adeline had a distinct feeling she was being tested. "I suppose I shall attend one or two more events after the Kirkland ball before returning. Not longer."

Hasmik's eyes met hers, challenging. "It's not too late to turn the false into something real."

"I don't know what you mean. It takes two to make this decision."

"Time is running out, *habibti*."

"Even if I agreed, which I do not, the duke has not expressed even the slightest desire to marry."

Or that he loves me. Love was the most important requirement. It was what she wanted, had always wanted. Her parents had it. Why couldn't she find it as well?

"Hmm. Then I do think Lady Heywood is

right when it comes to her godson. He may need…what do the English say…" She snapped her fingers as the word came to her. "Prodding."

Adeline held her breath. Their attempt to convince Warwick's godmother was hard to forget. "And if I don't want to prod the man? My plans were always to return to my cottage."

"Yet I sense conflict in you. Tell me the truth. Have your intentions changed?"

"No." *Yes. Sometimes.* She wasn't sure. That was the crux of her dilemma. Now that she had come to know the man, could she walk away forever?

Even more important, was she willing to settle for less than love?

• • •

Adeline met Mary at Gunther's in Berkley Square. Above the shop was a wooden sign that featured a pineapple, a luxurious fruit that was often used in confections, beneath the confectioner's name. The shop was bustling with customers, lords and ladies. It was one of the only places a lady could be seen alone with a gentleman in the afternoon as they enjoyed the sweet delights. A few waitstaff served those seated inside. Others carrying trays of sweets hurried across the road, dodging carriages, to serve customers who preferred to remain seated in their carriages or who wished to sit outside. Adeline had fond memories of her parents taking both herself and Mary to Gunther's. They'd sit outside under a shady tree as the waitstaff delivered thick custards and refreshing ices.

Wide-eyed, Adeline and Mary stared at confections behind the glass counter inside the bustling shop. Thick custards, ices, mousses, candies, and small cakes tempted customers of every age. The flavors were as varied as the sweets, chocolate, lavender, Parmesan, bergamot, chamomile, pineapple, saffron, and others.

"What would you like today?" Adeline asked Mary.

"Pistachio."

"Good choice. I'll choose lemon." The combination of the sweet and tart was Adeline's favorite anytime she visited here.

Once they ordered they sat at a table in the corner. Adeline set her reticule on the table. "Tell me what is so exciting that you insisted we meet here."

"I submitted my manuscript to Mr. Winter. He wants to publish it using my name—my real name."

Adeline's mouth parted and she reached out to clutch Mary's hand across the table. "Oh, Mary! That's wonderful news. I'm proud of you."

"I owe Warwick my thanks for the introduction."

"Yes, but you sold it on *your* own. Never forget that."

A shy smile lit Mary's face. "Yes, I did. Didn't I?"

Just then a waiter delivered their ices in glass dishes. Adeline picked up her spoon and smiled. "I'm honored to be your sister."

Mary wrinkled her nose. "Posh! I'm the lucky one. Now, what better way to celebrate than ices?"

They both raised their spoons. The lemon ice tasted even sweeter than Adeline remembered.

• • •

A week later, the Kirkland ball was upon them. If all went as planned, soon Adeline would be able to return to the country, free of Edwin's schemes. She'd told Hasmik she would stay for one or two more small parties, no longer. If Mr. Stan Slade sought a marriage with a daughter of the aristocracy, then he'd best find another match before then.

As they waited at the top of the ballroom stairs for a liveried majordomo to announce her arrival with the countess, Adeline took in the glittering scene spread out before her.

The colorful silks and satins of the ladies along with an abundance of precious gems of

diamond, ruby, sapphire, and emerald, sparkled beneath hundreds of candles in crystal
chandeliers. The gentlemen were dashing
with their striped and paisley waistcoats, crisp
cravats, and polished shoes. White pillars
graced the ballroom's entrance and marble
statues rested in oval niches. Artwork hung
on the walls in a display of decadent wealth.

Adeline smoothed her gown, the rich sapphire silk rippling beneath her hand. The
dressmaker was skilled, and the dress was
truly spectacular—the finest Adeline had
ever owned. Her hair was upswept in an elegant chignon and her maid had applied a
dash of rouge to her cheeks and lips.

"You are the mystery everyone is whispering about," Lady Heywood remarked.

"I've been in Town for some time now and
have been out and about, so hardly mysterious."

"Yes, you have been out and about—with
Warwick by your side. The duke has never
been fond of social events or any romantic
entanglement. Now he's been seen engaged
in both. You intrigue them."

It was exactly what she'd wanted. What
both had wanted.

"Smile. Chin up. Shoulders back. Remember to smile."

"Was I not smiling?" She sounded scared,
which scared her even more.

"I didn't mean to alarm you. You look stunning, my dear."

The lady's words reassured her. Rather than focus on the crowd before her, Adeline looked to the majordomo. A middle-aged man dressed in a red coat with gold trim, white breeches and stockings, and a powdered wig, he motioned for them to approach the top of the stairs.

His voice echoed off the marble pillars. "The Countess of Heywood and Lady Adeline Cameron."

Head held high, Adeline smiled as she descended the stairs.

Their progress was slow as they wove through the thick of the crowd. Eventually, others parted to allow them passage. She was aware of eyes watching her behind fluttering fans, while gentlemen nodded and smiled.

"Wonderful. It's as if you have never left Town," the countess said.

They reached Lady Kirkland, and the countess made the introductions. "This is Lady Adeline Cameron. I've had the privilege of having her stay with me this Season." Lady Heywood's voice was loud enough for those around them to hear.

Other women joined them, Lady Jersey and Lady Cowper, two influential patronesses of Almack's.

Lady Jersey fanned herself and smiled at

Adeline. "There is one Wednesday night assembly left of the season. I shall send you a voucher to Almack's."

Adeline knew vouchers were coveted. "You are too kind, my lady."

As soon as the two ladies departed to mingle with others, Lady Heywood drew Adeline aside. "A voucher! You did well, my dear."

"Lady Jersey and Lady Cowper are both kind."

"Posh! Kind has nothing to do with it. You are the talk of the *ton*. The patroness cannot turn you away."

"They anticipate the duke will attend as well, don't they?"

"Smart and perceptive. Warwick is quite besotted, and I can see why. You are beautiful inside and out, my dear." She clasped her fan to her chest. "I have no doubt that my godson will whisk you to the altar soon before some other buck has a mind to steal you from him."

Adeline wanted to hug Lady Heywood. Or cry. She was torn by conflicting emotions. She was prevented from hugging the countess by the intrusion of a too familiar masculine voice.

"Good evening, my lady. Adeline."

Adeline spun around, her happiness dissipating like a puff of smoke, and her stomach plummeting at the sight of her half brother.

"Hello, Edwin." Bile rose in her throat as she smiled.

Edwin was handsome enough with his fair hair fashioned in the *Brutus* style that was favored by Beau Brummell himself. The cut of his burgundy coat and gold embroidered waistcoat emphasized his athletic build. If one didn't know his personality, one could understand the young debutantes' interest in him.

"Good evening, Lord Foster," Lady Heywood said. "Pardon me while I say hello to friends."

Left alone with Edwin, Adeline squared her shoulders.

"I saw you speaking with Lady Jersey and Lady Cowper. No doubt the countess's influence has others forgetting about your heathen blood."

She let out a held-in breath. He truly wasn't worth her ire. "What do you want, Edwin?"

"Where is the lofty duke?"

"I imagine you will see him shortly."

"Are you sure? He's been noticeably absent and has made no appointment to see me."

"I am of legal age." At twenty-three years old, she didn't require his permission to marry.

"He should ask me for your hand in marriage. It's proper for him to do so."

"Is that why you are speaking to me? Or are you concerned about other matters? Have you found the funds to pay the money-lender?"

His lips twisted in irritation. "Do not think you have escaped unscathed, Adeline."

Fury and fear erupted within her, and she fought for control. "So you say. You should be focused on the earldom and your debt, not your half-heathen sister. As far as I'm concerned, *you* are not worthy of the earldom."

A vein bulged at his temple, and she knew it took him great effort not to raise his fist or his voice.

She was saved by Lady Heywood appearing by her side. Edwin bowed and made a quick retreat.

"What's wrong, Adeline? You look flushed. Please do not worry. We both know Warwick isn't known for his punctuality."

"Thank you for your concern. I'm sure he will arrive," Adeline said.

"Good. Until then, I say enjoy yourself, my dear. I won't be able to hold off all the gentlemen vying for your attention, and a spin on the dance floor never hurt a lady's confidence."

Directly following Lady Heywood's prediction of male attention, three gentlemen approached. She barely heard their introductions. A baron. A viscount. A marquess. She was tense over her confrontation with Edwin.

When Lady Heywood nodded in encouragement, the baron led Adeline off to the dance floor for a country dance. If the dance could take her mind off her worries, then she would embrace the dance with all her effort. She parted and met her partner, turned, and had just taken his arm when, through the length of the ballroom, she spotted Warwick at the top of the stairs.

She watched, entranced, as he approached Lord Drake and a group of other men and began speaking with them. The duke's tall frame stood out above the thick of the crowd. For a man who rarely graced a ballroom, he exuded an air of command and confidence, a duke who demanded obedience and respect. He didn't appear awkward or inept, but at ease as he spoke with his peers. His meticulously tailored black and white evening clothes were in stark contrast to the colorful coats and patterned waistcoats preferred by other men. His powerful build made her heart race, and the perfection of his features attracted more than one female eye.

But it was everything beneath the surface that captivated her as well. His keen intelligence. His regard for her thoughts and dreams. His consideration to help her sister.

He was hers.

For a little while longer, he was hers. In

bed the prior evening, she'd tossed and turned, thinking of her conversation with Hasmik.

Had her dreams changed?

She'd relived how his kisses and skilled fingers had made her feel, how easily she'd abandoned herself to the wild whirl of passion in his arms. It was incredible and freeing. Their charade had turned into more than she'd expected and a part of her, a frightening part, feared its ending.

Was she ready to part ways without experiencing more of the man?

CHAPTER FIFTEEN

Watching Adeline talk to other men, dance with them, smile at any of them, made Warwick's gut clench and a muscle tic by his eye. A roaring possessiveness coursed through him, and he knew he had no right to feel the way he did.

But he did.

Dammit. I do.

He was aware of his godmother's approach. "May I ask Lady Kirkland to announce your engagement to Adeline tonight, Your Grace?"

"No." He didn't miss the flash of suspicion in her gaze or the challenge in her voice. He looked away.

"What is going on between you two?"

"The same thing that goes on between any courting couple."

She accepted a flute of champagne from a liveried servant and took a sip. "She is right for you, Daniel. I see it now more than ever. Do not let her slip away."

Another man walked up to Adeline and engaged her in conversation. He very obviously peered down at the swell of her breasts above her bodice as she danced with him. Frustration boiled in Warwick's chest. He'd buried his face in the lushness of her flesh, tasted her. Rather than satiate his need, it had heightened it.

"Be careful, Daniel. You look like you're ready to challenge the chap she's dancing with to a duel. Or worse, a boxing match."

A bare-fisted match sounded like a good idea. "Will you do something for me?" Warwick asked.

"Anything."

He leaned down to whisper his request in her ear. The dance had ended, and his feet moved of their own volition. He tapped the shoulder of the man engaged with Adeline.

"I believe the lady promised me this next dance," Warwick said.

Two pairs of eyes turned to him.

Before either could respond, Warwick took Adeline's arm and led her away.

Brilliant blue eyes blinked up at him. "That was quite abrupt, Your Grace."

"Was it?"

"Quite."

"Have I done something to upset you?" she asked.

"No. Dance with me."

"I suppose people will watch."

"It's what we want, isn't it?"

The truth was he couldn't care about causing gossip at the moment. All he cared about was holding Adeline in his arms. He led her farther onto the dance floor just as the orchestra began the first strains of a waltz. He was vaguely aware of ladies gasping and tittering at the newest, scandalous dance being played at the ball. He'd have to thank his godmother later.

Adeline tugged on his sleeve. "Warwick! Are you sure about this—"

"Yes." He placed a hand by her waist and waited.

She allowed a long moment to pass before slipping a gloved hand in his and placing the other on his shoulder. A flicker of panic reflected in the blue depth of her eyes. "I haven't waltzed since last season."

"Neither have I."

She bit her bottom lip. "That isn't reassuring."

His gaze was drawn to where her white teeth tugged at her lip. He wanted to kiss her there, to ease her nervousness. Instead, he began to lead, and they twirled across the dance floor in perfect unison.

Her breath caught and her magnificent breasts rose and fell in her tight bodice. Her blue eyes rose to his. "You lied! You are an exceptional dancer."

"I've mentioned that my mother insisted on dancing instruction."

Her lips parted. "Yes, but the waltz is different and newer. You should have warned me."

"What would be the fun in that? Spontaneity attracts attention." He lowered his head and whispered, "See how they all watch."

Her eyes were wide as saucers. "You are not helping."

"Think of something else."

Her gaze never left his. "The truth is I'm finding it difficult to stop thinking about our afternoon encounter in my bedchamber. Have you thought of it at all?"

Hell yes. He'd thought of little else the past couple of days. Not even his work had been able to distract him. "It wasn't smart."

"I know. Our agreement," she said. "But I told you I didn't regret closing that door."

It was near impossible for Warwick not to pull her flush against him, to kiss her on the dance floor for all to see. To claim her as his.

Madness.

He pulled his attention back to the dance floor. On Adeline's lovely face. Her eyebrows drew together. "I'm feeling a bit breathless, Your Grace."

"It's the dance."

She shook her head. "But I am fit. I believe in vigorous exercise and walk in the park each day with Hasmik."

Vigorous exercise. He imaged another type of activity they could do together. Visions of Adeline's smooth, strong legs wrapped about his waist as he thrust inside her made him stiffen in his trousers.

Holy hell. Not here. Not now. He had little control when she was near. She was right. The dance wasn't helping. He tried to calm his own racing heart and quell his desire for the woman in his arms.

"It's working though," she said. "Everyone is watching us."

"Good." His voice was gruff.

Her gaze darted to the side. "Even Edwin is staring. And he's frowning something fierce. Am I a bad person for feeling satisfaction from his ire?"

"No."

He spun her and his legs brushed her skirts. His fingers spread and brushed the underside of her breast. His body felt heavy and warm. The dance was coming to an end. He was loathe to let her go.

"Warwick, I want to be honest with you. I want to do it again."

"Another dance?"

"Don't be silly. I want to kiss again. All last night, I couldn't stop thinking about how I fell apart in your arms."

She'd bring him to his knees right then and there on the dance floor. He stared in her eyes and knew it was no feminine trap, and that she was experiencing a burgeoning desire. It was more alluring to him than the wiles of a practiced courtesan. There was only one course of action. The dance had ended, and he led her to the open French doors in the pretense of gaining air. Then, when he was certain they wouldn't attract attention, he swept her right out of the ballroom and onto the terrace.

She gasped. "Warwick!"

Without releasing her hand, he hurried down the stairs and into the dim garden until they were secluded in the shadows of trees. Moonlight illuminated her upturned face. Her beauty tugged at his soul.

"You want to kiss again? Here? Now?"

"Yes."

Her eyes glittered with excitement and blossoming sexuality. It was impossible for any man to resist, and Warwick didn't try. His mouth swooped down to capture hers. She sighed, then melted into his embrace, kissing him back with a fervent passion that matched his own. A burning, consuming need exploded through his veins. He pressed her against an oak tree, and the low-cut bodice was down, and her lush breasts filled his hands. His thumbs traced the hardened nipples and her mewling sound reverberated like a firecracker in his skull.

"I'll combust if I don't have you here and now," he murmured against her lips.

"Yes. *Yes.* I feel the same."

His breath grew ragged as if he'd run the perimeter of the Kirkland's vast gardens. "No, Adeline. You don't know what you're saying."

Her fingers dug into his biceps. "I do. I feel a burning ache for you."

"Where? Show me?"

She clutched his shoulders and arched up, offering her breasts to his hungry gaze. Whatever constraint he had, snapped. He suckled and teased one rosy nipple, then the other. He pulled her between his legs, and she rubbed against him, seeking friction. He reached for the hem of her gown, touched her garter, desperate to feel the slick folds of her femininity. Desperate to plunge balls deep in her hotness and possess her once and for all.

She arched against his leg and moaned. "Oh Warwick."

"Warwick! I say Warwick. Are you out here?"

Warwick pulled away just as Lord Drake came around the corner. "What is it, man?" He moved to block Adeline from his friend's view. Sexual frustration raged inside him like a hot tide.

Drake took in the scene, but it seemed to make no impression on him. There was a wildness in his gaze. "The babe is coming! Christ! It's too early. Ana needs Adeline."

• • •

Adeline threw open the duke's carriage door before the wheels came to a full stop. She ran into the Drake residence and sprinted up the stairs. A housekeeper was waiting and led her straight into the bedchamber.

"Ana!" Adeline called out.

Lady Drake was on the bed. Pale, sweating, and in the throes of a painful contraction, she lifted a hand and cried out, "It's too soon. Dear God, it's too soon!"

Adeline hurried to her side and took her hand. "I'm going to examine you now."

Ana nodded, and Adeline lifted the cotton gown. She was already dilated, and from the strength of the contractions, Adeline knew the birth was coming fast. Then she felt the lady's swollen abdomen, and Adeline drew in a harsh breath.

The baby was breech.

Dear God. A breech birth complicated the delivery. Some doctors claimed only one could survive—the mother or the babe.

Adeline didn't believe in those odds.

Looking into the woman's anguished face, Adeline reached for her resolve.

Asvads! She prayed for her mother to guide her.

. . .

Another scream came from upstairs. Drake was in a panicked state. Warwick had to physically restrain his friend from bursting out of the room and heading for the grand staircase.

"Try to stay calm," Warwick said.

"Easy for you to say. The babe is early, too early."

"Nothing will happen. Have another whisky." Warwick splashed a good amount of the golden liquid into two glasses and handed one to his friend.

Warwick ran a hand down his face as he watched his friend pace the Aubusson carpet. It had been hours. He didn't know much about the delivery of babies, but he knew something was wrong from the screams and the apprehension on the housekeeper's face as she carried up buckets of hot water and clean linens.

"Life is so short, so precious. The gift of true love comes only once in a lifetime. If I lose her, I won't survive it."

Warwick was struck by the words. Jagged thoughts came to him in a flash. Adeline outside her home the first time he'd seen her. Adeline boldly shutting the bedroom door and kissing him after his godmother arranged to have them together. Adeline in the bookshop, sitting beside him, her blue eyes alight as they whispered behind a newspaper. He knew nothing about love. He knew mathematics and engineering and how to increase the efficiency of a train's engine. Then along came Adeline—a rare gift that came once in a lifetime.

Another scream and Warwick nearly had to tackle his friend to keep him in the room.

Then, mercifully, they heard the baby's cry.

•••

Drake sank to his knees by his wife's side. Warwick hovered in the doorway, not wanting to interfere in the private moment. Adeline nodded at him and headed for the doorway.

"Adeline," Lady Drake called out. "Thank you. You saved my baby."

Adeline smiled at the new parents, then stepped outside and quietly shut the door behind her. She looked up at Warwick. "It's a girl."

Warwick's gaze traveled over her from head to toe. Her dark hair had been styled in a chignon for the ball tonight, and wisps of unruly curls had escaped to frame her heart-shaped face. Perspiration beaded her brow, and blood stained her sapphire ballgown. She'd never looked more beautiful to him. He held out his arms.

"Oh Warwick." She sank into his embrace, her head resting on his chest. "I feared she would die. Or the baby."

His heartbeat thundered in his chest. "But

neither did. Both are safe and alive thanks to you."

She shuddered and his arms tightened around her.

"Come," he said. "I'll take you home."

She nodded, then stepped back. A frown marred her brow. "Wait! You're bleeding."

Warwick followed her gaze. He'd removed his coat hours ago and tossed it across one of the armchairs. He'd opened his wound when he'd restrained Drake from fleeing the study like a madman.

"It's nothing." It was just like Adeline to care for him after spending hours caring for Lady Drake and the baby.

She rolled up his shirtsleeve to study the extent of the injury. "Take me to your home instead."

CHAPTER SIXTEEN

The carriage stopped outside his house. If his servants thought it unusual for Adeline to attend the duke well after midnight without a chaperone, none showed it. Once Warwick informed Nelson and Mrs. Posner what had transpired at the Drake home and the birth of the earl's child, the butler and housekeeper had been eager to see to Adeline's needs.

Adeline was led to a guest chamber where a fresh, pressed dress from one of the servants had been delivered along with wine and food. A young maid helped her change out of her ruined ballgown before meeting Warwick in his ballroom workshop.

He'd removed his coat and waistcoat and had tossed them onto an armchair. Dressed in his shirtsleeves, cravat, dark trousers, and Hessians, he looked like a fierce pirate. Her gaze lowered to his arm where drops of blood stained the white linen of his sleeve. Her brow furrowed. Thankfully, she'd had the foresight to leave her prepared salve behind on her last visit to his home.

She stepped forward. "Roll up your sleeve."

"It isn't necessary."

"Do not be stubborn. I don't want my

prior treatment to go to waste if infection sets in."

"I know not to argue with you. Your salve and bandages are in the top drawer of my desk."

The newly healed skin had reopened, and Adeline hadn't exaggerated. The risk of infection was a concern. She cleaned the wound and applied a good amount of salve, then wrapped it in fresh bandages.

Once she was finished, he poured her a glass of wine from a small sideboard in the corner and motioned for her to sit on a settee. The piece of furniture hadn't been there the last time she'd visited his workshop.

"I had it moved here. I noticed a lack of seating for you."

"You were certain I'd return?" She settled on the plush blue velvet and sipped her drink. He leaned against one of his workbenches sipping his own glass of wine.

"More like hopeful."

When he said things like that, it made her want to reach for him, to kiss him. "I used the stethoscope tonight."

He cocked an eyebrow. "I assume it worked?"

"It was amazing. I could hear the mother's *and* the baby's heartbeats."

He pushed away from the workbench and sat beside her on the settee. Then, ever so slowly, he reached out to finger a loose curl that framed her face. Her lips parted, and he cupped her cheek and looked into her eyes. "You are amazing."

She closed her eyes, and he lowered his hand. She regretted the loss of his touch, the heat of his body. She'd never desired a man more than she did at that moment. He stoked a growing desire, and her whole being was filled with longing. Suddenly, she knew what she wanted. If they were to part soon, was she willing to walk away without knowing him intimately as a man?

"Warwick. I remember well our arrangement. But I think we should reconsider the terms."

"What do you mean?" He leaned against the back of the settee.

Even with the slight distance between them, he suddenly seemed far away.

"Why can't we be together? I'm not seeking to be your duchess, but to share your bed."

He swallowed. "As I said before, it's not a good idea."

"You mean it's not a good idea for you."

"No, Adeline. For you!" He shifted on the settee and leaned close, his green eyes flaring in striking intensity. "Every cell in my body aches for you. Whenever we are together, I want to kiss you. And that one time—that one short time—I was able to touch and stroke and kiss you the way I wanted, has been singed in my memory. I think of you every night. Every damned night when I lie alone in bed."

A thrill of excitement hummed in her veins at the unmistakable desire in his gaze. When she'd first met him, she'd initially thought him an academic, immune to the passions of the flesh.

She'd been wrong. So wrong.

He was as passionate as any red-blooded man. Even more than most. His restraint made him wildly attractive.

"Oh Warwick. I am a grown woman, fully capable of making my own choices. I choose you this night. I want to be your lover."

"Christ. There are consequences, dammit." He ran his fingers through his hair, pulled back the strands, then dropped his hand.

"I'm perfectly aware of the consequences. It's not my fertile time, and you can…you can withdraw."

"You trust that I have that much control?"

"I trust you." She leaned close and kissed him fully on the mouth.

Warwick kissed her back. Not just any kiss, but a consuming one. Her lips parted in supplication, and he swept inside to taste and tease. She clung to him, feeling the breadth and strength of his shoulders. Even in her inexperience, she knew there was something special between them, something as bright and hot as the sun on a glorious country day.

He lifted her onto his lap and trailed hot kisses down the column of her throat, lower still, to the swell of her breasts above the borrowed dress. She recalled the feel of his lips on her, and she wanted more. She squirmed on his lap, his hardness evident beneath layers of clothing.

His fingers went to the fastenings of her gown. The borrowed garment was a servant's dress, and as such, it didn't have dozens of hooks that required the assistance of a maid. As the fabric gaped, he placed kisses on every inch of skin. Adeline slid off his lap and slowly slid the garment off her shoulders, then over her hips. The dress pooled at her feet, and she stepped away. Warwick took in her every movement. His eyes darkened with unmistakable hunger, and a flurry of excitement made her limbs weak. She stood before him in her shift and corset. He looked at her like she was as beautiful as Venus.

"A man would have to be mad to refuse you. And despite what everyone may believe, I am not mad."

"I know." She turned and offered her back. "Help me with my stays."

"Gladly." The touch of his fingers as he loosened the ties of her stays made her breath catch. He placed a hot kiss on her shoulder that sent a shiver of delight through her. Her body ached for his touch, and she knew she wanted to be with him tonight.

Her nipples hardened beneath the thin fabric of her shift as she turned to face him. His gaze traveled her from head to toe before meeting hers. His expression was fierce, and she experienced a thrill that she could cause such a reaction in a man like Warwick.

"There's something special about you in your shift."

"You seemed to like it last time."

His large hand cupped her face and held it gently. "I liked it a lot. You were a vision then as you are now."

"I want to take off your shirt. It's only fair."

"I would not refuse you anything tonight."

She reached for his shirt and tugged it loose from his trousers. He helped her slip it over his head, then tossed it on his desk. Her greedy gaze took him in, and she swallowed. He was all lean muscle and power. A boxer's physique. His powerful shoulders were wide, and his chest had a sprinkling of hair. A trail of hair lowered down his abdomen to disappear into the waistband of his trousers. She wanted to see more of him, much more. Her fingers went to the placket of his trousers.

"Wait."

She lifted her eyes to his. "I've treated men. I've seen the male anatomy before."

"Not like this." He fingered a strap of her shift. "Let me see you first."

The shift slipped from her shoulders, grazed her hardened nipples, then fell in a wisp of fabric to her feet. She was aware of a brightly burning lantern on his desk, and suddenly, she wanted the room to be dim. The last time they were together, she hadn't been completely naked, and she worried he would think her olive complexion too dark. Prior insecurities rose in a rush.

His nostrils flared and he reached for her. "God, Adeline. You are beautiful. All that I've fantasized about and more."

Her worries eased, and her own curiosity about his body increased, and she grew bold. She had a strong urge to see him—all of him. She pressed a hand against his chest, her fingers trailing down to the muscled hardness of his abdomen.

"You are beautiful, too." She reached for a button of his placket, and this time he didn't stop her. Her fingers brushed the bulge of his manhood, and he groaned.

"Adeline."

Another button freed, and she watched, fascinated, as the tip of his erection was visible. A crimson head, smooth and thick. Then inches more until all of him was revealed to her gaze.

"Oh my." She touched the smooth head with her forefinger and a drop of clear fluid appeared. He moaned. She looked up. His eyes were closed, his expression tight. "Am I hurting you?"

"God no."

"You're right. You look nothing like my patient."

He opened his eyes and she saw stark hunger. For her. "I sure as hell hope not." He removed his trousers and kicked them aside. "Come close."

He pulled her roughly, almost violently, to him. At the first touch of naked flesh against naked flesh, they both gasped. Desire pooled low in her belly, deep between her thighs, and she throbbed for him. An invisible web of attraction had been building between them that had led to this moment. The future may be full of unknowns, yet only tonight mattered. This one night mattered.

His breath brushed her lips. "I swore I would be honorable."

"You are."

"Hardly. I am not thinking honorable thoughts right now."

"Good. Nor am I."

He shook his head, as if trying to clear his thoughts. "I can give you pleasure. Just like last time. And still not ruin you."

She ached for him. Being together was not ruin. "It's my choice, remember?"

"Then I will savor you tonight like you should be savored." He lifted her into his arms and lay her down on the couch. He took her mouth with a savage intensity, shattering thoughts, crushing promises, and leaving no doubt as to how badly he wanted her. His mouth didn't become softer as he kissed her, but even more feverish and demanding. When he finally dipped his head to her breasts, she was mindless with need. She gasped and arched in bliss.

One hand slid down her taut stomach to the swell of her hips, then lower still to her thighs. She squirmed beneath him, her body crying out for his skillful touch. Blessedly, he knew just what she cried out for. His fingers touched her between her thighs, touched her right where she was hot and swollen and pulsing. His mouth captured her groan. Her legs parted and he stroked the sensitive flesh. Need unfurled inside her, and her hips moved of their own volition. The friction was a delicious sensation, and every nerve ending in her body tightened in quivering anticipation.

"Warwick, please." She moaned his name not knowing what she was asking for.

"Easy, love." His voice was gruff and she opened her eyes to meet his heavy-lidded gaze. Whatever madness drove her, drove him as well.

He shifted above her, and his hardness slid down her slit. He looked into her eyes. "There will be pain. If I could take it upon myself, I would." Her eyes opened and she watched his handsome face above her, the fiery need in his green eyes, the tenseness in his arms as he held himself in control. For her. Her heart did a treacherous slide.

"I know." She understood. Whatever had brought them together was as inevitable as the tide.

The head of his hardness slid inside her an inch. Then another. She squirmed beneath him, wanton with need. Her breasts tingled against his hair-roughed chest. She smoothed her palms over his broad back, feeling the muscled power. Then he thrust inside her. She gasped at the invasion. She was wet and ready, but he was large.

"Are you all right?" His voice was hoarse.

She shifted her hips and the pain ebbed into a tingling pleasure. She understood mating but nothing prepared her for the fullness of him, the feeling of skin against skin, the wondrous feeling of...

One. "We are one."

He released a ragged breath against her cheek. "Yes, one."

She watched the planes of his face, the firm

jaw, the slash of eyebrows over green eyes, and her heart pounded with pleasure and with another emotion—love.

Was she falling in love with him? The thought barely crossed her mind before another followed. Could he ever love her in return?

"Warwick, I—"

He cut her off with a searing kiss that melted her heart and ratcheted her need. They became wild together, arching and thrusting, and she held on to him until her limbs quivered and passion rose in her like the hottest fire. She cried out as she peaked and soared to a shuddering ecstasy. He thrust once, twice more, then stiffened and pulled out as ropes of hot seed spurted across her belly.

. . .

Warwick's heart thundered in his chest. Withdrawing from the tight heat of Adeline's body had taken all his restraint. Warwick held her close to his heart, his limbs wrapped around her. Her eyes were closed, her lashes lush fans shielding her gaze. He caressed her arms, the side of her breast, her hips. He would never get enough of her.

Her lids fluttered open, and her brilliant blue eyes met his.

"Are you all right?" He needed to know

that he hadn't hurt her.

Her lips curved in a slow smile. "Wonderful. I'm wonderful."

He grinned like a simpleton. "I shall get you a clean cloth."

He dreaded letting her go as he fetched a cloth and dipped it in a basin of water. He cleansed the evidence of his lovemaking from her smooth skin. She reached for his arm. "Come back to me." She raised her arm.

"Adeline." Despite what she'd said, she'd been a virgin. Even more damning, he had no regrets or willpower. Damn, he wanted her again.

He returned to the couch and sat beside her. His gaze roved over her flushed breasts, the dusky-tipped nipples that he'd licked and sucked, the smooth abdomen and long legs, and the heaven he'd found between her thighs. He was afraid to hold her again, afraid he wouldn't be able to let go and would give in to the raging and swiftly building need he felt for her.

"No." She pressed a finger to his lips. "Let me speak first. I have no regrets."

"And your innocence?"

"What of it? I still plan to marry in the future."

The idea of her with another man caused a possessive roar in his head. *Christ! What is wrong with me?*

She swept her legs to the side of the couch and stood. She shook out the borrowed dress and bent to step into it. The sight of her naked backside and a glimpse of a lush breast made him hot and heavy in an instant. He closed his eyes. If he wasn't careful, he'd become obsessed or worse. Who was he fooling? He was already consumed.

This was wrong. All wrong. It was never part of their plan. "You may say you are not concerned with your innocence, but I have acted dishonorably."

"You are worried about your honor?"

"Yes."

She tilted her head to the side and regarded him, and her blue eyes were brilliant in the flickering lamplight. "I thought it might be from…from something else?"

"Something else? Like what?"

"Love." The word was whispered softly.

He scowled. "That is irrational. It's because we are of similar intellect and attracted to each other, both with strong biological needs."

A flicker crossed her lovely features, nearly a wince, but it was gone in a flash. He could almost feel the cold wave enter the room, and he realized he sounded like a cad. His struggle with feelings and emotions had come out harshly, and he wanted to explain, to fix things.

He stepped forward to gently touch her arm. "It was your first time, Adeline, and you must not confuse it with love."

"You are right, of course." She nodded once. "You needn't worry. Everything is progressing according to plan, and we can hurry now."

He tried to keep up with her change of topic. "Hurry?"

"Edwin confronted me at the ball. Time is running out for him, and he'll have to find another way to satisfy his debt. Our plan is working."

"Is it?"

"Your godmother believes you to be enamored of me. When will you tell her the truth about us?"

"I haven't decided."

"I believe I should make plans to return to Chilham."

That got his attention. "What? Why?"

"I've neglected the cottage and there is much to be done."

She was leaving? How had most of the Season passed so quickly? Before he'd met Adeline, the weeks had seemed a torturous and endless round of frivolous entertainment devised by a bored aristocracy. Now he was uncertain he wanted it to end.

"There is a need for a village healer."

He didn't want to part from her, not yet.

He rationalized his feelings. "Be careful, Adeline. Our arrangement isn't at an end. Until Stan Slade marries another heiress or daughter of the aristocracy, you are still at risk."

She bit her full bottom lip. His gaze lowered to her lush mouth. It was still swollen from his kisses.

"I understand," she said. "Like I said, Edwin must find another solution to his financial problems soon."

"Damn right, he will." He recalled the black eye and broken arm of his acquaintance. The idea of the moneylender anywhere near Adeline was unsettling.

"Will you also return to the country?" she asked.

Her fingers fastened the buttons on the front of the borrowed gown. She smoothed the bodice, and his gaze followed her movements like a randy boy.

"I suppose I'll return to Chilham. My work remains unfinished."

At the moment, he'd follow her anywhere. He finally understood the fixation of poets pouring out heart and soul, describing the charms of a beloved. He wanted to snatch a pencil from his worktable and write a sonnet about the richness of her hair and the deep sapphire her eyes turned when she came apart beneath him.

Insanity.

He had a mechanical and scientific mind. He didn't read poetry, let alone write it.

"We should start to be more mindful and not travel together. We wanted gossip, but we no longer require so much. It's best if you wait at least a week before returning."

He didn't care about propriety. He didn't want to be away from her, not yet. What he wanted was to join her on the sofa for another heated round of lovemaking.

She reached for her reticule. "Please thank your housekeeper for the dress. I shall return it straightway."

He barely heard her. Dresses didn't concern him. He wanted her to stay the night. Wanted to hold her as she slept and then wake her by kissing every inch of her silken skin. Bring her to orgasm by worshipping her flesh with his lips and tongue.

Fully dressed and clutching her reticle, she faced him. "Please ask Nelson to summon a hackney for me."

Warwick shook his head, forcing the erotic images from his mind. He took her arm. "It's late and we have cover of darkness. I shall escort you home."

CHAPTER SEVENTEEN

Adeline dumped shoes, stockings, shifts, and dresses into the trunk, not bothering to neatly organize each item. Her mind was just as disorderly. How could she think after her prior evening with the duke?

She'd tossed and turned in bed once she'd gotten home. She'd replayed images of her heated lovemaking with Warwick over and over, and she'd cherish their shared night forever.

What she'd told him was true. She had no regrets. The problem was she had fallen in love with him, but when she'd even mentioned the word, he'd visibly recoiled. Somehow their relationship had become a perilous one; for her to remain in London and stay by his side would be unwise. Eventually their charade would have to end, and she'd be left with a torn and tattered heart.

Instead, she'd told him she'd been away too long and needed to check on her cottage. What she truly needed was time and distance between them. Her emotions were a whirlwind whenever he was near. She'd been more affected by their lovemaking than she could have imagined, while he'd been concerned with his honor.

A knock on her bedroom door drew her attention. She went to open it to find Lady Heywood standing outside.

"I wasn't sure your maid was telling the truth. You are leaving?"

"It will be a temporary visit to the country. I shall return." It was not a lie. She would return. Mary was here and she wouldn't stay away forever.

"My goodness, I hope so. Have I done anything to make you uncomfortable, my dear?"

Adeline knew she meant the time she'd "accidentally" left her door open as she was trying on her ballgown. Despite Adeline's initial dismay when the duke had found her in a state of undress, it had turned into an unexpectedly pleasurable afternoon.

"You have done nothing wrong, my lady," Adeline said. "In fact, you have made the stay wonderful for both Miss Hasmik and me."

"I assume Hasmik will accompany you on this sojourn to the country."

"Yes."

Lady Heywood clucked her tongue. "I was enjoying her companionship. Miss Hasmik is a wealth of knowledge on many topics, and her stories of growing up in Egypt are fascinating."

Adeline took the lady's hand in hers. "I

want to thank you from the bottom of my heart for your kindness and hospitality. I promise we shall return."

"I believe you, but I must ask. Is my god-son aware you are leaving town? Even for a short trip, as you say?"

She lowered her gaze, not wanting to lie. "Yes, he knows." *The truth.*

"Is he accompanying you?"

"Not right away." *Still the truth.* Warwick had mentioned returning to finish his work.

"Hmm. I can only assume *he* did some-thing wrong. I know how stubborn the duke can be."

"He has done nothing improper." He'd been honest from the beginning. She had changed and lost her heart.

"Hmm. I find that hard to believe. Warwick has not proposed. To me, *that* is improper."

A stab of guilt centered in Adeline's chest. The countess had supported her from the be-ginning. It was on the tip of her tongue to confess everything.

Adeline's lips parted. "We...we—"

A knock on her bedroom door interrupted her train of thought. A young maid stood in the doorway.

"You have a visitor, my lady."

"The duke?" Lady Heywood inquired.

"No, my lady. The visitor is Lady Adeline's sister."

"Mary?" Adeline asked. "I will meet her in the parlor."

"I will leave you to your sister," Lady Heywood said.

Adeline clutched the ornate railing as she descended the grand staircase and hurried to the parlor. Mary leaped to her feet at the sight of her sister.

"Adeline. I received your message. Must you leave Town already? It seems like you just arrived. And what of the duke?"

Adeline held up a hand at the onslaught of questions. "One at a time, Mary." She joined her and they sat together on the settee. Lady Heywood's parlor was richly decorated with gilded mirrors on the walls and ornate sculptures on a marble mantel. She focused on a sculpture of a shepherdess, her mind twisting and turning about what to tell her sister.

Adeline met Mary's eyes. "It's true that I am returning to Chilham. I left the cottage in the hands of a local farmer. I was not to be away for long, and I should return to oversee the necessary repairs."

Mary gave a no-nonsense look. "How can you bear to be apart from the duke?"

Adeline cleared her throat. "Regarding Warwick, there is something you should know."

Adeline swallowed her misgivings. She never planned on telling Mary the full truth.

Even now, with two weeks remaining of the Season, she knew she couldn't confess all. The last thing she desired was for Mary to feel guilty. If she knew everything, Mary would be agitated, maybe even confront Edwin.

Adeline couldn't take that risk.

Adeline disliked Edwin, but he was Mary's full-blooded sibling. Mary lived beneath his roof and was dependent upon him for all her financial needs. Adeline wouldn't put that at risk.

She loved Mary and needed Edwin to care for her.

But she had to tell Mary something of her relationship with the Duke of Warwick. Her trip to the country, away from the man who was courting her, required an explanation. How much to confess?

Mary's face lit in anticipation. "Warwick proposed!"

"No."

"I know. He wants to act properly and seeks to ask Edwin for your hand beforehand."

"No, not that either."

"Then what?" Mary asked.

"Our courtship isn't an ordinary one."

"I never thought it was. Neither of you are ordinary. That's what makes it perfect."

"You don't understand. When I met Warwick, his intention was to put off marriage and focus fully on his inventions. His godmother, Lady Heywood, was pressuring him to marry and produce the expected heir to the dukedom."

Mary pressed a hand to her heart. "How terribly romantic! He met you and everything changed."

"It wasn't like that, either."

Mary didn't seem to notice the hesitancy in Adeline's voice. "I can only hope I meet a man who falls madly in love with me even after learning of my ambitions to work as an author."

Madly in love? She wanted to scream that wasn't true but bit her tongue. The word "love" associated with Warwick was a fantasy.

Then why did a restless tension coil inside her at the thought? Did she truly desire a future with the duke? If so, could he ever love her in return? Or would it be a marriage of convenience, a way for him to have the heir he needed?

For as long as she could recall, she'd sought a love match like her parents had known. Growing up, she'd always expected she could find the same, but as she grew older, she realized it was not as easy as in romantic childhood stories of knights and fair maidens.

"Our relationship was not as you believe. Warwick needed a reason to put off marriage for a time, and I agreed to aid him."

Mary stiffened. "What do you mean? I saw you with the duke. The air between you nearly sizzled at Lady Trehorn's party."

"You are mistaken. The only thing that sizzled at Lady Trehorn's gathering was the hot food on the banquet table. Warwick thinks of me only as a friend."

"A friend?" Mary's eyes bore into hers. "Don't be ridiculous. A man does not go out of his way to help a friend's sister find a publisher. A man does not stand up to a woman's half brother if he does not care deeply for her. A man doesn't look at a woman the way the duke looks at you if he thinks of you as only a friend. Warwick adores you!"

The vehemence in Mary's voice and the intensity of her gaze struck Adeline. Even more shocking, she wanted it to be true. She wanted Warwick to adore and love her.

She couldn't help but wonder: could their counterfeit courtship turn into a true betrothal?

• • •

The sight of the country cottage brought back a rush of feelings. Happiness. Relief. And a strange sadness. She knew what was responsible for the last emotion. Rather *who* was responsible.

She'd told Warwick to wait a week or longer before leaving London. There was no reason for her melancholy. Except for one.

She missed him.

They had spent weeks together and she had found herself looking forward to their meetings, their walks in the park, their intellectual conversations, the way he made her laugh, made her feel. Their flirtations to attract attention and their private kisses that had nothing to do with anything but their burgeoning desire.

She was never one to lie to herself. She had fallen helplessly in love with the man. The heart was a tricky organ. Ever since she was young, she'd wanted to find a man she could love, a man different than the aristocratic popinjays and the rogues of the *beau monde.*

Now she had found such a man and she wished she hadn't. Their passionate night together was impossible to forget, and she replayed their conversation over and over in her mind. She had no doubt that he cared for her, but he hadn't professed his love.

She didn't regret her actions. She was a grown woman who'd made a choice. She'd understood their agreement, had understood their one evening might not turn into forever. *She'd* propositioned *him.*

Hasmik opened the door, and they stepped inside the cottage, redolent with lemon polish. A pleasant breeze stirred the white curtains they had washed before they left.

"Mrs. Taylor has maintained the place well," Hasmik said.

"If only my father's steward had cared for it half as attentively."

"That man stole the earl's gold. Back home, he would be jailed as a thief."

Adeline knew Hasmik referred to Arabic law. The law was harsh with thieves, but those from wealthy homes fared much better with the corrupt judges than those from poor households. Some London magistrates were not much different and could be bribed.

Adeline began to unpack her medicine chest and arrange small glass vials of dried herbs on shelves. The cottage was clean, but it was still in need of numerous repairs before Adeline could use it for her intended purpose.

The roof was bare in spots and required repair before the winter. The banister leading to the second floor was loose. A large crack in the fireplace needed repair. Floorboards were damaged or missing in the drawing room, kitchen, and guest bedchamber. Outside the cottage, the garden gate was broken. Shutters needed painting. Flower beds must be weeded. The list was long.

She planned to turn the guest chamber into a sickroom where a patient or two could rest and she could check on them throughout the night if needed. It was far better than treating someone on the kitchen table.

She trailed her fingers along the back of a sofa in the front parlor then collapsed on the cushions. "You must be just as exhausted from traveling. Sit beside me for a moment."

Hasmik sat beside her and crossed her arms over her chest. "We didn't have to leave London so soon."

"I told Lady Heywood that I would return."

"Will you?"

"You know that I will visit Mary."

"Yes, but will you visit Lady Heywood? Or most importantly, the duke?"

"I don't know."

"You are thinking of Warwick now. I know you well," Hasmik said. "You never told me what happened that night."

"Which night?"

Hasmik gave her a don't-try-to-fool-me look. Adeline sighed. Hasmik was much more than her companion. She'd begun as Adeline's nursemaid, but Adeline hadn't looked at Hasmik as a nurse in a long time.

"The duke and I…we were together." Adeline felt her cheeks grow hot.

"Did he seduce you?"

"No. I persuaded him."

Hasmik arched an eyebrow. "A man who desires a woman does not need much persuading. And Warwick has wanted you for weeks."

"You're wrong."

"A blind woman could see it."

Hasmik's conviction made her feel oddly comfortable.

Hasmik stood and went into the kitchen to hang herbs on hooks to dry. Adeline rose and followed her. "I agree with the countess," Hasmik said. "The duke should 'come to scratch,' as she says."

On any other occasion, Hasmik's use of the English saying would have made her laugh. "You spoke with Lady Heywood about us?"

Hasmik rolled her eyes. "You know we talked. I resided under her roof, as you English say. Why wouldn't I speak with her about you two? She says the duke is enthralled."

Adeline experienced another rush of emotion. She knew it was misplaced. The duke wasn't enthralled or besotted; he had put on an act to convince his godmother that he was. As they had planned.

Hasmik knew the truth. Why was she acting as if things had changed? "Our intimate evening means nothing. Warwick never professed his love." Adeline lifted her chin. "I have more pressing matters to think about, and we have much work to do. The villagers need me."

Hasmik's unblinking gaze heightened Adeline's apprehension. "One day you must think of your own needs, Adeline. You cannot take in every stray or help every villager in need."

"I do not—"

"You deserve happiness, too."

A knock sounded at the front door.

"I'll see who it is."

"No, let me." Adeline jumped to her feet. For a fleeting instant, she wanted it to be Warwick.

She opened the door and found Max Simmons and his son, Jonathan, on her front step. "Mr. Simmons," she said in greeting. "Good to see you and your son. How is your leg?" She'd sewed a nasty wound on the carpenter's thigh—five dozen stitches as she recalled. Warwick had stood in the corner of the kitchen as she'd worked.

Stars! *Stop thinking of the duke.*

"I heard talk that you'd returned," Max Simmons said.

Adeline blinked. "How did anyone know?"

"Your coach passed the tavern. The town is small, and visitors are easily spotted."

"Are you ill?" Adeline's gaze traveled to his leg. His trousers covered his prior wound.

"No. We are here to help with your cottage."

"Why would you do that?"

"I haven't forgotten what you did for me."
His hand landed on his thigh. "I'm as good as
new because of your care. I never forget a
debt. Along with my son, I called upon
friends."

Adeline glanced past the man, and her
heart jumped at the sight of four young
men—farmers from the look of their worn
boots—hats to shield them from the heat of
the sun, and tanned skin. Three wives stood
beside the men and held buckets, brooms, and
mops. She smiled wide with joy.

"Come, Hasmik! I knew returning here
was the right decision."

• • •

Warwick had hired a hackney to take him to
the edge of the rookeries. His black lacquered
carriage would draw unwanted attention in
this area of town and this visit was not a social call. Here the homes were closer together
and not as well kept. Men and women in
worn clothing hurried about their business,
careful not to make direct eye contact. The
alleyways were dark, and shadows skirted
between the buildings.

Warwick drew immediate attention as he
entered the main room of the tavern. The tables were crowded with men in coarse
corduroy jackets and scuffed boots. Thick

smoke swirled to the ceiling and stained the rafters. Buxom barmaids wove between tables with tankards of ale and cheap gin.

He ignored the stares and found Stan Slade in a back room of the tavern, sitting by himself at a table. Slade was counting coins, a thick cigar in his mouth that he flicked back and forth with his tongue. His hair was slicked with pomade, and his flat black eyes focused on the money. A middle-aged man with a full head of dark hair and fine clothing stood before him. The man looked as pale as a sheet of parchment, and he shifted his feet as if he'd flee at the slightest moment or urinate in his pants. Stan ignored the man's discomfort, coins chinking on the table before him.

A huge, burly henchman with a broken nose and fleshy jowls that reminded Warwick of a mastiff, stood silently in the corner watching them.

The moneylender looked up from the coins to the man standing before him. "Is that all?"

"It's everything I've borrowed, plus more. It's all I have, Mr. Slade," the man said.

"You knew the terms of the loan. This does not cover the interest. I'm afraid I'm going to have to—"

Warwick slammed the door.

Slade's brows snapped together in irritation. "Who the devil are you?"

"Someone you're going to want to speak with alone," Warwick said.

Slade leaned back in his chair and the two front legs lifted an inch from the floor. "How'd you get past Peetie?"

"Your guard stationed outside? Peetie must fear me more than you."

Warwick hadn't fought the man. He saw no reason to enlighten the moneylender that Peetie took a bribe.

Slade threw back his head and laughed. "Arrogance is appreciated if it can be backed." He glanced at the pale-faced man standing in front of him. "Get out."

Needing no encouragement, the man sprinted past Warwick, yanked open the door, and closed it on his way out.

Slade shrugged, humor evident in his eyes. "One cannot always choose their business partners, can they?" Slade stayed seated. "Go on. Continue to amuse me."

"My name is Warwick."

The front legs of Slade's chair smashed against the floor. His expression hardened and he pointed a finger at Warwick's chest. "You are the one who is standing in my way."

"Since we've never met, I believe you are mistaken."

"There is no misunderstanding. I want Lady Adeline Cameron. It took cunning to get her brother squirming, and he assured me her hand in marriage. Then you interfered."

It took effort not to reach across the desk and yank the moneylender to his feet. He'd take great satisfaction in smashing his fist into his scrawny face.

His henchman took a step forward. Slade waved his guard back.

"If it's the lady I've taken, then you are right," Warwick said. "I am standing in your way and will continue to do so. I suggest you find another debutante to serve your needs. There's time left this Season."

"I don't want another. Her brother made me a promise. Unlike with you aristocrats, a promise, for me, is an unbreakable vow."

Warwick grit his teeth, his gaze never leaving the moneylender's. "Then it's good I never made you a promise. Stay away from the lady."

CHAPTER EIGHTEEN

Adeline tossed a bucket of scraps into a trough where a black-and-white pig waited. If he could wag his curly tail, she surmised, it would be vigorously wagging. "I missed you, Henry."

The pig looked up from his meal, oinked once, then went back to his food.

Two hunting dogs trotted to her side. Their tails wagged, and their brown eyes looked up at her, eager for affection. She took time to stroke their ears and smile at each of them. "I missed both of you, too, Remus and Romulus." Their owner hadn't returned for them, and Adeline decided she would keep them. She could never turn away an animal in need.

It was the end of a long day, and she was tired. Along with Hasmik, she'd scrubbed the cottage from top to bottom and rearranged furnishings to turn the spare bedroom into a sickroom. Other repairs had come along.

A week had passed and Warwick hadn't returned to Kent. Her treacherous heart leaped every time she heard a coach pass by the country road. Insecurities arose with each passing day, and her heart ached a bit more. He'd said he would return. Still, he never came.

Silly, Adeline. It was better this way.

When would the ache in the center of her chest begin to ease? Her head told her what she needed to do, but her heart was a different matter entirely. She walked to the end of the road to catch a glimpse of his country home. Not surprisingly, she could see no movement. She turned away just as the crunch of wheels on stone and the snorting of horses drew her attention farther up the road.

A coach was arriving. Not just any conveyance. Sunlight glinted off a black lacquered coach and the shiny coats of matching bays. Her heartbeat quickened as the coach turned the bend in the road, and a moment later, the duke's crest was visible on the black lacquered door. Without rational thought, she ran the remaining length of the stone drive to his home. She halted, a bit breathless, just as the driver hopped down to open the coach door.

Warwick stepped out. Adeline suppressed the urge to run into his arms.

"Your Grace!"

At the sight of her standing at the foot of his home, his brow furrowed and he hurried to her side. "Adeline. You are a sight for sore eyes. Is something wrong?"

"I saw your coach and came." She sounded foolish and she felt her face flush and her stomach drop. All her recent efforts to live her life without him had vanished as soon as she'd spotted his coach. Clearly, she had no willpower around the man.

"I'm glad you are here. I planned to visit your cottage straightway."

"You did?"

"Of course. Tell me what you have been up to."

Her words came out in a rush. Her relief that he had planned to visit her made her giddy. "Hasmik and I have had help with some of the cottage repairs. Do you remember the man whose thigh I stitched? He arrived with farmers and the roof has been repaired. It no longer leaks during heavy rain." She was babbling but couldn't seem to stop herself.

"Good. I'm glad to hear you have had help. It's also good to see you."

"I wasn't certain you would return."

"Why? My work on the high-pressure steam engine isn't complete. You told me to wait a week, and that was my plan, but then one of my stewards showed up in London and multiple ledgers needed overseeing."

"Your engine." A second coach had arrived and parked behind his. No doubt the engine was loaded inside. In her eagerness to see him, she hadn't even noticed it. Her voice sounded hollow to her ears. Was a greasy engine the main reason he was in Chilham? Or was it because he wanted to see her?

"I'd like to see for myself the progress you've made on the cottage," he said.

"Why?" Now she sounded like a petulant child.

"Because I want to know how I can help."

Her mind raced while her stomach tied itself into knots. "You want to help?"

He flashed a perfect smile. "Why not? I'm mechanical, and certainly capable of fixing a loose floorboard or two."

• • •

She was a sight for sore eyes. For as long as he lived, he'd remember Adeline's face when he'd stepped out of the coach. Her blue eyes had widened, and her full lips had curled in a welcoming smile. God, he'd missed her. He hadn't realized how exciting London could be with her by his side. Everything was brighter, more entertaining, more enjoyable — the park, Gunther's, the bookshop, even his intellectual meetings. She had a sparkling intelligence that matched his own and conversing with her was never boring. Rather it was scintillating. Even now, standing outside his home with two of his coachmen present, the desire to taste her, to touch his lips to hers, washed everything else from his mind.

A week apart had felt like a month...longer.

His meeting with the blackguard Slade hadn't improved his mood in Town. Warwick had a mind to challenge Adeline's half brother to a duel for the mere suggestion that he offer Adeline to the moneylender.

After she'd left for her home, he'd strode into his study. He'd told Adeline the truth about wanting to help her with her cottage improvements. Her goals were admirable, and her happiness paramount. His work was important. He'd always believed it to be true. But then he'd seen what she could do, first when she'd stitched the gruesome wound of a country carpenter, then when she'd saved Lady Drake's life and that of the babe. The high-pressure steam engine that awaited him seemed to be of less importance now.

He glanced at the tools he'd left behind, many scattered across the workbenches in his study. "Nelson!" he bellowed.

Nelson appeared in the doorway. "Your Grace?"

"I need a small chest to carry tools."

"To carry your tools? What for?"

"To help Lady Adeline. She has a loose banister."

Nelson looked at him like he'd lost his mind. "Shall I call for the village carpenter?"

"No. I'm going to do the repairs myself."

"You Grace? What of your work here?"

"It can wait."

"Your Grace?"

"I do not pay you to argue with me."

Nelson maintained the polished veneer of a proper English butler, but rather than sense disapproval, Warwick sensed something else entirely from the man. Approval. Admiration. "Right away, Your Grace. A chest for your tools."

. . .

It turned out that Warwick could fix much more than a crooked garden gate and a loose shutter. He had a bucket of nails and a hammer and was bent over as he secured the banister. The muscles of his back flexed as he worked, and Adeline could not help but stare and be distracted from her own task of organizing her medicine chest.

It was ludicrous. A duke turned into a carpenter. A man born into wealth and privilege who toiled over a loose banister with hammer in hand. A champion for a country neighbor.

Her hero. Memories of their shared night returned in a rush, and her heart squeezed in her chest.

Warwick stood and leaned on the banister, testing its steadiness. "There. Safe and secure." He grinned, his expression one of pride and satisfaction.

Her legs felt weak. They were alone. Hasmik had left for the village with one of the young farmers for fresh milk. She wanted to walk right up to him and kiss him. To lift his shirt over his head and press her lips to the corded muscles of his throat, his broad chest. For him to hold her.

"What else?" Warwick asked.

She swallowed, her throat as dry as cotton. "A floorboard is also loose in the guest chamber."

"I can repair it." He picked up the chest containing his work tools.

"I'll be right outside feeding the dogs." She left before she succumbed to weakness and did something foolish.

• • •

Adeline's panicked scream made Warwick's blood turn cold. He dropped his hammer where he'd been nailing a loose floorboard, sprinting out the front door. He ran past Remus and Romulus barking in their kennel and around the side of the cottage.

Adeline knelt on the ground. Blood covered her hands, a bright streak of red marring her cheek. Icy dread pierced his gut. Then he saw what she held. She cradled a pig. Not just any pig.

Henry.

"He's been shot with an arrow." Desperation tinged her voice.

Warwick dropped to the dirt beside her as

he inspected her for injury. "Are you hurt?"

"No. I heard Henry's scream and found him like this. He must have escaped his pen again and…and…" She broke down in a sob.

The arrow had pierced the pig's side. The animal was squealing in pain and breathing heavily. Warwick's first thought was that the pig should be shot and put out of his misery.

"Are you able to help him?" Warwick found himself asking.

"I don't know."

"Where's Hasmik?"

"She went to the village and won't be back in time." Tears welled in her blue eyes and spilled onto her cheeks. His throat ached, and he felt as if he himself had been pierced with the arrow.

Henry's head was cradled in Adeline's lap. "Who would do such a horrible thing?"

Someone who's hungry, thought Warwick. Still, hunting another's pig was not moral or legal. But then again, Henry had a habit of releasing his pen's latch and wandering away. Whoever had done this may have not known the pig belonged to someone.

Warwick's heart ached at Adeline's distress. She was the strongest woman he knew, and he hated to see her cry. "I've seen you work, Adeline. If anyone can save Henry, you can." He gently shook her shoulders to get her to look at him. "I'll assist. Tell me what to do."

She wiped her tears with the back of her hand. If he wasn't already kneeling by her side, the tortured look in her eyes would have brought him to his knees. "You're right. You can assist. Help me carry him inside."

· · ·

Performing surgery on a pig was no easy task. At two hundred pounds, they used a cart to transport the pig inside. Henry was strong, and Warwick struggled to hold the animal down on the kitchen table. The only reason he could restrain the pig was due to its weakened state.

He assisted any way he could, by handing Adeline clean cloths, hot water from a kettle, and items from her suture kit. Thankfully, the arrow hadn't gone through the pig and she'd carefully removed it. She'd given the animal herbs for pain as she'd worked, and the pig had finally ceased thrashing when she'd finished with the last stitch. Henry's raspy breathing filled the room.

Adeline washed her hands in a basin and wiped her brow with a cotton cloth. "We can move him to his outdoor pen. I'll need to watch him for infection."

Warwick lifted the pig onto the bed of the cart and wheeled him outside, then transferred him to a fresh bed of hay. Once they were back inside the cottage, he studied her face. "You did the best you could."

She bit her bottom lip. "If I hadn't been distracted, I would have seen Henry escape and he wouldn't have been harmed by a hunter."

"You cannot live by 'what ifs.' And you must not blame yourself for another's trespass."

"Thank you for all you did today," she said.

He opened his arms and she stepped into his embrace. "There is no need to thank me."

She rested her head on his chest. "Yes, there is. The first time you stepped onto my property, Henry barreled into you and hurt your arm, remember?"

It seemed ages ago.

"And he trespassed into your home, too," she said.

Warwick rested his chin upon her head and smiled. "Ah, I remember. He has a fondness for my pillows."

She laughed and looked up at him. He couldn't help himself. He dipped his head and kissed her, gently, tenderly, as if she were precious china. She kissed him back and rested her hand on his chest, her fingers curling into him, holding him. In an instant the kiss changed. He cupped her jaw, eased her head back, and explored the recesses of her mouth. Her kittenish moan and the feel of her soft curves pressing against his hard ones were enough to ignite an instantaneous fire in his blood.

His trousers pulled obscenely tight across his loins. He wanted to crush her against him and taste her lips and kiss her lush breasts. He imagined lifting her skirts to touch the smooth skin of her inner thighs. Lust vied with tenderness in a heady combination. He wrestled for control. She'd just experienced a trauma, and only a cad would take advantage.

He lifted his head and gazed down at her and knew he'd never forget the way she looked at that moment. Unmistakable passion burned in her blue eyes. Her lips glistened from his kisses and a lustrous lock of midnight hair escaped from her pins and rested between her breasts.

The front door opened and closed. Adeline's blue eyes widened, and her lips parted in surprise. Warwick released her and took a step back.

"Adeline!" a woman's voice sounded from the vestibule. "I found a grapevine on my way to the village. The leaves are tender and perfect to stuff with meat and rice." Hasmik stopped short in the entrance of the parlor. "Your Grace." She glanced at the smear of blood on Adeline's apron and her lips dipped downward. "What happened?"

"There was an accident. A hunter shot Henry," Adeline said.

"Henry?"

"Yes. He's resting in his pen after I surgically removed the arrow. His Grace assisted."

Hasmik's gaze pivoted to Warwick. "I see."

Warwick reached for his coat, which he'd tossed on the back of an armchair, and slipped it on. "I'll leave you two ladies to look after Henry. If you need me, summon me at once." He bowed on his way out.

CHAPTER NINETEEN

Adeline shifted the basket of herbs from one arm to the other as she raised the knocker. Nelson led her to the door of the duke's study and knocked.

"What is it?"

"You have a visitor, Your Grace. Lady Adeline." The butler opened the door and she stepped inside.

"Adeline. Is it Henry?" Warwick's brow creased and he stood from behind the desk.

"No. Henry's fine and resting in his pen."

He grinned. "Good to hear."

She couldn't help but notice the tingle of excitement she felt at the sight of his handsome face creased in a smile. Her heart thudded once, then settled back to its natural rhythm. She glanced at the papers on the surface of his blotter and noticed sketches of the lawn cutter he'd been working on. Had he made progress? Her interest was piqued. She still believed his "progress" was not always desirable, but she also understood his reasons for pursuing the invention. How different she felt from the first day she'd visited his workshop. She set the basket on the desk.

He eyed it. "I've no need for medicine." He rubbed the sleeve of his arm. "I'm cured, thanks to you."

"I know. I didn't bring my salve this time." She lifted the checked cloth covering her treasure. "I brought you something special to eat. Dolma—grape leaves and vegetables stuffed with meat and rice. There is also hummus and za'atar, Middle Eastern spice consisting of thyme and sesame seeds. Both are eaten with pita bread."

He glimpsed inside the basket, and she wondered if he would turn his nose up at the foreign food or embrace it.

"You cook as well as heal? What other talents have you hidden from me?"

His nearness and teasing nature caused her heart to flutter in her breast. "I don't cook often. Hasmik is talented in the kitchen. Dolma is her specialty."

"I'm famished. Time passes me by, and I often forget to eat when I'm working."

Her lips twitched. "I'm not surprised. Perhaps you should invent a clock that alerts you when too much time has passed since your last meal."

"You mean a small electric shock?"

"Goodness. Nothing that serious."

"Good to know." He walked around the desk and took the basket from her. "Come. I'm hungry and have the perfect place in mind to share a meal."

He led her outside and spread a blanket

on the grass beneath the shade of one of the large oaks on his property. She removed plates and food from the basket and served him. He chose one of the stuffed tomatoes first. At the first taste of the dolma, his brows rose. She waited and watched him, not wanting to miss his slightest reaction.

Would he like the Mediterranean dish? Or wrinkle his nose in distaste?

His green eyes met hers. "It's delicious. So much flavor." He ate with gusto, and she smiled in delight when he complimented her on the homemade pita bread. When she reached for the za'atar spice, he raised a hand.

"How do you eat it?"

"You must add olive oil to the za'atar, then dip your pita into the mixture to get the full flavor of the thyme and sesame seeds. Along with the hummus, it's one of my favorites."

She poured a small amount of olive oil into a shallow bowl and combined the oil and spice mixture. Then she tore a piece of pita bread, dipped it in the bowl, and offered it to him.

He bit into the bread, then his eyes met hers. "Extraordinary. English fare is bland in comparison."

Her heart did a pitter-patter. She should have known a man as educated as the duke would be willing to experience new cultures and foods. Edwin had turned his nose up at anything her mother had attempted to expose him to.

Warwick, on the other hand, helped himself to seconds of everything. She couldn't help but wonder how he would react to a visit to the diverse section of London. Would he think the sounds of the instruments, the dumbek, oud, and the duduk, odd? Would he be disdainful of the closeness of her mother's family and friends, the way they danced and talked in a mixture of English, Arabic, Armenian, and Greek?

She swallowed. It didn't matter. He was a duke, and she knew they wouldn't be together much longer. Eventually, he would have to return to London and his duties.

"I'm pleased you enjoy the food." It was a safe remark, one that didn't reveal the inner workings of her mind.

"Who wouldn't enjoy it?"

"You'd be surprised."

He swallowed the bread. "You mean Edwin."

"For one."

"He was always close-minded."

That was a kind way to describe Edwin. She didn't want to ruin the pleasant moment thinking of her half brother.

"Let us not think of him," Warwick said as if reading her mind. "How is Henry faring?"

"Thankfully, there is no sign of infection. We mixed table scraps with his feed and his appetite has returned."

"Ah, it must be a good sign when a pig wants to eat."

The humorous comment lightened the mood, and she chuckled and leaned back on her elbows. "Your gardens are peaceful and pretty."

A pleasant breeze cooled her cheeks and ruffled the tendrils of hair that had escaped her bun. Birds chirped in the tall trees, and colorful flowers of different hues—red, pink, blue, and white—bloomed in meticulous flower beds and scented the air with a heady perfume. Flowering shrubs lined the perimeter of the garden and secluded them from the outside world. His house was out of view, and she liked the isolation.

"I never have spare time to enjoy it," he said.

"Yet you have time to help repair my cottage and treat my pet pig."

"That's different."

"Why?"

A heart-pounding moment of hesitation passed before he finally answered. "Because it's for you."

The air stilled and her breath stalled. It was the closest he had come to expressing his feelings, and it was as if her entire future rested on that one pivotal moment. She stared with longing at him. His gaze met hers, and her heart turned over in response. Her whole being seemed to be filled with wanting.

If a few stolen moments were all they had together, then she was more than willing to seize the opportunity. A tangible bond existed between them, and, despite everything, she wanted to experience the man once more. All of him. She moved toward him, impelled by her own desire, and pressed her lips to his. She licked the seam of his lips and placed small kisses at the edge of his mouth.

He let out a long, ragged breath. "Adeline. I do not wish to take advantage." His hand glided up her back, then stopped by the base of her neck. Despite his words, his fingers tightened, holding her close. Pleasure rippled over her skin, down her spine. She willingly abandoned herself to the whirl of sensation. Her body craved more of his kiss and his hands. A golden wave of passion—and love—made her lighthearted with need.

Foolish man. "You're not." His magnetism was potent. What would it take for him to acknowledge she was a woman who could make her own decisions when it came to intimacy? She chose him.

• • •

Warwick gently lowered Adeline to the blanket and lay beside her. Wasting no time, he lowered his head and captured her lips in a searing kiss. At the first gentle thrust of his tongue, she made a low sound in the back of her throat that made his heart thump erratically. She clutched his shoulders and urgently kissed him back, their tongues tangling.

He lifted his head to look down at her. Her pink lips were swollen and moist from his kisses. Her blue eyes held his gaze, open and honest with need.

"Adeline, love. We can go inside."

"No. I don't want to wait."

Lord God, how lucky could he get?

Sunlight filtered through the tall oaks, and her skin glimmered. The light was a blessing. He would be able to see every inch of her, and his cock hardened even more with his desire for her. She was his Venus, his Adeline, and he wanted to lift her skirts and thrust deep inside the sweet haven of her voluptuous body.

He was suddenly a starving man wresting for control. He was not a rogue or rake, and she was a gift that must be savored. He'd foolishly believed that once he'd made love to her, his desire would wane. He'd been wrong.

He wanted her with a savage desire. And when she'd first kissed him, he would have dropped to his knees if he hadn't already been sitting. He reached behind her to unfasten her dress, and she helped slip it from her shoulders.

His lips traveled a path down her throat and his hands cupped her lovely breasts, then his lips followed. He tweaked her nipple and she made a sweet sound in her throat and arched her hips in a way that made him wild.

She helped remove his jacket; his waistcoat and the cravat followed. She pulled his shirt over his head and tossed it aside. His heart hammered as her gaze hungrily traveled over his chest, then her hands skimmed a path down and loosened the buttons that fastened the placket of his breeches.

When her fingers brushed the tip of his manhood, he groaned in an onslaught of lust so startling he shook with it. His arousal grew and he raised her skirts and ran his hands up her long, slender legs. His fingers found the slick folds of her womanhood and brushed against the swollen nub.

"Warwick," she gasped. "That feels incredible."

He could hardly think, and his body pulsed with frenetic need. He rose above her and replaced his fingers with the tip of his cock. She squirmed beneath him. "That feels even better."

He slid down the slick entrance to her body and sank a precious inch inside. Mahogany tendrils of her glorious hair spread across the blanket, and her throat arched. He kissed the slender column of her neck, and his lips traveled a path downward until he hovered above her breasts. He drew a nipple deep into his mouth as he thrust fully inside her.

He stilled. Her hot, slick channel gripped him. It took every ounce of effort to be still, to be sure he hadn't hurt her. "Is there pain?"

"Not this time. Only pleasure."

Only pleasure. Her words ratcheted his need and the roaring possessiveness in the center of his chest.

Her nails scratched down his back and gripped his buttocks, and his control snapped. With one forward thrust, he was deep inside her. *Sweet heaven.* She writhed beneath him, just as wild with her own lust.

She had to come soon. He wouldn't last. She threw back her head and cried out in bliss, her thighs gripping him tight. One more thrust and he was lost, pulling out as his hot seed spurted across her soft belly. He collapsed beside her.

They were half dressed, under a canopy of trees and a blue sky, and she'd come with him thick and heavy inside her.

She placed a hot kiss on his neck. "Just like last time, I don't have regrets."

Christ. The urge to stay buried in the sweetness of her giving body had been overwhelming. Even more frightening, his desire for her hadn't waned, only grown.

What the hell *was* going on between them?

He'd taken care of Stan Slade. Adeline was protected. He'd managed to put off his godmother and escape the Season unscathed. Why did he feel as if a fist squeezed his chest every time he thought of leaving her?

She turned his world upside down, and he hadn't realized how much he'd enjoyed being with her. She was easy to be with and intelligent. She hadn't gone into hysterics when she'd seen his country workshop, or his London ballroom converted into one. She'd enjoyed meeting with his intellectual friends. He found her mixed heritage fascinating. She was independent, beautiful—her beauty grew more vibrant every time he saw her. Her lips, her breasts, her eyes…

His godmother claimed he was besotted. He'd worked hard to convince her that he was, but somewhere along the way, it had become true.

• • •

Adeline shifted beneath Warwick and opened her eyes. He was lying on his side, his hand beneath his chin as he looked at her. "I must say this is a very pleasant afternoon."

Adeline tilted her head to the side and arched an eyebrow. "You must mean the food?"

"The basket lunch was delicious, but the

sweet that followed was even more so." He
pressed a hot kiss to her nape.

Adeline giggled. "Do you think Nelson
saw us?"

"No. But I wouldn't care if my entire staff
did."

"Warwick!"

"You're right. I wouldn't want anyone to
see you naked but me."

At his teasing tone, her love for him grew
even more. Was that possible? She may not
have regrets, but still, she would be foolish
not to protect herself. She pulled her gown
over her shoulders, then turned and offered
her back. "Please help me with my fastenings.
I have to check on my patient."

"Henry?"

"Yes, Henry." She needed to gather her
strength and her wits and leave the cocoon of
his arms. No matter what had happened beneath the shade of the tree, she had
responsibilities. Those duties would save her
from a bleak future after he left Chilham.

"When will I see you again?" he asked.

"We are neighbors," she pointed out.

"For now."

For now. The simple statement spoke volumes. Adeline claimed she would return to
London, but she was no longer certain. Even
though there were people who needed her
help in Town, she could not survive being

close to the Duke of Warwick and not being with him. Adeline had only her profession and her friendship with Hasmik. She knew deep down that a clean break from the compelling duke was for the best. If only it wasn't so painful. If only she hadn't fallen in love. A flash of wild grief ripped through her, and a sourness settled in the pit of her stomach.

Once her gown was fastened, Warwick stood and offered her his hand. "I'd like to come by tomorrow and check on your cottage and Henry." His large hand cradled her cheek. "Meanwhile, if you need anything, anything at all, come to me."

She swallowed tightly. She couldn't rely on him. Would not. Yet she found her herself nodding. "Yes, Your Grace."

. . .

Later that evening, Warwick was working on the pistons of the engine when he heard his housekeeper's outcry of delight a second before Nelson opened the door. Warwick glanced out the window to see a coach in the circular drive.

Moments later, a familiar voice sounded from the vestibule. "Hello, Nelson. Where is my godson?"

Warwick set aside a wrench and left his workshop to see Lady Heywood hand Nelson her cloak. Dressed in an elegant traveling gown of emerald adorned with Brussels lace, she brushed imaginary dirt from her skirt.

"Hello, godmother. What an unexpected surprise."

"I do get out and about, Daniel."

"Yes, but a visit to the country is much more than a routine house call. You should have sent word."

"Hmm. I did send word. It must not have arrived."

His suspicions rose. He'd bet all the gold in his coffers that she'd sent a letter just as she'd left London and it would arrive a day or more later. He led her into the drawing room and set her reticule on an end table just as his housekeeper entered and stopped short at the sight of the lady.

"Welcome, my lady. Would you like refreshment?"

"A spot of tea if you will," Lady Heywood said. "My throat is dry from the dusty travel."

"Yes, my lady. Cook prepared fresh scones as well." His housekeeper bustled from the room with her task.

"Oh dear. I hope my arrival will not burden your smaller staff in attendance here." His godmother settled on a gold and blue striped settee.

Warwick sat in an armchair across from her. "My staff may be few here, but they are highly efficient."

"From your lack of a waistcoat and coat," Lady Heywood began, "I take it you have been working."

"My lack of formal attire isn't why you are here, is it? Please tell me why you have left the remaining routs and soirees of the Season to travel all the way to the country."

"I missed you."

"I've been gone less than a week."

She sat stiffly on the settee. "Your manners have suffered, Your Grace."

"I won't disagree. It's the country air. Perhaps it's best if you say what is on your mind."

"Fine. I will be direct. Why did you allow Lady Adeline to leave London?"

He didn't wish to talk of Adeline or to address the reasons for her departure for the country without him. His tone sharpened with rancor. "I am not the lady's jailor."

Her scowl put him on edge. Apparently, she would have none of his attitude. "When will you propose to her?"

"My personal life is not—"

"Posh! Do not treat me with disrespect, Daniel. It will not work. I'm the one who cared for your bloody nose after a squabble with the aristocratic boys in the neighborhood. I am the one who visited you at Eton and welcomed you to my home for every holiday, and the only person who stood up to your parents on your behalf."

It was all true, dammit. Every word.

"Adeline will make you the perfect wife. I wasn't certain when you first brought her to London, but it didn't take long for me to realize the truth."

"That we are well suited?"

"No, you fool. That she loves you."

His heart stalled in his chest. *Is it true? Does Adeline love me?* She'd asked him about love, and he'd disabused her of the notion. Love was for poetic fools without an ounce of good sense. Not men like him. Men who prized academic learning over lust and poetry. Only his godmother had undertaken the effort to understand him, to accept him for all his eccentricities.

Her shrewd gaze never left his face. "I saw the way you looked at each other. Did something happen between you two?"

Yes, we made love. I almost came deep inside her, and it took every ounce of my restraint to pull out of her warm, welcoming body. He'd wanted to mark her as his own, to possess her every way a male could possess a female.

His jaw tightened. "We didn't have a falling out, if that is what you are asking."

"Listen to me, Daniel. If your intentions toward the lady are not proper, then you must not ruin Lady Adeline's chances."

"What do you mean?"

"Either propose marriage to the lady or release her to find happiness with another man."

CHAPTER TWENTY

When the clock pinged its fifth chime the following afternoon, a knock sounded on Adeline's door. She was surprised to find Warwick on her doorstep.

"My godmother paid me a visit," he said.

Adeline stepped outside and shut the door behind her. Hasmik was in the kitchen, and she didn't want her to overhear. "My goodness, so soon? Why?"

"She is meddling."

She bit her bottom lip. "What should we do?"

"Nothing. The countess will not stay long. She has friends and social obligations in London."

"You think to outlast her? Or that the solution to her visit is that simple?"

"I do. Time is on our side, and both of our family members will have to accept that our courtship is taking longer than most."

His reasoning made sense. They'd known each other for only two months. It wasn't entirely unreasonable. Only it felt like much longer. Looking up at Warwick's tall frame, it felt right, like they were meant to be together as much as the moon and stars. How ridiculous. He'd been honest from the beginning. It was her own desires that had changed. She'd never regretted allowing him to make love to her. For her, it had been much more than simple desire.

Warwick may be far from a rogue or rake seeking to bed as many beautiful women as he could, but he was still a man, and lovemaking may not have been as earth-shattering for him as it had been for her. She'd once overheard Edwin speak with his friends as they'd callously bragged about their sexual conquests. She wondered if it was the same for all men, including Warwick. Even if he didn't boast of his sexual relationships to others, had he felt the same connection, the same wonderful feeling of oneness she'd felt?

She was inexperienced, but she'd have sworn he cared for her more than a casual encounter. He'd made love to her with infinite tenderness and had ensured she'd received pleasure before his own.

"Are you on your way out?"

"I was headed to the village. A woman has a toothache."

"That is the reason I'm here. You need to know just in case you run into Lady Heywood in the village."

"Oh, I hadn't thought of that."

"What will you do?"

"You needn't concern yourself. I shall invite her to tea, of course, and convince her that all is well between us."

. . .

Adeline was tired after treating the goat herder's wife for her toothache. She was not a dentist and pulling a tooth was an unpleasant experience. Still, the woman was better off without a painful, rotting tooth.

She walked down the lane and her own cottage came in sight. She picked up her pace and looped the basket of herbs over her other arm. Henry was in his pen, dozing. Remus and Romulus barked, their tails down as she passed their kennel. She frowned at their incessant barking. It was unlike the dogs. They had been back to normal after her care. "What's wrong, boys?"

She opened the cottage door to find Edwin standing inside the parlor. Dread pooled low in her gut.

He faced her. "Those two beasts have been barking since I stepped onto this property. I have a mind to put both down."

Her breath stalled in her throat. "By God, what are you doing here?"

He stalked forward, his tall frame towering above her as he gave her a cold smile. "My brotherly duty is to check on my half sibling, even though she lacks manners and hospitality."

"You've never bothered to conduct your *brotherly* duty in the past."

"Not true. I've attempted to arrange your betrothal."

Her breath stalled. Her fingers curled into fists. He had nerve to show up unannounced once more and threaten her. "If that is the purpose of your visit, do not waste my time or yours. Your repetitiveness is straining my nerves."

She attempted to step by him, but he grasped her arm and yanked her toward him. Her shoes skidded on the hardwood floor, and she resisted his hold, but he was strong. He pulled her outside, then slammed the front door. Remus's and Romulus's barking intensified. Confined in their kennel, they were unable to protect her.

Edwin's eyes narrowed with menace. His breathing was hard. "You lied, Adeline. Somehow you have pulled off a fraud."

She yanked her arm out of his grasp and rubbed her forearm. Anger bubbled inside her. "How dare you!"

"I dare because I have every right as the earl and as your kin. If not a fraud, then why isn't there a reading of the banns announcing your betrothal to the duke?"

Despite her anger at his high-handed behavior, she was aware he spoke the truth. His position as the Earl of Foster gave him power. She chose her words carefully. "Some courtships take time."

His cold chuckle made her blood run cold. "Or is it because your mother was a commoner, a woman of mixed blood? It doesn't matter that our father was an earl." His gaze flickered over her with distaste. "Who would want you as their wife?"

"You cannot be serious."

He leaned close, his sour breath brushing her cheek. "A duke, no less! He must marry a blue-blooded heiress."

"Don't be an idiot. Our father found my mother worthy of marriage."

"That was a mistake the duke will not make. Warwick will find a true lady who will birth him sons with an impeccable pedigree."

Insecurities rose in Adeline at his cruel words — deep-rooted insecurities that crawled inside her chest like pestilence. The insecurities had begun after she'd first witnessed the prejudice her mother had faced from some of the *beau monde*. Prejudice that had been reinforced later. In fact, Adeline had experienced it only weeks ago in a Mayfair bookshop.

Warwick had stood up for her then, but when it came to the perpetuation of the dukedom, of the bloodlines of his children, Adeline knew convictions changed. The duke had made love to her twice, and not once had the topic of marriage even arisen. Worse, she'd fallen madly in love with him.

Was Edwin right? Was she not good enough for the Duke of Warwick? Were her mother's Arab roots distasteful to, or inferior for a duke? And why was she even thinking such thoughts when she had never intended to marry him anyway?

Warwick had never proposed. Never professed his love. Oh, she knew he desired her. But lust was far from love. She longed for that emotion. An old Armenian saying sprang to mind.

May you grow old on the same pillow.

If Warwick didn't love her, she would find another who would cherish her. She deserved love, no matter what Edwin claimed.

Edwin folded his arms across his chest. "The only man who will have you, Adeline, is Mr. Stan Slade. He is determined to marry into the aristocracy. A smart woman would use it to her advantage."

Frustration and anguish seared her chest. She faced him; her chin lifted. "Too bad the Season is almost over. Mr. Slade must find another woman. Meanwhile, you should leave, my lord."

Rather than leave, he shut the door behind him and faced her. "You leave me little choice. I had hoped to talk sense into you, but I now realize there is no reasoning with you. Pack your bags. There is a wedding you will need to attend."

Her fingers fisted at her sides. His stubbornness was infuriating. "Edwin—"

"It isn't your wedding I speak of this time."

"Pardon?" Her anger ebbed. The way he looked at her made the hair on her nape stand on end. "Who's?"

"Mary's."

She knew before he could explain. A savage gnawing clawed up her throat and made her nauseous. "You wouldn't."

"After I explained the financial loss and the devastation to her, she was receptive to the suggestion."

"How dare you! Mary is innocent. She doesn't understand."

"Quite the contrary. She fully understands. I followed your suggestion. I realized keeping her in the dark about the earldom's coffers was not advantageous. Once I informed her of the loss from the shipping endeavor and the debt incurred, she understood the consequences. I had hoped you would cooperate after Warwick failed to act, but now I am taking different measures. Mary is more malleable, and the debt must be paid, or Slade will retaliate."

Adeline was horrified that he would sacrifice Mary to the moneylender. "It is no secret you dislike me, have disliked me for as long as I can remember, but not Mary. Sweet, innocent Mary. She has her own dreams." Adeline bit her lip to prevent her revealing the truth about Mary's writing. She wouldn't betray her sister.

"You are sending a lamb to slaughter," she spat.

"If you had agreed, then there would be no need. Meanwhile, I am staying in Chilham at the local inn. I'll give you a day to pack your bags." His razor-like gaze scanned the cottage, and his lip curled in distaste. "From the number of your belongings, I'm being generous. Until then, you know where to reach me."

As he rode away, his spine stiff in his saddle, Adeline stood frozen on the porch. Her world had changed in an instant, and he'd devastated her life with one swooping tactical move.

She would do what she had to do. What she always did—look after others and, in this instance, she'd sacrifice everything to protect her sister.

CHAPTER TWENTY-ONE

Warwick urged the stallion to ride fast through the fields. The late afternoon sun was a low golden ball in the sky and lit acres of wheat fields. Lady Heywood hadn't stayed for two full days before declaring she must return. Before she'd climbed into her coach, she'd turned to him and brushed his cheek with her bejeweled hand. "Remember what I said, Daniel. You mustn't wait. Despite what you believe, time isn't on your side."

Her voice was hard to forget. He'd tried to immerse himself in his workshop. His work had distracted him for a half hour before he tossed down his wrench and headed for the stables. He needed to clear his thoughts, and a good hard ride through the fields should help.

But no matter how hard he tried to purge his godmother's voice from his mind, her words returned.

If your intentions toward the lady are not proper, then you must not ruin Lady Adeline's chances.

His intentions were to stick to their agreement. He had believed that was what Adeline wanted as well. She'd talked of her dreams to care for others, and those dreams didn't include a duke who immersed himself in machinery, and who often had grease under his fingernails.

She deserved more. A man who would adore and love her. A man who would stand by her and give her the family she wanted.

Let her go. Let her find happiness with another.

That was the rub, wasn't it? The thought of her with another made his skin tight and his gut clench. A different thought crept into his head.

Why can't I be that man?

He admired her intelligence and had no desire to stand in the way of her dreams. If she wanted to heal all of Kent, he would have no objection, dammit.

She could be as different a duchess as he was a duke. He'd never cared what the aristocracy thought of him.

But love was an entirely different matter.

Adeline wanted love. He had no experience with the emotion. His father had been distant and had rarely shown affection. His parents' marriage had been as frigid and cold as a block of ice, and they'd both taken lovers. They'd produced an heir, a boy whom they'd never understood. He'd been fascinated by books and knowledge and had nothing in common with his father. Rather than try to understand their son, they'd found him odd…

an embarrassment.

Lady Heywood had stepped in and attempted to take his mother's place, but as a boy he'd been starved for love from the duchess. His heart had been hollowed out for so long he'd grown to believe love illogical, a foolish fantasy written of by poets.

He cared for Adeline more than any other woman he'd known. He could offer her friendship, the dukedom's abundant coffers, his title...plenty of passion.

But not love.

It would have to be sufficient. *It had to be.*

He reined the stallion away from the fields and toward the path that led to Adeline's house. His resolve increased as he grew closer and the small cottage came into view. His heart pounded in anticipation of seeing Adeline. Of kissing her once on her sweet lips and stroking her magnificent hair. He felt right. Good. Happy.

Henry rested in his pen and the hounds wagged their tails in greeting. Warwick stopped to pat each of the dogs on the head before stepping onto the porch.

He raised his fist, but Adeline opened the door before he could knock.

"Your Grace."

Her cheeks were flushed, her blue eyes bright. She'd never looked more beautiful. "Hello, Adeline. May I come inside?" She bit her bottom lip, and he tried not to lower his gaze to her lush, pink lips or to recall how they trembled beneath him in the throes of passion.

Then she looked to the left, then right, as if she were expecting another.

"You seem surprised to see me."

"I thought you were someone else." Her brow furrowed, then she opened the door wide for him to pass.

He entered and shut the door behind him. She led him to the parlor and sat on the sofa. Rather than choose a chair across from her, he sat beside her. She didn't seem to notice. She tapped her foot. Her behavior was odd, and he watched her carefully.

"Is Henry well? The hounds?" he asked.

She blinked. "Pardon?"

"Your animals?" he prodded.

"Oh, the dogs are fine. Henry is as fine as before."

"You have new patients then?"

"No. Not here, that is. The shepherd's wife's tooth had to be pulled. She is sore, but there is no sign of infection."

"All good news then."

A trickle of sweat beaded on his brow. His stomach tightened. It wasn't every day that he asked a woman what he sought to ask Adeline. She seemed distracted as well. Maybe she sensed his unease?

He took her hand in his. Such delicate fingers capable of complicated surgery. Sure. Pretty and strong at the same time.

His thumb brushed back and forth across the back of her hand. She looked at him then, a flicker of surprise crossing her features. Her blue eyes met his directly for the first time since he'd come inside.

"Adeline, I need to ask you something."

"Have you reinjured your arm?" She reached for the cuff of his sleeve when he shook his head.

His eyebrows drew together. "No. Why would you think that?"

"From your presence here and your expression, I sense it's of importance."

"It is." He waited until she met his gaze once more. "I know we had an arrangement. An understanding. But Lady Heywood's visit enlightened me on a different matter. A complication."

Her brow furrowed. "What type of complication?"

He took a breath. "She pointed out that either I act or that I step aside for you to find another match."

"I see."

"No. I don't think you do. I do not wish to step aside or for you to find another."

"You don't?"

His heart drummed in his chest. He

slipped from the sofa to kneel. He took her hand in his once more. "Will you do me the honor of becoming my duchess?"

Her lips parted. "Pardon?"

She looked confused and uneasy. Perhaps he had failed to set forth his reasonings.

He gently squeezed her fingers. "I've given it much thought. It is a logical step."

"A logical step?"

"Yes. We are well suited. You are intelligent and diligent in your endeavors, just as I am in mine. We are attracted to each other. Many aristocratic marriages are based on much less."

"A well-suited aristocratic marriage?"

"Yes." A knot in his chest eased. She understood after all.

She sat upright. "No."

"No? Why?" It was not the answer he'd expected.

"I envisioned a different proposal, but nonetheless, it's too late."

"What do you mean it's too late? I don't understand."

She flinched. "Edwin returned a half hour before your arrival today. I shall return to London with my half brother shortly. I am to marry Mr. Slade."

"What?" It was his turn to be utterly confused. "Why would you agree to marry that moneylender? Don't you know that he is a blackguard?"

She turned her head to look out the window. "It doesn't matter."

He shook her hand until she met his eyes once more. "The hell it doesn't. What on earth could Edwin have said to make you change your mind?"

"It's of no consequence."

"No consequence! If money is the issue, you never need agonize about that again. Marry me instead."

"It's not that simple."

A muscle ticked by his eye. "Why, dammit?"

A flicker of anguish crossed her features. "Because if I refuse, Mary will take my place!"

Shock ran through him. A sudden furious anger pierced his chest. "Bastard. I should have expected as much from Edwin." He rose from his knee to sit beside her once more.

Adeline choked on a sob. "He has outwitted me."

He let out a breath, then ran fingers through his hair. "This can't be. How much is the debt? I will pay off Slade." Money was no object for him. The ducal coffers had grown under his care, and he was more than willing to use his gold to free Adeline.

She shook her head and bit her bottom lip. "It's not just the money. Mr. Slade seeks to marry into the aristocracy. The daughter of an earl, even one of mixed blood such as myself, will elevate his status. That's what he's after."

Warwick felt as if his cravat had tightened around his throat and cut off his air. Edwin had offered both of his sisters to satisfy Slade's ambitions of status and social standing? Rage bubbled in his chest, and he wanted to roar with fury. Had Edwin no conscience? He knew Adeline would sacrifice herself for her sister.

"What about my proposal?"

"If I cannot marry for love, then I will wed for family." Adeline stood.

Warwick rose. "Think about what you are saying."

She raised her chin and faced him. "Our arrangement is over. I only hope you have managed to delay your godmother's matchmaking tendencies until next Season." She stepped forward to brush her lips on his cheek. "Goodbye, Your Grace. I'm to leave for London tomorrow."

• • •

"The duke proposed?" Hasmik dropped her reticule on an end table and gaped at Adeline in the parlor. "What did you say?"

"I told him no." Adeline's voice sounded hollow, distant, to her own ears.

"Tell me why," Hasmik demanded.

"The duke listed his reasons. He failed to set forth the most important one of all." Hasmik had returned home and had found Adeline sitting by herself in the parlor, a glass of whisky in her hand. She remained on the sofa where Warwick had proposed to her less than a half hour ago, unable to muster the energy or will to move. After Hasmik's inquiry, Adeline had filled her in briefly.

"You speak of love?" Hasmik sat beside her on the sofa.

"I do. He failed to mention it." Her heart squeezed at the memory of his visit. A vulnerability had flashed across Warwick's face when she'd rejected him, one she'd never seen before. A dominant male, a duke no less, was not accustomed to being told "no."

Even without Edwin's demands—which took away her free choice, she would be hardpressed to accept Warwick's proposal. A man who loved a woman would profess his feelings. Warwick's reasons had not included those.

She was a sound choice for a logical man. A convenient woman who appreciated his intelligence and accepted his scientific endeavors. Someone who enjoyed his mathematical and scientific acquaintances. A woman who had her own ambitions and wouldn't get in the way of his.

Their relationship lacked what she'd always longed for: love.

"Are you certain of your decision?" Hasmik asked.

"I will not sacrifice Mary to Mr. Slade."

"She is a grown woman. It is her choice," Hasmik said.

"Is it? Or has she succumbed to Edwin's manipulations?"

"Mary is more intelligent than you give her credit for."

"Perhaps."

"Mary is older than you, yet you always feel the need to protect her. It is time for you to let go."

Adeline rubbed her temple. "I cannot let her ruin her life!"

Hasmik scowled. "You want to ruin yours instead?"

At Adeline's silence, Hasmik sighed. "You must know that I will support you and stay by your side no matter where that leads, even if I do not agree with your reasons."

Adeline's lips turned upward, and she embraced Hasmik. "Thank you."

Hasmik pulled back and raised a finger. "But as for the duke—"

Adeline shook her head. "What's done is done. I won't back out now. The duke can find another to fulfill his needs." If only the thought didn't cause her such despair and anguish.

"Sometimes it's hard for a man to comprehend his feelings or to voice them. You love the duke."

Adeline pressed a hand against her breast. Her misery was like a weight pressing against her chest. "I will not settle."

Unrequited love was the most painful emotion of all. Could she stand to marry a man who looked at her only as the most logical choice?

No sense worrying about it now. Edwin had taken away her free will by involving Mary. What a bloody mess.

Her half brother had won after all.

. . .

Adeline was silent for most of the trip back to London, her limbs limp with misery. A storm had made the roads treacherous, and they had to stop at the nearest inn. A dark and dreary common room matched her mood. Adeline ordered a tankard of ale and hoped to sleep in one of the procured rooms. Instead, she spent the night tossing and turning on a lumpy mattress. When she finally succumbed to slumber, she had nightmares of Mr. Slade.

She was wearing a black dress and veil to her wedding. Edwin walked her down the aisle, a satisfied sneer on his arrogant face, and when she reached the altar and Edwin lifted her veil and handed her to her groom at the altar, she fainted.

The next day, she had a roaring headache. She rested her head on the side of the coach and prayed the road would open up and swallow the carriage. She dreaded facing her family—both Edwin and Mary.

What would she tell her sister? That she valued her sibling more than she valued herself?

Truth.

That Mary had a better chance of finding a fine English lord who would love and adore her? That Adeline's Arab blood prevented many from wanting to mix their pure blue blood with her?

Double truth.

Years of her brother's taunting had eroded her self-worth. If Warwick didn't love her, what lord would?

Perhaps the best she could do was a greedy, wealthy moneylender like Stan Slade.

"We are here." Hasmik touched her hand.

Adeline startled. She'd fallen into an exhausted slumber. She lifted her head, which felt like it weighed a hundred pounds, and opened her eyes a crack. Her headache increased in intensity at the sight of the Piccadilly town house. She rubbed her temples. Gathered her courage.

Hasmik leaned forward and touched her

hand. "I'm worried about you. I can tell the driver to take us elsewhere until you are ready."

Adeline shook her head. "Putting off the inevitable will not stop it." She straightened her spine, smoothed her skirts, and squared her shoulders. The least she could do was to appear composed. Even if it was necessary to fake it.

Together, they climbed the porch stairs and Hasmik lifted the brass knocker once. The sound echoed in Adeline's head like a death knoll.

The family butler opened the door and nodded in greeting. "Lady Adeline. Hasmik." He opened the door wide, and they stepped inside the vestibule. "Please follow me to the drawing room, and I shall summon Lady Mary," the servant said.

"Who has arrived, Hawkins?"

At the sound of the lilting female voice, Adeline looked up the grand staircase to see Mary standing at the landing. Adeline's lips tugged in a smile.

"Adeline!"

Mary flew down the stairs and into Adeline's open arms. She hugged her sister, and her heart burst in her chest as she inhaled Mary's familiar rose perfume.

Mary's fair hair curled around her shoulders and down her back, her eyes wide.

"Edwin told me everything! I am not happy with you, Adeline."

Adeline sighed. "Please do not make this more difficult. I have made my choice."

Mary's lips thinned. "What about Warwick? Has the duke not proposed? I was sure he would by now."

At the mention of the duke, her throat welled, and she choked on a sob. She was ashamed of her reaction. She should have more control by now.

"Oh, forgive me." Mary's brows drew downward, and she took Adeline's hand and led her into the drawing room. She motioned for her to sit on a settee and settled beside her. Mary pulled an embroidered handkerchief from her skirt pocket and handed it to Adeline. "He's broken your heart, hasn't he?"

Adeline wiped her eyes. "It's not how you think."

"Regardless. I think I should've been a better sister."

Adeline lowered the handkerchief. "No! You are a wonderful sister. You have always been one. I don't deserve you."

"Do not be ridiculous. You have always been there for me, Adeline. I'm the older one."

"By only a few months."

"No need to remind us."

Adeline laughed. She blew her nose. Only

Mary could jest about the fact that the sisters were less than a year apart from two different mothers. "Edwin would never joke about it."

"Edwin is not here."

"Is he to arrive?" Adeline didn't look forward to seeing him, but they had business to attend to—her betrothal.

"Soon. I'm not pleased with him either."

"Mary, I've made up my mind about marrying Mr. Slade."

"Why, for heaven's sake? I don't need you to rescue me."

"I'm rescuing myself."

"How so?"

"You were right about the duke, but not as you think. Warwick proposed. But not for the right reasons. He never professed his love. He claims I am a logical choice."

"I see."

"Do you?"

"I know that as long as we were young girls, you sought to find love and marry. To be happy. Like our father and your mother."

"You understand then."

Mary bit her bottom lip. "Maybe a man like the Duke of Warwick considers love the same emotion as a logical choice."

"What do you mean?"

"In his mind, the two may mean the same."

Her sister's words struck her. The intellectual Warwick had never known love as a child from his own parents, only from his god-mother. Did he not know what love was? Had he confused it with what he understood and what he could comprehend—a like-minded intellectualism? In other words, a logical choice?

What did it matter anyway? Time had run out and whatever had existed between her and Warwick was at an end. She could think only of the future, a true future, and not one based on falsehoods or arrangements.

If she couldn't save herself, then she was determined to save Mary from a life of misery.

. . .

Warwick tossed down the hammer on the worktable. His breathing was labored, as if he'd spent an afternoon in the ring, boxing. He wanted to punch the wall. He counted slowly to ten, let out his breath, and hoped the sickening feeling in the pit of his stomach would ease.

Instead, it grew worse.

He'd believed returning to London would help the despair in the center of his chest. He'd been wrong. The high-pressure engine in the center of his ballroom workshop failed to hold his attention. His usual mental escape into the world of mathematics, physics, and heat transfer failed. His numerous inventions felt meaningless. His distracted mind held only one thought. Or one woman.

Adeline.

He went to his desk and idly opened his notebook and turned a few pages, thumbing through sketches of future inventions. He heard the ballroom doors open. His butler's voice was an echo in the recesses of his mind.

"Warwick."

Warwick blinked and focused to see his friend, the Earl of Drake, standing before him. Drake shook his shoulder. "I'd ask if you need a whisky, but I suspect you won't drink. How about a bout in the ring?"

Warwick scowled. "Boxing would be unwise. I'm unfocused. You'd beat me."

"That's the point."

Warwick wanted to be left alone. "Why are you here? You should be home with your wife and new babe."

"That's precisely why I'm here. My wife has heard the news."

"What news?"

"That Lady Adeline is betrothed, and it's not to you."

"Go away." Warwick's voice was gruff.

"Why didn't you propose to her?" Drake asked.

"I did!" Frustration bubbled in his chest, and he pushed back his chair. He banged his fist on the desk.

"Hmm. I see. I can only assume your proposal lacked finesse. Or is she marrying another man for different reasons?"

Warwick closed his eyes and let out a slow breath. "Perhaps it's both."

Drake slapped him on the shoulder. "Then do something about it."

Before Warwick could answer, the ballroom doors opened once more. This time, his godmother entered. Shoulders squared, chin high, she had the demeanor of a drill sergeant.

"If you would excuse us, Lord Drake. I'd like a word alone with the duke."

Drake bowed. "I am pleased to see you, my lady. Perhaps you can talk some sense into him."

Lady Heywood waited until they were alone. She walked to his closest workshop table, and her fingers grazed the wrenches, hammers, and screwdrivers. She picked up a wrench and turned to face him; her lips pursed in thought. "Life is too short to spend it alone with tools and a good amount of grease."

"Say what you mean to say and leave. I have work to do," Warwick said.

She pointed the wrench at him and he almost believed she would toss it at his head. "Go after her, Your Grace."

"I took your advice. I proposed. She declined."

"You love her."

"I do not—"

The countess held up a hand. "Your mother did you a disservice. I had hoped my love was enough to supplement."

"You are dear to me, godmother. But Adeline's refusal has nothing to do with love."

"Bah! It has everything to do with it. Go after her. Tell her you love her. Make it right."

Warwick leaned back against the desk. Was this desolate emotion love? He felt as if someone had reached inside his chest and hollowed it out with a dull spoon. Was she right? Did he love her?

For a man who believed in science, it was a fearsome emotion. Science had never failed him. Emotions had.

He'd never viewed marriage as anything more than a businesslike affair of the sort he'd witnessed in his own parents' relationship. Then Adeline had turned his world upside down. She'd changed him in ways he'd never believed possible, and the thought of her with a man like Stan Slade was as painful as the thought of his own life without her by his side.

He loved her.

Dear God, he *did* love her and needed her more than he needed air to breathe and water to drink. Nothing else mattered, not his inventions, his work…or science.

His godmother walked behind his desk and reached up to clutch both of his shoulders. "Hurry, Warwick. Before Adeline is lost to you forever."

CHAPTER TWENTY-TWO

"Why are you here?"

Warwick faced Lord Foster, Edwin, in the drawing room. Warwick had wasted no time getting to the doorstep of the earl's Piccadilly townhome and demanding to meet with him.

If Adeline was in the home, he hadn't seen her.

It served Warwick's purposes. He was here to discuss unsavory details with Edwin, and he didn't want anyone else as a witness.

"Why would you sell your sister to Slade?" There was an edge to Warwick's voice, one that simmered of barely restrained control.

Edwin's face screwed into one of anger and hatred. "I told you once before that our family affairs are not your concern."

"Since I intend to marry Adeline myself, I consider it my business."

"You arrogant bastard! You have always thought yourself better than everyone else."

"Not everyone. Just you."

Edwin raised his fist. Warwick blocked it before it made contact. He grasped Edwin's collar and yanked him close. "You were a bully as a boy, and you haven't changed as a man. Don't be an idiot. You haven't been able to beat me since we were thirteen."

If it wasn't under such grave circumstances, Warwick would find great satisfaction in besting the blackguard.

"I am the head of this house and as such, Adeline is my ward," Edwin ground out.

Warwick fisted Edwin's collar. "How much do you owe Slade? I'll pay him off. Not for you, but for her freedom."

Edwin sagged. "It's too late."

"Why? Just because the moneylender wants to marry into the aristocracy? If he's as greedy as they say, then money should suffice. He can find another wife."

"You don't understand. He wants Adeline."

Warwick grit his teeth and pushed Edwin away. "Then tell me where I can find him now."

. . .

The stench of cheap gin and cigar smoke wafted to Warwick as soon as he stepped foot in the gambling hell. It was a different one this time but had a similar feel. Despair oozed from the pores of the man sitting at the table across from Stan Slade.

Slade's black eyes glinted with avaricious anticipation as he held his own cards. The ever-present cigar dangled from his lips. Warwick didn't think the moneylender gambled, only took advantage of those who did, but perhaps he was bored tonight. Warwick recognized his victim, the third son of a marquess. How much did the bloke already owe the moneylender?

Warwick halted at the hazard table. "A word, Slade."

Slade never looked up from his cards. "I'm busy tonight."

"I'm not asking."

Slade lifted his gaze, his expression bland. When he noticed Warwick, one dark eyebrow arched upward. "To what do I owe the pleasure of another visit, Your Grace?"

"We spoke. I thought I was clear," Warwick said.

"Ah, you must be referring to my betrothed, Lady Adeline."

The word "betrothed" coming from Slade's lips was enough to stiffen Warwick's jaw. He wanted to smash the man's face with his fist. His hired lackey took a step forward. Slade waved his man back.

"I told you to stay away from the lady," Warwick said.

"And I told you her brother made me a promise," Slade countered.

"I know how much Lord Foster owes you."

"Then you know it's a significant amount."

"I will double his payment."

Slade removed his cigar and leaned back in his chair. "Why would you do that?"

"My reasons don't matter. In exchange for the payment, you will release Lady Adeline from the betrothal, and you will never bother her, her sister, or her family in the future." If he could exclude Edwin he would gladly do so. But Warwick knew it had to be the entire family, for Adeline's sake.

Everything was for her.

Slade's lips quirked. "I could ask for triple."

Warwick moved so fast, the man could only blink. He grabbed him by the throat, lifted him off his seat, and slammed him against the wall. When his lackey tried to intervene, Warwick shook his head. "Move and I'll snap his neck."

Slade nodded. Once more, the man backed off.

It was unlike Warwick to resort to physical violence, yet twice in one day he found himself using his strength to intimidate his enemies.

"You will take the offer. Or I will use my influence as a duke of the realm to ruin you socially and financially. No marriage to any daughter of the aristocracy will elevate your status. Do you understand?"

"Yes, dammit." Spittle sprayed Warwick's face. He didn't ease his grip.

"Good. Find a quill and a sheet of foolscap. I will dictate the terms."

CHAPTER TWENTY-THREE

Warwick spotted Adeline sitting outside on a stone bench in her garden. Mary had taken him to the French doors leading outside and pointed to where Adeline rested with her back to them.

Mary's eyebrows drew together, and her voice was steeped with concern. "She's been outside for more than an hour. She says she wants time alone. I'm afraid her solitude has much more to do with melancholy than clearing her thoughts. She has been weeping." She choked back a cry. "It's my fault, isn't it?"

He hated to see either his love or her sister cry. "Neither of you need worry anymore. I made things right with the moneylender. Stan Slade is releasing Adeline from their betrothal."

Mary gasped. She reached for Warwick's hand, her eyes brimming with tears. "How?"

"The details are not important. All you need to know is that both you and your sister are safe from that man."

"Thank you, Your Grace."

"It was the proper course of action. Will you please tell Adeline?"

"No!"

Warwick was taken aback at Mary's tone.

"You misunderstand, I—"

"You must tell Adeline, Your Grace. It's clear you care deeply for my sister. A man does not go to such trouble to save a woman if he does not love her. As such, you must also speak from your heart. She will accept nothing less."

"I—"

"Tell her you love her. Seize the opportunity. You *must* tell her."

Warwick nodded. Words escaped him at Mary's passionate speech. He prayed they didn't escape him when he stepped into the gardens.

He took a deep breath, filling his lungs with air. Mary was right. He had one chance to win Adeline, and failure was not an option. He wanted her with every fiber of his being.

He reached for the handle of the French door, turned it, and stepped outside. Lord Foster's gardens were well maintained. The hedgerows were well-trimmed, the lawn green and lush. Birds chirped and the sun shone brightly. Bees flew from flowering shrub to shrub. His gaze never left Adeline's back—the thick glossy braid caressing her shoulders, the soft curve of her cheek, the elegant swanlike neck.

He halted in front of her. "Hello, Adeline."

From where she sat on the stone bench, she shielded her face from the afternoon sun.

She turned to meet his gaze. He wanted to drop to his knee before her, rest his head in her lap, and beg her forgiveness for his stubbornness. Instead, he faced her with a weak smile.

"Warwick. I didn't think I would see you again," she said.

Her eyes were red-rimmed. His gut clenched at the thought of her crying. "Mr. Slade will never bother you or your family again."

"Pardon?"

"He has released you of the betrothal."

"How?"

"It does not matter."

"How?"

"I paid him three times what Edwin owed him." In the end, he'd been willing to pay whatever it took. Money meant nothing if it kept him from her.

She gasped. "Why?"

"Why else? For you."

"You sought out that blackguard? For me?"

"I promise I didn't do it for Edwin."

She let out a small laugh. "I don't know what to say."

Warwick dropped to one knee and cradled her small hands in his. "I love you, Adeline. I have loved you from the first moment I saw you—when I stormed over to your country cottage and was run down by your pet pig."

She stared. "Truly?"

He nodded. "I'm happy when we are together, and my heart aches when we are apart. I need you more than any invention, more than every book in my library. Reason has nothing to do with my feelings. I was a fool to claim it before. All I know for certain is that a future without you by my side is bleak and full of despair."

He reached into his coat pocket and pulled out a sapphire ring surrounded by small, brilliant diamonds. Sunlight glinted off the jewels. His gaze met her blue eyes. "This is my mother's ring. I would be honored if you would wear it. Will you be my duchess?"

Adeline's lips trembled and she threw her arms around him. "Yes! Oh, yes. I love you, Warwick."

He stood with her in his grasp and his arms tightened around her and held her close. "Please say it again."

"I love you."

"I'll never tire of hearing it."

• • •

"Are you sure you want to do this?" Adeline sat beside Warwick on the leather bench of his crested carriage as it sped through the city streets.

Warwick peeled back her glove to place a

kiss on the back of her hand. "Yes, as I told you multiple times. Are you worried I'll discover a secret you have been keeping from me?"

She laughed. "No. Just the other half of myself."

"Hmm. Now you have me more curious than before."

The carriage rolled to a stop, and Warwick helped her alight. They crossed Threadneedle Street and continued down a long lane. It was quiet today. Market day was once a month, a week away. Passersby walked the streets. She recognized more than one and they waved in greeting.

They came to a small house. Rather than knock on the front door, Adeline led him to the back garden. The street had been quiet, but the garden was full of people. This was the day of the week when friends, relatives, and acquaintances gathered to share a meal and spend a pleasant afternoon together. Even Lady Drake was present with her babe.

She could tell by Warwick's expression that he was surprised by the large group. Many were dressed in foreign garb of loose pants and brightly colored embroidered vests. The women wore vibrant gowns embroidered with gold thread.

"Family and friends get together every Saturday."

Warwick sniffed the air. "Something smells good." He turned to look in the corner of the garden where a man grilled skewers of lamb. He turned two skewers at once. The mouthwatering aroma of grilling meat scented the air.

"That's Harout. He prepares the best shish kebab in all of London."

Adeline took Warwick's hand and led him to a table laden with Middle Eastern delicacies. Shawarma, falafel, hummus, grilled eggplant and red and green peppers, olives, cheese, and freshly made pita bread.

Warwick's gaze traveled over the food. "I don't know where to start."

"Let me serve you."

She selected her favorite delicacies and handed him a plate. "You must try the shish kebab." She used the pita bread to slip the hot meat from the skewer. She added finely chopped parsley and diced onions, then handed it to him.

Warwick took a bite as Adeline held her breath. "Do you like it?"

"This is the best lamb I've ever tasted."

She smiled. "I'll tell Harout. You are most likely the first duke to eat his food."

Warwick devoured the shish kebab. People waved in welcome. Warwick grinned in return. "Is everyone always this friendly?"

"Always." She handed him a glass.

He took it and eyed it. "What is it?"

"Tispouri. It goes well with the lamb."

He sipped the anise-flavored alcohol. "Not bad." He studied the drink. "I'll have a bottle delivered to my home."

Lady Drake spotted them and walked over, cradling her baby. "I was wondering how long it would take for you to join us, Your Grace."

"I was waiting for Adeline to invite me," Warwick said. "Where is Lord Drake?"

"He is occupied with his steward today. Otherwise, he would be with me."

"He's kept this from me for years."

"Nonsense. He never believed you would be interested in my family." She winked. "But now that you appear to have a reason to visit, Lord Drake will be happy to accompany you." The babe began to fuss. "Please pardon me," Lady Drake said, shifting the baby in her arms. "She needs my attention."

"Of course," Warwick said.

Musicians had set up in the back of the gardens and now began to play. One strung the pear-shaped oud, another played the woodwind duduk with its double reed, and a third was skilled with the handheld dumbek drum. People cheered and clapped and began dancing in a line, holding pinkies and kicking their feet in unison.

Warwick set down his plate, his gaze riveted by the dance.

"Do you want to join them?" Adeline asked.

"It's unlike any dancing I know."

"If you can waltz, you can learn how to line dance."

She took his hand and led him to the back of the line. The dancers smiled in invitation. Adeline showed him the steps and, just as she'd anticipated, he was a quick learner. Soon, he was in complete harmony with the line, and they were laughing together.

At the end of the dance, she was breathless. Warwick left to fetch them a glass of tispouri. He stopped to speak to one of the musicians, then quickly returned. As they drank, she watched him. Warwick stood out from the others. Tall, fair-haired, green-eyed, his aristocratic bearing was as much a part of him as his intelligence.

Suddenly, doubts assailed her.

She bit her bottom lip. "Are you certain I will make you an acceptable duchess?"

"Tell me what worries you."

"These people are as much a part of my blood as my English father."

"And you think this is an obstacle?"

"I'm aware it could be."

He raised her chin with his forefinger and looked into her eyes. "Adeline, I could not be more certain that you will make a perfect duchess. If I could obtain a special license and marry you tomorrow I would. Waiting for the reading of the banns is making me impatient."

"Truly?"

"Yes. But I sense something else worries you as well. What is it?"

She glanced at those gathered in the garden, then turned back to him. "They need me. Many do not have access to a doctor. I know I wanted to stay in the village and treat the villagers, but I realize I'm needed here, too."

"Then we will do both."

"How?"

"Have you not noticed that I have many homes? My work can take place anywhere. I will go where you are needed. Where you will be happy."

Heat spread through her chest. "Oh, Warwick."

"I meant what I said. I need you, Adeline."

She needed him as well. He'd become a part of her life—a large and important part. She missed him when they were apart, and she enjoyed their intellectual conversations. And then there were his kisses...

Those she longed for most of all.

She placed her hand on his arm. "One more question. What did you say to those men?" She motioned to the musicians in the corner.

"I asked them if they would be willing to

play their instruments at our wedding break-fast."

He eyes widened. "Truly? You must know some of our English guests will be shocked."

"The only guest that concerns me is my godmother, and I know for certain she will be pleased. As for the rest, the wedding of a duke is the event of the season. If they do not approve, then they need not attend. But I expect they will. A typical English wedding breakfast is boring. I've attended my fair share. They will all be secretly fascinated. And jealous."

"You think so?"

"I have you. I believe they are already jealous of me, my love."

"Oh, Warwick," she said once more. How could she put her feelings into words? Rather than try, she stood on tiptoe and pulled him down to kiss him for all to see. His arms wrapped around her, strong and sure.

She'd found her hero and true love after all.

EPILOGUE

Adeline halted mid-step, her eyes widening. She touched her swollen abdomen. "The babe is kicking!"

Hasmik stopped on the country road and set down a basket full of clean, rolled bandages. "Let me feel." She pressed a hand against Adeline's abdomen, and her face creased into a smile as warm as the sun. "The baby is very active. It is a good sign." Her eyebrows snapped together as she studied Adeline's features. "Do you need to sit, *habibti*? You have been on your feet all day, treating the shopkeeper's son."

Adeline rubbed her low back. Her feet ached. She was six months along, and she felt as large as an ox. Even her ankles were as swollen as melons. Good heavens, how could she last another three months?

Adeline squinted into the horizon. "We are almost home. I can put my feet up then. Besides, Warwick will want to feel the babe kick."

She was right. Warwick's face could only be described as one of rapt fascination as he joined her on the sofa in their parlor and lay his large palm on her abdomen.

"She is lively," he said.

"He is enthusiastic. We will have our hands full."

"Mamma!" Their three-year old daughter burst into the parlor and ran full speed into Adeline's open arms.

"Hello, darling." Adeline kissed the top of their child's golden head. Her heart swelled as she cradled the little girl against her chest.

"Cara missed you," Warwick said. "I had to sneak her a sweet from the kitchen to calm her."

"Calm her or bribe her?"

"Is there a difference?"

Cara looked up. Her sea-green eyes, a perfect match of her father's, were clear and full of mischief. "Daddy played tea party with me and my dollies."

"Did he now?" The picture of Warwick sitting at Cara's child-sized table with her dolls while sipping imaginary tea from tiny porcelain teacups made her smile.

"He even held his teacup like a lady, with his pinkie raised," Cara said.

Adeline's heart melted another degree. "I'd like to have a tea party, too. Go and get your dolls ready for Mommy."

Cara jumped off Adeline's lap and ran from the room.

Adeline rested her hand on Warwick's larger one. "Thank you for playing with Cara while I worked."

"How is the shopkeeper's son?"

"Stitched and complaining. He will live. Meanwhile, how is your work on the engine's pistons?"

He shifted even closer to her on the sofa, and his fingers entwined with hers. "I'm ready to present my findings to the London Scientific Society."

"And your lawn cutting device?"

"Ready as well. Although I do not believe that invention will be as well received. Your argument about replacing workers with machines has merit. And those who do not personally perform backbreaking labor in their gardens with scythes all day long have little idea what it takes to maintain their vast lawns." He cocked his head to the side. "Are you certain you wish to travel to London with me?"

"My work can be performed everywhere, Your Grace. People need a good healer in the country and in Town. But your work must be properly presented to the world, and that can only be done in London." She'd discovered this when she'd been repeatedly summoned to treat the hardworking men and women in the diverse district of town.

"That's not what I mean. Can you travel?"

"I'm pregnant, not infirm."

"Adeline, if anything happens to either you or the babe, I couldn't bear it. I had no idea how empty my life was until I met you."

When he spoke like that her heart flipped over in her chest. "My place is by your side. Besides, Mary will be thrilled for us to visit."

Edwin had since learned Mary was a well-known author. Rather than prevent her from writing, he decided to act as if he knew of her secret profession all along. Of course, when he learned Lady Jersey was a champion of Mary's work, his mind had swiftly changed. Then gentlemen had begun to pay Mary visits and court her with flowers and chocolates. Edwin was at first resistant and had stayed in the drawing room during each visit. But one persistent suitor was the Viscount Hartwell, a wealthy, literary man who was fascinated by Mary's talent. Edwin, who had long forgotten about his woes with the moneylender, had come to realize the benefits of a match between his sister and a viscount, and had acted most amicably toward him.

Her half brother may be selfish, but he was no fool.

"And Lady Heywood will be happy to see you," Adeline said.

Warwick squeezed her hand. "She will be thrilled to see both of us, darling. My god-mother uses every opportunity to remind me that she was right and that I should have married you earlier."

"She was probably suspicious of our false

courtship from the first day," Adeline said.

"I finally gathered the courage to ask her. She claimed that she wasn't at first, but she grew more and more suspicious as the Season progressed."

"She is shrewd when it comes to the sexes."

He chuckled. "Shrewd? I will always owe her my undying gratitude. Finding you in a state of dishabille in your bedroom was life changing."

She parted her lips in mock horror. "How so? I was mortified."

His eyes twinkled with warmth. "Because looking back, I knew then that I could never part from you."

"Is that all it took?"

"That and so much more. You are my soulmate, Adeline."

"Soulmate? That sounds illogical, Your Grace."

He pulled her into his arms and kissed her. Only when she was breathless did he lift his head and tilt her face to his with tenderness. "A man cannot live on logic alone. But he can live for love."

TINA GABRIELLE'S SHISH KEBAB

5 to 6 lb. leg of lamb, boned, with fat removed, and cut into 1-inch cubes
3 cloves of minced garlic
¼ cup minced flat leaf parsley or 2 tablespoons crushed dried oregano
½ cup olive oil
¼ cup red vinegar or wine
¼ teaspoon cayenne pepper
3 onions, cut in quarters
2 tomatoes, cut in quarters
1 eggplant, cut into 1-inch cubes
red, green, and yellow peppers cut in quarters
salt and pepper to taste

Place cubed lamb in a large bowl with onions, tomatoes, peppers, and eggplant. Mix the olive oil, garlic, parsley, vinegar, cayenne, salt, and pepper in a separate bowl, then pour the mixture over the lamb. Cover and refrigerate overnight or for at least a few hours. Thread the meat onto skewers. Because cooking times vary, thread the tomatoes, onions, and peppers on separate skewers. Broil the skewers over a charcoal fire. Turn the skewers until the meat is cooked on all sides. Serve with pilaf and enjoy.

ACKNOWLEDGMENTS

Writers create stories in solitude, but publishing a book is a team effort. I'm thankful for all the wonderful people who have helped me along the way. I will always be indebted to my parents, Anahid and Gabriel, and miss them every day. They taught me to work hard and never stop believing in myself.

Thanks to my girls—Laura and Gabrielle—for believing in Mom. I'm eternally grateful to John for his never-ending support, encouragement, and love.

Thank you to Jeannie and Fran for their support of all my books.

Thank you to my agent, Stephany Evans, for your guidance and for always believing in me.

And a special thank you to my editors, Heather Howland and Erin Molta, and Entangled Publishing for all their work on my behalf.

Last, thanks to my readers. Without you, there would be no books!

Miss Julie Beaumont has exactly one *night*
to find herself a husband…

Cinderella
AND THE
DUKE

LYDIA DRAKE

The Weatherford Ball is the last chance Julia
Beaumont has to escape the clutches of her horrid stepmother. Any potential husband will
do—rich, poor, even a reasonably well-groomed
walrus. But all of Julia's matrimonial chances are
completely obliterated…thanks to the actions of
an infuriating and utterly rakish duke.

Gregory Carter, Duke of Ashworth, would
never risk his cherished bachelorhood by flirting
with marriage-starved debutantes. But one look
at the luscious and refreshingly clever Julia, and
he simply can't resist a stolen kiss—scandal be
damned. Then just as things start getting deli-
ciously interesting, the lady flees…leaving only a
slipper behind.

And it must have been one dandy of a kiss.
Because now Julia has proposed to *him*. After all,
the lady needs a husband, and this roguish duke
will certainly do. It's simply a matter of making
him the perfect scandalous offer…

*The rush is on for both gold and marriage
in this charming historical from
USA Today bestselling author Dani Collins.*

THE
Prospector's
ONLY
PROSPECT

After eight days in a cramped stagecoach, divorcée Marigold Davis already regrets her decision to come to Denver City to marry. She certainly didn't realize she'd signed up for mosquitoes, mud, and scores of rough men eyeing her like a hot meal on a cold day. But with her life in Kansas all but incinerated, Marigold needs a husband. Even if she's *not* the bride that gold prospector Virgil Gardner is expecting…

Virgil Gardner has a reputation as a grumpy hard-ass, and he's fine with it. He's also no fool—this is not the woman he agreed to marry. It takes a tough-as-nails woman to survive the harshness of a Rocky Mountain gold claim, and this whiskey-eyed, gentle beauty is certainly *not* the type. Now it's just a matter of how quickly she'll quit so he can find a wife who will stick. Someone who can care for the only thing he values even more than gold–his children.

But Marigold isn't about to give in. Cramped in a one-room shack. Berry picking turned into a bear escape. Or cooking for an entire crew of bottomless pits. She's got more grit than most. And just when Virgil starts to realize his replacement bride might be the treasure he's been looking for, an unannounced guest arrives…to change everything.

USA Today *bestselling author Eva*
Devon's bright, lively tale about daring to
be more than just a lady…

The Duke's Secret Cinderella

Charlotte Browne could just kick herself. What
on earth possessed her to tell the Duke of
Rockford that she is a lady? But something about
the duke's handsomeness and kind intelligence
makes Charlotte blurt out the teeniest, tiniest
falsehood. Now it's too late to admit she's just
plain Charlotte of no particular importance—
with cinder-stained hands, a wretched stepfather,
and no prospects for marriage…

Rafe Dorchester, Duke of Rockford, has done
what every self-respecting duke must do—avoid
marriage at all costs. But the only thing stronger
than the duke is his mother. When she lays down
the highest ultimatum, he'll need to find a duchess. Immediately. Only, when he calls on a
potential bride, he instead finds the pert, fresh-
faced Lady Charlotte. Rafe was warned to never
mix the business of marriage with pleasure, but
when it comes to her…oh, business would be a
splendid pleasure.

One passionate, illicit kiss sends Charlotte fleeing, leaving only a delicate blue ribbon behind.
For Rafe can never discover her secret, or it will
ruin her beloved sister's chance at marriage. But
the duke knows that when you've found the one
person that ignites you, body and soul, nothing
can keep you away.

AMARA
an imprint of Entangled Publishing LLC